PEGGY BIT HER LIP, KNOWING SHE HAD LOST THE argument. This was how it was among the three of them. Once two agreed, the third must go along—not in a coerced way, but because that was the irresistible pull, the strength, the sacredness of the Schuyler sisters' symbiosis.

And so it was now. "Will you help me, sweet Peggy?" begged Angelica. "I must elope now, before Albany is engulfed in fighting and we cannot make our way through battle lines to Boston. Before Papa comes home. All I need is the key to the front door. The windows are all too high off the ground for me to jump. Mr. Carter cannot approach the house with a ladder because of Papa's guards. I must slip away quietly, out the front door, timing my escape in between the sentries' rounds. You are the only one who can move with the stealth needed to get into Mother's room and remove the door key from her chatelaine without waking her." She squeezed Peggy's hand. Her radiant, dark eyes pleaded as much as her voice. "Please?"

Hamilton

★ AND ★

Peggy!

Hamilton

★ AND ★

Peggy!

A
REVOLUTIONARY
FRIENDSHIP

L. M. ELLIOTT

KATHERINE TEGEN BOOKS
An Imprint of HarperCollins Publishers

Katherine Tegen Books is an imprint of HarperCollins Publishers.

Hamilton and Peggy!
Library of Congress Control Number: 2017944492
ISBN 978-0-06-267131-8

Typography by Carla Weise
19 20 21 22 23   PC/LSCC   10 9 8 7 6 5 4 3 2
❖
First paperback edition, 2019

For all those little sister and smart-girl Peggys out there,
past, present, and future.
And, as ever, for Megan and Peter.

More than kisses, letters mingle souls,
for thus, friends absent speak.
—JOHN DONNE

Prelude

THE FIRST LETTER ARRIVES:

Alexander Hamilton to Margarita Schuyler
Morristown, New Jersey, February 1780

Though I have not had the happiness of a personal acquaintance with you, I have had the good fortune to see several very pretty pictures of your person and mind which have inspired me with a more than common partiality for both. Among others your sister carries a beautiful copy constantly about her, elegantly drawn by herself, of which she has two or three times favoured me with a sight . . .

You will no doubt admit it as a full proof of my frankness and good opinion of you, that I with so little ceremony introduce myself to your acquaintance and at the first step make you my confident.

1

PEGGY SCHUYLER KICKED OUT FROM UNDER HER heavy blankets, too preoccupied with a letter she had received to sleep. It came from an aide-de-camp to General Washington who proclaimed to be besotted with her sister Eliza—some silver-tongued man named Alexander Hamilton.

She shoved back the green toile bed curtains, gasping as frigid air pierced her linen chemise. "Good God! Can it possibly be this cold? Again?"

Teeth chattering, Peggy stirred the embers in the fireplace and dropped a split log from the basket onto them with as little noise as possible. It was still dark. She didn't want to wake her three younger brothers, slumbering next door. Endearing boys, but what a raucous rabble—especially the seven-year-old, Rensselaer, who had just gone through breeching and was racing around the house crowing about the fact he had finally graduated to wearing pants instead of dresses. For sure, he'd rouse little Cornelia, still in a trundle bed in her parents' room. And Peggy wanted to analyze Alexander Hamilton's words more closely, privately, without her mother insisting she read them aloud to the family.

The splintery wood sparked, sputtered, and caught flame as Peggy hurriedly bundled herself in shawls and slipped her feet into soft buckskin moccasins that the Oneida tribe once gave her father, General Philip Schuyler. They were artfully decorated with porcupine quills and blue-jay feathers.

Peggy never let her mother see that she had pilfered the colorful slippers from her father's closet. They were definitely not proper lady shoes. But her feet ached with a strange malady sometimes, especially on shivering days like this, and the moccasins were soft and forgiving. They also reminded Peggy of the vast New York wilderness just a few dozen miles north of their Albany mansion, and the elusive Iroquois who remained loyal to her father and the Patriot cause. Silently gliding through forests of towering oaks and chestnuts, they gathered information on Loyalist Tory Rangers who could strike the city at any moment.

Quaking, Peggy toasted herself by the fire. "It's cold enough for Hell to freeze over," she muttered. "All right, Lord, maybe this is proverb. Are you sending us a sign that our improbable Revolution may actually succeed? Please? If we just screw our courage to the sticking place?"

Peggy preferred quips to prayer, intelligent bargaining to pleading. Wit was her bayonet, her way of leading a charge. She detested the woman's role of patiently sitting, smiling like a painted fashion doll while men battled and argued philosophy that could end tyranny. But she knew talking out loud in this manner was ridiculous. Her imaginary conversations were a recent habit, born of being deserted by her two older sisters, with whom Peggy had shared her bed and her every thought for all twenty-one years of her life.

Born in less than three years from oldest to youngest, the Schuyler sisters had been a giggly, triplet-like brood, tight-knit and entwined. As a trio, they complemented and balanced one another, each recognizing and coaxing out

3

the best in the other two. Like pieces of those new jigsaw puzzles, only put together did the Schuyler sisters present a complete portrait, with the most beautiful and vibrant image of each clearer.

But Angelica had married, seduced by an ever-so-charming card gambler. And now Eliza, logically next in line to marry, was gone to Washington's winter headquarters at Morristown to visit their aunt and her husband, who was surgeon general to the Continental Army.

And Peggy? Here she remained in Albany, alone, feeling bereft not only of her big sisters' company but somehow of definition and purpose without her arms linked in theirs. She loved her little brothers and sister. But Peggy couldn't share her heart with them. They couldn't finish her sentences with her own thoughts the way Eliza and Angelica could.

Who was she without her big sisters? She had always been "and Peggy," introduced third whenever the Schuylers greeted guests to their family houses. Witty, elegant Angelica; kind, affable Eliza; *and* Peggy. Within the circle of family and friends she was always described according to her older sisters' attributes: "She's saucy like Angelica. She's artistic like Eliza."

As she stared at the flames, Peggy's hurt at being left behind turned to annoyance. It would be nice occasionally to be described purely as herself. In truth, with her sisters, Peggy was often reduced to confidante and accomplice. Rarely was she the center of anything. She was beginning to feel like Cinderella, always helping her sisters dress for balls she wasn't attending, relegated to chores. Peggy was forever helping their mama and watching after the increasing brood of younger siblings.

And here was this letter, from another male intruder into the Schuyler sisterhood who seemed to think Peggy would happily become handmaiden to a romance that would take away her middle sister, too. This poet-penned aide-de-camp, this Alexander Hamilton, who wrote to introduce himself and to make Peggy his ally in his courtship of Eliza. And the bait to lure her in was complimenting her person and mind as Eliza had depicted it in a pretty miniature painting? As if Peggy was so easily manipulated by flattery.

But the thought that had kept her tossing and turning? Eliza was obviously falling for this man. Normally her gentle sister would be far too modest to show her artwork to anyone. This was dangerous. Peggy must remain a watchful sentry to Eliza's enormous heart. She had learned the pitfalls of not being on guard for a sister the hard way with Angelica.

After lighting a candle, Peggy pulled Hamilton's letter out from its hiding spot behind the cushion of a wingback armchair next to the hearth. She tucked her feet up under her, huddled in her shawls, and began to read.

I venture to tell you in confidence, that by some odd contrivance or other, your sister has found out the secret of interesting me in every thing that concerns her.

Hmpf. As if the sweet Eliza was some calculating enchantress, fumed Peggy. She squinted at the parchment.

The handwriting was neat and elegant. One would never

5

know Hamilton had written his appeal in the middle of a war. Or in a camp laid waste by four feet of snow that refused to melt—where stubborn, stoic Patriots slept crammed together in tiny log huts, lying side by side with their feet to a fire, to share body warmth and make it through the night without frostbite.

I have already confessed the influence your sister has gained over me; yet notwithstanding this, I have some things of a very serious and heinous nature to lay to her charge.

Peggy fairly growled at that line. What could Eliza possibly be guilty of?

She is most unmercifully handsome and so perverse that she has none of those affectations which are the prerogatives of beauty. Her good sense is destitute of . . . vanity and ostentation. . . . She has good nature affability and vivacity unembellished with that charming frivolousness which is justly deemed one of the principal accomplishments of a belle.

Hmpf again. Well, all right, he had that correct. Eliza was all earnestness. She did not play games. She did not pull on heartstrings for amusement. No, that was Angelica. The famed "thief of hearts," as one officer had called her.

Peggy dropped Hamilton's letter. Her room filled with the memory of her sisters' mingled chimes of laughter. Their reading poetry aloud to one another's sighs of romantic appreciation. Their harmless gossiping about the dashing soldiers surrounding their father when he commanded the Northern Army.

That had all changed the summer of 1777. When New

York was burning and Americans were dying in apocalyptic numbers. When Angelica made her own defiant claim for liberty and breathlessly whispered, "I have a secret. Tonight, my dearest sisters, I elope with John Carter! You must help me escape."

PART ONE
1777

These are the times that try men's souls. The summer soldier and the sunshine patriot will, in this crisis, shrink from the service of their country; but he that stands by it now, deserves the love and thanks of man and woman.

—Thomas Paine, "The Crisis, No. 1"

ONE

Almost Spring

There is something in the behavior of [General Schuyler's] daughters that makes you acquainted with them instantly. . . . I sat among them like an old Acquaintance, tho' this only the seventh day since my introduction. . . . [The girls] would not let me leave them without some mark of kindness, and therefore loaded me with Grapes which they plucked fresh from the vines themselves.

—Tench Tilghman, aide-de-camp to General George Washington

"IT IS YOUR PLAY, MADEMOISELLE." JOHN CARTER smiled at Angelica as she hesitated over her cards. She and he were partners in a game of whist. Across the table, facing each other, Peggy and Eliza were paired against them.

Carter had laid down a six of spades, Peggy an eight of the same suit. To win the trick, Angelica needed to play a higher card than Peggy's but anticipate what Eliza might

11

hold in her hand. The deck from which they pulled was getting low. Her choice would likely determine the contest.

"Hearts is trump," he reminded her. "I wonder. What will be your trick?" A mischievous challenge flickered in Carter's blue-sky eyes. "Have you counted the cards in the previous rounds? May I hint at the solution?"

"Oh, but that would be cheating, Mr. Carter!" Eliza protested. "Partners sharing intelligence is against the rules."

Angelica flushed at his implication that she had not been keeping track of the played cards or analyzing her opponents' strategy—both key to winning whist. Lifting her chin, she lightly retorted, "*Chaque joueur doit accepter les cartes que la vie lui distribué. Mais une fois qu'il les a en main, lui seul peut décider comment jouer ses cartes pour gagner la partie. . . .*"

"Ahhhh." Carter nodded, not taking his eyes off her. "You have read the French philosopher Voltaire."

"I have read a great many things, sir. This may not be London, but we are still enlightened. You should see my father's library."

"I have not been invited."

"*C'est facile à remédier. Après ça tours, alors.*"

Eliza held her cards to her face like a fan and whispered behind them, "I hate it when you speak French, Angelica. You know how I struggle with it."

But Angelica did not break her gaze with Carter to respond.

So Peggy did instead. "All she said, sister, is that a player must accept the hand life deals, and only she may decide how

12

to play those cards in order to win her game with fate."

Eliza smiled gratefully.

Peggy didn't translate that Angelica planned to take Carter into Philip Schuyler's library after the card game. Eliza would be shocked at the implication of such a tête-à-tête. Perhaps Peggy would simply accompany them, claiming she wanted to retrieve a book from the two hundred shelved there. She'd been plaguing her pretty sister by shadowing her and her admirers to interrupt their wooing ever since Peggy was twelve years old and Angelica turned fifteen. That's when her eldest sister's first suitors had begun to flock to the family's hilltop Georgian mansion. It had been a favorite amusement for a preadolescent Peggy—when she first resented Angelica suddenly treating her like a child and crowding her out of their sisterly triumvirate by sharing secrets about her romances with Eliza but not Peggy—and the cause of much hair-pulling between them.

It was so odd. The expanse of years between them was so elastic, sometimes no space of consequence at all and other times feeling as insurmountable as a chasm. Now that she was eighteen and Angelica twenty-one, the difference felt like nothing. Although tonight, Peggy was feeling a canyon-wide draft of cold air between them again.

Angelica did not play her card. The look between her and Carter was searing.

To Eliza, Peggy said, "I suspect our Angelica is deciding whether to play an ace . . . or a jack . . . saving her ace of spades for the next trick." She paused. "I suggest your jack,

Angelica." Peggy gave her eldest sister a slight kick under the table to make her play her card while she looked pointedly at Carter to add: "It is always best to shed a knave."

He roared with laughter. "Touché! A hit, Miss Peggy, a palpable hit."

Peggy recognized that Carter was quoting from the sword-fight scene in the play *Hamlet* with his comment. She read, too, after all. Perhaps Carter knew that and was trying to play to her vanity about her intellectualism. She refused to take the lure. Peggy didn't much like the man. For one thing, he was born to British aristocracy. There was something too courtly, too frivolous, too showy about him in his beige-and-green-striped coat, his silk waistcoat embroidered with pink and green flower sprigs. He had actually donned an old-world wig for the evening, which hardly any real Patriot did.

Yes, Mr. Carter had reportedly fled England to join the cause. Yes, he was as beautiful a man as had ever graced their home. Yes, his European sophistication was exhilarating, especially for Angelica, who had essentially grown up in New York City when their father served in the colony's assembly. Now occupied by the British, New York City was forbidden enemy territory. The Schuyler sisters were relegated to their hometown of Albany. With its somber Dutch culture and architecture, trading outpost atmosphere, and narrow, muddy streets, it hardly compared.

So Angelica was restless—despite the young soldiers occupying the city's garrison and the parade of statesmen who visited to confer about the war with their father. Peggy's personal favorite had been Benjamin Franklin. He'd called her "wild Peggy." The way he said it had been more compliment than criticism. His sardonic commentary made her laugh.

As to Carter? Peggy just couldn't trust a man whose eyelashes were longer and thicker than her own. He also couldn't seem to answer to his whereabouts in the past few years without squirming a bit. Besides, he had been ordered by Congress to audit their father's military account books, to investigate its accusations that General Schuyler had mishandled the Patriot invasion of Canada the previous winter. That alone was enough to damn Carter in Peggy's mind.

She glared at him. The criticism of her father for the Canadian debacle was so unfair. No one had anticipated that Quebec would put up such a fight. Everyone assumed French Canadians would want to throw off British rule, too, even become the fourteenth American state. Yet, as commander of the Northern Army, Schuyler was blamed for Benedict Arnold and Richard Montgomery choosing to storm Quebec City during a blizzard and the disastrous retreat that followed.

Her father wasn't even there! He'd been ravaged by a horrendous flare-up of gout and remained in camp at the army's surgeon insistence. He was so ill Peggy's mother dared the harrowing journey north to care for him with her special teas. Peggy and Eliza had accompanied Catharine on that hazardous trek. Someone had to. Their mother was six months pregnant at the time—she could miscarry on the journey.

Thinking on the risks her mother had taken to save her husband's life and the poor untrained huntsmen-soldiers who slogged through the wilds of northern New York to take on British forces made playing the card game whist seem a superficial pastime indeed.

"Eliza"—Peggy broke the silence of waiting for Angelica's next play—"do you remember when we went to Ticonderoga to care for Papa?"

"How could I forget?" Eliza answered. "Oh my goodness, Mr. Carter, the things we saw."

Angelica frowned over her cards.

"Indeed so. But you were very brave, Eliza. Why, we nearly lost her at the very beginning of our journey, Mr. Carter. You see, our father had made himself deathly ill in service to our country. Knowing how concerned he is— *always*—for the welfare of his soldiers—even when he is racked with violent fluxes—we stopped first at our Saratoga farm to gather supplies for the fort. At Papa's own expense, of course. When we crossed the Hudson River, our wagon was so laden it tipped the flat-bottomed ferry. We nearly dumped our beloved Eliza into the currents. She would have been swept away, for sure."

"Good God, Miss Eliza! I am grateful you were spared."

Angelica shot Peggy a withering look, clearly annoyed that Peggy was hogging Carter's attention and sharing a story about an adventure she'd missed, choosing instead to stay in New York City to enjoy what would end up being its last season of Patriot balls.

Peggy ignored Angelica's glare to continue bedeviling her. "Oh, but that was only the beginning, Mr. Carter! For days, our wagon jolted along that path on the river's eastern shore. Whenever the wagon's wheels stuck fast in mud, Mama had to get out and yank on the oxen. Oh, how she pled with those stupid beasts. Eliza and I had to push from behind."

"What?" Carter asked. "You didn't have a military escort to help?"

"Oh no, Mr. Carter." Peggy smiled prettily to hide her inward smirk at her sudden mental picture of the immaculately dressed Carter trying to brave the wilderness road. Why couldn't Angelica see him for a popinjay fop? But aloud she said, "Following our papa's unselfish example, we only asked for one guide. We did not want to take any more men from the defense of our nation."

Peggy was about to continue her travelogue when she was suddenly beset with harsher memories of that exhausting, one-hundred-mile journey through the forbidding forests. She shivered involuntarily, even though she sat next to a fire blazing brightly in their ornate yellow parlor, soft with a florid Brussels carpet and cushioned chairs. How she, Eliza, and their mother had shivered back then—through bone-chilling downpours, and terrorized by the howls of wolves hunting in the thick, primeval woods all around them. What else, who else might be out there in the shadows was their constant question.

They had been so relieved to reach the safety of their

17

halfway point—Fort Edward—hoping for a cot and a hot meal. But the fort was a burned-out ruin, and the soldiers holding the skeletal fortification had no provisions. In pity for the bedraggled women, they managed to shoot a bear and cook it over open fires to feed them. That scorched fresh-kill bear meat had tasted better than any carefully dressed turkey presented in their mansion's elegant dining room. It tasted of staggeringly beautiful, untamed frontiers, of a gut euphoria at reaching safety after being in danger, of a freedom from Old Europe parlor-room niceties and banalities.

As Peggy had torn the meat off her roasting stick with her teeth, one of the soldiers proclaimed her as good a woodsman as ever a boy was. Catharine had been horrified. Peggy had grinned, grease running down her chin, loving the compliment.

Carter tapped his cards on the table, interrupting Peggy's musings. He laid them facedown, crossed his arms, leaned back, and tossed a dimpled smile of encouragement toward Angelica. Smooth, unblemished features; wide-set, luminous eyes framed by almost feminine brows. God, he was irritating with his sculpture-perfect face, his pampered refinement!

"Have you ever eaten bear meat, Mr. Carter?" Peggy asked abruptly.

He startled. "No, I have not, Miss Peggy." But he was clearly amused by the out-of-the-blue question. "Is it good?"

"Deeee-li-cious." Peggy drew out the word.

This time Angelica kicked her under the table.

Carter went back to dreamily staring at Angelica. The

man had recently finished his Congress-ordered audit and found Schuyler's records beyond reproach. But still he lingered about their house, like a bee drunk on honeysuckle. Peggy kept expecting her father to shoo him off. But Schuyler seemed to think Carter might be useful for intelligence gathering among Loyalists, since he was such a recent émigré from Great Britain.

That, at least, Peggy could understand. Having an ear to Tory homes was critically important. Longtime neighbors who remained loyal to the Crown had proven quite dangerous. Just a few weeks before, her father had uncovered a Tory plot to blow up Albany's powder magazine and set fire to the city. The wretches had even planted incendiaries all around town. Peggy had known one of the conspirators all her life.

But did this highborn Carter have what it took to be a spy? How Peggy wished she could volunteer for that job instead. She could dress up and act like a boy to hide her identity, just like Viola did in her favorite Shakespeare play, *Twelfth Night*. Shaking her head slightly, Peggy snapped herself back to their card game. "Angelica, play your card. We are all waiting."

"I would happily wait a century if your sister asked it of me," said Carter. "Frankly, each card she plays, Miss Peggy, brings our game closer to its end. A melancholy thing."

Eliza sighed, charmed. Of course Eliza would be charmed.

Ever so slowly, Angelica pulled out a card and laid it on the table. The queen of hearts. "Voilà! I believe hearts rule?"

A delighted grin lit up Carter's countenance. "The queen

of hearts commands all she surveys or touches." He bowed slightly.

Oh, for pity's sake. Peggy rolled her eyes. Angelica was a smarter player than that. There was no need to pull out such cannon fire for this trick. By Peggy's calculations, Angelica had the spades to win the play easily without resorting to a trump. It was pure flirtation. Deftly done, though, she had to admit.

"Well, with that move, we can only capitulate, Peggy." Eliza tossed down her cards and held her hand to her heart. She was in complete awe of her big sister's coquettish word-play.

Angelica stood. Shaking out her sapphire satin skirt and the tiers of creamy lace peeking out from her elbow-length sleeves, she asked, *"Voulez-vous voir la bibliothèque maintenant?"*

"Ah, oui!" Carter rose. *"Est-il permis d'examiner les volumes?"*

The impertinence! Did he have permission to examine the volumes, indeed. I should say not! thought Peggy. Seeing Eliza's hurt at being excluded once again by Angelica's French gave her an idea. "Eliza," she chirped, and purposefully mistranslated: "Mr. Carter was just saying how much he longed to hear you play the pianoforte."

How that sweet, heart-shaped face brightened. And how Angelica's clouded.

Again, Carter burst out laughing.

Well, at least he had a sense of humor, thought Peggy.

"Mademoiselle." He held out his hand to Eliza to escort

her across the parlor. Eliza giggled, blushed, and took it. She settled in front of a polished mahogany square-box piano, her billowing pink taffeta gown making a pretty picture against the room's gold-flocked wallpaper.

Eliza took a deep breath before beginning the Allegro first movement of a Haydn sonata. With nimble delicacy, her fingers danced up and down the octaves in crystalline runs. Then, with the piece's Andante, Eliza shifted moods, drawing out the expressive melody, lingering over its melancholy phrases. She swayed slightly as she touched the ivory keys, in complete communion with the lyrical movement, becoming a graceful personification of its airy, sublime tune.

Angelica and Peggy smiled at each other, all irritation between them extinguished. Their middle sister had that effect on them. Angelica and Peggy could be spit and rasp. Eliza was balm. She might not read as much as they. She might not speak French well, nor quip with their alacrity, but she far surpassed them in the arts and in the sincerity of her joys. Her music was magic.

Peggy glanced up at Carter, who stood directly behind Angelica. He was as rapt as they. Peggy softened. All right, he had a soul. Peggy always warmed to anyone who appreciated Eliza.

Coming to the end of her incantation, Eliza reluctantly pulled her hands back from the keyboard. She turned to face her listeners as they clapped—Carter impressed, Angelica and Peggy filled with affectionate pride.

"Sing with me, sisters," Eliza beckoned.

"Please, dear ladies, grant me that rapture," exclaimed Carter. "I will hold the image to my heart all my life, a shield against future unhappiness."

Angelica beamed.

Oh my, thought Peggy, how her sister succumbed to poetic rhetoric. How she wore her passionate heart on her sleeve. Who was Peggy to break it? She relented and decided to help rather than hinder Angelica's obvious love affair. She wasn't that good of a singer anyway. "Not I, Mr. Carter. I feel a bit hoarse. But Angelica has the voice of a seraphim angel."

Mouthing "thank you," Angelica swept across the floor to join Eliza.

The two conferred in whispers, holding their lips to each other's ears, their enormous nut-brown eyes and luxurious dark curls lovely mirror images. Peggy had the same eyes, the same curls—although hers tended to frizz—and the same dimpled cleft in her chin. But her sisters were graced with their mother's long neck, high cheekbones, and delicate jaw-line. Peggy had inherited their father's more aquiline nose, his slightly longer face and crooked teeth. Still attractive, she knew, but not as softly alluring. Whenever she saw her older sisters framed together like this, she felt a jealous pang, a fear of inadequacy. They were much to live up to.

Her sisters chose their aria. As Angelica's dulcet voice lilted through the room, Carter remained mesmerized.

"Can you play any of the music from *The Beggar's Opera*, Miss Eliza?" he asked when the girls concluded.

"Goodness, sir, no," demurred Eliza. The work was a

wildly popular satire of Italian opera, but scandalous in its featuring of London's thieves, prostitutes, and debtors' prisons.

"I know it!" Angelica piped up.

They all did, of course. But only Angelica would admit so.

"Please, then, permit me." Carter cleared his throat and began a cappella the lines sung by the rogue Macheath. *"Were I laid in Greenland's coast, and in my arms embraced my lass . . ."*

His tenor voice was as resonant and silky as any actor's Peggy had seen in New York City theater. She felt her left eyebrow shoot up in approval, an unconscious reaction that she knew gave away her thoughts.

The song was a back-and-forth between Macheath and the heroine. Carter strode across the floor to take Angelica's hands so they could harmonize together. She joined in singing:

"And I would love you all the day.
Every night would kiss and play,
If with me you'd fondly stray
Over the hills and far away . . ."

They stopped and simultaneously drew in a sharp breath. Before Peggy could interrupt, Carter leaned over and kissed Angelica. On her mouth, lingering, searching, in a way that made Peggy blush for her sister. Angelica did not draw back.

"Sir! What is the meaning of this?"

"Papa!" the girls squeaked.

None of them had heard the enormous back door of the hall open, their father handing his cloak and tricorn hat to Prince, his personal attendant and the enslaved servant he trusted to greet all guests to the mansion. Nor had they heard

23

Schuyler enter the room. They were that bewitched by Carter's musical seduction.

"I repeat, sir," Schuyler bellowed. "What is the meaning of your behavior?"

Tall, muscular, lithe, their father—when he wasn't ill—exuded a commanding prowess. He'd spent years traversing New York's upper lakes and dense forests—first learning to trap and trade with the Iroquois, then as a colonel in the French and Indian War. The Oneida—one of the Iroquois Confederacy's six tribes—had named him *Thoniondakayon*, one who walks young with old wisdom. With such bearing, rarely did Schuyler need to raise his voice.

Angelica's creamy, soft hands balled into fists at her side. Peggy could imagine Angelica's silk-slippered foot stamping with indignation under her gown—a gesture that always preceded impassioned speeches about her rights, peppered with quotes from Thomas Paine.

Schuyler's shout brought their mother scampering down the staircase, from where she had been putting her thirteenth child to bed. Having lost six children in infancy already, Catharine tended her babies with an anxious carefulness herself, despite having several enslaved female attendants who could help.

"Kitty." Schuyler turned to her. "Why were you not chaperoning?"

Catharine looked with bewilderment at her daughters before answering in her blunt Dutch-housewife way: "I expect them to safeguard one another's virtue."

"They have failed one another in that tonight."

"How so, sir?"

"I just caught Angelica . . . here, in our parlor . . . behaving . . . allowing this man liberties."

Catharine frowned. She wagged her finger at Angelica as if she were a toddler. "I should have known. I have never been able to teach you proper modesty, daughter, or proper restraint."

Angelica's face turned red with humiliation. "And who was it failed you in that regard, Mama?" she shot back. "When Papa was courting you?"

Peggy's and Eliza's mouths popped open at Angelica's salvo. No one had ever dared acknowledge the fact she had been born only five months past her parents' wedding day. A shocked silence fell. The clock ticked; the fire in the hearth popped and threw sparks; one of the grooms could be heard calling for lanterns to be lit in the back courtyard.

Angelica stood her ground, smoothed her skirts, and took advantage of her command of the stage. "I love him, Papa."

At that Carter gasped. But it took him only a moment to regain his gallantry. He bowed low. "General Schuyler, may I ask the honor of your daughter's hand in marriage?"

Eliza about swooned at the romance of all she was witnessing.

Peggy inwardly groaned. Angelica seemed more defiant than beguiled by love. She longed to ask her sister what in the world she was thinking.

But Schuyler's reaction was immediate and vehement. "Good Lord, man. No!"

"Papa!" Angelica wailed.

"My beloved child," he began.

"I am no child!"

"Then do not act like one, Engeltje." When their father used the original Dutch version of their Christian names, the sisters knew they were in serious trouble.

"I do not have time to debate this," he continued, holding his hand up to stop Angelica's protest. "Canadian Oneida have warned me of British plans. As soon as the roads thaw, they will invade New York, coming south from Quebec down Lake Champlain. General Burgoyne has amassed eight thousand British and Hessian solders. One hundred pieces of artillery. Those numbers triple ours."

"*Goede God*," murmured Catharine.

"He is also recruiting Senecas, Cayugas, Onondagas, and Mohawks as scouts and New York Loyalists to join his ranks.

"At dawn, I must ride for Philadelphia to meet with Congress. First to deal with the nonsense this man"—he gestured toward Carter—"was sent to investigate me for. And then to plead for more troops, more horses, more salted meat, more ammunition." He rubbed his forehead. "I swear Congress expects us to fight on nothing but self-sacrifice and rhetoric."

Schuyler paced, worrying more to himself than to the other people in the room. "The war could be lost right here in the coming weeks."

"But, Papa," Angelica interrupted him, "this has nothing to do with Mr. Carter and me."

Absorbed by impending catastrophe, Schuyler didn't hear her.

"Papa?"

He paced on.

Angelica reached out and stopped him. He blinked, then focused on his daughter. Somehow his voice gentled. "You cannot marry this man, Angelica. I am not even certain of his real name. Carter is an alias. I have just learned that he fled England because of a duel. Perhaps over a woman. Perhaps over a gambling debt. I do not care which. This man is not for you."

Oh, Papa, thought Peggy sadly. How could he know so little about Angelica's willfulness? Now that he'd commanded her obedience and denied her wants, Angelica wouldn't give a fig what he might uncover about Carter. Intrigue would only make her suitor more romantic and tantalizing in Angelica's mind.

Schuyler swung around to face down Carter. "Be gone, sir. Do not return to this house. You are no longer welcome around my daughters."

TWO

Spring

Colonel Richard Varick to Major General Philip Schuyler

Albany, April–May, 1777

Dear General:

It is reported here that the Enemy are preparing to come up the River [from New York City]. You may easily conceive how Mrs. Schuyler feels on the business, however, we have almost induced her to vacate. . . .

Last night brought an account of [British] frigates and transports . . . above Peeks Kill. The ladies were in a distressing situation for an hour or better and I am getting boxes made [for packing] for fear of the worst.

[We are] in very sanguine expectations of receiving some letters from you . . . but our most earnest wishes were disappointed, which induces the ladies to think that you are . . . unfortunately fallen into the hands of the Tories.

—I am Dear Sir, Your Most Obedt & Very Hblsevt, Richd Varick

28

"RIDER APPROACHING THE HOUSE!"

The cry by one of Schuyler's guards sent the Schuyler family scrambling from their breakfast to the window.

"It's an express messenger!" shouted twelve-year-old John. He pressed his nose against the glass as his younger brothers, Jeremiah and Rensselaer, climbed on his back to look. "He's wearing blue and buff."

"Praise God," murmured Eliza, taking Peggy's hand. "Maybe it's finally a letter from Papa." The family had been worried sick about their father now that the British had sailed up the Hudson River. There had been no word from Schuyler at all. What if he had been taken prisoner?

The horse was lathered, its breathing labored. Whatever the news, it was urgent enough to gallop. A reassuring note from their father would not necessitate pushing a horse so hard.

In the past days, they'd been bombarded by unnerving reports of British ships and troops moving quickly toward them, of Loyalist Tories torching barns in the night and kidnapping Patriot leaders. The guards placed around the Schuyler mansion to protect the home and family of the Northern Army's commander were jumpy. Most of them were old or semi-crippled from wounds—probably of little help in real trouble.

The rider's face was grim as he handed a packet of letters to the sentry. Then he galloped away down the drive toward the fort at the northwest peak of town, where Patriot troops were encamped. Given its strategic location near where two major waterways met—the north-to-south-flowing Hudson that stretched from just below Canada, all the way to New York City, and the west-to-east Mohawk—Albany had become the center for troops guarding against British invasion from Canada.

Peggy hoped the poor horse made it. The Schuyler estate was a mile outside the south end of town. The animal was clearly exhausted. Turning from the window, Peggy caught Angelica's eye. She, too, was tense, obviously recognizing the delivery was unlikely to be happy news.

As Lieutenant Colonel Richard Varick left the dining room to collect the letters, Catharine shooed her children back to their meal. "Your hasty pudding will grow cold," she chided. "Mary worked hard to make it for you."

Already finished with her porridge of cornmeal, molasses, milk, and butter, Peggy reached for a slice of bread, made of wheat from their fields in Saratoga. Before the war, their table had also been graced with salted meats and smoked fish at breakfast. But even the richest ate more lean these days, given the food shortages made by two armies foraging. The Schuylers still had preserves made from her father's hybrid plums, though, which he'd cultivated to be sweeter and fuller than the standard. Peggy wondered if her father would ever be able to return to the life he most loved—that of a gentleman farmer, overseeing his crops. Fighting had already dragged on for two years.

Varick reentered, sorting the mail. A gangly twenty-four-year-old, her father's military secretary was all hotheaded idealism, a Dutchman from Hackensack, New Jersey, who had instantly thrown off his law apprenticeship to join the cause. He was fiercely devoted to Schuyler. Peggy had grown fond of him for his emotional outbursts. Right before the rider interrupted their meal, Varick had been hammering the table with his fist and damning John Adams for attacking her papa's military judgment.

"Anything for us, Colonel?" Catharine asked.

"No, ma'am," he answered, distracted with one of the letters. For a few moments the only sounds were silver spoons scraping against china and a rooster sounding off in the courtyard out back.

"*Godverdomme!*" Varick bolted up out of his chair, shaking his head as he hastily reread a dispatch from Connecticut.

"Mr. Varick, what is it?" In her anxiety about its contents, Catharine forwent her usual reprimand for someone using the Lord's name in vain.

Varick looked up from the paper, his gray eyes wide, his face pale. "The British have destroyed our supply depots at Danbury."

Everyone moaned. The Patriots couldn't afford to lose one musket.

"How bad is it?" Peggy asked.

"I hate to say, miss. I do not wish to alarm you."

"You are alarming us more, Mr. Varick, by not divulging the details," Angelica weighed in. "And pretending we are not strong enough to know facts simply insults us."

"As you wish, miss." Sheepishly, Varick glanced down

31

at the paper. "They torched seventeen hundred tents, five thousand pairs of shoes, four thousand barrels of beef, five thousand of flour, sixty hogshead of rum. They also set fire to the town. Danbury's meetinghouse and forty of its homes are ashes."

Godverdomme indeed, thought Peggy.

"Five thousand boots burned when so many of our soldiers march barefoot?" Catharine shook her head. "How did we leave such stores undefended?"

Varick dropped the dispatch to the table. "Forgive me, Mrs. Schuyler." He bowed formally to her and then to each Schuyler as he said, "Miss Angelica, Miss Eliza, boys. I think I'd best issue orders for Albany residents to strip all lead from Albany's roofs and windows and melt it down for musket balls." He saved his final bow for Peggy. "Miss Peggy," he added with a shy smile.

Then he dashed out the door, all earnest flurry.

Her brother John made a face at Peggy and teasingly thump-thumped his hand against his heart. Eliza giggled.

"Colonel Varick is just grateful for the respect I show him," Peggy snapped. "You should be, too, for how much he helps Papa!"

Oh, why did Congress keep their father bogged down in Philadelphia continuing to answer partisan questions about last year's failings in Canada? He should be in Albany, readying his army! It was nonsense. Petty politics. Regional squabbling kept alive by sanctimonious, puritanical New Englanders! They just didn't like the fact her father was Dutch!

"Poor Papa," she said aloud. Maybe the letter said something about his whereabouts. Peggy reached for it just as John did. But Peggy snatched it up first.

"At least share it out loud," her younger brother grumbled as she scanned its contents.

But Peggy was so stunned by the heroics described in the letter, she kept reading until the twelve-year-old hit her with a well-hurled hunk of bread—right on her forehead!

"I say, good shot!" Jeremiah shouted, as he and Rensselaer guffawed.

Peggy's face flamed. "Oh, you're going to regret—"

"Margarita!" Catharine interrupted. "What else does the dispatch say?"

Peggy glared at her brothers before regaining her deportment. "You remember General Benedict Arnold, Mama?"

"Of course. After his brilliant defense of Valcour Island in Lake Champlain last fall, your father considers him the nation's bravest commander."

"Well, he has amazed again. When he learned of the British and Tory treachery at Danbury, General Arnold rode through the night in a rainstorm to set a trap for the British as they made the march back to their ships. He and the local militia managed to build a breastwork of wagons, rocks, and dirt and then lay in wait.

"Arnold's horse was pierced with nine musket balls during the fight. Finally it fell, the general caught in his stirrups. A Redcoat rushed toward him, bayonet ready, shouting at him to surrender." Peggy quickly skimmed the next few lines. Holding up her fist, she read dramatically, "'Not yet!' the brave Arnold exclaimed, and pulled out his pistol and shot his enemy dead, before extricating himself from his horse and escaping into the nearby swamp."

The boys jumped out of their seats, shouting, "Huzzah!"

Jeremiah skipped around the table whistling "Yankee Doodle."

Eliza laughed and clapped on the beat.

"Thank God General Arnold is on our side," said Catharine, reaching for more bread and plum preserves.

How could she think of eating? thought Peggy. "Excuse me, everyone, but you do know where Danbury is, don't you?"

"Near Peeks Kill," answered Angelica. "Right where those British frigates have been seen."

The boys froze.

Peggy nodded. "Exactly. Presumably on their way upriver to attack West Point."

Slowly, Angelica finished her sister's thought. "And if they take West Point, that gives them control of the lower Hudson River . . . all the way down to New York City. The river there is deep enough for any of their seagoing sloops and men-of-war to traverse."

"Controlling the Hudson," added Peggy, "is the perfect way to decapitate us—cutting New England off from the rest of the states. Just like Mr. Franklin's 'Join or Die' cartoon of the severed snake warns us." Peggy considered the situation with growing alarm. "You know, if General

Burgoyne comes down from Canada and manages to seize Lake Champlain . . . then heads downstream to Fort Ticonderoga and can take it . . . Burgoyne will be free to keep moving south, which brings his eight thousand troops to . . ." Peggy trailed off.

None of them had to verbalize the obvious meeting point for the two British armies—Albany. Thousands of British soldiers, bent on taking control of the country and crushing the Revolution and its Patriots, converging right where they sat.

Eliza covered her mouth, her large, soft eyes wide in fear. The boys plopped down in their chairs.

"Tush, child." Catharine reached over to pat Eliza's hand. "We must have faith." Even though her voice quavered, she worked to stanch Eliza's nervousness. "Your papa says Fort Ticonderoga is impregnable. It is shielded by cliffs too steep to climb and by the lake, which our Patriots have barred with a chain of thick logs moored by double iron links and sunken piers."

"That's right," crowed John. "Papa said that the king's whole armada couldn't break it apart."

"There, you see, my dear?" Catharine crooned to Eliza.

"You know the other thing that raid on Danbury would do, don't you, Mother?" Angelica asked, an insolent edge to her voice. The tension between mother and daughter since Schuyler had banished Angelica's card-playing suitor had been like the stinging pop and spark of fabric brushing together. "It would embolden all Tories in that district.

Right along the road Papa will need to take to make it home from Philadelphia."

"Oh, Angelica, don't," whispered Peggy. "Don't frighten Mama on purpose." When Angelica was angry, she could go for the most vulnerable part of her adversary. Peggy had experienced that plenty during their squabbles.

But Angelica ignored her. "I suppose if they capture Papa, they would take him to the British prison ships in New York harbor. Mr. Carter has written me appalling accounts—of so many Americans prisoners being crowded together into the ships' holds that they almost suffocated for want of air. The pork and bread given them is unfit for humans, riddled with weevils. If they receive rations at all. Sometimes they go for days with nothing. Men afflicted with dysentery, dying in their own filth."

"Angelica!" Eliza whimpered, pushing away her pudding.

Angelica didn't pause, not even in pity for Eliza, which told Peggy just how much she wanted to rattle their mother. "The Redcoats terrorize Patriot officers for fun—condemning them to be hanged, making them ride coffins to the gallows, with ropes round their necks. Only to be told at the last min-ute, in front of a jeering crowd of the city's Loyalist Tories, that they are to be spared."

Ashen, Catharine rose slowly from her chair. Peggy expected her to rail against Angelica's bringing their father bad luck by even suggesting his being apprehended by the enemy. She was Old Dutch superstitious that way. But instead Catharine asked, "You have been in communication with Mr. Carter?" Her voice was icy.

Angelica answered her mother's cold imperiousness with hot defiance: "Papa only forbade him from this house. He said nothing of our exchanging letters. And you know, Mother, Mr. Carter has the ear of General Washington's staff, a Lieutenant Colonel Hamilton in particular. Mr. Carter is to be a commissary for the army. Replacing that flour, those boots burned by the British at Danbury? That is now Mr. Carter's job. As Papa himself said, an army that is starving or doesn't have ammunition cannot fight. In fact, it is now rather unpatriotic to speak ill of Mr. Carter."

She stood up as well, eye to eye with Catharine. "I still want to marry him. It is my right. Our Declaration of Independence says all men are created equal. That all of us have God-given, unalienable rights to life, liberty, and the pursuit of happiness. Mr. Carter makes me happy."

Catharine snorted. "You ignore an important line in that document, Engeltje. As you just recited, the declaration says that *all men* are created equal. We women are still subject to the law of our husbands, and"—she emphasized the next words—"our *fathers*."

She stepped away from her chair and rested her hand on the chatelaine at her waist—a decorative silver belt clasp that held all the keys to the mansion's cabinets and doors. "Your papa has forbidden your marrying this renegade. So I will be locking up the house from now on, for your safety." She forced a brittle, authoritative smile. "And for your *future* pursuit of happiness."

She looked to her sons. "Finish your breakfast, children. In this crisis, it is a crime to waste food." With that Catharine swept out of the room. From the hall came two loud clicks as the bolts shut on the front and back doors.

That night, Angelica reclined in one of the wide window seats of the sisters' bedroom, silently gazing out into the darkness. Eliza embroidered one of her intricate pictures in thread. Peggy sat on the edge of their bed, swinging her legs and reading aloud to them—*Pamela: Or, Virtue Rewarded.*

"*Well, but, Mrs. Jervis, said I, let me ask you, if he can stoop to like such a poor girl as me . . .*" Peggy broke off reading and hurled the Richardson novel against the wall. "I know you wanted to hear it, Eliza, but I cannot read this insipid rubbish again!"

Aghast, Eliza cried, "You shouldn't throw a book, Peggy! You'll break the binding."

"Oh, Eliza, we should do more than just break the binding of that novel. Don't you remember that its heroine is almost raped by the master of the house, when he disguises himself as another housemaid to climb in bed with her? Then he claims he loves her but his family won't let him marry her because of the social chasm between them?" Peggy flopped back on the bed, kicking and flailing her arms. "For pity's sake!"

Normally Peggy's outrage with vacuous prose would have won applause from her oldest sister. But Angelica continued to stare out the window. Quietly, she said, "And there you have my plight."

"Oh my goodness, Angelica." Eliza dropped her hoop-bound cloth. "Have you been . . . have you been . . ."

"Attacked? By Mr. Carter? No. But my heart, my happiness are attacked, most assuredly. And if Mother had her way, she would marry me off to some boring idiot. Some mild-mannered Dutchman, I imagine. A Mr. Varick, for instance."

"Oh, Angelica, Richard Varick is not that bad," replied Peggy.

"Would you want to marry him?"

"No!" Peggy made a face. "But that's not the point, and not what Mama has suggested."

"Just wait. She might." Angelica spoke without turning from the window.

"What are you looking at?" Eliza asked. "Are . . . are you watching for Redcoats? Do you think it possible they will make it up here so fast?" Eliza's voice was climbing into an anxious soprano. "Remember New York City? Within ten minutes of the first sighting of a British gunship, the whole bay was filled with boats. Like all of London was under sail and afloat. One minute none and a half hour later, thirty-two thousand Redcoats."

"Beyond West Point, the river is not deep enough for troop transports," Peggy said, trying to assuage her fears.

Angelica seemed oblivious. "Well, they can certainly land at Kingston and then make the march up in a few—"

Suddenly, Angelica sat bolt upright, placing her hand on the windowpane. "He's here," she whispered.

"Who? Papa?" Eliza scampered to the window to look out.

But Peggy guessed instantly. Not their papa. Carter.

Angelica swung excitedly out of the window seat. Her sudden movement and her voluminous skirts would have knocked Eliza over had Angelica not caught her by the elbow. "I have a secret," she burbled with excitement. "Tonight, my dearest sisters, I elope with John Carter! You must help me escape."

Eliza fainted.

After much fanning and coaxing, Eliza came to, propped up by her sisters, in a rainbow heap of petticoats, disheveled curls, and tears on pretty faces. "Don't leave us, Angelica," Eliza whimpered. "We won't be the same without you."

"Think about this carefully, Angelica," Peggy urged. "Papa told you this man is a gambler, a debtor! A murderer maybe!"

"That's rumor and Papa's provincial opinion. No, Peggy. John told me all about the duel. It was over the honor of a lady who had fallen desperately in love with him. John was trying to protect her good name."

"How gallant," murmured Eliza.

"But Angelica"—Peggy continued to push for reason— "why did he have to flee England? Men fight duels all the time without having to run away."

"For the Revolution! And he's heading to Boston now that the port is liberated. Things are happening there. The Sons of Liberty are there." Angelica grew more and more excited as she spoke. "Don't you remember what it was like in New York City before the British Army invaded and occupied it? All those plays, the dance classes, the balls, the fox hunts, the concerts?

"Remember listening to all those impassioned speeches at the Liberty Pole on the Common about liberty and human capabilities? Didn't it make your mind soar? And stir your blood? Remember George Washington's spectacular parade through the city when he was made the supreme commander of our armies? The fife and drums, the dress uniforms, all those young men, the gorgeous horses."

"Of course I remember!" Peggy interrupted. "Papa rode right beside General Washington in that parade. You are forgetting Papa, sister. Think how you will break his heart by doing this. Right at a time our countrymen need his full attention! Look at all the British maneuvers going on. Our city may become the critical battlefield of the war. Things will hardly be dull around here. Mark my words."

"Blood, cannon fire, and pain, yes." Angelica nodded, sobering. "But no glory for us. No matter how much you and I might want to fight in the war, we cannot, Peggy. Women are not allowed to lead a charge." She shrugged. "But I could help persuade foreign dignitaries to go back to their country and send us arms, gold, ships, and men. Emissaries from France and Spain are sailing into Boston to talk to our leaders and decide whether to support us. Mr. Carter will be talking with them, too, to find supplies for our armies. You know I would be good at such conversations. That way I can be a real part of the Revolution."

She flashed that disarming smile of hers. "Plus, if you are so worried about Papa, remember that his most vicious critics are from Boston—Samuel and John Adams. Perhaps I can charm them into relenting a bit."

Peggy sat back on her heels. She had no retort for that.

Eliza had been looking back and forth between her sisters as they debated. "Do you love him very much, Angelica?"

Angelica laughed, almost as if she were surprised by the question. Clasping their hands, she drew her sisters to the window and pointed. Way down their hill, toward their private dock, was a silhouetted rider. He held the reins to a white horse, illuminated by a full moon that also sprinkled light onto the river's dark waves, making them glitter and look magical rather than menacing.

"How could I not love him?" she whispered, laying her cheek on Eliza's head. "He is like Perseus, freeing Andromeda from the rock to which her parents had chained her." Together, Angelica and Eliza sighed—just like they did over poetry.

Peggy bit her lip, knowing she had lost the argument. This was how it was among the three of them. Once two agreed, the third must go along—not in a coerced way, but because that was the irresistible pull, the strength, the sacredness of the Schuyler sisters' symbiosis.

It had always been that way, particularly with expeditions that required some daring—from climbing trees in the orchard to sneaking down to the Hudson to watch sailors landing at the family wharf. Typically, though, whatever aspect carried the heaviest punishment if caught by their parents seemed to fall to Peggy.

And so it was now. "Will you help me, sweet Peggy?" begged Angelica. "I must elope now, before Albany is engulfed in fighting and we cannot make our way through battle lines to Boston. Before Papa comes home. All I need is the key to the front door. The windows are all too high off the ground for me to jump. Mr. Carter cannot approach the house with a ladder because of Papa's guards. I must slip away quietly, out the front door, timing my escape in between the sentries' rounds. You are the only one who can move with the stealth needed to get into Mother's room and remove the door key from her chatelaine without waking her." She squeezed Peggy's hand. Her radiant, dark eyes pleaded as much as her voice. "Please?"

Peggy waited an hour, until the house was asleep. Then, leaning forward, walking toe to heel, she crept silently across the broad, bleached floorboards of the upstairs hall. Her papa had once described to her how Oneida warriors could come within a few feet of deer they hunted, without the animals knowing. Wearing his moccasins, Peggy had quickly perfected the silent glide.

Creeeeeaaaaaaaaaaakkkkk, the door to her parents' room

groaned as Peggy pushed it open. She froze, holding her breath as her mother rolled over. Waiting, waiting, waiting. Finally her mother gently snored again.

Peggy exhaled. Heart pounding, she tiptoed to her mother's dresser. Atop the polished wood was Catharine's chatelaine. Besides her keys, the ornate waist-chain held a thimble and needle case, a medicinal funnel, and miniature portraits. The tiny painting of Angelica was particularly pretty. What would Catharine do with it after her daughter so flagrantly defied her? What would she do with Peggy's once she discovered her role in the betrayal? Oh, this was all family treason, and for a man Peggy didn't trust at all. What was she doing?

Peggy hesitated but then shook her head to rid her mind of such misgivings. Like Caesar, she had crossed the Rubicon. The die was cast. No retreat now. She pocketed the chatelaine. There was no way to pull the door key off without rattling the chain. She'd have to slip back in again to return it before dawn, doubling her chances of awaking her mother.

Toe to heel, toe to heel. Peggy was almost safely to the door again when she heard, "Ma-ma-ma-ma-ma-ma." Eighteen-month-old Cornelia sat up in her cradle and crooned, pointing to her big sister.

Peggy shook her head at the child and put her finger to her lips in a hushed *sssshhhhhhhhhhh*.

Catharine stirred. "Mmmmmmmm," she mumbled, half awake.

Cornelia chortled. "Up, up, up, up," She grabbed the edges of her cradle and began rocking it back and forth.

"Go back to sleep, little one," Catharine murmured.

"Ma-ma-ma-ma-ma-ma."

Catharine groaned, nestling deeper under her blanket. "Sleep, Cornelia."

"Ma-ma-ma-ma-ma." Cornelia rocked harder.

She'd be caught! Hastily, Peggy scooped up her tiny sister. The toddler laughed and grabbed fistfuls of Peggy's hair.

"Shhhh, shhh, shhh," Peggy pleaded.

Yawning, Cornelia stretched abruptly, yanking Peggy's curls.

"Ouch!" Peggy mouthed.

Cornelia giggled.

Taking a deep breath, Peggy forced herself to stay calm. Slowly, gently, she swung the child and hummed into her ear.

Cornelia yawned again, bigger.

"Thaaaaattt's iiiiiit," Peggy whispered in a singsong voice, "gooooooo to sleeeeeeeep."

Cornelia's eyelids fluttered.

"Goooooooooo to sleeeeeeep."

Cornelia's head fell back against Peggy's shoulder. She had drifted off.

Ever so carefully, Peggy laid Cornelia back down in her cradle and worked her hair out of the toddler's grasp. She straightened and turned for the door—and about jumped out of her skin.

Catharine was watching her.

"Mama!" she gasped.

"You are so good with the child, Peggy. So good with people when they are sick . . . or in need." Catharine lay back on the pillows, obviously exhausted and still half asleep. "I am so tired, child. Worrying about your papa and what I should do if . . ." She almost drifted off. "Come here." She patted the bed.

Trembling, Peggy sat on its edge, careful to keep one hand atop the pocket filled with Catharine's keys to keep them from jangling.

Catharine took her other hand and held it. "Goodness, child, you're shivering. You are not with fever, are you?" She held Peggy's hand to her own face to test its temperature. Satisfied Peggy was not sick, she continued sleepily, "I remember when Eliza had her nightmares, you were the one to talk her out of . . . out . . . of . . ." Catharine's eyes closed. After a moment, she snored again slightly, that blissful heavy breathing of deep slumber.

Peggy made herself count to sixty before slowly sliding her hand out from Catharine's.

Her mother hadn't questioned Peggy being in her bedroom. Clearly, she trusted that her daughter had heard the toddler cry and out of kindness and goodness came in to rock her back to sleep. Peggy felt sick to her stomach. Catharine would probably never entirely trust Peggy again—once she discovered Angelica gone and thought back to this moment. What an enormous sacrifice Peggy was being asked to make for Angelica. Choosing her sister's love over her mother's better prove worth it!

Angelica was waiting at the top of the stairs, wrapped in her dark cloak to conceal her in the night. But nothing could dim the shine of joy, of adventure, on her face.

Taking her hand, and Angelica clasping Eliza's, Peggy led them in soft tiptoeing down the stairs, their arms lifted and arched gracefully as in the dozens of allemandes and reels they had danced together in their parlor.

Clllllliiiiiicccckkkk. The bolt unlocked. The night air spilled in, smelling of freedom, of intrigues, of endings and beginnings.

They looked left, then right. No sentry they could see—the watch must be pacing the back of the house. Without a word, the three sisters embraced in a long, tight hug, hearing one another's breath, feeling one another's heartbeats. Just as they had done when they were little and jumped into the sweet-cool lake by their Saratoga country home.

Then Angelica pulled away and fluttered down the hill, knee-high fog rising to wrap her in mystery until she reached Carter and the luminous white horse he held for her. Even Peggy giggled girlishly with Eliza as they watched Carter leap off his own horse to sweep Angelica up onto hers. Their horses pranced and pawed, impatient to go. Angelica looked back to her childhood home and waved to her sisters. Her cloak fell back as she did, revealing she wore her favorite scarlet ball gown. Then she disappeared, a blaze of brilliant red rushing along the river.

"Like dawn in russet mantle clad," whispered Eliza.

Peggy looked at her in surprise.

"I remember your quoting that once, from something. And I always liked it." Her big sister smiled at Peggy. "Angelica has ever been our brightest light, hasn't she, blinding us slightly to each other's?" Eliza pulled them inside and quietly closed the front door. "Truth be told, Peggy, I thought that bear meat rather delicious myself. As much as our journey north to nurse Papa terrified me, I thrilled to some of the adventure of it, too. I just don't have your courage to say it."

Again, Peggy assessed Eliza's gentle face with some astonishment. She wouldn't have ever guessed that Eliza might define her headstrong impulsiveness or tendency to shock people as courage. Or that the vein of wild that coursed through Peggy's soul might trickle through Eliza's as well. In that regard, she had always felt more kindred with Angelica. Somehow that realization made the ache she was feeling at her eldest sister's flight a little less sharp.

Peggy smiled at Eliza. "Help keep Cornelia quiet if she wakes as I put Mama's chatelaine back?"

Eliza took a deep breath and nodded solemnly.

Peggy took Eliza's hand and together, now a duo, they tiptoed back up the staircase.

THREE

Summer

Philip Schuyler to General George Washington
Albany, June 30 and July 5, 1777
Dear Sir

Should our Troops at Tyonderoga fall into the Enemy's Hands,
I fear they will be able to march where they please, unless
a greater Force is sent me . . . If any Tents can be spared I
beg your Excellency to order them up and whatever Cartridge
paper you can, for we have next to none on this Side of Tyonderoga. . . . If any intrenching Tools can be spared, I wish to
have two hundred Spades . . . we shall be in a disagreeable
Situation with little else besides Militia . . . If it is possible, I
wish your Excellency to order us as many Artillery men and
Field pieces to this Quarter as can be spared . . .

I am Dear Sir most respectfully
Your Excellency's obedient humble Servant.
Ph. Schuyler

"ELIZABETH! MARGARITA!"

"It's Papa!" Eliza jumped up, dropping her needlework. "Thank God! He's home."

Peggy stayed rooted. Since Angelica's elopement, their mother had banished the girls to their bedroom. Their father's voice sounded more like cannon fire than joyous greeting.

"Margarita! Elizabeth!" he boomed again.

Eliza's face flushed. "Do you suppose him angry?"

"Yes, I suppose him angry." Peggy took her sister's hand.

At the bottom of the wide, grand staircase stood their father, hands on hips, his boots and breeches splashed with mud from riding at a hard pace. Behind him, his aides carried in boxes of papers and maps to his study, just off the mansion's back courtyard entrance. A few feet beyond was Catharine, arms crossed, fuming. Peggy could imagine easily the conversation her parents had just had. Nothing upset Catharine more than displeasing Philip.

Her father was in full uniform. Congress must have cleared him of the criticism that Philip had botched the Canadian expedition. Peggy knew her mother would be aggravated by that as well. More than once, Catharine had said she hoped her husband would just quit. Many other generals threatened to do so, insulted by Congress second-guessing their stratagems or promoting less-qualified men over them purely for political reasons.

But Philip Schuyler was stoic and loyal. He believed in duty and the personal honor it brought a man.

Peggy noted all this as she descended the stairs, and

50

spotted the potential for a diversion. "Papa! You are in your general's uniform—congratulations! You have been restored to command?" She smiled hopefully.

But Schuyler glared back, her flattery missing its mark. "I am. Which makes my having to deal with a betrayal within my own family in the middle of these coordinated British attacks even more egregious. General Burgoyne is reported a mere three miles from Fort Ticonderoga! We cannot lose it—Ticonderoga is like a floodgate—closed we are safe, open we drown in Redcoats. I am in desperate need of reinforcements and ammunition to hold it. But General Washington must also block a movement of British regulars out of New York City. Never have we been spread so thin!"

Peggy felt a flash of resentment for Angelica and her timing. Peggy had feared this precisely—that reprimand. God forbid their sisterly insurrection endanger America's by distracting their papa.

"Your mother says neither of you will explain what happened or where your sister is."

The girls remained silent. They had pledged to not divulge anything until Angelica contacted their parents herself—to give her time, so that no rescue party sent out by their father would find her before the marriage knot was tied.

Schuyler sighed. "I have no choice, then, but to separate you two for questioning, as I would any confederacy of traitors." He took Eliza's hand and led her toward his study. "Come in here, Eliza." He turned to look at Peggy. "You." He pointed to a chair against the wall between his study and the door leading to their back courtyard. "Wait there."

Peggy sat. Closing her eyes to steady herself for her own interrogation, she turned her face up to the warmth of early morning summer sunlight spilling through the enormous window. This corner was actually one of her favorites in the house. With the window open, she could catch the scent of boxwood and flowers blooming in the formal gardens adjacent to the house and the sweet promise of recently turned earth in the vegetable gardens beyond.

She drew a large breath to pull in those delicious smells while Schuyler's aides hurried past her, bringing in their last armload. Eliza remained just inside the door while Schuyler quickly dealt with issuing some orders. Then Peggy could hear Varick open a paper the aides had brought in and splutter with aggravation.

"What is it, Richard?" Schuyler asked.

"Sir! It is a proclamation from General Burgoyne to the people of New York."

"And what does Gentleman Johnny puff himself up to proclaim?" Schuyler sarcastically used the affectionate nickname the British had given their aristocratic general.

Before Varick could answer, Schuyler's personal secretary, John Lansing, joked, "It is a wonderment he took the time to write anything. Rumor has it he spends all his nights drinking champagne with his mistress. Gentleman Johnny carries thirty wagons of wine, personal possessions, and clothing—as if he was going to a ball rather than a battle!"

The aides laughed.

But Varick did not. "There is nothing gentlemanly about this proclamation. He accuses us of tyranny! Us! He claims we persecute Loyalist Tories as surely as the Spanish Inquisition! He incites them and their Iroquois allies to take up arms against us. To attack and do as they will. He threatens us—with devastation! Wrath! Famine!" Varick read a horrifying description of the hell Burgoyne planned for the Patriots, ending with the British general's claim, *"I shall stand acquitted in the Eyes of God and Men in executing this vengeance against the willful outcasts."*

Peggy heard Eliza plop down into a chair, her wide skirts ballooning around her with a little pop.

"For God's sake, man, you've frightened the child." Schuyler appeared at the study door, calling for Catharine. She bustled in, all worry and motherly care. With that, Eliza's part in Angelica's rebellious love affair seemed all forgotten.

That had always been the way of it with their gentle middle sister. Their parents' ire seemed reserved for the other two, sometimes doubled in fury since what came to Angelica and Peggy included the dose that should have been for Eliza. Peggy would be in for it later. It was a good thing she loved Eliza so much, or she'd box her ears.

Sighing, Peggy stood up to gaze out the window. Outside, the family's stablehands scurried to sponge down and get water to the winded horses Schuyler and his aides had ridden. In the midst of the hubbub, Peggy noticed a stranger wander into the courtyard. Schuyler's guards should have

53

challenged him. Any man could be an assassin these days.

Muttering to herself about incompetence, Peggy went to the door and eyed him.

The man was lean, his face gaunt and smudged, his clothes soiled and patched. Thirtyish, Peggy estimated. He had taken off his frayed hat and was nervously clutching it to his breast as he stared up at the mansion, tracing its breadth with his eyes, his mouth slightly ajar. Peggy had seen that look of awe in many a tradesman who had approached her home for the first time. He was obviously no assassin.

"May I help you, sir?"

The man startled and brought his gaze down to her. He blushed as he saw her face.

Peggy smiled, touched—she preferred such unspoken compliments to the flowery pronouncements of men like Carter. She bobbed a curtsy appropriate for a more aristocratic visitor, and as she performed the feminine bow with its pre-scribed downcast look, she noticed that his toes had broken through his worn shoes and were bloody from his journey. But she knew better than to embarrass him. "You look as if you have traveled far, sir; may I offer you some water?"

"Aye, miss, please. But I think I best speak to the general first."

"He is with his staff right now. But in a bit I am sure he will be glad to speak to you."

"Begging your pardon, miss, but truly someone needs to look at these right away." He pulled from his dirty brown jacket a packet of crisp, sealed letters, emblazoned with sweeping writing.

Peggy gasped as he laid them in her outstretched hand. They were addressed to Sir Guy Carleton, the royal governor of Canada—official British communiqués! "Where did you come by these?" she asked in astonishment.

"Well, miss, I reenlisted upon hearing of the Danbury raid." He drew himself up taller, as if at attention and reporting for duty. "'Tis my fourth enlistment, so they made me a sergeant. In the Sixth Dutchess County Regiment. Sergeant Moses Harris, that's me." He tapped his chest with his thumb. "Anyway, Major Brinton Paine—you must know him, miss?"

Peggy twitched with impatience, but she knew she needed to honor the pride of this simple man who had risked his life so many times already for the cause while richer Patriots sat in their warm houses, wearing soft slippers, and opined. "No, sir, I have not had the pleasure of knowing Major Paine. That county is a good bit south from here."

"Aye, miss, on the Hudson just above West Point." He pointed south.

She couldn't help smiling. "Yes, sir, I know the area. And these letters?"

"Oh, right-o. You see, Major Paine sent me on a scout. I, by accident, all of a sudden like, fell into a party of exhausted Loyalists. They were lying beside the cascades at Wappinger Creek, fast asleep. That's why I didn't notice them at first; the grasses were up around them." He shook his head. "A fool I was. They could have killed me sure."

"And . . . these letters?"

"Of course, miss. I am trying to explain the way of it. Them Tories jumped up—like crickets when you almost step on them. One grabbed me by the throat. But I talked a good game, no worries there. I learned that from dealing with my accursed Loyalist uncle—a Gilbert Harris by name. He owns the Thousand Appletree Farm, what he stole from my pa back when—"

"Sergeant Harris," Peggy interrupted. "The letters?"

He nodded but persisted in telling his story in the manner he wanted: "I learned to pretend with my uncle that I agreed with his cur-like opinion of the Crown, figuring someday he might drop unsuspecting a bit of information we Patriots might need. So I convinced those blokes that I was a Loyalist like them were. We sat back in the grass. I revived them with a bit of peach brandy I had on me. That's when they told me our patrols had been giving them good chase. They were afeard of going farther. They had been on their way here, to Albany. They were to give those letters to a traitor in the city, who was to get them to the lobsterbacks in Canada.

"So I told them I was heading this way already and would gladly undo your father, the general, and his damned rebels by delivering their missives for them." He grinned. "So here I stand, miss."

Peggy grinned back. No fool, this rustic man. "Come

with me." Carrying the letters like a sacred chalice, she and Harris approached Schuyler's study.

Inside, Eliza sat penitent, in a Windsor chair tucked in a corner. Her frightened face was almost the color of the green brocade wallpaper. Their papa was surrounded by several aides, Varick, and Lansing. Studying a map laid out across a table, Schuyler was placing pieces of his favorite backgammon set to trace what he suspected would be Burgoyne's next moves toward Ticonderoga.

"Really, sir, I think Burgoyne's outrageous proclamation needs to be publicly rebuked so the citizenry do not panic," Varick was saying, pounding the table and rattling the backgammon disks. "The last thing Albany needs is a flood of terrified refugees from the country, looking for protection within the city walls. We have no food or shelter to spare."

"Perhaps we can confiscate houses for them from suspected Loyalists," Lansing suggested.

"Papa?"

Schuyler looked up with a scowl. "I do not have time now, daughter. I will speak with you later."

"But Papa"—she held out the letters—"this man has intercepted British communiqués. Sergeant Harris," she prompted him. Harris was again looking up, gaping at the mansion's ornate dentil crown molding and all the books in Schuyler's library. She cleared her throat loudly. "Sergeant Harris!"

He jumped a bit.

Schuyler straightened. "What have you there, Sergeant?"

Harris snapped into duty mode, saluted, and told his story again, this time mercifully trimmed. "I thought the letters urgent, sir," Harris concluded, "since they risked three couriers on the same errand." He shook his head. "There's sure to be mischief in those letters you need to know of, General."

Quickly, Schuyler rounded the table, took the letters from Peggy, and turned them over. "Good man," he murmured to Harris. "You have not broken the seal."

"No, sir. T'wouldn't have done me no good or changed my mind about getting them to you. I cannot read."

Schuyler clapped him on the back. "Sir, you have more good sense than half the Continental Army's senior officers. You are absolutely certain your deception held? The Tories were convinced you'd deliver these letters for them?"

"Oh, yes, sir."

"And so you shall, then. If you have the courage for it?"

"Sir?"

Peggy could see immediately what her father planned. If Schuyler could open those letters, read them, but then reseal them and get them delivered so the British would never suspect he knew their plans, he could prepare for their attack, perhaps even set up an ambush of his own.

Schuyler explained as much to Harris.

Harris grinned. "That would stick it to 'em, sir."

"Indeed." Schuyler smiled back. "It would mean you would have to continue pretending to be a Loyalist. If they

58

figure you out, you will be hanged as a spy."

"We all will hang if we don't win this fight, won't we, sir?"

Schuyler nodded and considered Harris for a moment. Peggy could tell her papa admired the sergeant's grit. "Perhaps we should stir the pot a bit, Sergeant. I'd like to send along a little feint that might pull some British troops out of Burgoyne's invasion force—thus lowering his numbers a bit to our advantage."

He paced, holding the precious letters. "I shall compose a letter to General Washington, proposing I send General Stark's brigade north to invade Canada. Everyone is afraid of John Stark. The man is insane—terrifying in the best way. We can hope Governor Carleton will panic and recall some of Burgoyne's men to defend Montreal and Quebec."

"But didn't Papa already try going into Canada?" Eliza whispered nervously to Peggy. "It didn't go well."

"It's a ruse," Peggy murmured into her sister's ear, as her father continued pacing.

"Oh." Eliza looked at Peggy with gratitude. "Of course it is."

Schuyler abruptly turned to face Harris. "You will need to claim that you came upon a Patriot courier when you were on your way to Albany to deliver these letters the Loyalists gave you. Say you managed to convince that Patriot courier you would deliver his messages. To me. But that you went straight to the Loyalist agent instead so that the British would know what we 'rebels'"—Schuyler made little quotation marks in the air on the last word—"were plotting. Does that make sense?"

"Aye, sir." Harris nodded.

"It makes you a bit of a double agent, Sergeant. Is that too confusing for you to keep straight under"—Schuyler hesitated—"under stringent questioning?"

Harris snorted. "No, sir."

"Good man! All right, then." That agreed upon, Schuyler could continue. "I have Oneida scouts, and a few friendly watchers in Canada, but I have been hoping for just such an agent like you, Sergeant Harris. To intercept British messages. Such intelligence gathering could be the trick that saves us.

"You see, sir, General Washington now plans a purely defensive war, engaging the enemy only in small hit-and-run skirmishes. Full-out battles are suicide. The British regulars and Hessians are professional soldiers. They outnumber us. They outgun us. So, we will seek to disrupt and perplex them. We'll cut their supply lines. Raid their outposts at night. Take what we need, then disappear, using our forests and rivers as shields. Like we did at Trenton. We'll wear them down by forcing them to maneuver constantly, trying to locate us.

"But all this will only work if we have solid intelligence of where the British are and what they are planning. I have been building networks to do that. Reliable couriers, that's the key."

Schuyler glanced down at the letters again. Each was closed tightly by red wax that had been pressed with a heavy seal, ornamented with the Crown's distinctive emblem. Any break in the impressed image would tell the recipient the letter's contents were compromised—opened and read along its delivery route.

"The design of these crests is more intricate than what I have seen before," Schuyler muttered. "I don't have time to re-create it today. I must open them without breaking the seal."

He unlocked his writing desk, folded down the tabletop, and reached for a long, thin knife in one of its slots. "Colonel Varick, light that candle. I suspect we haven't a moment to lose."

Schuyler was so intent on finding out what was inside those communiqués, he didn't waste time shooing his daughters out of the room. Fascinated, Peggy watched him roll the flat, razor-like blade in the candle's flame, heating its steel.

She knew exactly what he was doing. When the knife was hot enough, it would actually melt the wax as it sliced under, so that the seal would lift without breaking. The motion had to be quick and confident, though. The slightest jostle would crack the wax. Resealing it had to be done carefully as well—by holding the letter close to the flame to soften the wax enough that it would stick again when pressed. But not so soft that the wax bled a telltale trickle. A sure hand was paramount to it all working.

Peggy winced seeing her papa's hand shaking, making the candle flame dance. Sometimes he trembled like that during attacks of gout.

When the knife glowed, Schuyler tucked it underneath the letter's folded flap, up against the red seal. But he paused. "Damn," he cursed, pulling it back out again. He rubbed his hands together.

He looked toward Varick for help, but before the Dutchman could move, Peggy stepped forward. "Let me do that for you, Papa." Without thinking about how surprising her actions were, she reheated the blade for just a moment and then with a graceful flick of her wrist, swiped the hot steel underneath the seal, popping it open—perfectly intact.

She handed him the communiqué.

Schuyler and all the other men stared at her, stunned. "How did you know how to do that, child?" he asked.

Oh Lord. Peggy froze. She hadn't thought about having to explain that she'd perfected that trick as a youngster to snoop on Angelica. She'd been left behind as being too young when Angelica and Eliza first attended balls. Furious, Peggy started opening and then resealing ardent letters from Angelica's swarm of new admirers. Peggy had outgrown that bit of little sister tomfoolery long ago. But that probably wouldn't matter now, considering she was already in trouble for helping Angelica elope.

Now everyone would think her devious, unworthy of trust. She opened her mouth to find some quip to defend herself. But nothing came out.

Schuyler frowned. "Colonel Varick, have you been gossiping?"

"Indeed not, sir. On my life!"

"Margarita, have you been prying about my study? What happens in this room is the business of the Continental Army."

Peggy felt the color drain from her face.

It was Eliza who saved her. "Oh, Papa," she said, rising and brushing off her skirts. "Our Peggy is a wonderment. She has read almost everything here in your library and probably knows almost as much as you do." With careful nonchalance, she swept toward her sister, and put her arm through Peggy's. "Hadn't you better see what the letter says, Papa?"

Eliza was right. Peggy had underestimated her.

Schuyler shook his head slightly. "Yes. Yes. What am I thinking?" He read greedily as Peggy gave Eliza's arm a squeeze in thanks.

"Good God," he breathed. "Burgoyne is planning a three-pronged attack. As he marches down from Canada, and the British in New York City sail up the Hudson, he orders a Colonel Barry St. Leger to invade western New York at the same time! Leger will attack Fort Stanwix from Lake Ontario to gain control of the Mohawk River. And then lay waste to all the villages along it on his way to Albany."

Schuyler dropped the letter to the table. "I don't have enough troops or guns to fight on three fronts at the same time. We will be crushed."

A horrified silence filled the room.

"Quick, man." Schuyler waved Lansing to the table. "Pen and paper. At all costs we must hold Fort Stanwix. It's guarded right now by a handful of ill-trained lads. Order two hundred soldiers to reinforce them immediately. Now, we must copy these British communiqués and get them to General Washington so he knows what I am about."

He turned to Sergeant Harris. "Go to the kitchens, sir, and tell them to give you a good meal. You will need sustenance before you continue on to deliver these letters to the Loyalist agent in town. The couriers told you where to find him?"

"Aye, sir, that they did."

"Did they divulge his name?"

"Aye, the trusting bastards." He laughed. "His name is William Shepherd."

"Shepherd!" blustered Varick. "I know the man! Let us go arrest the traitorous cur!"

"No, you mustn't," Peggy blurted out. "He must think all is safe, so we can continue using him, Colonel Varick, without his realizing that he is to play our fool."

Harris nodded. "This one a smart'un, sir."

About time someone noticed, thought Peggy.

"Indeed, so I am learning, Sergeant." A slow smile spread on Schuyler's face as he looked at Peggy. "Now, daughter, can you open these remaining two? My hands are unsteady today."

Oh, the sudden pride Peggy felt.

Their papa had always favored Angelica with his conversation about politics, not Peggy. Could this moment change that? The night she eloped, Angelica said she hoped her marriage would allow her to participate in the Revolution in a tangible way—influencing her husband's dinner guests and visiting foreign dignitaries. Was it possible that Peggy's tendency to nosiness, her capacity for shrewd observation—which many dismissed as sarcasm or as inappropriate for a woman—could actually help her serve the cause of liberty?

Hushed at the possibility, Peggy held out her hand to receive responsibility.

But just as her papa passed the letters to Peggy, an express rider rushed into the room, red-faced, soaked in sweat.

"General Schuyler, sir!" he shouted breathlessly. "Ticonderoga has fallen. Without a shot fired. And our troops—all three thousand of them—disappeared. Without a trace!"

FOUR

❧ ❧

Midsummer

Alexander Hamilton to [New York delegate] John Jay
Pompton Plains [New Jersey], July 13th, 1777

The stroke at Ticonderoga is heavy, unexpected and unac-
countable. . . . [W]hat, in the name of common sense could
have induced the evacuation? I would wish to suspend my
judgment on the matter; but certainly present appearances
speak either the most abandoned cowardice, or treachery. . . .
All is mystery and dark beyond conjecture.

I am Dr Sir
Your most Obed servant
A. Hamilton

CRAAAACCKK!

Crack-crack-crack!

Peggy shot up in bed. That was musket fire.

"There! The tree line. See 'em?"

Peggy could hear the sentries outside shouting. She jumped out of bed to run to her mother's room.

She and Catharine were in the family's Saratoga country house to pack up precious belongings and to gather what stores of wheat and flax they could before Burgoyne's army overran their fields. The fall of Fort Ticonderoga and the disappearance of Patriot troops supposed to guard it had thrown New York into panic. Those three thousand soldiers made up a third of all American troops—if they were prisoners or, worse, gone over to the enemy, the fight for liberty would be all but dead and hopeless.

And Burgoyne was on the move—heading straight for them.

Her papa had raced to Fort Edward, desperately marshaling what little troops he had left to mount a defense against the British invasion. He urged Patriots to quickly harvest their crops—or burn them—and to drive their livestock into the relative safety of Albany. This biblically harsh sacrifice would starve the approaching Redcoats, who expected to live off the land as they marched. But it could also starve all New Yorkers. That wheat and corn was to be their food supply during the coming winter.

Believing she should, by example, inspire the populace to obey her husband's orders, Catharine had ridden north *toward* the enemy. She clearly didn't recognize or care about the danger, since Catharine had carted along little Cornelia as well as Peggy.

Eliza had been left behind, safe in Albany, supposedly

67

to keep an eye on John, who had threatened to join up as a drummer boy the instant Catharine left. Of course, rarely did Catharine enlist Eliza in manual labor like packing china or even overseeing their enslaved servants doing it.

Being dragged to Saratoga felt like punishment for her part in Angelica's elopement. As Peggy had expected, Eliza's sensitive and inoffensive nature had brought out Catharine's motherly protectiveness. She'd actually accused Peggy of coercing Eliza into participating in Angelica's escape! She'd patted Eliza's face as she said, "I know you'd never have imagined such mischief, child. " When Eliza tried to defend Peggy, her mother replied, "What a kind soul you are to try to cover up your little sister's treachery."

Typical. When Catharine made up her mind about something, there was no changing it. Take, for instance, their still being in Saratoga. Catharine had foolishly lingered an extra day after receiving word from Schuyler that he needed the estate's carpenters and blacksmiths to build—with all speed humanly possible—carriages for forty small, unmounted cannon General Washington had managed to send. Without carriages, the guns were useless. Catharine had hovered, urging the workmen on.

What had she been thinking? She and Peggy were in the isolated house all alone. Schuyler and his troops were thirteen miles and a ninety-minute express horse ride away. All they had to protect them was Colonel Varick, who had accompanied them, and a few guards posted outside.

All this swept through her mind as Peggy sprinted into

her mother's room, nearly tripping over her nightgown in her hurry.

Craaaacccckkk.

Crack. Crack.

Catharine was already at the window. "Here, daughter." She shoved little Cornelia into Peggy's arms. "We have a few hours until dawn. Hold her while I fill the last boxes. I have some precious things I wish to wrap myself."

"What?" Peggy shook her head violently, setting Cornelia to crying. "There is fighting right outside in the woods. Forget the boxes! We must go now, Mama!"

Catharine lit a candle. "No. We must do as I promised. We cannot flee without the provisions we loaded in the wagon. And I do not wish to leave my china for those heathen Hessians the British have hired to kill us."

"For pity's sake, Mother! Your housewifery will get us killed."

Craaaackkk.

The front door burst open. Someone raced up the stairs.

Good God. Peggy almost tossed Cornelia at her mother in her scramble to grab up the loaded flintlock pistol laid out on a table in case of emergency. Peggy pointed it toward the door, cursing her hands for shaking. She'd never hit her mark.

"Mrs. Schuyler!" Varick called. "Douse that light!" He dashed into the room, waving his arms.

Crack! Crack-crack.

Varick blew out the candle and pushed Catharine away

from the window. "Please do not make yourself a target, Mrs. Schuyler." He peered out into the darkness.

"Who is attacking us?"

"We think Mohawks allied with Burgoyne and Loyalist brigades. Stay here!" He rushed out.

The women huddled on the bed as Catharine rocked Cornelia. "But Philip negotiated a peace with all the Iroquois tribes to not make war against us," she whispered. "Your papa has known many of the Mohawk sachems all their lives."

"Yes, but those Mohawks have also known all their lives the local Tories who are mustering units like the Royal Greens. And you know, Mama, some settlers encroach on the Iroquois hunting grounds. I heard Papa say the Mohawks believe that if the British retain control of America, the king will keep their borders sacrosanct."

"I suppose we cannot count on anything anymore," Catharine murmured.

No, certainly not, thought Peggy. Not if Ticonderoga—considered impregnable—had fallen. If the rumors were true, British gunboats had blown apart in a mere thirty minutes the floating breastwork that had taken the Continentals ten months to construct. And somehow they'd hoisted enormous cannon up the sheer cliffs of Sugar Loaf Hill to point them straight down into the fort.

Clearly anything could happen.

Crack! Crack-crack.

Trembling with terror, Peggy rose and took up post

against the wall next to the window. For a few agonizing minutes, she watched the flash-fizz of igniting gunpowder that preceded each shot. Peggy held the heavy pistol out away from her body, knowing it could easily misfire and explode, tearing apart her hands. She clutched the wooden handle, keeping her thumbs braced up against the cock to keep it closed and her fingers off the trigger loop. Her breath came quick and shallow. Peggy felt faint. Would she really have the courage to aim and fire and split open an attacker's chest?

What if there was more than one? To reload took pouring gunpowder into the pan and down the muzzle, ramming in a grease patch and ball. She didn't know how to do all that quickly. If more than one enemy came through that door, she, her mother, and her little sister were done for.

The back-and-forth firing abruptly stopped. In the dim moonlight filtering through the windows, Peggy eyed Catharine nervously. Did that mean the attackers were gone? Or were their protectors captured?

Peggy raised the pistol, took aim at the bedroom door, and pulled back the cock. "Aim small, miss small," she whispered to herself, repeating what she'd heard Schuyler tell her brothers. "Aim small, miss small." Her quickened pulse throbbed in her head.

"Mrs. Schuyler! Miss Peggy!" Varick ran up the stairs. "Do not be afraid." He popped through the door.

Peggy gasped and lowered the pistol. *Thank God*. Feeling like she was about to vomit, she leaned over, trying to breath normally again.

"Oh my Lord!" Catharine cried.

Peggy looked up.

A Mohawk stood behind Varick.

"Get back! Get back!" Peggy shrieked at the colonel. Raising the pistol again, she fumbled to cock it.

"No! No, Miss Peggy!" Varick rushed toward her. "Stop! He is a friend!" He pulled the pistol away from her, gingerly putting it down on the table. "It's all right. He stopped the others. It is all quite extraordinary. Regret overcame this man." Varick gestured toward the warrior. "He convinced his compatriots to stop. He came to us a few moments ago to say his kin had been enticed by a promised reward bounty for the capture of General Schuyler. Honestly, Burgoyne is a devil, tempting, exploiting—"

Sensing one of his outraged and rather verbose tirades coming, Peggy interrupted. "What caused his regret, Colonel?"

"He wishes to tell Mrs. Schuyler himself. Given the circumstances, I could hardly refuse. Sir?" He called to the Mohawk.

The warrior stepped through the door. Even in the dim light, Peggy could see his face was painted for war. She tried not to instinctively recoil in trepidation. His fierce and strong presence filled the room.

Slowly, Catharine rose.

The Mohawk bowed his head. She curtsied.

"When I was a young," the warrior began in a deep voice, "I often tired on the hunt. The aunt of your husband let me sleep in her barn. She gave me fruit from her trees. I do not agree with your husband, *Thoniondakayon*, and his fight against our father, the king. But I will not harm his family in the night." He bowed again. "I lay boughs of peace at your feet."

Then he withdrew, making no sound except the click of the downstairs front door as it opened and then shut.

"Quite poetical, don't you think?" murmured Varick. "I regret that we fight them."

"Who ordered their attack?" Catharine asked.

"Local Tories, most like. They are greatly emboldened with Burgoyne's approach. They'd like nothing better than to kidnap General Schuyler and turn him over to the British. Or keep you as hostage to control him. We must evacuate you at dawn, madam."

Without skipping a beat, Catharine turned to Peggy. "That is still a few hours from now. We can finish packing."

The rising sun warmed Peggy's left side as their two-wheeled calèche jolted down the road. To the right were still-dark woods, their tangled undergrowth a mystery of potential ambush. She tried not to think about that, or whether she would ever see their beloved country house again.

How many games of hide-and-seek had she played there with her siblings among the lilac bushes her father had brought back from England and planted in a welcoming lane from the Hudson to their front door? How many bluebird nests in tree cavities along their fields had she peeped into?

73

What joy it had been to lie in the meadow grasses and look up, watching the young birds' exquisite sky-blue plumage blend into the azure heavens above. Oh, and spotting the brook trout darting through the waters of Fishkill Creek as she hoisted her skirts and leapt from rock to rock to cross to the wilds along its western side. The gorgeous wild hydrangea blossoming there along the far bank. The glorious green cool that enveloped her as she stepped onto that shore and into the deep forest shade.

Her heart would break if she never saw all that again.

Peggy sighed and focused on the ears of the horse pulling the little carriage in which she sat with her mother and Cornelia. An odd twitch could signal that the horse sensed trouble she did not. Behind her, their heavily loaded wagon creaked. Varick and a guard rode alongside it, nervously checking the bushes as they passed. A third man rode one of the cart horses to steer it. In this slow, weighted-down train, they were, as any frontier huntsman would say, roosting turkeys begging to be shot for dinner.

For several hours they rode in careful, anxious silence, jumping when any squirrel shook leaves as it leapt from branch to branch. At midday, about halfway home, they heard ahead of them a bone-chilling cacophony—dozens of voices raised in panic.

Peggy pulled the horses to a stop. The pair stamped and snorted and shied backward, alarmed.

"What in God's name?" Catharine breathed.

Varick pulled out his saber and, brandishing it, rode ahead.

"Well, that's likely to get him shot," Peggy muttered. But she didn't hear any musket fire. She strained her ears. What she could make out were shouts of impatience, anger, fear. As if a horde was crushed together on the narrow road.

From behind them came the thundering sound of fast-moving horses. Peggy whirled around in her seat as their two guards pulled out the flintlock pistols they carried.

"Whoa, whoa, whoa." The three approaching riders yanked back on their reins. They were in a hodgepodge of plain clothes, their mounts thick plow horses. They were no military couriers.

"Don't stop here, miss," one of them said. "Burgoyne is coming, thanks to that idiot Schuyler."

Her father—an idiot? "What do you mean, sir, by calling General Schuyler that?" Peggy shot back. How dare this man criticize her father?

"Schuyler and St. Clair sold us out at Ticonderoga. Played traitors."

Peggy started to rise up and strike at the man with the carriage whip she held, but Catharine grabbed her by the arm and kept her down in her seat. She shook her head, reminding Peggy they were outnumbered. Better to remain anonymous. Catharine kept her voice calm. "Goodness, why do you say that, sir? What proof is there?"

"St. Clair has just shown up with some of his army at Fort Edward. . . ."

"Oh, thank God," Peggy couldn't help but exclaim.

"Don't thank God for it," the man replied. "St. Clair is

a cowardly devil. Burgoyne is laying waste to everything he sees because General St. Clair slunk out of Fort Ticonderoga in the middle of the night, without so much as putting up an hour's fight."

"But now it all makes sense!" Peggy blurted. "Now that he's brought his troops to reinforce Fort Edward. Surely St. Clair evacuated Ticonderoga to save his men from capture or certain death—to fight another day. Don't you see? If the British did indeed manage to aim cannon directly down into our fort from adjacent cliffs, their artillerymen could see every movement our boys made inside. They didn't stand a chance. So the evacuation was . . . brilliant! He saved a third of our army."

"Begging your pardon, miss," the second rider spoke up, "but that is simpleminded. Obviously you haven't heard the truth of it. Those twelve-pounders weren't filled with cannonballs but with balls made of silver. That's right—silver! We heard that them Redcoats shot pure silver into the fort— to bribe that bastard St. Clair into handing over Ticonderoga. People say he's come to Fort Edward to divvy up the riches with his conspirator, that old arrogant Dutch fart Schuyler. We ought to string the pair up, right now."

Peggy was speechless. She had heard vicious attacks of her father before, but nothing this ludicrous. Or this threatening.

"Silver balls? Hogwash, sirs." Catharine spoke, polite but firm, even though Peggy could feel her quivering with anger, squashed as they were together on the calèche's board

76

seat. "As we speak, General Schuyler is marshaling militia to fight Burgoyne. He is begging Congress for more Continental troops and ammunition. He is using his own money to supply the meager troops he does have. Meanwhile he has ordered his men to block all roads and waterways that Burgoyne must use—to fell trees across paths, to break up bridges and dam up creeks so they flood into impassible swamps. It has taken the British two weeks to go a few miles, has it not? That is because of General Schuyler. A traitor would not do all that."

She cleared her throat before adding, in her best lady-of-the-manor voice, "Now, where are you heading in such haste? Surely to join up with a New York militia to defend us?"

Peggy admired her mother striking such a steely attitude. If she weren't so afraid, she might have smirked, knowing what a dressing down by an imperious Catharine felt like.

The men squirmed in their saddles. "We be from Massachusetts. And our crops need harvesting," said the second rider. "We are for home."

Peggy wondered if they had deserted and stolen the plow horses on which they sat.

"Your country, *we*"—Catharine gestured to herself and Peggy—"need you."

"I already did my time," the first rider snarled. "I froze and starved this past winter and nearly died of the pox inoculation the army made me take. And for what? For twenty Continental dollars. All that paper money is good for is the outhouse. Which reminds me . . ." He kicked his horse to nudge it close to their wagon. "What's in here? Any food for a hungry veteran?" He reached over and caught the edge of the tarp covering their provisions.

Schuyler's two guards cocked their pistols as Peggy shouted, "Leave that be!"

Cornelia wailed.

Everyone froze in the standoff, until Catharine slowly stood, balancing herself as the calèche swayed with her movement. "That happens to be supplies we have gathered for the army. We carry them to Albany for the troops mustered there to fight Burgoyne. We do so at the request of *my husband*—General Philip Schuyler—who is, by the way, in constant conference with His Excellency, General George Washington."

As her words sank in, the first two deserters froze like startled deer. The third rider, who had remained silent, rolled his eyes. "Now you done it. Washington executes men what steal food." He tipped his hat at Catharine, before saying to his compatriots, "She's right, boys, now's not the time to quit. Remember that lad telling us Benedict Arnold has arrived to command the militia being called up? I'll follow him. He be the bravest man this side of Hades." He kicked his old horse into a heavy trot, calling over his shoulder: "Come on."

His companions watched him go. "The fool," the first rider grumbled. "I ain't going. I'm headed home to save my wheat and protect my family. What about you?" he asked his remaining friend.

"Aye, I'm with you."

They turned their horses for the woods.

The cowards! If only Peggy could join up. She'd show them what loyalty to the cause looked like. And oh, how she'd duel men who dishonored her papa with such lies!

Only when the riders disappeared from view did Catharine collapse back onto the seat. "Let us find Colonel Varick, child. Quickly."

Five minutes down the rutted road, they found it swarming with cows, hogs, sheep, and farmers trying to herd them around a clog of wagons stuck fast in mud. The woods grew so close to the path, many of the animals were caught up in thick brambles. They thrashed and kicked, grunting, mooing, bleating, as their herdsmen tried to cut back the thorny thickets to release them. Their own faces bled from deep scratches where branches had whipped up in the fray, slicing open the men's skin.

In the road, other frontiersmen were pushing carts and shouting curses at one another. Women stood nearby, their children clutching their skirts and whimpering. A boy held Varick's horse. The colonel was down in the mire, yanking on a wagon wheel as a hulking old man shoved its back.

There was no getting around the tangle. Those wagons simply had to move.

Making it all worse were more families and livestock stalled in a merging pathway, coming from the northwest, out of the forest. Fear and rage and life-or-death impatience were splashed along their faces. Peggy felt her skin prickle with anxiety. The British and Loyalist raids they were fleeing must have been horrific to spark this much terror. These were hardened frontiersmen who braved many soul-breaking hardships to hack out their rustic farms on the edge of the wilderness.

She was about to take Catharine's hand for comfort when Peggy thought she recognized a distant cousin of their vast extended Schuyler family. "Mama, isn't that Ann Bleecker?" She pointed to a young mother, kneeling in the grasses, wailing. A little girl clung to her, sobbing.

"Goodness, it is." Catharine frowned, witnessing the woman's anguish. "Go see if we can help her."

Peggy clambered down and hurried toward Bleecker. She could see a baby lying on the ground. As she drew closer—and just as she realized with horror that the poor baby was dead—an elderly farmer grabbed Peggy's arm. "Don't get no closer, missy. That baby died of the runs. You be one of the general's daughters, aren't you? I recognize the good Mrs. Schuyler." He nodded toward Catharine.

"Y-y-yes," stammered Peggy. She tried to pull herself loose of his grip. She couldn't just this leave this poor woman.

But the elderly man held fast, seeming to read her mind. "Not nothing you can do for Missus Bleecker. She won't even let friends near her yet. She's mourning her babe. When she's through, we'll bury the little lamb and then keep moving to Albany. The babe sparked a high fever. So if we're going to get the curse of whatever tore her up with dysentery, the die is cast for us. No need for you to endanger yourself. Your papa been good to me. I tenant on your Saratoga lands. I can't let you get sick, missy."

He looked sadly to the weeping mother and her children. "This is what happens with bad water, food that spoils on the road. Damn the bloodybacks. Damn the Tories what help them. They torched all the farms round us. Beat a widow trying to douse the flames. Bayoneted her son. A young woman, name of Jenny McCrea, has been murdered, rumor has it by Torries or a Huron with them. She were engaged to a Loyalist officer—someone on their side! If that be true, no one's safe." He gestured to the swarming crowd. "That be what's fulminating all this."

Right as he pointed, the wagon Varick was struggling to uncork from the mire popped free.

Cries of "Huzzah!" "Thank God!" "Move on!" echoed into the woods.

"Go on now, missy." The old farmer gently turned her to head back to her carriage. "Your mama needs you."

Peggy staggered toward Catharine, sick to her soul. Eloquent words and lofty beliefs in the rights of man, of an individual's God-given ability to think for him or herself, had spawned their Revolution. This, though, was how it was fought. In vicious attacks neighbor to neighbor; in fear; with rumors spawning panic, hatred, and retributions. And this was what it cost—refugee children dying on the roadside as their parents fled enemy armies thinking that would keep them safe and alive.

As Peggy crawled back onto the seat and their calèche rolled forward, she swore that if she did nothing else, she would stick fast to her family to watch over them. She prayed she'd have the nerve to protect them when it really counted.

FIVE

Late Summer

Albany, August 8th
Philip Schuyler to the following:
To Governor Clinton (New York)
[W]hat reinforcements of Militia are we likely to have? . . .
Yesterday, the time expired of a regiment of Continental
troops, they marched off, nor could I prevail on one (man) to
remain., altho I offered twenty dollars bounty if they would
engage.

To Governor Trumball (Connecticut)
[N]one of your militia has yet joined us. I wish it may be
remembered that I have made early & repeated application for
assistance; that I have only had about one hundred from your
State, and those deserted a few days after their arrival.

To the Committee of Berkshire (Massachusetts)
We are very weak . . . If the enemy gets as far as this place it

*will soon be lost. . . . If [your militia] come an hour too late it
is the same as a year.*

*I am with Great Esteem & Regard your most obed.
Hble Servant, Ph. Schuyler*

SAFELY BACK IN ALBANY, PEGGY STOOD IN THE WIDE
hallway of her family's mansion, smiling at two Iroquois
warriors. Their Kahstowah headdresses of three eagle
feathers—two pointed up and one hanging down—had
quickly identified them as Oneida. Their arms also bore the
Oneida's tattoo of a rock in a fork, their sign as People of the
Standing Stone, a symbol of their endurance and constancy
to one another. With them were seven Caughnawaga who
had journeyed from Canada to speak to her father.

Philip Schuyler had ridden hard through the night from
his new headquarters just south of Fort Edward to meet the
Indian delegation. Clearly the Caughnawaga had critically
important intelligence to have traveled so far, and considering the increasing attacks on frontier settlers and American
scouting parties, it was crucial Schuyler reinforce his friendship with the Oneida. Of the Six Nations of the Iroquois
Confederacy four had allied with Burgoyne—the Mohawk,
Seneca, Cayuga, and Onondaga. Only the Oneida and the
Tuscarora stood with the Patriot.

"General Schuyler will be here in a moment," Peggy
said, bobbing a curtsy. "He begs your pardon for his delay.
An express messenger brought grave news my father must

respond to immediately." She repeated herself in French, knowing the Canadian Caughnawaga were more likely to understand that language.

The men nodded.

Even though this was the first time Peggy had been trusted to welcome such an important group, she spoke with more confidence than she might have if addressing American officers. Part of that came from the fact she had grown up meeting Iroquois leaders and watching her father, as New York's Indian Commissioner, negotiate with the tribes. At one such conference, the Oneida had even given her sister Eliza a tribal name meaning One of Us. The Iroquois were like that—embracing of family. They also elevated women above men in many ways. Clan mothers chose the tribal chiefs and had the authority to remove them if those men did not fulfill their duties to the matrons' liking. Women councillors attended conferences on war and diplomacy and had the vote to block a decision if they felt it endangered their kin.

Would her new nation offer her the same voice? Peggy wondered.

Aloud she asked, "May I provide you some food or drink?" The delegates shook their heads. She gestured for them to sit in the many Windsor chairs along the hall's paneled and lavishly papered wall. But the men remained standing, tall, on watch.

The eldest among them smiled back at her. He was older than her father, but his bearing was still imposing. Most likely a sachem, a chief. He wore the typical breechcloth and leggings, but also a white-man's hunting shirt he had decorated with Iroquois beadwork. Silk ribbons once imported from England were tied below his knees to ornament and keep in place his buckskin leggings. He was a walking display of the easy mingling of cultures on the frontier that had also created European-born men who fought with tomahawks and traveled by canoe.

So Peggy was not surprised when he spoke in perfect English, saying, "I remember you, daughter of *Thoniondakayon*. You cried when your father would not let you run in a race with our warriors for a silver armband he gave as prize after a peace talk."

"Oh dear," Peggy murmured. She didn't remember that, but it sounded like something she might do. Once when she was very young, Peggy had been furious that the Oneida had pulled her father into their ceremonial dance but refused to include her. They had all laughed, but in a kind way, when she had tried to smear her face with paint as they decorated her papa's. The Iroquois were like that, too—they joked easily among themselves and with those they considered friends.

How they had teased one of George Washington's aides two years before, during the "Great Peace," when the Six Nations had agreed to stay out of the conflict between the English and the then colonists. An Onondaga chief announced that he would adopt Lieutenant Tilghman since he was Washington's emissary. But to really become a member of his tribe, Tilghman must take an Onondaga bride.

Peggy laughed out loud remembering. She spoke quickly to explain herself. "I was just remembering when the Iroquois honored one of General Washington's officers with adoption and the promise of the chief choosing him a bride."

"Yes. I remember," the sachem replied with a smile. "He was sad when your sister offered to stand as bridesmaid—not the bride. I think his heart was for her."

Peggy nodded. Tilghman had been crestfallen, clearly quite taken with Eliza. He had been the only man she'd ever noticed look more at Eliza than at Angelica.

"Is that daughter of *Thoniondakayon* here today? She sang like a mockingbird last time we met."

Eliza had joined the Oneida women when they gave a concert for the people of Albany watching the peace proceedings. "I am afraid not, sir. She is with my other sister, who has married."

How Peggy was missing Eliza now. Catharine had sent her to the relative safety of Boston, to visit Angelica, whose elopement she had forgiven after Angelica had fled to her grandparents for help, counting on their fond indulgence. Angelica was smart that way. Indignant, their grandparents had arrived at the mansion and berated Catharine for being intransigent. After a great deal of tears and shouting in Dutch, Catharine had finally relented and acknowledged Angelica's marriage to Carter—or whatever his real name was.

But Peggy had heard her mother say, as she kissed Eliza

and tucked her into the carriage for Boston: "If that English-man is not treating your sister well, you bring her home."

Catharine might forgive, but she did not forget.

The Oneida chief interrupted Peggy's thoughts: "You are grown now, Miss Schuyler. You are like the great trumpeter swan that has shed its gray for white feathers and a strong song."

Touched, Peggy's hand flew to her heart. "Thank you, sir."

The Caughnawaga looked at him with a questioning glance. It was so strange to Peggy that all these tribes living so close together could be so foreign to one another. But then again, a Congregationalist fisherman from Marblehead, Massachusetts, had naught in common with a Dutchman from New York and even less with the country gentry of Virginia—even if they shared the same language and desire for independence. The Six Nations' cooperative confeder-acy among diverse and autonomous tribes for mutual trade and against common foes was a good model for the Patriots' fledgling United States.

"The chief was kind enough to compliment my matu-rity," she said, translating for them: *Le chef a la bonté de faire un compliment sur ma maturité.*

The Caughnawaga told her that they heard wisdom in her voice as well.

Again touched, Peggy lowered her gaze and curtsied, just as Schuyler hurried out from his study. Pulling his uniform coat on as he came, her papa was followed by Varick and Lansing. "Get these to express riders immediately," he ordered Lansing as he hurriedly scribbled his signature and handed the letters back to his secretary one at a time. "To His Excellency. To General Lincoln. To Ethan Allen, and these begging for militia reinforcements to Governor Clinton, to Governor Trumbull, and this to the Berkshire Committee. With all haste, man! Or we are done for."

She caught her breath. Peggy had never ever heard her father so pessimistic. She also had never seen Schuyler so exhausted. She noted him limping slightly, and prayed that his gout would not attack him now. They all needed him.

"Sirs." Schuyler bowed low to the Oneida and Caughnawaga and said solemnly in their dialect, "Welcome. How are you, my friends?"

"We have come, brother, to ask how matters are with you and Father Washington."

"I will not lie to a great chief. They are dire indeed. Please." He gestured for them to sit. This time they did.

The Oneida chief motioned for Peggy to sit as well. She glanced to her father for approval. He was surprised but nodded permission. Peggy settled into a chair, smoothed her skirts into their smallest circumference, and tried hard to suppress her excitement, to not to move at all, lest he change his mind.

"You must have news of great import to have traveled so far for us." Schuyler looked at the Caughnawaga. He repeated himself in French. "Please, proceed. *S'il vous plaît, procédez.*"

The Caughnawaga told of what they had seen in their country—that Burgoyne was eight thousand strong, including tribesmen and Canadians. A thousand Tories had joined as well. Some British regulars were left at Quebec, fortifying that city against any counterattack from the Patriots.

Schuyler nodded. "Yes, this we had heard from others. I am grateful you corroborate it."

He asked a few clarifying questions, of exact positions, the condition and supplies for the troops. Then the Oneida sachem added: "You fight more than Iroquois. Mississauga, Huron, and Chippewa cross by canoe from Canada in great numbers now to add their tomahawks to the British."

"Good God." Schuyler fell back in his chair. "I wonder if they will join the British siege of Fort Stanwix?" he muttered to himself.

After a moment, he sat up. "Sirs, what kept me this morning was an alarming report from the west. The British landed a force at Oswego from Lake Ontario. They marched east to attack Fort Stanwix. Their plan is to gain control of the Mohawk River, then sail down it to Albany—at the same time Burgoyne's troops arrive here to attack our city."

"This is a cunning plan," said the Oneida chief. "Two packs of wolves hunting one deer from two sides will always kill their prey."

"Yes. So you see it is imperative that Fort Stanwix not fall. To that end, I asked the leader of that county's militia, a General Herkimer, to gather his men and hasten to reinforce the fort. But this morning I learned that he and his men were ambushed and cut to pieces."

"By?"

"By the Royal Greens and five hundred Mohawk and Seneca warriors." Schuyler paused and sighed. "They say old Herkimer was shot through the thigh in the first volley. But the brave old man dragged himself to a stump where he propped himself and smoked his pipe to dull his pain so he could continue to direct his men. But alas, they were not prepared for such fierce combat." Schuyler's voice broke as he added, "These men are just farmers, who laid down their scythes during haying, and ran to defend us. Entire families are lost. The dispatch rider told me one father witnessed the death of seven of his nine sons."

Schuyler put his hand on the Oneida chief's shoulder. "And I must tell you, sir, that many of your tribe flew to help our militia. But your brave warriors were killed as well. Perhaps as many as seventy."

The Oneida bowed his head. After a long moment, he said, "A chief must bear many sorrows, brother. We will honor Herkimer and his fighters with our warriors."

"Thank you. But I am afraid we have little time to mourn. I must again ask your help," said Schuyler. "Will you send scouts to determine the situation at Fort Stanwix? I need to know how many British troops and how many of their Mohawk allies surround it. I have no scouting parties of my own to spare. The few we have risked have been ambushed."

"Before I risk my people more, I must ask the truth of

something the British have shouted to the Iroquois Nations. British chieftains say they command the Hudson River waters. That they have taken Philadelphia. That your Congress has fled and scattered like milkweed, leaving you without leaders, no council. The British say this will allow them to crush you in a few weeks."

Schuyler's mouth dropped open. "No! None of that is true. But that confirms what General Washington has feared were the British plans. Thousands of Redcoats have been loaded onto transport ships and departed New York City. But we knew not for where. General Washington must move with all haste to protect Philadelphia!"

Schuyler stood, rubbed his forehead, and muttered, "This means His Excellency absolutely cannot spare a single man to me now." He staggered a few feet and stopped. "Nothing to help me reinforce Fort Stanwix or to protect the families of Tryon County."

"What about General Arnold, Papa?" Peggy whispered. "He was so effective in riding to Danbury's defense."

Surprised, Schuyler swung round to look at her. "My very thoughts, daughter."

"Ah yes," the Oneida chief said to her with a smile, "a trumpeter swan."

With that, the Caughnawaga and Oneida left, but the day was far from done.

An hour later came a great banging and shouting at the front door. Varick rushed from Schuyler's office as Peggy peeped out from the parlor where she had retreated to draw portraits of the chiefs from memory, sketch pad and charcoal in hand. Cautiously, muskets ready, the guards opened the door to reveal a group of agitated Patriots from Albany's watch. With them, bound and much bruised about the face, was Moses Harris.

"We caught us a Tory spy!" cried the leader of the ragtag bunch. "We want General Schuyler's permission to hang him!"

Feigning enormous gratitude and amazement at their clever capture, Schuyler announced he would question the prisoner first. He hauled Harris into his office and slammed the door shut—leaving Peggy, Varick, and the Patriot watch in the hallway, much disappointed.

"Well, sirs," Varick blustered, clearly insulted by his exclusion, "I have questions about who you think might provide supplies for the troops."

"Oh, there are a brace of Loyalists around here with ample chicken coops and cattle we should confiscate," one watchman answered.

As Varick asked about beef and eggs, Peggy flounced into the parlor, fuming. The Oneida and Caughnawaga had just pulled her into their conference, even complimented her wisdom. How could her father continue to infantilize her?

Peggy threw herself onto one of the couches.

"Ouch!" She'd landed on her sketch pad and the tin box holding her charcoal. Peggy stood up, grabbed it, turned around while rubbing her backside, and flung the box. Damn it and all the demure feminine arts that she was reduced to!

The box sailed, crashing against the door leading to Schuyler's study and scattering charcoal bits everywhere.

Peggy sighed. Catharine would scold her for that mess. She stomped to the corner to pick up the pieces. As she collected shattered bits that had fallen up against the doorjamb, she heard voices! Muffled. But she could hear the deep baritone of her father and Harris's answering country lilt.

Quickly Peggy pulled a footstool up to the door. It was closed, of course, but there was a large keyhole. She faced herself toward the parlor, pretending she needed that perspective to capture its entirety in a sketch, and leaned over to eavesdrop as best she could.

Dampened, she heard:

"I delivered them letters to the Loyalists' man here in Albany, just like you directed, General. There was a bit of questioning to endure—nothing like what those Patriot ruffians done me that brought me here to you today. You should reward those lads, you should. Most men wouldn't hold up against their . . . interrogation."

Peggy could hear the scrape of a chair, probably Schuyler pulling up right next to Harris. "Go on," her father said.

"So it were simple to hoodwink him. The fool asked me if I'd like to serve the king as a messenger from Montreal to New York. And I hemmed and hawed a bit, sir, afore I gave over. Didn't want to look too ardent, that'd be a giveaway I were up to something. What sane body would go on such an errand?"

"Good man," Schuyler said.

"Then I told him about my uncle, that Tory cur what stole the apple orchard from my pa, may he choke on the cores. . . ."

"Mr. Harris, please, I am afraid today is dreadfully rushed with urgent news on all sides."

"Right, sir, sorry. So, the fool told me to go to my uncle's and his conspirators would send word there. I thought that right remarkable, till I learnt my uncle was in deep with our enemy all along. Round midnight, my uncle took me to his barn. And do you know that old bastard has a secret passage to a tiny room he built in the center of the haymow to hide it. I had to keep me head ducked. There were three British officers, mind you, all cramped up inside as well. They told me they needed a trusty courier to go to General Burgoyne and back."

Peggy heard the chair squeak and Schuyler say, "And . . . ?"

"Well, sir, I went straightaway to Burgoyne. That were your and my plan, after all. The general—handsome bloke, I must admit, and very jolly. He was with a pretty strumpet, but he put down his glass to talk with me. He gave me a canteen with three heads—one for drinking water inside, and two concealed ones, where he tucked two messages. Just like a chipmunk stuffs nuts into a hidey-hole. Then he told me to head back to Albany—Shepherd would carry the messages to the Redcoats in New York City.

"But then those fellows in your hall apprehended me. I told them I was fleeing into Albany for sanctuary, like all them other refugees. But someone recognized me, what with my going back and forth and all, and started in with questions. No fooling good Patriots, General. I count my lucky stars they didn't string me up afore bringing me to you."

Schuyler lowered his voice to an urgent whisper, and Peggy had to put her ear right to the keyhole to hear: "Mr. Harris. Do you still have that canteen?"

"Oh, yes, sir. Right here!"

"Miss Peggy!"

Startled, Peggy fell forward out of the chair to her knees, and her sketchbook slid across the bleached, scrubbed floor to stop at Varick's boots. Horrified, she held her fingers to her lips and looked at the colonel pleadingly. What could she say; what excuse for eavesdropping like this?

But Varick just scrambled to lift her, and flushed as he drew her up and steadied her. "Are you hurt, Miss Peggy? Shall I get you water?" He led her to a chair and hovered as she sat down.

Had he not seen what she was doing? Why was he smiling at her like that?

A different kind of horror swept Peggy at that moment. Could her little brother John be right? Poor Colonel Varick. She felt nothing in return.

Schuyler bellowing for his aide saved her from Varick's infatuated concern. The colonel backed out of the room, gazing at her with that silly grin.

Shamelessly, Peggy put her ear back to the keyhole just in time to hear her father explain that he and Harris had agreed to maintain his cover by sending Harris to Albany's prison, ostensibly to await trial. Within a few days Schuyler would send private instructions to the jailer to release him, secretly, during the night.

"Will that work, sir?" asked Harris.

Peggy heard her father clap Harris on the back and answer, "We have done it before." He opened his study and called the Patriot watch, who manhandled Harris out the front door.

From the window, Peggy watched them drag Harris down the hill. Her father had allayed their disgruntlement at not getting to lynch their captive by pressing a few shillings into each of the men's hands and explaining that a public hearing and execution would strike more fear into the hearts of Albany loyalists. As they disappeared, she noticed a cloud of dust and then a rider cresting the hill.

"Papa!" Peggy called. "It's another express!"

This dispatch brought terrible news: Burgoyne and his British Army had reached Saratoga.

But to Peggy, the next express was even worse. Two mornings later, as Schuyler swung himself into his saddle to ride to Saratoga to prepare for a do-or-die battle, in galloped a messenger from Congress. Schuyler leaned over to take the letter from the rider.

His face fell as he read. After a moment, he dismounted, landing on the ground heavily. His expression made Peggy tremble with uncertainty and anticipation of god-awful news.

"What is it, Philip?" Catharine asked with alarm. "Is it about Angelica? Eliza?"

Schuyler handed the message to his wife. "John Adams and the New Englanders have won their campaign against me. Congress relieves me of command."

The bastards! "Oh, Papa, I am so sorry," cried Peggy.

But Schuyler did not answer. He stumbled toward the house, limping badly.

SIX

❧ ❧

Early Autumn

Philip Schuyler to General George Washington
Stilwater [New York], August 15th, 1777
Dear Sir

It is extremely chagrining to me to be deprived of the Com-
mand, at a Time when we shall . . . face the Enemy; when
we are on the point of taking such Ground, where [Burgoyne]
must attack to a Disadvantage . . . —When an opportunity
will in all probability occur, in which I might evince that I am
not what Congress has too plainly insinuated by their Resolu-
tion, taking the Command from me.

I have the Honor to be Dr Sir with every Sentiment of
Respect & Esteem Your Excellency's most obedient humble
Servant.
Ph. Schuyler

"HORATIO GATES? THAT ONEROUS TOADY?" VARICK fumed. "Congress is going to replace you with him? That lazy, selfish . . . ?"

Schuyler help up his hand to stop his aide. "Yes. And he will need you, Richard. I have suggested you for his staff."

"No, sir." Varick shook his head. "I will not leave you for General Gates. That man has taken two weeks to sashay his way up here being wined and dined while we are in such peril. No, sir."

"Colonel Varick." Schuyler sighed. "Your country needs you, no matter who the commander."

"But sir, it is too unfair. You were the one to weaken Burgoyne by impeding his march. You rallied our militia. We are ready for this fight because of you. Gates is good for nothing other than politicking, his glasses slipping down that long nose of his as he pens poison. In fact"—Varick stood as if to make for pen and paper himself—"I think they should know that you . . ."

"Richard, sit down." Schuyler motioned to a chair. "I need you to focus on the work at hand. There is still much to be done. The battle at Saratoga will start any day now. I will not give in to resentment and fail to serve my country when she most needs me. Nor should you. We must do as I have told others: keep up our spirits, show no signs of fear, and act with vigor."

"But Philip, why do you continue working yourself to the bone for people who only disparage you?" Catharine railed.

"Because, Mama"—Peggy finally spoke—"if he doesn't, Burgoyne will take Albany, take the Hudson, and our Revolution is done for. Only Papa seems to really understand the critical nature of our geography and anticipate British strategy. Colonel Varick didn't include in his list the fact Papa was the one to save Fort Stanwix and stop the British forces advancing down the Mohawk River. Because of Papa, we only have one British army to fight instead of two at once."

"That was not me, daughter. That was Benedict Arnold."

"You are too modest, Papa. You sent General Arnold to the fort's rescue."

"Yes, but he devised the ruse that saved the fort."

"Because of the Oneida you sent ahead to scout the situation at the siege," she countered.

But indeed Arnold's trick had been a brilliant, life-saving, perhaps country-saving deceit. After a nineteen-day siege and threats to butcher them when the fort inevitably fell because of their refusal to surrender, the Americans inside were running out of water, ammunition, and hope. Arnold was within forty miles of it when he met up with the Oneida scouts sent by Schuyler. They warned Arnold that he was outnumbered two to one by the British force of Redcoats, Loyalists, Hessians, Senecas, and Mohawks.

So Arnold sent in a false messenger to terrify his enemy instead, his plan like something out of *The Iliad*. Threatening to hang his brother if the man didn't agree, Arnold ordered a captured Loyalist to run to the British and claim Arnold was coming with a vast army. The Loyalist did as Arnold demanded—staggering into the British camp, crying out that he had just escaped and showing as proof his coat, riddled with musket ball holes he had shot himself. Arnold was coming with fury and a thousand men, he panted.

An hour later, one of the Oneida scouts ran in, claiming he, too, had managed to evade Arnold and *two* thousand well-armed Americans. Then a third supposed escapee raced to the lines, this time insisting Arnold was pursuing him with *three* thousand troops.

The Mohawks and Senecas—already mourning the fact that they were fighting other Iroquois tribes they had called brothers for several generations—decided to quit the siege. They withdrew into the surrounding wilderness. Arnold's fighting prowess and do-or-die courage was already infamous and intimidating to the British as well. Despite the fact his soldiers were a mere 150 yards from the fort's walls, St. Leger marched his regulars back to Lake Ontario.

"Truly, Papa"—Peggy pressed her point—"you must give yourself credit."

Schuyler shrugged, shifting the foot he had elevated on pillows. "As General Washington says, we will only win against Britain's professional soldiers with frontier-style cunning. He himself has saved his forces by using decoys and evacuating into fogs."

Catharine noticed Schuyler wince as he spoke, and put another pillow beneath his leg. His gout was plaguing him badly. "Rest, Philip. If you are not better on the morrow, I am fetching the surgeon to bleed you," she said. Then she left from the room to prepare him willow-bark tea.

But Peggy knew there was no resting for her father. He had a full day ahead of him, meeting with delegations who still sought his expertise and advice.

"Is there anything I can do to help you, Papa?" Peggy asked. What she really wanted to do was to ride to Congress and thwack them all—just as Shakespeare's Beatrice railed against the courtier casting pernicious attacks on her sister's honor: *O God, that I were a man! I would eat his heart in the marketplace.*

Schuyler smiled wanly at her. "Find a way to pour that willow tea your sweet mama is brewing for me into a chamber pot?"

Albany's leaders arrived, bustling in, clad in self-importance and dark, Dutch-modest frock coats, no hint of lace frippery. Peggy knew their speech would be heartfelt but boring. She slipped out of the house to enjoy what she loved most about "The Pastures," as Schuyler had named his estate—its grounds. She could spend hours in their flower gardens and as a child had delighted in petting the soft fleece of the young lambs or playing a dangerous game of tag with the goats who loved to butt intruders. The estate always felt so alive. Now, standing on their hilltop, she happily breathed in the fresh breezes blowing up the river. The air carried a hint of crispness. Scanning the far coast, she could even spot a few maple trees mottled with the first splashes of orange. The beauty of early Autumn along the Hudson belied the danger marching south along its wake.

Perhaps some of the apples in the orchard were ready. Rather than going to sit in their formal gardens as she had planned, Peggy fairly skipped to the acres of fruit trees on the north side of their estate. Bordered by Beaver Creek, the orchard hummed with the chorus of honeybees drifting from tree to tree and the laughter of small waters cascading to the river below. It was one of her favorite spots—riotous with pink and white blossoms and their perfume in the spring, a paradise of shade in the summer heat, and a bower of sweet, ripe fruit to be plucked in the fall.

The very first tree she came to slumped over with the weight of its red apples. She pulled down one the size of a man's fist, and bit into tart sweetness. Heaven. Peggy bit again, her teeth breaking off a quarter of the apple whole. She munched noisily, juice running down her chin, blissfully happy, like an ancient druid tree-worshipper. She wandered from tree to tree, picking a few more choice red orbs, tucking them into her pocket as she devoured her apple. Then she sucked its juice from the core. Mmmm-mmm-mmm.

She turned and startled to see little Cicero, the stable boy.

Embarrassed, Peggy wiped her face with her handkerchief. She pulled one of the apples she'd stuffed into her pockets to hand to the lad. "They are quite wonderful this year."

He took it solemnly.

Cicero had only recently come to the Schuyler family,

hired out by a widow in Albany. She was an elderly lady who had remained loyal to the king in her parlor conversation and, as a result, had been thrown into financial upheaval in a city controlled by Patriots. The Revolution was costing so much in human lives. The old woman was politically harmless, her Loyalist stance bred by having family still living in Great Britain, a strong faith in the Church of England, and fear of the unknown. Peggy speculated the transaction had also wrenched poor Cicero away from all the people he loved. "Is there something I can help you with?" she asked gently.

"No, ma'am. There's a man down to the wharfs what wants to speak with the general. But I'm afraid to go into the house with all them gentlemen folk."

"Won't the man come to the house?"

"No, ma'am."

"Why not?"

"Didn't say."

"Well, it cannot be important, then," Peggy said. She took a bite of another apple—a smaller, more appropriately dainty bite. "Try yours, Cicero. They're perfect."

"Begging your pardon, miss, but the man, he say it urgent. He say if I cannot get to the general to ask for the clever young lady. The one so interested in—he made me repeat it so I got it right—'so interested in candles and knives.'"

Peggy about choked. "Where is he exactly?"

"By your papa's wharf."

Racing down the steep hill to the Hudson, Peggy burst onto the large common grazing pastures along the river bank, owned by the Dutch Reformed Church. The fields were usually deep in green grasses and peaceful. But now they were trodden and muddy because of the hundreds of half-starved cows driven into the city by terrified settlers fleeing the British Army.

At first, the refugees had jammed Albany's streets with their wagons and livestock, encamped there with nowhere else to go. Besides blocking all carriage traffic, the garbage and waste of so many people and animals living outdoors threatened to spread disease. So the city fathers had ordered all their cattle pastured here, their owners lodged wherever they could beg a roof or in houses the city confiscated from known Tory Loyalists. It had been quite a fight to separate the farmers from their cows. Unaccustomed to being so confined and in such a large mass, the animals were restless, anxious—an echo of the city and its frightened refugees and residents.

Peggy met an almost deafening mooing as she set the cattle running ahead of her.

Reaching the wharf, she was surprised to see how crowded it was as well, with people hurriedly loading boats and rafts. Usually their dock received sloops belonging to her father or doing business with him—most tradesmen and fishing boats went upriver to the city's two large wharves or the seawall that calmed the Hudson's currents into a still harbor. She asked one of the dockworkers the reason for the hubbub.

"We're heading south, miss. Word is Loyalists plan to set fire to the city right as Burgoyne approaches."

Peggy backed away, chewing on her lip. If her father's intelligence was right, sailing south wasn't exactly safe, either. She needed to find out what Moses Harris knew. She kept walking, scanning faces.

She finally recognized him, dressed in fisherman rags, trying to braid rope. Peggy had spent enough time around her father's ships to see the spy-courier really didn't know how to make rigging. Anyone who knew a thing about boats would spot that he was an amateur. But clearly he wanted to be incognito. So Peggy slowly wandered toward him, pretending to inspect the fish being hauled up in baskets.

"Hello, miss." He stood and tipped his hat. "Would you be interested in some oysters I brought up from downriver?"

"Why, yes, sir, I would."

"This way, then; I be keeping them in the shade."

She followed him away from potential listeners. "Wouldn't it be better for you to come to the house, Sar . . ." His frown stopped her from saying his rank or name.

"No, miss. I'm taking a chance being here at all. After being hauled off to the Albany dungeons, all sides know me face. It were necessary, I know, for the general to allow me jailed—part of the game—but I cannot be caught again here. I am dizzy with all the lies I have told. I fear making a mistake in my story. Although a bit of outraged innocence can get you out of a heap of trouble. Remember that if you get caught in a bear trap yourself, miss."

"Whatever do you mean?" she breathed.

"Well, you take a bit of a risk, coming here to talk with

me, miss. There are still plenty of Loyalists and turncoats in this city. If they realize you be talking to me, well . . ." He shrugged.

Peggy couldn't help looking over her shoulder.

"But here's what you do," Harris continued. "Them last letters I took to Burgoyne—the ones your father stuffed with lies and false orders to throw the Brits off our scent—they so fooled Burgoyne he thought he'd caught news that would be General Washington's undoing. So he ordered me take them all the way to St. John's. Canada! Once I got there, half-starved and footsore, mind you, the British royal governor and his men accuse me of treachery. Everyone accuses me of that. I am getting a bit tired of it, miss, truth be told.

"So I tore open my shirt, I did, and bared my chest, telling them to shoot me then and there. It was worse'n than death, I said, to be suspected of disloyalty to my king." He laughed. "I so impressed them they gave me some new messages for Burgoyne."

"Goodness, I'm not sure I could playact that well." Peggy laughed.

Harris grinned at her, pleased. Then his smile faded. "Of course they regretted their decision and sent runners after me. I escaped them and got to my uncle's. But that old cur has begun to suspect me, too. Some of his villains dragged me off to an island in the big swamp east of Sandy Hill. They strung me up on a tree to get me to confess, only letting me down as I saw stars and black and St. Peter at the gates. They did that to me three times. Three! That last time," he muttered, shaking his head, "I thought for sure I'd die. So I committed a betrayal."

"Oh no; you didn't tell them of your mission, did you?"

"What? Of course not, miss." He looked at her indignantly. "But I did betray my brothers, the Masons." He shook his head with sadness.

Peggy knew secrets were vitally important to the ancient fraternity of Masons. The order was full of rituals, symbolism related to the symmetry of stonemasons' tools, and promised their members a path to moral certainty.

"I was so afeard swinging from that branch," continued Harris, "that I gave our sacred hailing sign of distress—with a dying man's hope that someone there might be a brother Mason. And you know what?" He paused theatrically, the consummate storyteller. "The captain of that gang were one himself. He cut me down." He studied her a moment. "I'd show you the signal, miss, but I sworn an oath."

"That's all right," Peggy reassured him. "I don't think anyone would believe me a Mason anyway."

"No, I suppose not, miss. A pity, that. You would make a good one if you weren't wearing skirts." He grinned. "Please tell the general that I will wait with Mr. Fish in Easton."

"A Mr. Fish?"

"Aye, miss. He is the go-between the general set for me."

There was a prearranged go-between now? "You have been to the house since I last saw you?" Peggy asked with surprise, annoyed that she had not known of it.

He shrugged.

Hmpf. "Well . . . do you have anything for my father?"

Harris looked all around, took his hat off to scratch his head, looked up at the clouds as if he was thinking about a price to request of her. From the edging of his hat he pulled out a letter folded thin, which he dropped into the basket of oysters. Putting his hat back on, he lifted the basket up to her, as if for her to inspect.

Following his move, Peggy turned over a few of the oysters and retrieved the twig-thin note. Without thinking, she started to tear it open, so greedy she was to be part of the spy-ring intrigue. But Harris cleared his throat and shook his head slightly.

Of course. What an idiot! Peggy clasped her hands together and bowed slightly. "That is a fine price for the oysters, sir. My mother will be pleased. Send a bushel to the house and Mary will pay you," she said loudly.

Harris bowed. "Thank you, miss. I'm grateful, miss," he responded, adding in a hoarse whisper, "Tell the general it needs of a cipher. I saw paper with holes cut in it, very random like, lying atop General Burgoyne's desk. Like little windows onto the letters underneath."

Straightening, he tipped his hat, murmuring, "Tell your father to check any British courier he catches for silver bullets with a screw top. They be sticking tiny messages in them and telling men to swallow them whole if they are captured."

Musket balls stuffed with tiny messages? Ingenious! But swallowing one if caught? Peggy felt herself choke at the idea.

SEVEN

Mid-Autumn

Colonel Richard Varick to General Schuyler
Camp near Headquarters, ½ mile west of Saratoga,
September 1777
Dear General,

Burgoyne now gives out that he intends to attack us . . . I
should bless my stars and think myself completely happy were
you at the head of this army but . . . I am resolved . . . Every
man's countenance seems to bespeak courage . . . we trust
ourselves to Providence and make our Dependence on the Dis-
poser of all Events Whose Intention it never was or can be to
subjugate a free and Loyal people . . . God bless you, my best
wishes ever attend you and your family. I am with respects to
Mrs. Schuyler and Miss Peggy, as ever dear general your most
affectionate humble servant.

Rich. Varick

"MARGARITA!" SCHUYLER CALLED.

Peggy was roosting in her favorite spot—one of the wide window seats of the upstairs hall, where she was watching eagles skate the winds along the opposite shore of the Hudson and trying to capture their gliding freedom in her sketch pad. Alarmed by her papa's shout, she dropped it to the floor and hurried down the stairs.

Schuyler was pacing the parlor, skimming a letter, agitated. But what frightened her most was the fact Catharine was in tears. Her mother never cried. "What is it?" Peggy asked anxiously. "Is it Colonel Varick?" She didn't realize that her mother had become so fond of him.

"The British have burned our house at Saratoga," Catharine wailed.

"What?" Peggy looked to her father for confirmation.

He nodded, grim.

"According to Colonel Varick," Catharine began, fighting off little sobs, "the rascals first tore down our fencing to corduroy the roads. Then they stripped our fields. Ground *our* corn into meal in *our* gristmill for *their* horses. Stole our ox and pigs. Then their *Gentleman Johnny* Burgoyne"—she said the nickname with outrage—"after guzzling champagne and cavorting with his mistress through our home, he torched our entire estate—our beautiful house, all the barns, the smithy, and the mills!"

"He left one of the sawmills standing, at least, my dear," Philip murmured, preoccupied with the letter he held.

"Oh yes, and the necessary. Do you not see the message

112

in leaving your outhouse standing?"

Schuyler looked up from the paper, taken aback by his wife's bitterness. "My dear, you will upset yourself. Margarita, I called you to help calm your mama. She will make herself ill. I must respond to this quickly."

He sat down at a writing desk and dipped a quill in ink, thinking aloud: "Varick must ride with all haste to salvage whatever iron scraps he can from the charred remains. Nails, barrel rings, blacksmith tools. Whatever grasses remain uncut must be hayed. I hope the British didn't think to dig up the turnips and potatoes."

Peggy sat and took her mother's hand and patted it soothingly. But Catharine would not be comforted. "Oh, I left behind all that lovely green tea we imported before all this fighting started. And the pineapples and coconuts." She looked at Peggy and cried, "Why didn't you remind me, daughter, to retrieve those from the cellar?"

Who cared about coconuts when their entire world was burned to the ground? What was wrong with Catharine? This was entirely unlike her. Her mother only acted like this in the early stages of pregnancy—when she was all anxiety and vomit. *Wait.* Peggy suddenly remembered hearing Catharine retching a few nights ago. She'd just figured her mother was suffering from the unsalted meat. They all had far more stomachaches than they used to because of the war's shortage of salt that preserved and kept their food edible. Could she be pregnant yet again? Peggy slid back a bit, realizing that if her conjecture were true, this was exactly the kind of moment that might unleash her mother's nausea.

Schuyler sealed his letter and limped to the entry to call for a courier. He was not well. This flare of gout had infected his foot and crept up his calf, making each step an agony for him. But he stood tall as he said, "Kitty, we must bear this heavy loss as best we can. But it sits quite easy on me, my dear. Truly. Because we won the battle. Burgoyne surrendered!"

Peggy leapt to her feet. "Papa! Why didn't you say so? We won?"

"Yes! We held the field at the second engagement. The losses are many, and the war goes on, but the British forces are reduced by five thousand Redcoats and Saratoga . . ." He finally broke into a smile—a big one. "Saratoga is our victory. Our first large battle won! General Washington is hoping that we have now proven to the French that we can fight and survive so that they will join us in this war against the British empire."

Peggy flung herself into a hug with her father. Now *she* was crying—tears of joy, exultation, relief. For months they had lived in terror of the Redcoats attacking and burning Albany to the ground, and dragging Schuyler off in chains, or worse. "Congratulations, Papa!"

"Little thanks your father will receive," Catharine whimpered. "Even though Gates didn't leave his tent once during the battles, that usurper will be credited."

"And General Arnold, my dear," Schuyler countered. "Benedict is the one who rallied the troops for the charge that broke the British lines. Although our hero is badly injured. He may lose his leg." He straightened his cravat. "I must pack. I ride at dawn."

"Where are you going?" Catharine demanded.

"To the surrender ceremony. I wish to see Burgoyne give up his sword."

Catharine finally pulled herself together. "But Philip, my dearest love," she began gently. "It will not be to you."

"No," Philip said flatly. "But I will see it done. And thank my . . . the men." He called up the stairs again, this time for his sons.

When told the news, the three boys whooped and danced. "HUZZAH!!!" they shouted again and again.

Schuyler put his hand upon the shoulder of twelve-year-old John to stop his cavorting. "You will come with me, son. You should witness this."

"What?" The word just jumped out of Peggy's mouth. "Why John?"

Because he was the oldest boy? She was the one who had helped open British communiqués, survived insult and threat by deserters to bring supplies safely home on a road thronging with panicked refugees. She had helped open sealed enemy letters and proved she could keep war secrets, and even met with a spy! Why should her obnoxious little brother get to see this hard-won and costly moment of triumph?

Peggy took a deep breath to keep from saying what she was really thinking and, with as much politeness as she could muster, asked: "Please, Papa, might I go, too?"

Schuyler looked at her as if she had demanded he pluck the moon from the sky to hand her. "I need you here, Margarita." He shifted his glance to Catharine and then back to Peggy, clearly indicating he was worried about his wife's condition.

So she *was* with child—again! "Oh, Papa, for pity's sake, she's already birthed thirteen babies. She doesn't need me." As soon as she said it, Peggy's hands clapped to her mouth, as if she could stuff the offensive, insensitive words back in. "Papa, I'm sorry," she whispered through her fingers. "I . . . I . . ." She thought she would collapse under his glare. "Mama." She turned to Catharine. But her mother was staring out the window, a few tears still sliding down her cheeks. Had she heard? Or was Catharine caught up enough in her sorrow and anger about her house to have not really taken in Peggy's words?

Ashamed, Peggy froze. Her eyes cast down and her face burning, she waited. But Schuyler didn't answer her outburst. When she finally dared to meet his gaze again, she saw the most profound and damning disappointment with her. Being struck with a horsewhip would not have affected Peggy more. Her knees went wobbly.

Without a word, Schuyler strode from the room and up the stairs to pack.

But John took the opportunity to stick his tongue out at her before he turned to follow their father.

Schuyler didn't speak to her that night, either. But the next morning, as Schuyler swung himself onto the back of

116

his favorite white charger, he took a moment to cup Peggy's upturned face in his leather-gloved hand. "I know you will take good care of all my concerns here, Peggy. I depend upon you." He kissed her forehead.

Only when he rode away did Peggy realize that General Philip Schuyler had stripped himself of his military dignity and right to claim glory for a battle victory by dressing himself in civilian clothes.

Two days later, Peggy and Catharine stood on their marble stoop with Rensselaer and Jeremiah, who held little Cornelia's hands as she unsteadily tiptoed about, still learning to walk. They were all clad in their best afternoon receiving clothes. Despite her morning sickness, Catharine looked quite lovely in a quilted pale-yellow skirt and long blossom-embroidered jacket. She'd draped a sheer, ruffled neck-handkerchief artfully over the top of what Peggy now recognized was her expanding torso. Peggy fidgeted in her lavender gown—its skirts looped up *à la Polonaise* in puffs of stiff silk taffeta. Her bodice was lined with the finest ruffled linen peeking out of her neckline, and a row of petite black satin bows marched down its front. The dress itched. Horribly.

They were awaiting the arrival of Burgoyne and his entourage. The Patriot Northern Army was marching the defeated British and Hessian troops into Albany—where their surrendered five thousand soldiers would be imprisoned while arrangements were made to transport them south to prisoner-of-war camps or to Boston, from whence they'd be deported to Britain. But Burgoyne and his staff, the Hessian commander and his German officers? Philip Schuyler had invited them all—all!—to stay at their mansion.

Peggy had been flabbergasted when Catharine told her. How did Papa expect his wife to entertain Burgoyne without throttling him? Papa wasn't even coming to help. He remained in Saratoga, with John, to rebuild their country house before winter set in. Peggy couldn't get past the cruel irony that while Schuyler would freeze in a tent to reconstruct his estate, the man who had torched it would be sleeping in her papa's warm feather bed.

Peggy heard fife and drums announcing the approaching parade. She spotted American officers riding abreast with their British counterparts, dingy blue and buff juxtaposed with bloodred and gold. Weary Continental infantrymen marched behind, shouldering their heavy Brown Bess muskets.

"Are we to provide for the guard as well, Mama?" Peggy asked, stunned.

"Yes. They will encamp on our back pastures to prevent Burgoyne escaping." She hmpfed. "I cannot imagine the man making such an attempt since he will be enjoying our bed and our wines. More likely, our soldiers will need to watch against the poor, wretched refugees who crowd Albany, who have lost everything to British attacks. They might decide to revenge themselves on Gentleman Johnny."

Hosting people they loathed, making their house vulnerable to a totally justifiable attack by the victims of those guests? Peggy couldn't help asking, "Tell me again, Mama, why we must do this?"

Catharine sighed. "That is what your father wishes. So that is what we shall do."

From the tone of Catharine's voice, Peggy knew better than to ask how *she* felt about those orders. Peggy wondered how her forthright mother would hold her tongue with Burgoyne, the man who had destroyed so much of what she loved. How would Peggy?

With courtly flourish General Burgoyne bounded up the stairs and bowed low to Catharine, taking her hand and kissing it. He was, as reported, handsome and elegant. Burgoyne was a playwright as well as a soldier. Looking at him now, Peggy could more easily imagine him in a London opera house balcony than on a battlefield. Although, by all accounts, he had stayed with his troops throughout the cannonade and bloodletting—his hat pierced by a Patriot sharpshooter. Even so, Peggy was not impressed with the man.

She was more interested in eyeing the Hessian, Baron von Riedesel. German mercenaries were feared as cold, calculating killers. The baron's attire certainly presented him as a menacing would-be conqueror with polished above-the-knee boots and a tall peaked brass miter helmet, pressed with a rearing lion crest for his Hesse-Kassel king. But his intimidating aura was diluted by what came behind him—a young, doll-pretty woman with blue eyes, golden hair, and two cherubic little girls clinging to her skirts. She cradled a baby with a halo of duck-down soft curls.

"My wife," the baron introduced her, "Baroness Frederika Charlotte Louise von Massow, and my daughters Augusta, Frederika, and Caroline." The baroness curtsied with distinctly aristocratic grace in her elaborately trimmed riding costume.

Peggy was floored. How could a woman drag such wee babes onto the battlefield? For love? Peggy assessed her German husband again—handsome, commanding surely. There must be gentle affection somewhere in his soul to warrant this noblewoman endangering her little ones. For a moment, Peggy's visceral dislike and fear of Hessians softened.

But then Augusta, the oldest child—perhaps six years old, Peggy speculated—chirped: "Ooh, Mutter, is this the palace Vater was to have when we defeated the damned rebels?"

At dinner that night, the baroness worked hard to make up for her daughter's rude question. "Your husband is the kindest man I have ever met, madame," she said to Catharine, "even at court."

Peggy bristled at the condescending "even at court." Laid before this German woman, her brood of children, and close to twenty officers who had ordered atrocities against her fellow Americans, was a meal fit for any king's court. Quail with chestnut stuffing, oranges, pasty of venison, roast beef, spiced peaches in brandy, plum pudding. Foods Peggy and her siblings had not seen for months, and certainly the Patriot foot soldiers out back guarding them may never have tasted in their entire lives.

"The day of the surrender," the baroness continued, "General Schuyler embraced my girls, and told them not to cry, then escorted me to my husband—oh, I was so relieved to see him alive! He was safe with General Burgoyne." She gestured to Gentleman Johnny, who was cutting his mutton on the tabletop, seemingly oblivious to the gashes he was leaving in the mahogany.

"We witnessed such horrors," she murmured, her delicate hand trembling as she reached for her wine. "Not to discuss during such a lovely dinner." She took a sip for fortification. "Your husband, understanding that I would be embarrassed to eat with so many gentlemen, invited me and my daughters to his tent for dinner."

Catharine was about to take a bite but put down her fork abruptly to ask, "Do you mean to say that General Gates did not include *my husband*—the general who had raised the troops for this battle—that General Gates excluded *my husband* from the official surrender dinner?"

She looked from face to face for an answer.

Peggy burned with the same indignation for her father. Oh, if she could ever get Gates in a room alone! But then she remembered Schuyler's parting words as he left for Saratoga—that he depended on Peggy to take good care of all his concerns. Her papa's honor was everything to him. He would want this meal marinated in old-world etiquette, as proof of American diplomacy, and that Patriots were not backwoods ruffians.

Peggy forced herself to say something to alleviate the tension. "I imagine, Mama, that in his infinite graciousness, Papa would decline any invitation from General Gates in favor of saving this lady and her children discomfort."

The baroness seemed to recognize Peggy's stratagem. "Yes, surely, madame. It is clear your husband is first a gentleman and a father."

Catharine forced a smile. "He is that."

"Indeed, madam, he is beyond gracious," interjected Gentleman Johnny. "When we met I expressed my regret at the event which had happened, and the reasons which had occasioned it and . . ."

Event? Peggy couldn't let him get away with reducing the burning of her home to a pleasant euphemism. "What *event*, sir? Do you mean the torching of our home and barns and mills and storehouses?" She did at least manage to wrap her comment in a vaguely subdued tone she knew Eliza would use. What would Angelica say? Peggy wondered. Her eldest sister would likely tear Burgoyne apart with her wit—or flirt brazenly with him.

She glanced at Catharine, expecting a look of reprimand, but Catharine simply smiled at her. Was that a rare encouragement of Peggy's cheekiness? Was this her chance to finally duel with one of her father's enemies, to fight with her wit, the one weapon allowed her? She couldn't get to Congress or the Adams brothers, and had been too outnumbered and threatened by the deserters on the Saratoga road to beat down their slanders of Schuyler. But here she was in her own home, with the chance to parry with this arrogant Brit.

Like Carter had been the night of the card game, Burgoyne seemed more amused than insulted by Peggy. She would make Gentleman Johnny pay for that, too, she swore.

"Why, yes, Miss Peggy," Burgoyne answered. "Your father desired me to think no more about it. He said that the occasion justified my orders. You see, the buildings were being used as protective barricades and shields by the Colonials and—"

"You mean our *American* troops?" she interrupted.

Burgoyne laughed. "Yes, Miss Peggy, quite right. The soldiers of *the American Army* were firing upon us from the protection of buildings on your father's estate. To protect my men, your father's buildings had to be removed. General Schuyler, with great courteousness and understanding of military matters, said that according to the rules and principles of war, he would have done the same."

"Really?" Peggy asked, feeling her eyebrow shoot up archly and hoping it revealed that what she was about to say was sarcastic, no matter how polite the words. "How magnanimous Papa is. We all try to emulate his largesse."

Burgoyne's answering smile was wry, and his eyes twinkled; clearly he caught Peggy's jab. He stood and raised his glass, playing along. "To the Honorable General Schuyler and his gracious family."

Mirroring their commander, the officers stood and

thumped the table as they said, "Hear, hear."

At least Peggy had managed that hit for her papa's honor.

"I have been most impressed by the mercy of all the Americans," the baroness said, continuing the thread of conversation. "During the battle, when a terrible bombardment trapped us in a house with many wounded, we desperately needed water. Nobody wanted to risk going to fetch some, because the rebel enemy . . . forgive me . . . because the *Americans* shot every man who went near the river. We are much in awe of your marksmen, madame."

"That would be Daniel Morgan's riflemen, probably," Peggy offered. "They are quite legendary." Peggy was fully aware that Morgan's line, shooting from treetop roosts, had taken down a dozen Redcoat officers. She knew she was being rude, callous even, but the fact of their being at her table and treated to such deferential entertainment considering their swath of destruction and cruelty to Patriot New Yorkers was too insufferable for her to simply smile and offer them more baked rolls.

But the baroness went on, "Finally a soldier's wife offered to go. The reb . . . the Americans did not hurt her. We would have perished had we not had that water." She cleared her throat. "I must add that when I rode into your camp, after our army's capitulation, I feared jeering, or . . . or worse." She hesitated. "But not one American glanced at us insultingly. In fact, your soldiers bowed to me. Some even looked with pity to see a woman with small children there. I . . . I am afraid that might not have been the scenario had the reverse been true and your men were our prisoners of war."

Peggy's instantaneous reaction popped out of her mouth: "And that, Baroness, is why we fight against you."

Silence fell around the table. Several officers froze, forks midway to their lips.

Peggy turned defiantly to her mother, expecting to be sent to her room.

But all Catharine said was, "More wine, anyone?"

Peggy took a big gulp herself to keep from laughing out loud in triumph.

Burgoyne and his entourage finally vacated, a week later— after Catharine had emptied their cellars to feed them and the encamped American guard had plundered their chicken coops, dug up their root vegetables, torn down fencing for shelter, and milked their cows dry in the night. Gentleman Johnny did not apologize for the wreckage, but he did leave behind a beautiful pair of shoe buckles ornamented with lines of brilliant diamond-like paste baubles—for Miss Peggy, he said, "a most spirited and delightful child."

Child! So Burgoyne got the final cut in their verbal swordplay.

As Catharine handed them to her, she said, "What a tribute to the fine hostess you have become, my dear. I will be sure to tell your papa."

Peggy eyed her mother, trying to gauge if there was a double and disapproving meaning to her words. Catharine had never said anything about Peggy's impertinence at dinner. Nor had she punished Peggy for egging on her little brothers—nine-year-old Jeremiah and four-year-old Rensselaer—to charge through their bedroom, where a dozen British officers were billeted, and to shout, "You are our prisoners!" before dashing out and slamming the door behind them.

"Mama?" Peggy began.

Catharine just patted Peggy's cheek and said, "Pack those in a bit of silk and keep them as souvenirs to show your own children someday—all that's left of Gentleman Johnny here in America."

EIGHT

Late Autumn

General George Washington to Alexander Hamilton
Head Quarters Philada: County 30th: October 1777
Dear Sir:

It having been judged expedient by the Members of a Council of War, held yesterday, that one of the Gentlemen of my family should be sent to Genl: Gates in order to lay befor him the State of this Army; and the Situation of the Ene(my) to point out to him the many happy Consequences that will accrue from an immediate reinforceme being sent from the Nothern Army; I have thought (it) proper to appoint you to that duty, and desire that yo will immediately set out for Albany . . .

I wish you a pleasent Journey And am Dr: Sir Your most obt. Servant Go: Washington

"MISS PEGGY, I SIMPLY DO NOT KNOW WHAT TO do," Varick said with exasperation.

Peggy tossed aside her needlework. She was botching her

design of roses anyway. Eliza was the artist with the needle. Peggy would stick to her watercolors and sketches. She was sitting by the hearth in the family's less formal yellow parlor to toast her feet by the fire against the sudden, sharp cold of November in upstate New York. Her foot had been bothering her again. She was praying that the needles of pain were simply a reaction to the frigid temperatures and not a harbinger of inheriting her father's malady. It was too terrifying a thought to contemplate.

"I am sorry, Mr. Varick, what did you say was the matter?" Peggy pulled her feet off the stool to tuck primly beneath her skirts. She hadn't really paid attention when the colonel first blustered into the room.

Catharine had gone to Saratoga to help Schuyler rebuild their country house and left Peggy in charge of the household. Everyone was turning to her now for direction and to negotiate squabbles. It was proving a heavy, and insufferably boring, responsibility for the nineteen-year-old. Especially thinking on the Boston dinner parties and balls her two older sisters were probably enjoying. Before she knew it, Peggy might be covered with fire dust, just like the ever-suffering Cinderella!

Peggy had tamped down her resentment of being left behind by her sisters as long as her papa was in Albany and there was the chance Peggy might help him with Patriot espionage. But now that he was in Saratoga, she felt adrift, without purpose. This running of a house was supposed to be her goal in life, she knew, but what a small dream it felt in the context of the Revolution. She suddenly longed to share in whatever action her sisters were seeing in Boston. Even if it was just watching Angelica sweet-talk European financiers into supporting the rebellious Patriots.

Varick began again: "Mrs. Schuyler requested that I send to Saratoga our whitewash brushes, but Mary refuses to give up the one she has. And Charles forgot to put the apple cider Mrs. Schuyler wanted into the wagon that has already left with the stovepipe and chimney irons your father has been waiting for. I fear your mother will be most dissatisfied when the shipment arrives and the cider is missing."

Sighing, Peggy pushed her dark curls back off her forehead, trying to look authoritative. "Surely, Mr. Varick, some of our tenants in Saratoga would have brushes."

"Most were burned out of their homes, too, miss."

Of course. Peggy wasn't thinking. Most every farm around Saratoga had been laid waste. "Damn Burgoyne," she muttered.

"Miss?"

Peggy stood and made herself smile graciously, as she knew Catharine would. "I'll convince Mary to give up her brush, and if you put it in the wagon with the cider tomorrow, Mama won't mind about the cider being a day late."

"Thank you, Miss Peggy." Varick beamed at her.

Peggy tried to ignore his admiring gaze. She liked the man, truly, a great deal. But Richard Varick had none of the dash, the daring, the wit—the savoir faire—of the heroes of her books and which, in her loneliness for her sisters and their conversation, Peggy was coming to realize her heart craved.

So she was careful to keep their conversations to business. Surely, though, there was something more interesting than paintbrushes to talk about. "Is there anything else Papa needs, Mr. Varick? Anything related to our great cause of liberty?"

"Oh yes, miss! I gather one of General Washington's aides-de-camp, Alexander Hamilton, is here in Albany. He has come to see Gates about releasing troops to reinforce General Washington's Continental forces to the south. Since Philadelphia—unfortunately—has fallen to the British, General Washington is trying to blockade them and hold the Delaware River to starve them of provisions."

"Really?"

"Yes, miss." Varick lowered his voice. "And I have it on authority that Gates is so bloated with self-importance—now that he is hailed as the victor of Saratoga—that he is refusing the young Hamilton's entreaties. In fact, General Arnold suspects Gates of trying to convince Congress to replace General Washington with *him*. Just as he stole your father's command of the Northern Army. What better way for Gates to accomplish that than to deny Washington needed troops and let him fail in Pennsylvania?

"The man is so conniving! He does not acknowledge Benedict Arnold's role in our victory at Saratoga and even ordered Arnold off the field during the second battle so that Gates alone won glory."

Peggy would have dismissed such gossip if she hadn't witnessed such petty rivalries herself, firsthand, in the fate of her father. So many of the delegates to Congress and the army's generals seemed far more concerned with elevating themselves than with actually defeating the British. This could not happen—not now that the Patriots had won their first decisive victory after two years of humiliation and disaster, not after so many had died.

"I am going to see Benedict Arnold," she announced, charging toward the door.

"Miss?" Varick looked at her questioningly

Peggy stopped, recognizing that it was not the place of a young woman to rush off to see a general, sounding like she wanted to discuss politics. Although it galled her to do so, she racked her brain for more acceptable motivations. Arnold still lay in Albany's hospital, critically ill, his leg shattered. "Your speaking of General Arnold reminded me that I should visit and ask after his health, the poor man. "

Varick smiled. "A visit from a beautiful young lady would surely do his heart good, miss." He raised his eyebrows meaningfully, hope all over his face.

"And a basket of apples," Peggy added as if she hadn't heard. "Surely, the general would appreciate some good fruit." With that she hurried from the room.

As her horse climbed the steep hills bordering the west end of town to the stone-walled garrison and hospital, Peggy was stunned by the crowded horizon of tents, shanties, and smoldering campfires stretching before her. She knew the Northern Army had more than doubled Albany's population of 3,500 people. But until she actually saw it herself, she hadn't realized what putting a tent city atop a town of four hundred houses would look like. The hospital was jammed with hundreds of sick and injured Americans. Hundreds more were being tended in private homes and the Dutch Reformed Church, which had turned its sanctuary into a medical ward. Albany hadn't exactly been picturesque before the war, but now it looked like one of Dante's circles of hell.

Peggy dismounted, handing her horse's reins to a private on post. Immediately, she held to her nose the sachet bouquet women carried to survive street smells. The stench of camp cooking, makeshift necessaries for four thousand men, animal dung, trash, and mud was overwhelming. She nearly retched.

As she approached, Peggy trembled at the sounds emanating from the hospital—the large H-shaped building seemed to pulse like a gigantic hive, humming with moans and weeping. She forced herself forward, step by step, her heart jumping at each outcry of anguish from within. She reached the threshold and beheld dozens upon dozens of mangled men, lying on straw, elbow to elbow, contorting in pain, whimpering for a drink of water. Others lay so still, crawling with green bottle flies, they seemed already dead. Many were missing limbs and were wrapped in bandages that oozed blood. The air was putrid with the smells of rot, dysentery, stale whiskey, and tincture of myrrh.

Peggy gasped, swayed, and dropped her basket, apples bouncing and rolling away. She caught herself on the doorway and damned her corset, her mind chanting *don't throw up, don't throw up.* She looked down, away from the horrors, and fought blacking out. In the swirl of her almost faint, she saw a hand pick up one of the scattered apples. She made herself focus on that hand as it picked up apple after apple to drop back into her basket. *Plunk . . . plunk . . . plunk.* Then the hand lifted the basket toward her and a voice said kindly, "There, miss, it's all right. Take a deep breath."

Peggy followed the hand to an arm to a face—a beautiful, sweet-child face of a foot soldier. No beard, not even the hint of stubble on that smooth skin. Her gaze met green eyes framed by baby-soft tendrils of honey-brown hair. As young as he was, those eyes carried a sad wisdom of having already seen far too much of the world.

"Thank you, sir," she murmured. "I am ashamed of my weakness."

"Don't be, miss; we are a terrible sight for a lady such as yourself." He smiled, the kind of innocent dimpled smile that made a mother easily forgive a child waking her in the night. "I believe you dropped these?"

Peggy looked down to take her apple basket and bit back a gasp. The boy had only one arm.

"Who are you here to see?" The boy kept talking as she fought to collect herself and to not tear up at his injury.

"Gen . . . General Arnold," she stammered.

"Lucky man. He is back where the officers are being tended. Would you like me to show you?"

Peggy nodded.

"I think I best take you to our commanding surgeon

first. General Arnold can be a mite prickly. If he is having a bad day, that doctor will know it. Follow me, miss." The boy swept his one hand out as graciously as if guiding her to a ballroom floor for a minuet.

Fleetingly, Peggy wondered if the boy would ever be able to dance again.

The hospital was enormous—two stories high, with forty wards. Keeping his hand on her elbow to steady her, the boy picked their way through rows of pallets and groaning men. Good thing, because when she saw a doctor begin to wind the crank of a huge screw into the skull of a patient, she nearly fainted again.

"Good Lord, what is that doctor doing?"

The boy grimaced and turned her to face away. "I'm sorry, miss. I should have taken you a different way. But don't worry. The surgeon's just trepanning a fractured skull. To relieve some of the pus and blood."

"Wh-wh-what?" Peggy was sure her face had turned as green as the boy's eyes.

"Oh no, miss, seriously. It will relieve the pressure and give the soldier a chance. He would die otherwise for sure. You'd be amazed by what a man can live through."

"Miss Schuyler, what are you doing here?" The hospital's surgeon-commander approached, wiping blood from his hands hurriedly. Peggy recognized Dr. Thacher from her long-ago trip to Ticonderoga to nurse her father.

"I bring General Arnold greetings from my father and some apples from our orchard. May I see him?"

"Hmm. General Arnold is quite peevish. The femur was shattered. Yet he refuses an amputation, which leaves him in great pain and in danger of infection." He paused, considering if she should really see Arnold or not. "But I hear he is also quite the wooer of women, so he is like to better behave with you. This way." Dr. Thacher strode away.

Peggy hurried to follow, but not before thanking the youth. "Godspeed, sir," she whispered, and handed the lad an apple. He held it to his heart and bowed.

Catching up to the surgeon, she asked, "Will that young soldier be all right?"

"As long as he doesn't catch camp fever," Thacher muttered in reply. "He's one of the lucky ones. He has education and can earn a living with his mind. These other poor men, who can no longer do manual labor having lost an arm . . ." The doctor shrugged. "That worry is for after we win our liberty."

He stepped into a small room. "Here we are. General Arnold," he called. "I bring you a visitor."

Benedict Arnold's scowl turned to surprise as he saw her. He struggled to right himself in his bed. His leg was held together by a wooden press, and he winced and grunted as he dragged the cage-like contraption along the mattress.

"Let me help you." Peggy instinctively hurried to pull the pillows out and retuck them more comfortably behind his back as he sat up.

Arnold looked up at her with intense gray eyes. He was dark in complexion and hair and possessed a strong, athletic build, rather indecently exposed in his open nightshirt and his bared, broken leg. He was so . . . hairy. She blushed and pulled back.

"Thank you, Miss . . . ?"

"Miss Peggy Schuyler, General."

"Ahh." He nodded. "You must be Philip's youngest. Colonel Varick told me of you when we served together at Saratoga."

At this, Peggy more than blushed. She could only imagine what mush Richard Varick might have said.

Arnold chuckled. "You are already too much woman for him, Miss Peggy, I can tell."

"Sir!" she exclaimed, flattered and shocked all at once.

Arnold waved her toward a camp chair. "Accept the praise, Miss Peggy. Do sit down. How is your father?"

"At our homestead in Saratoga, rebuilding."

"We should have had him at the battle. Perhaps I would not have been shot through this leg yet again, had he been issuing orders that day." He looked down at it and muttered, "Would to God the musket ball had passed through my heart instead."

"Oh, sir, you must not say so! Our nation needs you. My father says you are the bravest and most cunning of all the army's officers."

"So says General Washington as well." A voice spoke from the door. "Romantics such as you or I may wish for a brilliant exit, a glorious death in battle. And certainly valor such as yours, General Arnold, seems above this terrestrial world. Yet, His Excellency has great need of your talents, sir."

Arnold straightened. "Colonel Hamilton."

In walked one of the prettiest men Peggy had ever seen. A dark green sash across his buff-and-blue waistcoat marked him as an aide-de-camp to George Washington. Small and willowy, his complexion milky and his hair red-gold and thick, the man would have commanded admiration anywhere. But what was most striking about him were his enormous violet-blue eyes that scanned everything in the room, including her, quickly and keenly. She'd never seen eyes that color or that hungry before.

"Fair nymph." He bowed low. "*Enchanté.*"

Peggy stood and curtsied, a bit surprised by the flirtatious tone and Shakespearean-florid greeting in so stark a setting. "*Moi aussi,*" she answered to let him know she understood French.

"Oh-ho. Beware this man, Miss Schuyler. He is famous for his love affairs," warned Arnold. "I hear he is paying serious courtship to Kitty Livingston—a cousin of yours, I believe."

"Merely letters, sir," the colonel responded. "It is but a childhood friendship."

"So you say, sir, so you say." Arnold chortled—a laugh more appropriate in a tavern than in front of Peggy. "Have you news for me, Alex?"

"Yes, sir. I wish to ask your advice before I negotiate with General Gates again."

Arnold visibly stiffened and his scowl returned as he muttered a damnation of Gates.

"It is most urgent."

Arnold nodded. "Thank you for these apples, Miss Schuyler."

Both men looked at her expectantly.

They would dismiss her that quickly? Peggy frowned. "Perhaps my father could be of assistance as well, sirs?"

"General Schuyler? I am afraid I do not have time to ride all the way to Saratoga to see him," said Hamilton. "I had to cover sixty miles a day for five consecutive days to reach Albany. I will need to push myself at the same pace to get myself back to General Washington. Plus, my mission concerns troops no longer under your father's command, miss. But please do give him my highest regards when you see him. His Excellency's as well." The aide-de-camp bowed low, elegant even in his mud-splattered uniform, but with a definite air of impatience.

Silence.

This after her father had done so much, lost so much? Peggy's eyebrow shot sky high. Emboldened by her sparring with Burgoyne, she replied, "Your 'highest regards,' sir, would be your taking the time to give them *in person* to General Schuyler, whose efforts preserved the troops you now need. But I suppose the war makes all of us rude out of necessity." She nodded rather than curtsied and made her exit, grinding her teeth with anger for her father.

Interlude

WE RETURN TO THE WINTER OF 1780
AND HAMILTON'S FIRST LETTER TO PEGGY:

Alexander Hamilton to Margarita Schuyler (continued):
Morristown, New Jersey, February 1780

There are several of my friends, philosophers who railed at
love as a weakness, men of the world who laughed at it . . .
whom your sister has presumptuously and daringly compelled
to acknowlege its power . . . I am myself of the number. She
has . . . overset all the wise resolutions I had been fram-
ing . . . and from a rational sort of being and a professed
contemner of Cupid has in a trice metamorphosed me into the
veriest inamorato you perhaps ever saw.

. . . It is essential to the safety of the state and to the tran-
quillity of the army that one of two things take place; either
that she be immediately removed from our neighbourhood, or
that some other nymph qualified to maintain an equal sway
come into it.

SOME OTHER NYMPH. PEGGY SAT UP ABRUPTLY. THE shawls she had snuggled into as she sat cross-legged in the armchair fell back. The frigid predawn air of her bedroom cut into her being—even though her hearth had been roaring for the past half hour as she reread the letter from her sister's new suitor, this aide-de-camp named Alexander Hamilton, this man who hoped to solicit Peggy's aid in his courtship of Eliza.

"*Nymph!*" she repeated aloud, her breath fogging, a cloudy echo puff of her voice. The word lit an alarm beacon.

Peggy stood and paced. Hamilton's letter had prompted her to remember so many things that had happened since the war began and Angelica ran off with John Carter, shattering the world Peggy had known and loved. Now this single word triggered the memory of her visit to the wounded General Arnold in Albany's hospital, after the Battle of Saratoga, two years prior.

Eliza's new suitor was the aide-de-camp who had interrupted their conversation!

Peggy had been struck then by the aide's flirtatious tone, his flowery, Arcadia-poetic language in a hospital, a place of pain and harsh realities. But she'd been so irate at his not taking the time to pay respects to her father in person that she'd buried his identity as not worthy of remembering.

Peggy's eyebrow rose in appreciation, recalling Hamilton's enormous violet-blue eyes, their piercing, searching scrutiny. Typically, so handsome a man would be completely monopolized by Angelica. Well, good for Eliza! Maybe now that Angelica was married, Eliza's more subtle beauty and gentle heart would be the Schuyler nectar drawing suitors. Then perhaps it would be Peggy's turn.

Because surely it was her turn, wasn't it? Peggy had survived the terrors of Burgoyne's invasion. She'd witnessed their father's humiliation when General Gates replaced him just in time to win a battle that Schuyler had prepared the Northern Army to fight. She'd cared for him as he grieved the attacks on his honor and sank into ill health. She had helped nurse the tiny baby brother who was born and struggled for each breath, his little body shivering and twitching. And she'd comforted her mother when that baby died five months later.

Why did Peggy always have to be the responsible one among the three Schuyler sisters? Pacing once more—feeling smothered, snuffed—Peggy reread Hamilton's last line about Eliza: *By dividing her empire it will be weakened and she will be much less dangerous when she has a rival equal in charms to dispute the prize with her. I solicit your aid.*

That was an invitation. Backhanded, to be sure, but an invitation nonetheless. To the winter headquarters of the Continental Army. To the intimate circle surrounding General George Washington, to the subscription balls and banter his officers reveled in as tonic to the deprivations and disasters, the forebodings of the war. To experience those evenings and camaraderie firsthand, not just vicariously through letters.

She had held the fort at home long enough. Peggy was

going to join Eliza at the house their aunt and uncle were renting near this year's winter encampment. They wouldn't mind another niece. Dr. John Cochran was always up for merriment and family gatherings.

Peggy fairly danced in her moccasins to the window. Its drawn curtains glowed as sunrise seeped in around its edges. She yanked back the damask brocade to gaze out at a horizon of frozen white, glinting in the dawn's golden rays. Snowbanks started glittering one after another in a wave of jewel-like sparkle as the sun climbed, spreading out light across the Hudson River toward her, until the earth beneath her window was blinding in reflected, mirrored luster. Shading her eyes, Peggy scanned the fairy-tale-beautiful world, awash herself in morning light and a sense of adventure.

But her smile began to fade as she surveyed the unrelenting view of snow, some of the drifts higher than a horse's head. The Hudson River was solid ice many feet thick. Had been for weeks and weeks since late November. There were reports that all harbors, bays, and rivers, both saltwater and fresh, from North Carolina to Maine, were frozen over. No ships were sailing anywhere. Her father's spies had told him that Loyalists in New York City were actually skating and driving ox carts across the harbor to and from Staten Island.

The heavy snows had been nonstop, starting in November—four of them—and followed by seven more in December. One blizzard, right after the new year, had lasted days, packing gale-force winds that collapsed houses and dumped four feet of fresh snow on what was already piled knee-deep on the ground.

The trek to Morristown, New Jersey, would take three dangerously long days pushing a pair of horses to draw a sleigh atop the snow at top speed. The temperatures could be killing for them, for her. No raiding parties were out given the below-freezing cold. Even so, she would have to pass close to enemy camps and hunkered-down sentries.

Eliza had made it through safely, Peggy reassured herself. Although her big sister had been incredibly lucky that one of January's six snowstorms had not hit as she traveled. Peggy glanced to the heavens—gray clouds, thick, muscular, glowering, menacing. Was she so starved for witty conversation, ballroom flirtations, and her sister's company to risk potentially dying in a snowdrift somewhere?

Peggy drew in a deep breath as she also considered the fact Philip Schuyler had just left for Philadelphia. No longer a battle commander, he had been elected to the Continental Congress by New York—people who knew and trusted him, unlike the New Englanders who had assassinated his character. Catharine could certainly run the house without Peggy, but what if her mother had to join Schuyler? What about the boys and Cornelia? John was almost fifteen, but he was usually at the center of whatever mischief the boys drummed up.

Wavering, Peggy weighed Hamilton's letter. She pushed her mind back again to her meeting him. How much sisterly protection did Eliza really need from this man? She closed her eyes to repaint the scene. There was poor, broken General Arnold in his bed, clearly in terrible pain. But he had snapped to military alertness as soon as Hamilton mentioned he needed General Washington's advice. Before that moment . . . *hmm* . . . before that there had been a bit of good-natured teasing about . . . about . . .

Peggy gasped, remembering Arnold playfully telling her to beware Hamilton! *He is famous for his love affairs.* Or infamous?

Was this man trifling with Eliza's trusting heart? Lord knew he had been quick to flirt with Peggy.

In a flash as quick as gunpowder, she was at her bedroom door. Peggy didn't care whom she woke. She shouted down the stairs for Prince, who basically ran the mansion and negotiated the worries and chores of the ten other enslaved servants when her papa was not there. Given the chaos of the war, the threat of Tory Rangers, food shortages, the constant in and out of soldiers, Prince had become a guardian, really. They all had come to rely on his judgment as much as Schuyler did.

Until a few weeks ago, she could have called on the faithful Richard Varick to help her. He had just returned to Hackensack, his New Jersey hometown—after an embarrassing good-bye. Peggy had hustled the man out the door for fear of his asking a question she didn't want to answer. He could have arranged Peggy's passage and a safe military escort to Morristown easily and eagerly. But perhaps it was just as well. He probably would have insisted on coming along to protect her. Blushing and spluttering all the way.

No, with Prince's advice she would figure out how she could make this journey. She was going to Morristown. Eliza needed her.

PART TWO
1780

The winter of 1779 and '80 was very severe; it has been denominated the "hard winter," and hard it was to the army in particular, in more respects than one. The period of the Revolution has repeatedly been styled "the times that try men's souls." I often found that those times not only tried men's souls, but their bodies too. . . .

At one time it snowed the greater part of four days successively, and there fell nearly as many feet deep of snow, and here was the keystone of the arch of starvation. We were absolutely, literally starved;—I do solemnly declare that I did not put a single morsel of victuals into my mouth for four days and as many nights, except a little black birch bark which I gnawed off a stick of wood. . . . I saw several men roast their old shoes . . . some of the officers killed and ate a favourite little dog that belonged to one of them.—If this was not "suffering" I request to be informed what can pass under that name.

—Nineteen-year-old private Joseph Plumb Martin

NINE

~~~ ❧ ~~~

Winter

Military Journal, Dr. James Thacher,
January 3, 1780, Morristown

We experienced one of the most tremendous snowstorms ever
remembered: no man could endure its violence many minutes
without danger to his life. . . . Some of the soldiers were actu-
ally covered while in their tents and buried like sheep under the
snow.

SSSSSSSSSSSSSSSSSSS . . . SLOOOOOSHHHHHHHHH . . .
sssssssssssssss . . . slooooooooshhhhhhh.

For hours, the only sound Peggy had heard was the
sweep of her sleigh along the ice-crusted snow, the horses'
struggling trot, and the wind. No birds. No squirrels leap-
ing from branch to branch, scattering ahead of her. Nothing.
The world was frozen, suspended in cold and silence.

She wrapped the beaver pelts up around her face so that
only her eyes peeped out from the fur. The sun was low in

the sky now. If they didn't make Morristown within two hours, she and the two men escorting her—Private Hines of her father's guard and Lisbon, the enslaved servant her father most trusted with his horses, his sleds, and the safety of his family when traveling—might freeze to death on the road in the killing night cold. What had she been thinking?

He that outlives this day, and comes safe home, will stand a' tiptoe when this day is named. Peggy thought of Shakespeare's Henry V, convincing his troops to stay the course against their enemy, promising them legendary memories. "All right, Lord," she murmured, "I absolutely promise that if I make it safe to Morristown that every year on this day I will say my hosannas."

She had felt so jaunty when they left Albany. Peggy had been bundled happily, sucking in the brisk air, the sun bright, the sky a spring-promising blue. The winds had tasted of freedom. But south of Kingston, in deserted countryside, Peggy may have murdered a pair of kindly draft horses. Not directly, of course, not by her own hand, but it was her fault that the sweet old mares might perish.

A tear crept out of Peggy's eye and stung her wind-chapped face thinking on the catastrophe. On their second day, when they came to the frozen Wallkill River, Lisbon urged the horses onto the ice to cross. They'd just witnessed another sledge do the same safely. But halfway across, one of the mares spooked and reared, its hooves piercing and cracking the ice as it came back down, plunging both horses into the water up to their chests.

Such accidents happened frequently enough in their frontier world that Peggy and Lisbon knew what to do to save the horses, the sleigh, and themselves. But it had to be done quickly, within moments—or the horses would fight to save themselves and break the ice further, sinking the sleigh and all of them. Or the poor animals would simply expire from the shock of the frigid waters.

"Hurry!" Peggy had cried, tumbling herself off the back of the sled-carriage, where the ice was still solid.

She could hear the horses swimming with their front legs to stay afloat. Panic in their eyes, snorting with terror, the mares stretched their necks out, straining, with their heads sliding back and forth on the unbroken ice in front of them. Thank God the ice was so thick—the horses were engulfed in a self-contained hole cut by their hooves. The white ice around them remained unshattered—for the moment.

"The plank!" Peggy cried.

The men yanked out a flat beam that had been put on the back of the sleigh for this very kind of emergency. They rushed to slip the long board against the horses' chests, bracing it on the solid ice beyond the animals' circumference. The mares could then scramble up onto the wood and lunge out of the water. But the peril would not be over with that—the horses would need to hasten forward to jump the sled over the hole, so that it did not sink in the water as well.

"Quickly!" Peggy urged. The men rushed to the horses' heads, knelt, grabbed the bridles, and pulled, hard, as they scrambled backward, slipping and sliding themselves.

"Come on, girls! Walk on! Get!!" Peggy shouted and clucked.

With the brute muscle and force of fear, the heavy old mares wiggled their knees onto the wooden flooring and then, pushing up, sprung and popped out of the water, sprays of ice shooting off them.

"Trot on! Trot on!" Peggy shrieked as the men ran, careening along the ice, dragging the horses with them. They didn't stop sliding and skating until they all—humans and horses—scrambled up onto the bank, heaving.

Swiftly, Lisbon wiped down and rubbed the wet horses to get their circulation going, talking to them gently as he worked. But the frost was settled into their legs and the mares could only stumble into Poughkeepsie, wheezing. There, a tavern owner took them, promising to do his best to warm them up and save them. Had he not been a Patriot, Peggy might have been stranded there. But her father's good name—or perhaps in truth it was the good repute of his riches—convinced the man to swap out a pair of horses to pull her to Morristown. On Schuyler's credit and her promise, the new pair of horses would be returned to him, or her father would pay the tavern keeper 200 pounds, or $20,000 in Continental currency.

Private Hines had whistled at the price. It was a fortune. The Continental Army was paying him only six dollars a month—and that only if Congress actually coughed up the wages, preferably in hard coin and not its grossly devalued paper money. But that was how precious horses had become in the war-ravaged land.

What if she maimed this pair of horses, too? Or killed them with the cold. Peggy glanced back to gauge the shadows cast on the Watchung Mountains now behind them and to the east. She knew they were nearing Morristown—finally. Washington had chosen the village specifically because the mountain range shielded it from British scouting parties and attack. But the sun was going down. Soon they'd be engulfed in darkness and plummeting temperatures.

"We'll make it, miss," Private Hines shouted to reassure her through the scarves wrapped around his head and face. A forty-year-old who'd been assigned to the easier job of Schuyler's guard after he'd suffered a ruptured hernia, Hines always hunched with some pain. But he seemed devoted to her father, having grown up in the city of Albany. Private Hines had volunteered for the journey, crossed sheepskins across his chest to withstand the winds, and now braced himself on the rails behind her seat, ready to shoot at anyone who threatened her.

Peggy nodded, grateful, and turned around. Her feet were prickling with cold, and she knew that soon she'd be shivering all over.

Another mile dragged on with nothing but thick forest and snow.

Then, what seemed a miracle. Peggy spotted a lone, thin figure standing atop a stump, backlit by the sunset. It seemed to have wings, opening and closing, like an angel. A guardian? Or one of death? Peggy held her breath. Was she so cold she was hallucinating?

But within a few more yards of the sled sliding along, she realized the figure was a sentry. He was slapping his arms to keep warm, and the shawl of his linsey-woolsey hunting shirt was flapping up and down with the motion of his desperate flagellation.

"Ho! Stop and identify yourself!" the sentry shouted in a thin voice as three other fellows dashed from out of a lean-to they'd fashioned of sticks, and aimed muskets at them.

"Peace, lads," Private Hines called. "We're friends."

Peggy flinched at the sight of the soldiers' ragged appearance. Their breeches and wool stockings were torn and patched. Thin, worn blankets were tied as tight as possible around their bodies with twine. She could barely see their gaunt faces through the towels they'd tied over their tricorn hats and under their chins to cover their ears. One had wrapped whatever pitiable shoes he wore in scraps of cloth. Another—the boy couldn't have been more than fifteen—stumbled in tall Hessian boots he'd obviously commandeered from a dead foe, which were far too big for his feet.

But to Peggy, they were possibly the most beautiful creatures she'd ever seen.

"This is Dr. Cochran's niece, come to visit him," Private Hines called out.

"What's the password?"

"No idea, son," Hines called back.

The soldiers didn't move, eyeing them.

"You going to keep a lady cold and caught in nightfall?" Lisbon demanded.

Peggy was grateful for his bold question and protectiveness of her. But she knew some might not respect an enslaved man being that brave and confident. He had always been like that. Lisbon should be a soldier, thought Peggy, even though she knew her father disapproved of Black troops.

Three of the soldiers lowered their guns. The fourth kept his Brown Bess aimed.

The man on the stump asked, "What's the name of the good doctor's wife? Not her Christian name. What her family calls her?"

Peggy pulled the beaver pelts from her face. "G-G-Gitty," Peggy said. The shivers now had her and she was shaking all over.

One of the sentry posts smacked the arm of the man still pointing his musket at her. "Now look what you gone and done. You must have given her fright. The poor lady is a-shivering."

The angel-soldier jumped off his stump, landing thigh-deep in snow, and waded to the sleigh. Pointing down the hill and then to the right, he explained to Lisbon how to find the Cochrans' house. He touched the brim of his hat to Peggy, saying, "Give my respects to your uncle, miss. He saved me from a rattlesnake bite. My skin turned blood-orange. One side was completely paralyzed. Thought I was long gone to Hades, but Dr. Cochran rubbed the bite with mercury ointment and made me drink a quart of olive oil. And here I be."

He was standing close enough to the sled that in the eerie silence of that snow-muffled forest she could hear his stomach whine and roll over and over in a long, anguished growl. And in the fast-falling twilight, she caught the flash-grimace of starvation pain on his face.

"Oh, sir, please, let me share the dinner I packed from home. I fear I have eaten most of it on the road here. But there is a little roasted chicken and some biscuits left, and dried apples."

Peggy nearly cried at the response on their faces. The boy swimming in those enormous boots gasped and staggered forward. The man who'd been last to lower his musket bit his lip and rubbed his eye, looked away and wiped his nose with his sleeve, trying to mask his tears. Damning herself for gluttony, she pulled a basket from under her blankets.

The head sentry's hands trembled as he reached for her offering. "Much obliged, miss," he choked out, and then carefully divvied up the food equally among them before handing her back the basket.

As Lisbon clucked the horses and they slid away, Peggy heard them saying grace.

Ten minutes gone and they were engulfed in darkness, but not far below and beyond them in a gentle valley, candles were being lit inside houses she couldn't yet see, little beckoning stars. Finally, in rising moonlight they reached the village and the little white-clapboard house on its edge that held her family—just as snow, big lacy flakes, began to drift down from the heavens.

"Hello in the house!" Lisbon shouted.

The front door opened and out spilled light and warmth, relieved joyful greetings, her uncle, her aunt, Eliza, and then Angelica, too! Peggy had had no idea that her eldest sister had traveled to Morristown as well. No letters with that news had made it through to Albany.

The Schuyler sisters! All together again!

Swept up in a tight embrace of laughter, kisses, and taffeta, Peggy was scooped out of the sled, out of the night, into the little house and its glow.

"That was the cussedest, most foolhardy . . . what a nincompoopa!"

Despite her face being so frozen she could barely feel it, Peggy grinned. "Good evening, Uncle Johnny."

"Good evening, indeed," fussed the blunt Irish-American surgeon as Eliza guided Peggy to a chair by the fire. "Quick, girls, pull off those boots and stockings. Rub her feet down. Brisk now. That's it. The child is like to be frostbit."

Dr. Cochran poured a golden liquid into a glass, waiting for Peggy's hands to stop shaking with shivers so he could hand it to her. "And what if you hadn't made it through, and lay in a snowbank somewhere? You'd be nothing but a pretty corpse, you would. Not found until the thaw when the crocus sprouted. I can hear the poetic laments for you now. And all for the thought of basking in some sunshine of jollity!"

"But I did get through, uncle," she answered gleefully,

despite her teeth chattering.

Cochran snorted. "Aye. The faeries looked after you, sure, Miss Meaghan-fay-Meaghan." Hearing him use his Irish endearment of her name, Peggy knew he was amused as well as worried. "Here, now." He took her hand, blew warmth on it, and handed her the goblet. "Drink this. All of it. Straight down."

"What is it?" Her nose wasn't working yet, either. It certainly didn't look like olive oil, although she was as paralyzed with cold as if she had been rattlesnake-bit.

"Rum." He finally grinned himself.

"Rum?" she asked with surprise. She'd never been allowed spirits other than Madeira before.

"She'll smell like a pirate, Uncle John," Eliza whispered.

"And so she should, with the antics she's been up to!" Cochran crossed his arms. "Drink!"

Angelica winked at her. "Go on."

Peggy downed the searing liquor. Suddenly she felt her toes.

"Now then," began Angelica, leaning over and taking Peggy's face in her hands. "You have come just in time, little sister. There is a ball tonight!"

Peggy could hardly believe her good luck.

Angelica straightened back up. "No time to unpack your trunk. But I have the perfect dress for you."

Peggy nodded happily. How many times she had longed to borrow her eldest sister's exquisite gowns!

"Perfect dress for what?" Cochran demanded, placing

the decanter on a table and coming back to the hearth to keep watch on his patient.

"For the ball!"

"What? No, madam. This child needs to stay by a fire."

"Oh, Uncle J," Angelica crooned, "what better way for her to warm up than to dance?" She threaded her arm under his and squeezed it. "Eliza and I will keep watch over her."

Peggy nodded. Angelica always made the best arguments.

Cochran hesitated, then blustered, "You are full of the blarney, you are, Mrs. Carter. And dangerously so, I might add. To think I saved the Marquis de Lafayette from his wounds at Brandywine, only to have him almost expire from merrymaking at your Boston home. There was hell for me to pay with His Excellency for letting that lad's departure to France be delayed because of overconsumption at your table. Washington was desperate for Lafayette to plead our cause to the French king."

"Surely the marquis will return with good news from King Louis this spring," Eliza interrupted. "Don't you think, uncle?"

"Good Lord willing. We are surely in need." Cochran inspected Peggy again. "There. I see some rose in your cheeks now." He smiled.

Peggy nodded. All better now. Always better when the Schuyler sisters were together, plotting merriment.

"Then she is absolutely fine to accompany us to the ball." Angelica pressed her point.

Peggy nodded emphatically. "Please, uncle?"

Cochran ignored Peggy and continued fussing at Angelica. "Do you want her developing quinsy? Is good-timing that important to you that you would risk your sister's health?"

At that, Angelica finally bristled. "It is important for morale. General Washington endorses these assemblies himself, as you well know, uncle. He and thirty officers have paid four hundred dollars apiece to subscribe to a series of balls."

"Four hundred dollars!" breathed Eliza.

"Yes," Angelica continued, "quite a financial sacrifice on their part to create a happy diversion for the officers in camp. Your gallant Colonel Hamilton told me just the other day that he only draws sixty-dollars-a-month salary. So this subscription has cost him more than a year's commission. Poor man." She looked pointedly at Eliza.

Peggy frowned. Even in the haze of the rum saturating her body and mind, she wondered why Eliza's suitor would be telling Angelica about his wages.

"Poor man, *pshaw*," Cochran snorted. "The man is living on air these days anyway—he doesn't need money." He smiled at Eliza, but talked to Peggy. "The lad comes to deliver a message from His Excellency and this one," he gestured toward Eliza, "opens the door. Shot through the heart, he was, at first sight. Every night since I come home weary from the hospital and want to stretch out on the settee for a wee bit of rest before supper and what do I find? It occupied by these earnestly chatting lovers."

Eliza's face flushed pink. But she rose to join her sister's argument. "Oh, uncle, if the officers are paying that much for a night of diversion from all their cares, we must all go to provide them partners on the dance floor."

Uh-oh, thought Peggy. Eliza was already too protective of this man. Good thing she had come.

Cochran paused, softening as everyone did at Eliza's sweet-natured concerns. He walked to the window and pressed his face against the panes. "It's snowing again. Hard. What is this—the fourth storm this month? On top of all that came before." He watched a few more moments. "From the way it's coming down, it will probably drop a few more inches." He looked back to the sisters and to his wife, who had just entered with a bowl of soup for Peggy. "Gitty, my love, talk some sense to these girls."

"About what, my dear?"

"This infernal ball!"

"Oh, doesn't it sound wonderful?" The plump little lady brightened. "I hear the general has asked the military bands to come with French horns and flutes. Won't it be marvelous to have more than just a violin?"

"NO!" Cochran roared. "This child cannot go. She has been out in this below-freezing weather for days. She must go to bed by a stoked fire. Immediately!"

Peggy frowned. Now that her face was unfrozen, she felt her lips pout. She started to open her mouth to protest, but Angelica put her delicate hand on Peggy's shoulder and shook her head slightly. Looking up into her sister's beautiful face, Peggy recognized a look of warning that said Angelica had a salvo ready. So she stayed silent.

"Oh, uncle, it's far too early for bedtime," Angelica scoffed, adding, "What time is it anyway?"

"Wh-wh-what?" Cochran seemed oddly flustered by the question. He glanced out the window, ostensibly to gauge the fall of darkness for his answer. "I suspect half past five."

He paced back to the hearth, hands on his hips, looking at Angelica with a sudden nervousness. Then he surveyed Peggy carefully before asking in a completely new tone of voice, "What think you of the outing, lass?"

Peggy hiccuped.

Instantly, Angelica gathered her up, taking Eliza's hand, too, and danced them out of the room toward the stairs. "Wait till you see how pretty she'll be, uncle," Angelica chirped from the hallway.

"I'll be driving that sleigh, I will," Cochran shouted after them. "I've bandaged too many a local girl tossed into the snow out of overturned sleds, driven helter-skelter by rogues! Lovesick officers! Idiots!"

The girls giggled and swept up the stairs as one.

"Why did you ask him the time, Angelica? And why did that change his attitude?" Eliza whispered.

"Let's just say, sister, that our beloved Uncle Johnny lost his pocket watch at gaming tables while visiting me in Boston, in a way the retelling would make him blush! He definitely would not want Aunt Gitty to know of it."

TEN

Winter: The Same Night

The ball was opened by his Excellency the General. When this man unbends from his station, and its weighty functions, he is even then like a philosopher, who mixes with the amusements of the world, that he may teach it what is right, or turn its trifles into instruction.
—*Pennsylvania Packet*

His Excellency . . . danced upwards of three hours without once sitting down. Upon the whole we had a pretty little frisk.
—*Brigadier General Nathaniel Greene*

AS GUESTS ARRIVED, SHAKING SNOW FROM THEIR outer cloaks, Peggy hid in a corner, her back turned to the dance floor. She was desperately trying to yank up her dress and fluff out some of the lace ornamenting the neckline of the ball gown Angelica had put her into. If one could call it a *neck*line. Cut tight from the shoulders, the ruby-colored satin dropped to her waist in a wide-open V that was filled by a stomacher of overlapping rows of puffed, creamy lace. Along its top and from under the edges of her shoulders peeked a diaphanous fringe of neatly embroidered silk organza— floaty, gorgeous, but so . . . so revealing.

Plus, Angelica had tied her stays so tight and the stomacher was so stiff, Peggy's breasts were compressed and pushed up in the most embarrassing manner. She was terrified they might escape during one of the dance's bows or skipping circles. If only she could pull the stomacher up a bit, she thought, as she squirmed and tugged. Or maybe she could tuck her breasts down some. . . .

"Huzzah! Here she is—Aglaea herself."

Startled, Peggy whirled around, her hand still stuck in the top of her dress.

The man chuckled, quickly lowering his eyes, and bowed. "Miss Schuyler."

Peggy dropped her hands to her sides, mortified, hastily curtsying. As she rose, she realized with horror who stood before her: Alexander Hamilton.

"Finally, I have the honor to meet the last of the three Schuyler Graces." His violet-blue eyes quickly flicked up and down her figure as he added, "I see the Greeks were right; the youngest is aptly named splendor."

Did he think she didn't see his amusement at her, that rapid undressing look, or his rather shameless smirk? Peggy felt her eyebrow shoot up although she kept her answer ballroom-courteous. First, to let this cocky aide-de-camp know that she knew precisely the reference he was making to Greek literature. "You are too kind, sir. I would hardly claim the role of superior beauty that mythology grants the youngest of the three Graces. But Eliza is surely the middle Grace—Euphrosyne—the epitome of delight and joyfulness. Don't you think?"

"Indeed, Miss Peggy, your sister Eliza is all that." His smile twitched—with surprise, a tinge of admiration?—before he continued, "Her lovely portrait of you certainly captured your beauty. She did not warn me, however, of your—"

"My education?" Peggy interrupted, but her tone was light, almost flirtatious. What was the matter with her? There was just something about this man that invited such frothy repartee.

"Your quick wit," Hamilton bantered back.

"We have met before, you know," said Peggy.

He frowned. A moment of uncertainty clouded his smooth, fair face and then dissipated. "I think not, mademoiselle," he said. "I would not forget you."

Using her French to emphasize her point, Peggy told him that it was indeed true they had met and that he had called her a nymph: "*Mais c'est vrai. La dernière fois que nous nous sommes rencontrés, vous m'avez appelée une nymphe.*"

Hamilton crossed his arms, stepped back, and shook his head. But he grinned, intrigued. "Impossible. You are a nymph, *certainement. Mais une telle beauté est inoubliable.* Your beauty is completely unforgettable."

165

She shrugged. "Whether you care to admit it or not, we have met."

"Perhaps in a dream, then?" he quipped.

"Hardly. More of a nightmare, I'd call it."

Hamilton clutched his chest. "A nightmare? Ouch! Shot through the heart, Miss Peggy." He squinted at her a bit, searching his memory, which gave her a moment to assess him. He was trim and delicate, not much taller than she, but his lithe build kept him from seeming short. And as beautiful as those huge, intense eyes were, they were close-set. The bridge of his nose was also low, almost like it had been pressed flat by a hot poker, so that when he frowned, his eyebrows seemed to truly knit together. It was, above all else, an expressive face—his moods probably easy to read despite any efforts he might make to hide them.

Finally, Hamilton confessed that he simply could not remember. "Clearly a moment of madness on my part. Please tell me why our meeting was almost a nightmare?"

Now Peggy frowned slightly as memories of the injured at Albany's hospital rushed into her mind. "It was in Albany. At the hospital. I was speaking with General Arnold and—"

"That was you?" he asked with genuine surprise. "I am very sorry, Miss Peggy, but"—he gestured toward her as he continued—"you look very"—he paused—"very different now, mademoiselle."

Peggy flushed. "It is Angelica's dress," she blurted.

"Ah, it has her . . . aura. But it is most becoming on you, Miss Peggy. You will most certainly achieve what I had hoped with your presence—denying your sister's absolute sway over our hapless officers by dividing our attentions."

"Oh, I doubt that," Peggy answered without thinking. She had become so accustomed to playing second fiddle, to Angelica especially.

He cocked his head. "You are too modest."

"Not really," Peggy said with a small laugh. "Just honest. And speaking honestly, you might remember that day we met, I was rather annoyed for my father that you did not bother to go see him in Saratoga when you visited General Gates. It was my father who set up our army to be able to vanquish Burgoyne. You know that, don't you?"

Hamilton was taken aback. "I . . . I . . . my mission was so rushed, Miss Peggy. And politics . . . Congress . . . your father at that time . . ."

"Was persona non grata?"

Suddenly, Hamilton looked very young as the realization sank in that he may have once deeply insulted the father of the woman he was now courting. "I hope General Schuyler will not hold that against me."

"Papa is not like that." She paused, noting Hamilton called her father "general" even though he no longer served as such. "That is if we—his three Graces—tell Papa not to be." Peggy was not ready yet to make things easy for this man in his pursuit of Eliza. The aide-de-camp had much to prove.

Hamilton considered her a moment before speaking again—clearly unsure of stratagem. He chose sincerity. "I will depend upon your mercy, then, Miss Peggy. Because surely no man has been as struck through with love as I am with admiration and feeling for your sister's generosity of spirit and beauty."

Well, she thought, no verbal strutting in that, no claiming that against his better judgment was Eliza luring him into love—as he had bantered in his letter. She'd give him a chance at least.

Hamilton clearly observed Peggy soften. "Have we negotiated an alliance, then?"

"I will discuss it with my sisters, my fellow Graces," Peggy quipped, defaulting to ballroom playfulness. "Perhaps we must cast dice to read the future regarding you. Will there be some at the card tables tonight?"

Hamilton followed her lead. "If not, I will ride to the soldiers' huts to find some! May I escort you to your sisters, Miss Peggy? You must not stand in this corner, hiding your glory." He held out his hand.

She took it. As they crossed the sanded floorboards of the recently built army storehouse that would serve as the night's dance hall, Hamilton added, "We must find you an appropriate suitor. No Hephaestus for my Aglaea."

Peggy made a face. "I would hope not! The deformed, cast-off lover of Aphrodite? Wasn't he her half brother, too?"

Hamilton laughed outright. It was an honest laugh. Peggy liked it.

"I can see finding an appropriate match for you is going to be quite the challenge, Miss Peggy. But tonight will be a good start. Tonight's snowfall seems to have kept most ladies at home. They are not blessed with the Schuyler sisters' intrepidness. There are a mere sixteen ladies to almost sixty officers. I hope you are ready to dance."

"Oh, look!" Eliza caught her breath and squeezed Peggy's hand. "The general!"

At the threshold stood His Excellency, General George Washington. The room hushed.

Tall, broad-shouldered, lean, with long-stretched, muscular legs, Washington towered over all the other men in the room. He bowed his head to the assembly, noble yet unassuming, as he quickly began the circuit of greeting everyone. On his arm, barely reaching his chest, was his diminutive wife, Martha, or Lady Washington, as the soldiers fondly called her. She was slightly plump, and her heart-shaped, dimpled face carried a sweet impishness in it.

"I so wish to be like her," Eliza whispered as she waited with Peggy and Angelica for their turn with His Excellency. "She is kind to everyone, even preening fools. Aunt Gitty told me that when Mrs. Washington made it through the snows to camp, all the Morristown ladies donned their most elegant dresses and jewels to call on her. They arrived at the arranged time and there she sat, in a very plain brown dress of homespun, a neat frilled cap on her head, and no ornamentation except a miniature portrait of her husband hanging from her neck.

"Mrs. Washington was knitting stockings for the soldiers!"

Eliza laughed lightly. "The ladies were quite stunned that she was not all done up as they. But Mrs. Washington was her amiable, cheerful self, chatting about her pity for the poor, naked soldiers, and 'my old man,' as she calls His Excellency. Her knitting needles were going the whole time, a ball of yarn in her outside pocket. She was careful to make her guests feel at ease with her welcoming conversation. Yet they were ashamed of their idle hands. They left and immediately started up several sewing circles."

Eliza beamed, bouncing slightly on her toes as the Washingtons neared. "Oh, and she also told me that she keeps more than a dozen spinning wheels going round the clock at Mount Vernon. Imagine. We must talk to Mama about doing the same in our barn. Mrs. Washington has learned to design her own dresses, too, with what can be found here in our states. No reliance on Europe. We can do that, Peggy. She made two dresses of cotton, striped with silk—the stripes coming from ravelings of old, crimson damask chair covers. Isn't that marvelous!"

"*Hmpf.* Well, I don't think I will be making gowns for myself out of frayed furniture," mumbled Angelica. "And someone should tell her to take that enormous satin bow off the bodice she wears tonight. It does nothing for her figure."

Eliza and Peggy looked at her with shock. Their eldest sister's sense of humor had always been rapier sharp, but never catty, never envious or mean.

Noticing their surprise, Angelica murmured, "I can't believe I just said that."

"Eliza, my dear." Martha Washington held out both hands to clasp Eliza's and kissed her on the cheek. "You look absolutely radiant. I'm sure our Alexander is swooning. There is much talk about you two among the general's family."

Eliza blushed.

Martha Washington turned to Angelica. "Mrs. Carter, what a lovely dress."

And then she came to Peggy. "This must the youngest of the Schuyler sisters. Your sister brags much upon your talents, child. I look forward to our friendship." She turned to her husband. "Mr. Washington."

"Yes, my dearest?"

"This is Philip Schuyler's third daughter we have so looked forward to meeting."

Peggy felt her knees go weak as His Excellency approached, took her hand, and bowed. "I am relieved to see you have made it here safely, Miss Schuyler. I hope your trip was not too taxing. Although I can imagine the dangers and the discomforts you experienced. I am truly sorry that we are not able to better guard and maintain the roads for our fairest visitors. The best we have been able to do is send the infantry out to tramp down the snows so sleds can pass." His voice was resonant, deep, but breathy, as if he pulled in air with effort. Peggy knew his brother had died of consumption, and the general's face was pockmarked, a lingering sign of having survived smallpox. Don't let this man become ill, she thought. The country would not survive General Washington dying.

Aloud she demurred, "No, sir. Not too uncomfortable. The trip was simply long."

"Ah, you are as your uncle described—a spirited young woman. Bravo. He is quite proud of you, you know. And protective. Good Dr. Bones was beside himself when he learned that you had embarked on this journey. I thought he might demand I send out a regiment to collect you."

"Dr. Bones?"

General Washington nodded. His smile was drawn tight across his lips—he was reputed to rarely laugh outright or grin, but he was clearly entertained with a memory of her uncle. "We call him that because of an amusing song he sings to lift our mood. I don't know what we would do without his medical acumen and his jokes."

"He is a man of great mirth, indeed, sir." Peggy marveled at how Washington looked at her so deferentially, so full in the face with his gray-blue eyes, as if he had all the evening to spend listening to her, as if there were not dozens of far more important guests impatiently awaiting his attention. "I should not monopolize you, Your Excellency."

"I suppose you are right. And yet truth be told, I would far prefer retreating to a corner to talk with you, your sisters, and my beloved wife. May I beg a dance with you later?"

Dancing with His Excellency, the supreme commander of the War of Independence, the man all fighting Patriots depended on to lead them to victory, to protect them against starvation and disease, and to save them from hanging as traitors! "Yes, please, sir," she answered.

General Washington bowed again with sincere court-liness. Seemingly unaware of—or perhaps studiously ignoring—the effect he had on people, His Excellency moved on to the next group eagerly awaiting an audience with him.

To begin the dancing, Washington led Lucy Knox, the wife of his trusted artillery general, out in front of the assembly for a minuet.

"Now there is someone worth talking to," Angelica said to Peggy. "Mrs. Knox is quite the scholar. Everyone in Boston talks about it. That's how she met her husband. She frequented his bookshop constantly. He advised her on what to buy and read next. He is a self-made intellectual, you know. His knowledge of cannonade and warfare is completely gleaned from reading books. Isn't that marvelous—a wondrous irony if ever there was one given how he has bested the most trained of British artillery units. Mrs. Knox's father, on the other hand, was a royal provincial governor of Massachusetts. He was incensed when his daughter fell in love with a poor man—no pedigree or breeding, a mere merchant. And a Patriot! Her parents completely disowned her when she married. Lucy gave up everything—wealth, her family—for love."

"For love of General Knox?" Peggy couldn't help her surprise. It was a marvel much discussed that Knox weighed something like three hundred pounds while the Continental Army starved.

Hamilton was standing beside the sisters and the Cochrans

and laughed at Peggy's astonishment. "One cannot predict love, Miss Peggy," he said.

Eliza blushed again. Peggy realized her sister was going to be blushing on and off all night long.

"Aye, child," Cochran chimed in. "For his part, General Knox is besotted with his bride, despite her dollop of autocratic tendencies and fits o' passion. He is a good soul and laughs along with jests at his expense. The night before we attacked those blasted Hessians at Trenton, our men stood for hours. Standing in sleet, wet to the bone, waiting to cross the Delaware River clogged thick with ice, in nothing but rowboats—their apprehension grew like a rising fog. His Excellency sensed it and dispelled their fears by teasing General Knox. Before setting foot into a boat in which General Knox already sat, His Excellency prodded him with his boot. 'Shift yourself over, Harry,' he said, 'but do it slowly or you'll swamp the boat. And don't swing your'"—Cochran winked for the word—"'or you'll tip us over.'"

Peggy laughed. She knew she shouldn't at such off-color jokes, but she delighted in her uncle's outrageous sense of mischief.

"Dr. Cochran!" protested Aunt Gertrude.

"Now then, Gitty, it's just a bit of fun that His Excellency did a-purpose to help the lads laugh a bit. The question— 'What did the general say?'—went down the line of those poor, freezing bastards, followed by hearty laughter and renewed energy."

"Honestly, husband," she reprimanded him. "The girls."

Cochran winked at Peggy as the military band, augmented with some fiddlers, French horn players, and flutists from Morristown, raised their instruments.

According to custom, the musicians were waiting for Mrs. Knox to select her music. A ball's opening minuets followed a strict, formal ritual. The ranking gentleman and the most important lady present danced first, followed in descending order of social standing by other couples, one after the other. Each pair danced solo, performing for the assembled watchers. It was theater not for the fainthearted. A minuet's steps were complex, intricate, requiring the two dancers to move in symmetrical patterns across the entire dance floor, away and then back to each other—so there was no hiding mistakes or clumsiness during those five minutes of music. Dancers were expected to glide as if they skated along ice, four steps to six beats of melody, while never breaking their gaze from each other and ignoring the witnessing throng that analyzed and gossiped about them.

"Watch this," murmured Hamilton with obvious awe. "His Excellency is as good a dancer as horseman."

Mrs. Knox called an old favorite, the "Philadelphia Minuet," and the musicians began a 3/4-time melody that Peggy knew well from her dancing classes. Mrs. Knox and the general did "honors" to the crowd and then to each other—sinking, slowly, by bending their knees, heels together, their arms extended slightly in an open arc, like birds sunning

175

their wings. Then they promenaded, his right hand palm up holding her left hand, palm down. Forward then backward in small tiptoe steps, a pause as a foot was held up, heel down, another slight plié bend of the knees, and repeat.

Halfway through the minuet, they drifted apart, mirroring each other in Z patterns that pulled away to opposite corners of the floor. A few elegant jetés switching from one foot to the other midleap, a few hops ending with one foot extended, toes pointed, always on the beat, always exactly together.

Finally reunited, hands held, General Washington returned Mrs. Knox to their opening position, parading backward, to conclude with an elegant bow.

Everyone applauded. Women sighed and murmured how they hoped the general would ask them for a dance as they awaited the next brave pair to step onto the floor. General Greene led out Widow Ford, whose home served as headquarters. Washington took the floor again with the vivacious twenty-four-year-old Caty Greene. Senior officers performed one after another, and then it was the turn for the next tier of importance, the general's "family"—his five aides-de-camp. There was a long silence and pause as his cohorts turned to Hamilton.

"Go on, Hammie. The general typically puts you at the head of our table opposite him. So you must have rank," prodded Tench Tilghman. Peggy had recognized him instantly—he was the Marylander who Washington had sent to Albany five years earlier to help Schuyler negotiate an alliance with the Iroquois Confederacy. His hair was now graying, and the ten or so years' difference between him and Hamilton showed clearly.

"Yes, you're our little lion," teased Robert Harrison, another thirtysomething Marylander on the general's staff. He elbowed Hamilton.

"Of all of us, you best know the ways of Cupid," added an Irish-born doctor named James McHenry, who now acted as secretary to Washington. "And what better way to show it than by the minuet." He ribbed Hamilton. "Besides, your head is totally in the clouds these days, my friend, so you will float across the floor."

Eliza blushed.

"It is true, my dear." Martha Washington took Eliza's arm. "I heard from one of the Ford children . . ." She paused and explained to Peggy, "Mrs. Ford is kind enough to rent her house to the general for his headquarters, but she and her four children remain in residence as well. Her eldest son told me that Colonel Hamilton shares our daily password with him so the boy can visit friends in the village and still gain entry to his own home after dark. These poor villagers, we certainly disrupt their lives."

"Madam, I beg you not to share this story; it will show me for the fool I am," Hamilton pleaded.

"Oh, you must tell, then, Lady Washington!" said McHenry.

Martha laughed, like a charming little bell pealing. "It seems our Colonel Hamilton's mind—which we all so admire—completely failed him after a visit with our dear Eliza. He was so preoccupied he could not remember that day's password. Had Master Ford not snuck out and whispered it to him, our guard would never have let Colonel Hamilton reenter. He would have spent the night like that tomcat I named after him, yowling at the perimeters of the house, looking for a way in."

Hamilton's friends guffawed and punched his shoulder.

"A tomcat?" Peggy asked.

"Yes, Miss Peggy," Harrison answered. "Our young squire has been looking for love ardently."

"And now, it seems he has found it," Martha concluded. "Come, Colonel. The minuet awaits you."

Peggy stepped back so nothing but air stood between Hamilton and her sister. Yet Hamilton hesitated. Peggy suddenly realized there was a shadow of panic on his face. Did he know how? There was no faking a minuet, no way to simply mimic a partner's movements. One had to know the steps, had to have internalized the rhythms, as they weren't always obvious with the music's phrasings. Peggy knew nothing about Hamilton's background—whether he would have had the advantage of a dancing master. She glanced at Eliza.

Her sister's luminous rich-brown eyes were fixed on Hamilton's and radiated reassurance. Eliza nodded ever so slightly at him, smiled, and mouthed, "It's all right." Hamilton took a deep breath and took her hand.

It was magic.

Eliza swept out onto the floor with a poise that stunned

Peggy. Such confidence—the likes of which she had never witnessed in her middle sister before. As Eliza turned, the pleated train of her *à la française* dress sailed in pretty swells behind her, like a swan on still waters. At first Hamilton moved with stilted, stiff dignity. But with each lilting phrase of the flutes, each near pass with Eliza, each momentary brush with her beautifully billowing skirts, each fleeting touch of hands, he gained a buoyancy, a beauty of step that was breathtaking. Their movements gained harmony until together, Eliza and her suitor embodied the musical metaphor of courtship that the minuet was first designed to celebrate and display.

It was all palpable, poetic urgency as they slowly spiraled toward each other in gradually shrinking circles for that exquisite moment they touched, right hand to right hand. Two delicious rotations with their hands held and then the bittersweet agony of withdrawing, hands still outstretched and beckoning, a plea for reuniting, before they had to repeat those separating snake patterns of steps away from each other. Even then, never did their gaze break—Hamilton's an insecure hunger, Eliza's a shy acceptance. When they did their final honors to their spellbound audience, Peggy could see that Eliza and Hamilton breathed in-out, in-out in tandem— the strings of their souls now tuned to match each other's pitch, their hearts' pulse now beats of the same melody.

The poise Peggy had noted in Eliza—it wasn't mere confidence, she realized. It was the power of love, the largesse gained by coaxing out the best of another human being, the promise of being there during dangers and unknowns, the leap of faith needed to take a risk together. In that minuet, Peggy witnessed her sister give her enormous heart to Alexander Hamilton.

No one dared follow that heart-wrenchingly gorgeous minuet. So the band struck up a lively 6/8-time piece called "Lady Washington's Quick Step" for the contredanse, or "country dances"—where couples danced together in long facing lines, men on one side, ladies on the other. For hours Peggy danced. Hop-step-step, forward-back, clap-clap, circling and changing places, skipping down the outside lines, weaving and threading through chains of dancers.

Laughter, breathlessness, joy. This was what she had been craving.

She danced with Tilghman, Harrison, another aide-de-camp named Robert Kidder Meade, the captain of Washington's personal guard, Major Gibbs, another dozen lads whose names she never caught, and His Excellency's very own nephew, a tall, pretty boy named George Augustine. Hamilton partnered her twice as well, but mostly he tried to occupy Eliza.

Around midnight, General Washington asked for Peggy's hand to a dance. Trembling at the honor, Peggy followed him to the lead couple position, at the top of the two lines. There, it was her privilege to call the song. She hesitated—many dance songs had been renamed to political references or to honor battles. Her choice would be akin to a man making a toast. She caught Angelica's eye. Her sister stood with Hamilton in the third couple position. Angelica returned her gaze quizzically, as if to say, *Everyone's waiting, little sister.*

Peggy looked back to the general, and with her chin lifted and her eyebrow raised, she called for "Burgoyne's Defeat." Even over the fiddlers, she could hear it—the general chuckled. So clearly he did know that her papa had contributed just as much as Gates to that critical battle!

The next eight minutes were perhaps the best of her life to that day. She and His Excellency—the legendary General George Washington—joined hands with the couple next to them, circled to the right, then to the left, let go, cast off so that she and the general walked down the outside of the two lines, to rejoin at the funnel's bottom and parade back through. Then they moved down to the position of second couple for the repeat. As she joined hands with Angelica for a four-person circle, her big sister leaned over and whispered, "Excellent choice!"

For such a tall man, Washington was remarkably light on his feet, catlike in grace, and completely delighted with the spritely melody. Peggy memorized the feel of every turn, every bow, every skip with him. She knew that if they all came out of this war, independent, alive, and whole, she would recount the privilege of "*getting a touch* of General George Washington"—as all the women that night called the experience of dancing with the man in whom they placed all their hopes and trust their very lives.

At the end of their dance, she was limping a bit. She had

been dancing for hours at that point. She didn't care. But General Washington did. "Miss Schuyler, I must insist that you sit for a moment. We have taken advantage of your generosity. You dance with such grace and good humor, we have all forgotten that you arrived just this evening, after hours of hard, cold travel. You must be exhausted."

"Oh no, sir, I could dance for hours more." She beamed up at him.

"Then I defer to your mercy, for my legs are fatigued." He guided her to a chair.

She knew it was a gracious lie and sat gratefully.

"Gentlemen," Washington called, holding his hand up to silence the musicians. "We must pause for a moment to allow our gallant ladies to catch their breath and our wonderful musicians to rest their fingers."

All sixteen ladies smiled with relief, and suddenly looked tremendously tired. As they fluttered into seats, Washington announced, "I have been waiting to bring out my punch until such a break." He motioned to the servants standing along the walls, who promptly carried in a large bowl. "A glass for everyone, and then a toast."

When everyone held a tin mug or glass filled with aromatic liquor, Washington raised his and said, "To liberty, our fellowship, and most particularly tonight to the ladies who braved the fiercest winter of the century to bring us happiness."

"Hear, hear!"

One sip and Peggy's eyes watered and throat burned.

Tilghman, Harrison, McHenry, and Meade had all ended

up standing near Peggy and Angelica. Tilghman noticed her grimace at the punch. "Be careful of that, Miss Peggy, there is quite a bit of whiskey, rum, and Madeira in that."

She sniffed at it, preparing to try again, and decided against the adventure. "Perhaps I'll just hold it," she said.

"Oh, I'll take that off your hands," said McHenry. "We mustn't waste such excellent spirits in this awful winter."

The aides noticed Eliza and Hamilton across the dance floor, talking.

"Hamilton's a gone man," quipped Harrison.

"How could he not be?" said Tilghman. "Miss Eliza has the most lively dark eyes I have ever seen. They radiate good temper and benevolence."

Angelica and Peggy looked at each other knowingly. They had suspected in that visit Tilghman made to Albany that he was smitten with Eliza.

"Poor Cornelia," Tilghman murmured. "I hope Alex didn't break her heart."

"I warned her," brayed McHenry. "I told her that one man is oft more dangerous to a woman than a whole army. And I could tell she was a passing fancy. She has turned, as I suspected into, '*a mere rant, th'effusion of a brain oppress'd with love's distempered train.*'"

"Quoting yourself, Mac?" Harrison asked with a laugh.

"Ah no. 'Twas penned for Hammie by our dear friend Samuel Blachley Webb last month. It is nicely turned, so I memorized it. He wrote all the right sentiments: '*She's but—sweet sir, nay do not fret, She's but—a beautiful brunette.*'"

Peggy did not like this McHenry at all. Was he the source of Hamilton's letter calling love a weakness? Who was Cornelia? And what about Hamilton's flirtation with Kitty Livingston that Benedict Arnold had mentioned?

But before Peggy could ask the aide-de-camp who he was talking about, before she could rise up to protect her sister, the music started again. McHenry pulled Peggy back into the crowd, as people again gathered to frolic on the dance floor.

Peggy tried to keep her eye on Eliza, to gauge her interaction with Hamilton. But her watchful eye was always drawn to Angelica, even within the lovely sea of dancers. Angelica kept surfacing like a beautiful shimmering fish. Her dress was slim and form-fitting despite her recently giving birth to a baby girl and the most elaborate of any that night—a cream-tissue taffeta shot-through with silver metallic threads, its skirt ornamented with ribbons of twisted silk gimp. Peggy wondered fleetingly where Carter was—in the flurry of getting her primped and dressed and into the sled and back into the snow for the ball, Peggy hadn't thought to ask.

Of course, that night, since there were four men to each woman, the ladies partnered with many officers besides their husbands. So Peggy wasn't shocked that Angelica danced with the same abandon and flirtatious effervescence she had before she married. Not even when she noticed Hamilton draw Angelica in a bit too close as she pirouetted under his arm, not even when they lingered in that allemande turn, when couples' arms entwined in a pretzel-like clasp. That night, against the bitter cold dark of the worst winter anyone could remember, snow falling yet again, and the sure knowledge that come spring, their desperate fight against the British would renew, everyone danced with a do-or-die kind of exuberance that might have scandalized in peacetime.

At two a.m. the revelers scattered through the snow back to their quarters, the ball over. Peggy, Angelica, and Eliza bundled together in their sled, exhausted, Eliza flushed with the kiss Hamilton had pressed to the palm of her gloved hand. As their sleigh pulled away, they could hear Washington's aides-de-camp defiantly singing to the heavens the Patriots' cheeky takeoff on the British grenadiers traditional fight song:

"Vain Britons, boast no longer, with proud indignity,
By land your conquering legions,
your matchless strength at sea,
Since we, your braver sons, incensed,
our swords have girded on . . ."

As the male voices reached the song's final line, Peggy linked arms with her sisters, and laughing with rebellious abandon, the Schuyler women shouted with them:

"Huzzah, huzzah, huzzah, huzzah, for war and Washington!"

ELEVEN
∾

Early Spring

Alexander Hamilton to Eliza Schuyler
Amboy, New Jersey, Thursday Forenoon, March 17, 1780

If I were not afraid of making you vain, I would tell you that Mrs. Carter, Peggy, and yourself are the dayly toasts of our table . . . though as I am always thinking of you, this naturally brings Peggy to my mind who is generally my toast. Capt Beebe is here and talks of her sometimes; but I won't give my consent to his being her favourite. I don't think him clever enough for her; he sings well and that's all.

ELIZA WAS SPRAWLED ON HER STOMACH ON THEIR bed, reading aloud from Hamilton's letter. Pausing, she looked up to ask, "Which one is Captain Beebe, Peggy?"

Peggy was trying to remember herself. "I think he is an officer in the Corps of Sappers and Miners. I only danced once with him. A sweet but rather short, stocky man. Talked a bit about the importance of trenches." She made a face.

"Not exactly scintillating. But he did have a lovely voice. I recall that now. He sang for the assembly when His Excellency gave the musicians a few minutes to enjoy some grog and let their fingers rest."

"Oh, was he that man who sang that heartbreaking love song?" asked Eliza.

"I thiiiink so?"

"Awwwwww." Eliza put her hand over her heart.

"He most certainly was." Angelica spoke up. "And he completely sank the mood with it, remember? A sapper and miner, indeed. Best beware of him, Peggy, he's a sap, all right."

The girls laughed. Peggy was overjoyed to hear the carillon peal of their joint amusement once more. How she had missed the sound of her sisters' mirth and their interconnected thoughts—like the harmonies and synonymous beat of a song. It was a hard price to pay for growing up—not hearing that daily. Was romance and marriage really worth splitting and scattering the three of them? Angelica's husband certainly was not convincing her that the bittersweet sacrifice was worth it. And Peggy still wasn't positive that the jocular Alexander Hamilton was devoted enough for the loyal and loving Eliza.

Angelica was pacing, lightly rocking her four-month-old daughter, who slipped in and out of slumber peacefully. Her firstborn, a two-year-old named for their father, was toddling about the bedroom, protected from being hurt if he fell by a padded, helmetlike pudding cap.

Peggy sat cross-legged in a settee, rubbing her toes to push out the ache in them. The pain was getting more frequent and more annoying and frightening. She needed to ask her uncle about it. The discomfort was jabbing, knifelike, in her joints. Just like Papa. But she said nothing, not wanting to disturb their sisterly conclave. She had so missed them.

Angelica's lullaby rotation brought her to her youngest sister's side. She reached out with her free hand and fondly twirled one of Peggy's curls. "Just think, little one, General Washington's aides-de-camp toasting you. You are quite grown up now."

"Indeed she is! Perhaps I should be jealous that Peggy is, hmm . . . wait a moment . . ." Eliza looked down to the neat handwriting: "Alexander says, and I quote, *This naturally brings Peggy to my mind who is generally my toast.*"

Angelica abruptly let go of the tendril of Peggy's hair with what felt like a little yank. Peggy frowned and rubbed her scalp, saying, "It is only because he thinks he has enlisted my help in his courtship of you, Eliza."

"Does he say anything about the prisoner exchange he is negotiating?" asked Angelica. "Mr. Carter is hoping a friend of his will be released. He thinks he can cajole the man to help procure supplies for General Washington from the islands. They were childhood friends in England."

"Wouldn't that be treason for a British officer to engage in trade and smuggling to the Patriots' benefit?" asked Peggy.

"Only if he returns to Great Britain after the war." Angelica laid her daughter in an awaiting cradle. "Besides, it's simply good business, my husband would say," she added with a sigh, straightening up.

"When does Mr. Carter return to us?" Eliza asked.

"Not for a while. The winter has been so harsh he has to travel farther and farther south to find any provisions at all." She wandered back to the window and gazed out, again petting Peggy's hair absentmindedly. "Lord, Lord, it looks like it might snow once more. Isn't it almost April?"

Peggy and Eliza exchanged a raised-eyebrow look at Angelica's uncharacteristic melancholic tone. Both of them were growing worried about their beautiful eldest sister's happiness.

After a moment, with forced lightness, Angelica asked, "What else does your ardent suitor write?"

Eliza read on: "*The express arrived with your dear billet under cover of one from your guardian. I cannot tell you what extacy I felt in casting my eye over the sweet effusions of tenderness it contains. My Betseys soul speaks in every line and bids me be the happiest of mortals. I am so and will be so. You give me too many proofs of your love to allow me to doubt it and in the conviction that I possess that, I possess every thing the world can give.*"

"Oh my, Eliza." Peggy sighed now. "That is quite beautiful." To herself, she added a mark in the positive column in her tally of whether Alexander Hamilton was worthy of her loving sister.

But Eliza looked stricken.

"What is wrong with you, you silly goose?" Angelica asked. She crossed the room to sit beside Eliza on the bed.

"I should never have let you tell me what to write in my last letter, Angelica. I will never pen something as good. He will discover me a fraud!"

"It won't matter once he is allowed to hold you in his arms, and . . ." Angelica trailed off with a mischievous smile.

Eliza turned absolutely crimson. Then she whispered, "But maybe he won't want me if I cannot keep up with his wit. Oh, Angelica, you can't ever leave us again. You must stay and help me know how to speak to him."

"Oh, for goodness' sake, Eliza, just speak from your soul," Peggy reassured her. "That is poetry enough. Your sincerity is one of your greatest charms, and carries a beautiful eloquence, because it is genuine."

For a moment Eliza brightened. Then Angelica asked, "Has Alexander spoken to Papa yet?"

"I . . . I don't think he has. He planned to stop in Philadelphia either on his way there or back from the prisoner exchange." She glanced down at the letter and skimmed it. "Surely he would have mentioned meeting with Papa if he had." Her face puckered up again and she burst into tears.

Peggy made a what-are-you-doing face at Angelica and added herself to the bed's pile of Schuyler sisters. "You mustn't be so afraid, Eliza. You'll worry yourself sick. Honestly, if this man doesn't approve of your words, he doesn't deserve you and you don't want him. There are plenty others who would find your words intoxicating honey."

That statement turned out to be worse than what Angelica said. Eliza wept in earnest now. "But I don't want any other man. I love Alexander—since the moment I saw him."

"Oh dear," Angelica murmured. She gathered Eliza into her arms. "Then you shall have him, my pet. I will *teach* you how to write playful letters, so that you can write them on your own as second nature. Letters that promise much but not all. Letters that tantalize enough to keep him feeling not quite satisfied and needing to continue his pursuit. It can be as simple as where you place a comma. For example, place one between an adjective and Hamilton's name in a formal phrase. Instead of starting your letter 'my dear sir,' write it this way: 'my dear, sir.' It will catch him off guard. He'll start looking for other little hidden endearments.

"Now that won't be so hard." She pushed Eliza's hair back from her pretty, tear-streaked face. "Will it?"

Eliza smiled and shook her head.

"Angelica, honestly, leave her be!" Peggy pleaded. "Eliza's own sentiments are perfect."

"Oh, it's all right, Peggy," Eliza said. "I'm grateful. And once . . . once Alexander and I are married . . ." She paused and her voice hushed. "Once we're married, we'll be together and I will be able to show him how much I love him."

"Oh really, little sister?" Angelica teased.

"I didn't mean that! I meant . . ." Eliza sat up, clasping the sacred letter. "I mean like this. Listen to this next part: *'The good Meade had the kindness to tell me that you received my letter with apparent marks of joy and that you retired with eagerness to read it. 'Tis from circumstances like these we best discover the true sentiments of the heart.'*"

Angelica laughed again. "So he has spies watching you. That's good!" Then she shook her head. "Those aides-de-camp are such a pack. Lord knows how they will survive being separated when he weds you."

"Papa will say yes, won't he? Alexander isn't exactly, isn't . . . he is new to America. He has no connections."

Angelica snorted—a most unladylike and unusual sound coming from her. "No connections? Alexander has His Excellency's ear. He is probably the most trusted aide in Washington's family. Of course Papa will approve."

"Eliza, listen to me," said Peggy. "No, better yet, listen to what Hamilton just wrote you. You don't need to worry. You don't need to deal in flirtation or artifice. He loves your—how did he call it—the true sentiments of your heart."

"You can say that, Peggy, because you are as clever as Angelica. And it's not just me who is intimidated by his intellect. Remember that sweet letter I received from Kitty?" Eliza bounced off the bed, nearly knocking down little Philip on her way to the writing desk. She pulled out a letter from their friend and distant cousin. "Let's see." She quickly read the paper. "*I have purchased your apron* . . . no, no, not that part . . . here: *assure Colonel Hamilton of my best wishes . . . . I would endeavor to say something in behalf of this poor letter, pray do not let Colonel Hamilton see it. His forte is writing I too well know, to submit anything I can say tonight to his inspection . . .*"

Angelica waved her hand in dismissal. "I love dearest Kitty, but she is in danger of turning into a simpering old maid."

"Angelica!" Eliza and Peggy exclaimed at the same time.

"Well, she is." Angelica shrugged. "Kitty is closing in on twenty-nine years of age, isn't she? She had her chance with Alexander, back when he had just arrived from Saint Croix and was studying at Elizabethtown Academy and staying at their house. He told me he wrote her the most ardent letters at the beginning of the war, calling her goddess, damsel, promising to attack windmills in her service. And she spurned him. Her loss. He now belongs to you, ladybird." She pointed to Eliza.

Peggy burned to ask Angelica why Alexander Hamilton—their sister's lover—was telling *her* about his past love affairs. Clearly the man was a gossip. But what was Angelica up to with such conversations? Did she always have to insert herself in every situation and relationship around her? Besides, Hamilton had written wanting Peggy as his confidante, hadn't he? Peggy felt a sudden swell of her childhood competitiveness with Angelica. She didn't like the feeling at all.

"What about Cornelia Lott?" Eliza whispered.

So that was the Cornelia whom McHenry had referenced at the ball while Eliza and Hamilton danced their mesmerizing minuet. Peggy sat up.

"She is Caty Greene's close friend. Why do you ask?" To Peggy, Angelica seemed suddenly evasive. Her nonchalant question was clearly hypothetical since she kept talking. "Now, that Caty; there is someone who made a rather remarkable marriage in her General Nathaniel Greene, don't you think? A man fifteen years older than she, not particularly well-educated. He wheezes and walks with a limp. And he's a Quaker, mind you! Who could have foreseen that a man coming from the pacifist Society of Friends would take up arms and become one of our most important and brave generals? General Washington has great faith in him. They have become close friends. Clever girl, that Caty . . ." Angelica trailed off, lost in thought.

Now Angelica was going to imply that the totally delightful Caty Greene was cunning in her affections? Why was she being so peevish? "I don't think there was anything calculating in that match, Angelica. I think the general adores her and she just fell in love," said Peggy. "I really like Caty. She's completely engaging in conversation, and has such a joyous nature. Warmhearted and exuberant. But there's nothing frivolous about her. Frankly, she reminds me of you."

The look Angelica gave Peggy was so sad it took her breath away.

"Yes, I suppose," Angelica murmured. She stood and smoothed out her petticoats. "Now, to your reply, sweet Eliza. Take up your quill. Let's think of winter and the cold of separation. How, when dear Hamilton returns, spring will bloom, and in your heart . . ." She smiled. "What? What would you say? Think about the promise, the flowering, the flush of life hiding beneath those wretched snowbanks longing to be awakened."

Eliza dipped a quill into her inkwell. "Oh goodness." She looked up in surprise. "The ink has frozen!"

"Then we will warm it up by the fire and melt it with

the heat of your thoughts," Angelica quipped.

They all laughed—that wondrous chime.

As Eliza stirred the hearth's fire to make it roar, and Angelica held the inkwell near the flames, rubbing and rotating it in her hands to unstop the liquid, Peggy returned to the window.

A few days before, through the frosty panes, she had been able to hear, very faintly, fifes and drums in the distance. But not military parade music. Jigs and "Yankee Doodle." General Washington had proclaimed a day of rest to celebrate St. Patrick's holiday and to honor the parliament of Ireland for its own growing protests and potential revolt against the tyranny of Britain. The general had even given the men a hogshead of rum to enjoy.

Nearly a quarter of the soldiers shivering and starving and stubbornly surviving the winter in log huts they'd built in nearby Jockey Hollow were recent Irish immigrants. Their loyalty to America's cause would certainly strengthen with Washington's tribute to their heritage and his applauding their home country rattling England's chains.

Her uncle Johnny had also shared with Peggy a startling fact that he had come to recognize as he kept records of all the illnesses and the men he treated in the hospital. His journals revealed that nearly three out of four men in the Continental Army had been born someplace other than America—England, Ireland, Germany mostly. Many of them were paid substitutes for rich men who were born in the colonies and with roots dating back a few generations. Africans—slaves and freemen both—were beginning to fill the ranks as well. The enslaved were promised freedom papers after the war.

The American Army may have begun with homegrown Patriots and their eloquent writings or audacious protests, but it was becoming a fighting force of immigrants—like Alexander Hamilton.

Peggy looked toward the Ford Mansion, sitting atop the hill outside the small courthouse town of fifty houses and two churches. She knew that in its first floor things were happening! Washington and his aides were receiving and writing letters, worrying over dispatches, pleading Congress for money to clothe and feed the soldiers, trying to convince locals to sell them meat or eggs or dried fruit at a reasonable price, speculating about what the British forces might be up to in New York City, perhaps even planning the spring's first attacks on the Redcoat strongholds.

How she longed to be part of that! Not worrying over the wording of love letters and whether a man would find them engaging enough.

She sighed heavily.

"What's wrong?" Eliza looked up from her letter, uncertainty on her face again.

Peggy smiled at her. "Nothing. Just thinking about . . ." She searched for a plausible fib. "I was remembering . . ."

"Captain Beebe?" Angelica quipped.

"No!" Peggy gazed back out the window, finding her

cover. "I was remembering the story Kitty told in that letter. About those two British regiments raiding their home."

"Oh yes, wasn't that just awful," breathed Eliza. "Thank God their father escaped capture. Can you imagine how terrifying that would be?"

"Yes, their poor family," murmured Angelica. "Ever since their father became the Continental governor of New Jersey, their house has been repeatedly attacked and pillaged."

"Didn't Kitty say the rogues have even stolen all the house's door hinges to melt down for musket balls?"

"I was actually marveling at how Susannah kept her head to save her father's dispatches," said Peggy.

Her sisters laughed.

"She always has been frisky, that one!" Angelica commented with obvious respect.

During a recent raid, infuriated that Governor Livingston had escaped into the night, British soldiers ransacked the house looking for any letters or records that would reveal Patriot secrets. To stop the Redcoats threatening her family, Susannah offered to help them look. She led them from place to place, finally coming to the locked secretary where she knew her father filed his precious correspondence. Standing with her back to it, Susannah pleaded with the soldiers to spare *her* secrets, that *she* had hidden there love letters her parents knew nothing of. If they promised to leave those notes alone, she would take them to her father's important papers. Beguiled, the Redcoats nodded and followed her to the library, where she climbed a ladder to the highest shelf and pulled out old law briefs her father had written before the Revolution's outbreak, neatly bound and official-looking.

"Wouldn't you have loved to have seen the look on those Redcoats' faces when they opened the governor's old law papers and found they had been bamboozled?" laughed Peggy. "And by a *girl*!"

Even though Peggy jested, Susannah's little triumph was an important one. Having watched her papa carefully veil the wordings of his communiqués with General Washington in case of interception, and seeing how excited Schuyler was when his spies like Moses Harris brought him messages that revealed British plans, Peggy knew how vitally important Susannah's save had been. Her clever ruse had probably protected information about Patriot troop numbers, encampments, ammunition levels, where they got their supplies, where their scouts patrolled—all insights that could have helped the British or their Loyalist allies plan ambushes or kidnappings.

"I wonder if I would have been that ingenious," she wondered aloud. "That defiant."

"You?" Eliza asked with a grin.

Angelica laughed. "Oh yes, baby sister, you would be. We have no doubt."

TWELVE

Spring

Philip Schuyler to Alexander Hamilton
Philadelphia, April 8th, 1780
Dear Sir

Mrs Schuyler . . . consents to Comply with your and her
daughters wishes. You will see the Impropriety of taking the
dernier pas [elopement] where you are. Mrs. Schuyler did
not see her Eldest daughter married. That also gave me pain,
and we wish not to Experience It a Second time . . . I shall
probably be at Camp In a few days, when we will adjust all
matters. . . . Beware of Communications to this quarter which
you would not wish the world to know. This hint will prevent
you from writing but by a safe hand.

I am Dr Sir sincerely Yours &c &c
Ph. Schuyler

"DO NOT WORRY, MY BOY. YOU HAVE MANY OTHER, far superior talents!" called George Washington. He tossed a leather ball up and down in his hand, waiting for his nephew to take position for a throw. Hamilton had failed to catch any of the general's passes and given up.

"That's right, Hammie. Such as whistling all the tunes of love," cooed McHenry.

"Or walking on air," teased Harrison. "Our little lion has exchanged his roar for wings."

Hamilton flung himself down at Eliza's feet. "Do you witness this? For you, my charmer, I endure such abuse." He laughed as he spoke, but Peggy detected a pink glow of embarrassment on the aide's creamy complexion as he mumbled, "It's not as if I had time for ball games while working my mother's store."

Peggy was learning quickly about her soon-to-be brother-in-law. How sharp his mind, how quick he was to romanticize or to take offense, how passionate, poetic, and mercurial. He was orphaned early on the Caribbean island of Saint Croix—abandoned by his father, and his mother later dying of fever. An immigrant trying to make his own hard-won name, Hamilton was the epitome of what America promised. But Peggy hadn't before thought about the day-to-day impact of such a harsh and lonely childhood—like not knowing how to toss a ball back and forth because no one had taken the time to simply play with him.

Hamilton noticed Peggy's gaze. He smiled back, chagrined, recognizing she had heard his grumble.

General Washington pulled back his arm and hurled. The ball flew, fast and straight like a rifle shot. His nephew sprinted back and back, then jumped up to grasp the hurtling ball, crashing onto the ground with laughter.

"Good Lord, what a pitch His Excellency has," exclaimed McHenry.

Martha laughed. "Don't ever let him lure you into a game of billiards. Or a sword fight. He does both as well as he throws. Oh, and he has been known to wrestle friends to win arguments. A negotiation he learned during his time exploring and surveying the Ohio wilderness with Seneca and Delaware Indian guides."

Washington strode over to his nephew and pulled him off the ground, clapping him on the back. "Well done!"

The aides-de-camp applauded.

"He makes it seem so easy!" Hamilton complained.

"Never mind, dear boy," Martha said to him. "Mr. Washington is just letting off a little steam." She looked back to her husband. "Playing catch reminds him of what we are fighting for—peace and family, home. He misses Mount Vernon horribly. He has not seen his own home for five years now."

"Oh my, how sad," Eliza murmured.

Martha nodded without stopping her sewing. "He's not the only one who mourns his absence from home." She paused, wistful, then made herself speak lightly. "Even his dogs! Lord love them, how his hounds look for him—Venus, Truelove, Madam Moose, Tippler, Vulcan. Oh, what a bad dog that Vulcan is—he stole an entire ham right off the table one time. I wanted the general to chastise him roundly and all he did was laugh." Martha chortled. "He simply has a soft spot for children and dogs."

"I can testify to that." Hamilton spoke up. Rolling to a sitting position, he turned to his fellow aides. "Do you remember that ridiculous little terrier wandering between the lines during the Battle of Germantown?"

"Remember? I was the one who had to walk it back," protested Meade.

"You made quite the sight walking under a flag of truce with that tiny, hairy dog tucked up under your arm," Hamilton joked.

"A perfect target I was!"

"A target of ridicule most like!" Hamilton countered.

The men roared.

"Sirs, what are you talking about?" Martha asked.

"He didn't tell you, madam? General Howe's dog got loose and ran away from the British camp and ended up in ours. We wanted to keep it as a trophy to demoralize Howe—print far and wide that even his dog chose liberty over British tyranny! But your husband insisted he be returned. His Excellency took the animal to his tent, fed it, brushed it, and wrote a note to his enemy saying that the dog had accidentally fallen into our hands and that he had the pleasure of returning it to the general with his compliments."

Martha nodded. "That sounds like my old man. And very

like him not to tell of such an act of kindness." She pulled in a long, deep breath. "Can you smell that wild rhododendron? How it reminds me of Virginia along the Potomac."

They all breathed in together at her prompting.

It was indeed a glorious spring day, the air balmy. Pink dogwood trees wreathed the hills encircling Morristown and seemed to be popping open with perfumed jubilation before their very eyes. Overnight, meadow grasses had turned from ashen winter gray to lush emerald. Washington and his family couldn't help being beckoned by such weather. They'd spilled out of the Ford Mansion to bask in the warm afternoon sunshine, escaping for a few hours the blizzard of dispatches that were only increasing as the roads thawed and the likelihood of British attack grew.

Washington's mood had lightened considerably that week because he had finally received a communiqué from the Marquis de Lafayette. The gallant young French aristocrat general had returned to the French court at Washington's request to beg assistance of the king. During one of his nightly visits to the Cochrans' parlor, Hamilton had shared that Lafayette was safely back on American shores, having crossed the Atlantic without being captured by British ships policing the coast. He was making his way from Boston to the army's New Jersey headquarters.

Washington had cried when he read that letter, said Hamilton, without any trace of jealousy in his voice. Peggy had noted it, impressed. So he was capable of loving a friend selflessly. Another mark in her tally in favor of her sister's suitor.

Hearing the men laughing in the meadow like schoolboys at recess, the Schuyler sisters had come out to watch, bringing their own stitching with them. Martha had enlisted their help in producing linen shirts for foot soldiers. Now that the snows had finally melted, she had been able to find some linsey-woolsey for the task. They sat on stumps with Martha while the aides-de-camp sprawled along the ground beside them, happily chewing on new-soft blades of grass. Washington and his nephew continued tossing the ball.

Obviously flustered by Hamilton's nearness and more accustomed to stitching decorative embroidery than utilitarian seams, Eliza pricked her finger with her needle. She gave a little yelp of pain. Hamilton pulled out his handkerchief to wrap it and kissed the tiny wound.

Peggy sighed impatiently. She was truly glad to be doing something useful for the threadbare Patriots—especially when remembering those starved sentries the night her sleigh approached Morristown. But, oh, how she itched for some task more intellectually stimulating than sewing. Her gaze wandered, catching Hamilton as he slid his hand under her sister's hem and crept it up her shoe to gently caress Eliza's ankle. He was trying to be secretive but Eliza certainly wasn't helping with that. Her pretty face was crimson.

"Papa!" Eliza gasped at seeing Philip Schuyler coming

up the road toward them. He had arrived in camp two weeks earlier.

Peggy bit her lip to not laugh at how far Hamilton jumped back away from Eliza's skirt at the sight of their father. He literally landed on his backside at least a foot away.

But his friends guffawed.

"Now if you had moved with that alacrity before, you would have caught the general's pitches," teased McHenry.

Schuyler waved as he approached. He carried a satchel full of papers. Ironically—given the fact her papa had begged for similar supplies and reinforcements when he commanded the Northern Army—Congress had appointed Schuyler head of a committee to investigate Washington's claims that he desperately needed more money, more food, more ammunition, more horses, more shoes, more muskets if he was to wage any kind of battle in the coming months. Congress dismissed their commanding general's petitions as hyperbolic. Within an hour of arriving at Morristown, Schuyler had found ample evidence to send back to the delegates supporting Washington's pleas for help—cementing the friendship that already existed between the two men.

Hamilton leapt to his feet. Schuyler had only recently agreed to his marriage proposal. He bowed low and nervously to his fiancée's father. Washington stopped tossing the ball to lope his way over to the group.

"General," Schuyler said, and nodded.

"General," Washington answered, and nodded in salute as well.

"I am sorry to interrupt, sir, but I have just done an evaluation of your artillery." He shook his head. "We have enough for about five minutes of fight. With your permission, I . . ."

Washington held up his hand. "Do you hear that?"

From the direction of Jockey Hollow, where the army was encamped in a thousand log huts, came the sound of a musket shot. Then another and another.

Everyone froze.

Washington cocked his head, straining to hear.

"To arms, sir?" Hamilton asked excitedly.

But Washington was smiling. "Listen."

More shots, but also whispering over the two miles were shouts—hundreds of shouts! *Huzzah! Huzzah!*

"It must be the marquis," breathed Washington. And then he grinned—ear to ear—one of the few times General George Washington would ever show that much unabashed relief and joy—or his false teeth.

Lafayette brought news as resurrecting as the spring: the French fleet was on its way to Newport, Rhode Island, bringing six thousand infantrymen under the command of Count Rochambeau to fight alongside the half-starved and bone-thin Continental Army. Wherever Lafayette walked for the next few days, hope bloomed in his wake as rampantly as the wildflower spring beauties carpeting the woods. That was especially true when he, Washington and his aides, and the family's ladies went to Jockey Hollow for a celebration dinner with Colonel Webb, of General Stark's brigade.

Soldiers stopped whatever they were doing to cheer him as loudly as they did Washington.

"*Mon Dieu*, my dear Hamilton, there are so many of them!" Lafayette stood at the top of a hill looking down at the regimented rows of one thousand twelve-by-sixteen-foot log huts that had kept the Continental Army from freezing to death during the long, hard winter.

"The men had a terrible time felling the trees and stacking the walls during those January blizzards," Hamilton answered him. "Far worse than Valley Forge."

"*C'est impossible!*"

"No, it is true, my friend. This past winter . . ." He shook his head. "The men had to chop and lathe and fit those logs while thigh-deep in snowdrifts. And more snow coming down. Of course, the threat of dying in the elements will drive a man to do just about anything." His voice was grim.

"Oh, but surely also *esprit de corps, fraternité*! These men, these Patriots! They have hearts *énormes, oui?*"

"They also have enormous—"

"Dr. Cochran!" Aunt Gertrude cut him off before he could utter another bit of anatomy, slapping his arm.

The men pressed their lips together, sniggering.

"Ah, good old Dr. Bones," said Lafayette with his warm smile. "I would say the same of you. Did you know, my dear"—he looked down at Peggy, whom he was escorting, her hand resting in the crook of his arm—"that your uncle saved my life at Brandywine? We were in retreat. A Briton shot me in the calf. Dr. Bones carried me on his back out of the crossfire. We both nearly were captured. Then he operated on me in the middle of the battle to save my leg."

"Aw, well, good sir"—Cochran blustered a bit—"that's just my job. Besides, His Excellency told me to take care of you like you were his own son. I couldn't disappoint him."

"You are as modest as you are expert with that knife, sir. Ooh, that knife!" Lafayette held his hands out the length of a sword in jest.

"Nay, sir, it was merely a three-inch blade I needed to extract the bullet."

"It felt like a bayonet!" Lafayette laughed.

"Had you been old enough to really drink the whiskey, you might not have felt it! French champagne does not have the same . . . errr . . . medicinal properties."

"Ahh, *mais c'est superbe!* When the war is won and we are all legends, I will return to France victorious and ship a case to you, dear Dr. Bones."

Peggy looked up into the Frenchman's face with unaccustomed shyness, startled by a tingle of infatuation and the realization Lafayette was the kind of man she could fall in love with—courageous, mischievous, hungry to learn, sophisticated yet still excited by every new experience. Too bad he had a wife and baby back home in France. She had met him briefly two years before, when Lafayette passed through Albany and conferred with Schuyler regarding Oneida he wished to employ for scouting. Like everyone, Peggy had been completely charmed by his effusive idealism and unabashed affection for men he admired. The twenty-two-year-old was also disarmingly handsome—high forehead, wide, arched eyebrows over eyes that seemed perpetually delighted or intrigued, pronounced, round cheekbones, a dimpled chin, and full, red tulip lips.

Their meal over, the party was walking through the log-hut city, greeting soldiers. It was a steep climb up and down the hills for the petite Mrs. Washington, and she begged a rest, sitting down on a log in the shade. "Forgive me, sirs, I am not blessed with legs as long as yours!" She motioned for the Schuyler sisters to join her. "Do tell us more of your stories, Colonel Webb, as we catch our breath. You had me in amazement over dinner about that silver bullet. How could a man swallow a musket ball?"

Just like her father's spy, Moses Harris, had warned! Peggy leaned forward to hear every detail.

"Well, ma'am, it just goes to prove that sometimes luck plays as much of a part in our fight as good stratagem, begging Your Excellency's pardon, of course."

Washington laughed gently. "It's true, Colonel; sometimes our fate is left to Providence or to our dearest friends." He nodded toward Lafayette, who beamed, standing behind Peggy.

Webb began his story: "We came into some important intelligence purely because of mistaken identity given two men having the same name. When the British sailed up the Hudson River from New York City with the plan of joining Burgoyne to take Albany, those grenadiers were under the command of Sir *Henry* Clinton. We, of course, were answering to our Governor *George* Clinton. A few of my men were out on a scout and fell in with a man dressed in civilian clothes. He asked who their commander was. When told 'Clinton,' he requested an audience—saying he had important information. But when he stood before the governor, his face turned white and he blustered that he had been confused, this was not the man he was looking for, and then hastily swallowed something! Given his strange behavior, we questioned him, and after a bit of persuasion and a potion to make him vomit, we found the ball. It was hollow with a top that screwed off, and it contained a tiny message from Burgoyne."

"My goodness," murmured Martha. "What a marvel. What will these spies think of next?"

Washington smiled ever so slightly. Oh, how Peggy longed to tell him that she had opened British communiqués and conferred with a spy herself. Peggy sat back, thinking. Her papa would return to Philadelphia and Congress after his work requisitioning supplies for the Continental Army was concluded. Someone needed to be in Albany in case Moses Harris showed up again. She hadn't considered that before; she'd been so happy with her sisters and listening to the convivial sparring among the aides-de-camp. That would end, of course, when fighting renewed. She should go home. Good-bye sewing, at least.

"Tell again about the little fifer," Martha prompted Webb.

"He is here, Lady Washington. Would you like to meet him?"

"Oh yes. Yes indeed! What pluck that child has," she said to Eliza, who sat next to her. "Wait till you hear this story."

Webb sent one of his lieutenants for the boy, asking he bring along his fife to play for the Washingtons. Then he began his story: "My men were given the task of destroying lumber stacked on the east end of Long Island that the Redcoats would use to build their winter barracks. Anything to slow them up and give them a bit of discomfort, right, General?"

Washington nodded.

"It was a daring raid," Webb continued, "considering all the Redcoats we were trying to slip by. I and two dozen of my men were captured. Including the lad. He was only ten years old at the time, and much afraid."

Only ten, thought Peggy. Two years younger than her brother Jeremiah, who was such an innocent. Was their cause that desperate that they had to take such a young child into battle, risking his capture and imprisonment? Peggy felt herself frown in anxiety for the boy and what Webb would relate happened to him.

Webb rubbed his face, remembering it. "I have to say, Your Excellency, this abated my hatred of the lobsterbacks a bit. Some of them anyway. Seeing the lad's youth, our British captor asked him who he was." Webb chuckled. "And our little hero, his name is Dick, ma'am, straightened himself up to his full four feet and answered proudly that he was one of John Hancock's men and fought for General Washington.

"Impressed with his hardiness in such circumstances, the colonel sent the boy outside, where he would be given food. Within moments, we heard quite a row. A British drummer boy, many years older and twice Dick's size, had evidently insulted His Excellency. Even in the camp of our enemies, young Dick felt he had to defend his commander. He'd pinned the boy to the dirt and the Briton was crying mercy: 'Get off, rebel, get off!'"

Webb chuckled. "In deference for his stout heart, the colonel set our boy free. I, on the other hand, had to wait for a prisoner exchange! Ah, here the lad comes now."

A cherubic boy, blond hair flying, cheeks flushed, darted up the hill, to stand gaping at George Washington.

The general smiled warmly, and took off his cocked hat in salute. "I believe we have the honor of meeting perhaps the youngest, nay even bravest, soldier of the Revolution. Your name, sir?" he asked gently.

"R-R-R-Richard Lord Jones, Your Excellency," he squeaked.

"An honor to make your acquaintance, Fifer Jones." Washington approached the boy and bent over to address him. "May I ask the favor of a song for my dearest wife?"

The boy nodded his head furiously.

Peggy worried the poor lad might faint, he was so over-awed at meeting Washington. But he closed his eyes to concentrate, and as soon as the first notes of the American version of England's anthem lilted from his little soul, Fifer Richard Lord Jones was transformed, his voice angelic.

"God save great Washington, Fair Freedom's chosen son;
Long to command.
Next in our Song shall be, Guardian of Liberty,
Louis the King
Terrible god of war."

Lafayette sprung to his feet. *"Vive la France! Vivez l'Amérique! Vive George Washington!"* He rushed to the lad and, kissing him on both cheeks, exclaimed, *"Quand tu seras grand, mon garçon, tu dois venir à Paris en ambassadeur!"*

The boy drew back, chewing on his lower lip—a nervous habit Peggy's youngest brother had when he worried he was in trouble with adults. Peggy realized that the torrent of French had left the fifer afraid he might have displeased the important entourage somehow. She hastened to translate for the boy. "General Lafayette is so touched by your praising his homeland and king that his native tongue overcomes him. He says that someday you could be an excellent ambassador to France." She rose to whisper in his ear, "You did very well. Smile now."

The boy heaved a sigh and gave a trembling smile.

Martha Washington couldn't help herself and swept up the little soldier into a tight embrace. Then, remembering the dignity demanded by a young boy, she let him go and pulled from her pocket a three-dollar bill printed by the United Colonies, July 22, 1776. "Thank you, sir fifer. That was better entertainment than any theater the general and I have seen. Even *Cato*," she added with a mischievous look at her husband. *Cato*—a play about a Roman senator who gave up everything for love of country—was the favorite of all good Patriots, especially George Washington.

The boy's mouth dropped open and he took the paper money as if it were a sacrament.

The marquis remained overcome. "After this war is done, you must come to France. *Je vais te présenter au directeur musical de l'Opéra de Paris!*"

The boy frowned. "I don't want to go to France," he whispered to Peggy. "I follow His Excellency. He's my man."

Peggy smiled at him reassuringly. "Mine, too. The marquis was only complimenting your voice, saying it was as lyrical as professional opera singers in Paris."

"Oh, that's all right, then," he murmured.

Lafayette held out his hand to shake American-style, and in his palm shone three English shillings. "*Merci, mon frère.* I am indebted to you."

The fifer stared. Peggy assumed it was out of awe once again—sterling British money was like treasure since Continental paper dollars had collapsed in value—it cost $400 to buy a hat, for instance, if it could be found. But little Richard Lord Jones shook his head.

Lafayette frowned, his feelings clearly hurt.

"Go ahead," Peggy prompted. "The general makes you a generous gift."

The boy turned his earnest eyes toward Peggy. "Them's devil bobs."

"Oh no." She shook her head and couldn't help laughing. "You show no disloyalty taking them." Knowing Lafayette wouldn't know the slang term *bob* for shillings, Peggy quickly explained to Lafayette the fifer's worry that he would be showing disloyalty to their Revolution by taking British money: "*Il ne manqué pas de respect, Général, il a peur que l'argent britannique semblerait déloyal.*"

The misunderstanding cleared up, the boy took his money and Lafayette saluted him.

Now Lafayette gaped—at her! "*Mon Dieu!* You must forgive me, mademoiselle. I had forgotten your command of French."

Now it was Hamilton's turn, with Eliza on his arm, to laugh. "It seems many of us have made the mistake of not remembering our first meeting with Peggy. That surely would not happen today!" He winked at her.

"Our Peggy is brilliant," murmured Eliza with sincerity, but her face begged Peggy to not expose her clumsiness with French.

Peggy shifted the compliment and the language. "I have simply grown up, that is all. Much like our beloved Eliza."

"You should have more admirers than Colonel Hamilton and myself, mademoiselle! Hmm." Lafayette thought a moment. "*Ah, oui!* I have the perfect match. Do you remember my countryman Colonel de Fleury? He was with me on that journey to Albany."

"Oh, you will remember him," said Hamilton. "He . . ."

But Peggy recalled. "He was the man hoping to sink Britain's navy with little self-propelled boats that would explode when they bumped up against its ships."

Hamilton frowned. Peggy realized from his reaction that she shouldn't know about the boats. She'd be sure not to tell him, then, that she had overheard it, lingering on the stairs outside her father's study, eavesdropping.

Lafayette seemed to have no such concerns, however. "*Oui, oui, incroyable!* Few ladies are truly interested in his military inventions. You must come to Newport, Mademoiselle Peggy! Fleury returned home as I did to convince our countrymen to support America. Now he sails to Rhode Island with Rochambeau. There they will revitalize before we march into glorious victory together!"

Smiling with infectious delight, Lafayette added, "Fleury has yet to find love. My own marriage to my beauteous Adrienne was arranged. I wager we can contrive a romance to rival my brother Alexander's with your sister! *N'est pas?*" He looked to Hamilton and then exulted, "*Merveilleux!*"

Peggy shook her head. She had reveled in her time in Morristown, it was true—the balls, the revolutionary talk—but now she was resolved to return to Albany to watch for spies.

"Now that—my soon-to-be little sister—is a perfect match for you! Far more appropriate than old Captain Beebe."

Peggy started to ask—with a new defensiveness and embarrassment at not having attracted more interesting suitors—why Hamilton was so interested in her love life, when Martha Washington pulled her aside.

"My dear, I will consider it a favor to me if you would travel to Newport as another pair of ears." Martha lowered her voice. "Listening to you a moment ago so deftly undo misunderstandings prompts me to ask it."

Martha pulled them a little farther away and continued, "The general cannot speak French, a deficit he feels keenly. Given his father's early death, he was not granted a college education. What my husband knows he taught himself. There was no time for French. That is one of the many reasons he is so dependent upon your sister's fiancé." She nodded toward Eliza. "Colonel Hamilton's eloquence and fluency makes such a difference for my husband. The general will keep him close by his elbow through talks with Rochambeau, who I gather speaks no English.

"Accuracy of translation can be a matter of life or death, peace or war, success or disaster in moments of history like this. That is the power of words. My husband learned this in the most tragic of ways. Many people, in fact, blame him for starting the French and Indian War because of it."

Peggy looked at her quizzically. How could one person possibly be blamed for an entire war?

Reading her mind, Martha nodded. "It's true. Before the war was formally declared, George was in a terrible fight at Fort Necessity. He was young. It was his first command. He positioned his men badly. Many were killed. He had to surrender." She sighed. "The terms were written in French, badly translated to English by one of his junior officers, who did not understand the paper claimed that in a previous skirmish, in which a French officer had been killed, my George *knowingly assassinated* a French nobleman, an official of King

Louis's court. To the French, that was a barbarous insult, requiring retribution and all-out war."

She took both Peggy's hands and waited until Peggy met her gaze before continuing. "Colonel Hamilton will be by the general's side during these strategy talks. But there will be many other conversations among French officers that might bear important nuances. And certainly social connections and comfort always make for tighter alliances, my dear. I heard my old man say that Mrs. Carter's husband will be the commissary for the French army. She will want to join him, surely, at Newport. So you could travel to Rhode Island with your sister. I would ask Mrs. Carter my favor, but"—Martha paused—"I think in her effervescence she might not notice the littler comments that sometimes bear the most fruit." She squeezed Peggy's hands. "May I enlist your help?"

"Almost like a spy?" Peggy whispered eagerly.

Martha's return smile was warm and motherly. "Let's say as a lovely female of diplomacy with a good memory for conversation and a wise eye for recognizing implications."

Peggy smiled, feeling her eyebrow shoot up. Far better than sewing!

THIRTEEN

Summer

Journals of French officers under Rochambeau:

The fair sex here is really unusual in its modesty and sweetness of demeanor. Nature has endowed the women of Rhode Island with very fine features; their complexion is clear; their hands and feet generally small . . . One sees few malformed women . . . They all like dancing, and they engage in it unpretentiously, as is their manner in general.

—Baron Ludwig von Closen, Rochambeau aide-de-camp

We were frequently invited to private houses. There seemed to be a rivalry among the residents to see who would serve the richest fare and have the largest number of guests at dinner.

—Baron Gaspard de Gallatin

JOHN CARTER SLAMMED DOWN HIS GLASS OF Madeira, his wine sloshing onto the tablecloth. Peggy realized the man was drunk. But if her sister was embarrassed, it did not show. Angelica continued to smile regally, keeping her eyes glued to her husband, as if what he was saying was profoundly interesting.

Peggy sat across from her in a small clapboard house that Carter was renting in Newport, Rhode Island. They were not alone. Lafayette had arrived with messages for Rochambeau from Washington. But the French army had landed only a few days earlier and was frantically fortifying the harbor and town, having spotted the British fleet lurking off the coast. Lafayette's meeting must wait. Most men would have been insulted by that dismissal by his own countryman, but the ebullient Lafayette instead happily accepted Angelica's dinner invitation. He brought with him his own brother-in-law, Vicomte de Noailles, and Hamilton's most dedicated jester, McHenry, who was now Lafayette's aide-de-camp. Plus, his old friend the Marquis de Fleury, the Frenchman he planned to matchmake with Peggy. She had to give Lafayette credit. Fleury was—well, in a word, gorgeous. Disarmingly so.

"So I told them," crowed Carter, "when they were dining at my house—captives, mind you—and they still dared to raise a glass to the king—I told them that for every village and farm that Burgoyne and his officers and German devil Hessians had pillaged and set fire to, that we should behead one of their officers. Then we'd put those heads in small barrels, salt them, and ship them all back to England at once. That certainly would send the king the message that his henchmen don't belong in America any longer!" He pounded the table and guffawed. "Well, you should have seen Baroness von Reidesel's pretty little face crumple. She looked at me as if I were some monster!"

A stunned silence fell around the table. Of course most everyone there felt the same outrage at British atrocities, but the gory suggestion of pickled heads was a bit barbaric. It was particularly cruel for Carter to needle the young baroness in such a way, since her Hessian husband was in Boston as a prisoner of war.

Peggy felt her stomach twist. Was he that uncouth and mean in the way he talked to Angelica in private? She could find no clue on her beautiful sister's party-perfect expression.

And what was he trying to accomplish with these French noblemen with such bragging? Carter's emotional ties to the nation's cause seemed thin at best. Maybe if he had taken up arms for America—like the immigrants Hamilton or McHenry—rather than making a profit off supplying her army, Peggy might feel differently. But right now his posturing seemed . . . seemed . . . Queen Gertrude's line in Shakespeare's *Hamlet* was all that came to mind: *The lady doth protest too much, methinks.*

She glanced around the table. Lafayette and his French officer friends seemed frozen in time. This was awful. Why didn't Angelica say something? She looked again at her beautiful, whip-smart older sister, those wide dark-mahogany eyes. They glistened. Angelica was fighting off tears.

All right, this was up to her. Peggy quick-searched her own mind, but it was actually the Frenchmen's slightly baffled look that guided her. Carter's little speech was so outrageous, she could tell they were questioning if they had really understood his English words!

She turned to Fleury and said, "What an excellent metaphor for the English losing their heads—being so confused by American bravery and tactics that their heads might as well have been in barrels." She repeated herself in French so he understood her precisely, and then finished it with a light laugh.

The men laughed politely in return. Angelica's eyes kissed her.

"Major." Peggy hurried to change the subject before Carter could speak again. "I have been admiring that medal about your neck. May I?"

Fleury leaned forward so that the medal and its chain fell toward her. He leaned a little closer than she had expected, smelling of leather and shaving soap. She tried not to be distracted by his typically French good looks—thick dark hair, a lean face with a strongly cut jawline, a long straight Roman-statue perfect nose, and a wide, full-lipped mouth. There were already laugh lines around his dark eyes, but his tanned skin was taut. Not a youth—a man in his prime.

Peggy concentrated on the medal, suddenly embarrassed and hesitant.

On the face of the medal, a soldier dressed like a Roman centurion stood amid ruins, holding an unsheathed sword in one hand and in the other a flag, pointed down so that his bare feet trampled it. At the base was Fleury's name. Along the top, she read aloud, "*Virtutis et Audacle Monum et Prae-mium.*" She paused and then translated, "Commemoration and reward for courage and boldness."

"*Vous savez aussi le Latin?*" Fleury complimented the fact she knew Latin as well as French.

"A little," she answered shyly, not looking up.

"Mademoiselle Peggy, you know not this story?" Lafayette asked. "*Mon Dieu!* This man is one of the Revolution's great heroes. Congress struck this medal in honor of Fleury's courage at Stony Point. Only General Washington was before so honored. Turn it over!"

On the back, etched in the silver, was Stony Point: a clover-shaped fort atop a jutting cliff, surrounded by water. Again, Peggy translated the motto along the medal's top rim: "*Aggeres Paludes Hostes Victi.* Victory over fortifications, marshes, enemies."

Fleury nodded as she glanced up into his face. Words stuck in her throat at his penetrating look.

All Americans knew about the daring raid on New York's Stony Point. Less than fifteen miles south of West Point, the craggy peninsula jutted into the Hudson River. Taken and heavily fortified by the British, who called it "Little Gibraltar," Stony Point gave the Redcoats command of the river from there south to New York City. It also gave the British the perfect launch point to attack West Point—the American stronghold that protected the northern portion of the Hudson River stretching to Albany and beyond.

Exactly one year before, July 1779, at midnight, a group

of handpicked Americans had managed to scramble up 150-foot cliffs and take the fort. Their surprise attack victory had been an enormous morale boost to all Patriots.

"Oh my" was all Peggy could demur in sincere admiration as she dropped the silver medal, which suddenly felt searing hot. "You led that bold venture?"

"*Non. Pas moi.* General Wayne."

"Oh, my dear marquis," interjected Lafayette. "You are too modest. I have learned an English proverb about hiding one's light beneath a bushel."

Fleury looked at him quizzically.

"Light is not to be hidden, but revealed! Like freedom! Lift the basket, *mon ami!*" Lafayette grinned. "Let me." He turned to Peggy. "Perhaps the marvelous details have not been told yet entire to the nation. This was an attack extraordinaire. Such risks. In darkness. In silence. *Absolument.* Unloaded muskets. Fixed bayonets only. This was to be a deadly hand-to-hand duel."

Peggy was transfixed—as if Lafayette was Homer recounting Odysseus's legendary journey.

"The approach was hellish. Waist-high water in the marsh. Then rows and rows of spikes! The British had stripped the cliffs of all trees and turned them to spears, anchored in the hills. Twenty brave Patriots were assigned the 'Forlorn Hope'—the task to cut gaps through those rows of spears so that the marquis and his men could slide through and—*voilà!*—climb the battlements.

"Need I tell you, Mademoiselle Peggy, that the odds of

success were minuscule. Of death immense! *Imaginez*: The men of the Forlorn Hope chop with their axes. Their blows awake the Redcoats. The British fire down onto our courageous men. Many are killed. General Wayne is struck in his head and falls. But our marquis, our Fleury, rallies his men. He charges through the tiny gaps in the spikes cut at such a price of blood and death. Then he, our Fleury, is the very first to leap over the fortification! He fights his way to the British flagpole and tears down the hated Redcoat flag."

Lafayette pointed to his friend's chest. "And there it is, commemorated!"

Everyone at the table was riveted by the retelling. The enslaved servants had hung by the door, decanter and trays in hand, listening, too. Lafayette looked around at his audience with great satisfaction, his face pink from the excitement of the tale.

Fleury merely smiled. Then he shrugged. "All were brave. The glory belongs to all. When he thought he might die, dear General Wayne demanded to be carried into the fort. He said if his wound was to kill him, he wished to die at the head of the column."

Lafayette interrupted, "Perhaps this is why his men call him 'Mad' Anthony."

Fleury laughed. It was a nice, deep rumble. "*Toutefois*, he was our inspiration. The message General Wayne sent to His Excellency that night was brief. The best example. He said the fort was ours. Our officers and soldiers behaved like men determined to be free. *C'est tout*. That is all."

Carter destroyed the spell. "I hear that Washington offered a bounty to the first man to enter the fortifications. Five hundred dollars if the rumor is correct."

"Strong proof of the danger!" Lafayette exclaimed, trying to keep the atmosphere heroic.

"A small fortune," said Carter. He leaned back in his chair and eyed Fleury. "I hope you spent it well, and gave yourself a just reward for the risks you took." His tone was overly playful.

Fleury frowned slightly and looked to Lafayette.

With some embarrassment, Peggy clarified. "Mr. Carter wonders how you celebrated that victory, given General Washington's reward." She repeated herself in French.

"Oh, I did not keep the money," said Fleury. "I divided it among my men. We shared the danger. We share the reward."

Without realizing she was doing it, Peggy sighed deeply.

This time, Angelica kicked her under the table.

A few weeks later, Peggy sat in a carriage with Angelica and Carter, waiting for a large delegation of Oneida, Tuscarora, and Caughnawaga warriors to ride into Newport to meet Rochambeau. Their papa had sent them from Albany, to be reassured that the French forces had indeed joined the Patriots. The British were claiming the alliance between France and the United States was a lie.

Peggy had brought her sketchbook to record them. She was flipping through drawings she had made of Oneida sachems when Fleury trotted up on a tall bay horse. He was stunning in the uniform of the Saintonge Regiment: white linen breeches and canvas gaiters, a white coat and waistcoat piped and faced in dark green, with matching cuffs and vertical rows of gilt buttons.

"*Bonjour,*" he called, nodding at Angelica and Carter before riveting that intense gaze of his on her. The French troops had been so busy settling into quarters, constructing barracks, and building fortifications around the harbor she had talked with him only briefly a few times since the dinner party. Her face was carefully shaded beneath her wide straw bonnet, yet she felt her cheeks turn pink—much to her self-conscious annoyance.

"I did not know you are an artist *aussi*, mademoiselle."

Peggy smiled nervously, forgetting to close up the sketchbook.

Noticing her younger sister's uncharacteristic reserve, Angelica spoke for her. "She is actually quite good." Her big sister scooped up the book and held it out for the marquis to peruse before Peggy could protest.

"*C'est magnifique!*" Fleury exclaimed as he pointed to one sketch of a chief with feathers festooning his head, a fur crossing his chest, and sandal leathers coiling up his calves.

"You do not wear your medal this afternoon, Marquis," Carter commented.

"I wear it for special moments." He smiled warmly at Peggy. "My dear friend Lafayette told me the night I meet the Schuyler sisters was such an occasion."

"You are too kind, monsieur," said Angelica, nudging Peggy to say something, anything.

Words stuck in her throat until Fleury said, "General Rochambeau has gold and silver medals to give the chiefs today. On them is King Louis on his coronation. I hope they will like?"

"Oh, they will see it as an honor and a sign of respect." Peggy found her voice finally. "The Iroquois commemorate their peace treaties with gifts. They revere symbolism. Two different-colored rows in a wampum belt, for instance, means that the two tribes support each other but neither will interfere with or dominate the other. The belts are quite beautiful, made of tiny beads of whelk and quahog shells."

"I didn't know that you knew so much about the Iroquois, Peggy," said Angelica.

"Well, we've grown up with them." She wondered how Angelica couldn't know them as well as she did, but then realized her big sister was trying to give Peggy the stage. That recognition pulled her up short. How many times had Angelica done that for her before and Peggy simply hadn't seen it because of little-sister insecurity that she could never be as captivating or clever as Angelica?

She smiled gratefully to her big sister before continuing. "I hope you have the chance to really talk with them, Monsieur Fleury. They are so brave, but also so loyal to family and to those they believe in. They keep to their promises. And they are kind." She turned to Angelica. "Remember Polly Cooper?"

Angelica nodded. "Tell the marquis," she prodded.

Peggy glanced up at Fleury, gauging his interest. She had yet to learn if he valued human stories as much as military ones.

"*S'il vous plaît*, mademoiselle."

"Well," she began, "the winter before last, when our troops were starving at Valley Forge, the Oneida gathered six hundred baskets of their own corn and carried them all the way from New York. A clan mother, Polly Cooper, came along to show the troops how to grind the kernels and boil the meal into a soup mixed with fruits and nuts. Their white corn must be prepared a certain way or it makes people dreadfully sick. The Oneida probably saved hundreds of lives with that generosity. It meant their own people ate less that winter. Mrs. Washington gave Polly a beautiful black shawl as thanks."

"*Incroyable!* That and courage. Both! Lafayette told me that his army would have been devastated, he a British prisoner at Barren Hill, had it not been for the Oneida."

Peggy nodded. She knew this story, too. Washington had sent Lafayette to monitor British movements, but local Tories alerted the Redcoats. The Brits sent out eight thousand men to capture Lafayette—nabbing him would be a tremendous propaganda coup. They outnumbered the Patriots four to one. It would have been a catastrophe had not a forward scouting party of Oneidas and Patriot riflemen heard the Redcoats' horses coming along the road and opened fire on the British line from the woods. With that screen, Lafayette was able to rush his troops across the Schuylkill River—holding hands so the current wouldn't drag them downstream. Lafayette's second in command only survived because two Oneida managed to grab and carry the injured French aristocrat to the river just as two British cavalrymen were descending on him.

"Here they are now," Carter said, and pointed.

Nineteen sinewy men rode into camp, near naked given the late summer heat. They rode erect and tall and essentially bareback—only blankets for saddles and ropes for bridles. One foot was bare in deference to the French general. Their simplicity contrasted starkly with Rochambeau's entourage, at attention, in their high boots and spotless, buttoned-up, gold-braided uniforms, broiling in the American sunshine. Suddenly the regally clad Europeans looked a bit ridiculous to Peggy.

She spotted the Oneida sachem who had led the delegation to Albany and with whom she had shared family memories. She could tell Rochambeau was speaking, greeting them, but she couldn't hear. "Oh, I wish I were closer," she murmured.

Without missing a beat, Fleury leaned over and extended his arm toward her, saying, "*Permettez-moi.*"

Peggy stared at him. Allow him what? To swing her up onto the horse with him? Riding on a horse with a man was . . . was . . . so familiar. Her parents would be scandalized.

"Go on," whispered Angelica.

Yes! Why not? Damn propriety. This was the Revolution.

Peggy stood, held up her arms, accepted the Frenchman's embrace, and jumped, letting the marquis swing her up onto his saddle. The seat was padded with royal blue wool. With its cushioning and her massive apricot-colored skirts, Peggy settled easily, her legs dangling to one side, the marquis's arm about her waist to steady her. She faced forward as primly as possible, trembling with a sense of adventure. She felt more than heard the marquis's rumble of laughter as he rearranged his battle sword to swing farther back on his hip, away from her.

As he clicked his tongue to move his horse forward, Peggy heard her brother-in-law warn: "Careful, Marquis, that one carries a sword as well—of wit. Beware! You won't see it until she nicks you with it."

"*Un homme bon à être pourfendu,*" Fleury murmured into her ear.

A good man to skewer, Peggy translated for herself. Ha! She laughed—a triumphant, defiant little peal. Fleury admired her keen tongue? Suddenly anything felt possible.

Fleury discreetly kept them to the back of the gathered crowd as he moved his horse close enough for Peggy to hear. Her Oneida friend was speaking and her papa's translator was explaining the sachem's English words in French to Rochambeau: "We are astonished that the king of France sends his troops to protect the Americans in an insurrection against the king of England, their father."

In French, Rochambeau answered: "The king of France protects the natural liberty that God has given to man. The

Americans have been overloaded with burdens, which they were no longer able to bear. King Louis has found their complaints just."

Her papa's linguist explained Rochambeau's statement in English and then, in turn, Peggy's sachem translated to his companions. How she itched to help with this back-and-forth in three languages.

Rochambeau continued: "Several of your neighbors, deceived by the English king, have made war upon the Americans. He has said the Americans are our enemy. That is false. The Americans are our friends. We come to defend them. It will please King Louis very much if you will join us in making war against the English."

The sachem nodded solemnly. "We lament the choices of our brother Iroquois. But the Oneidas and Tuscarora, at every hazard, will hold fast the covenant chain with the United States. We promise this. We will keep the hatchet in our hands for our brethren the Americans. With them we will be buried in the same grave or enjoy the fruits of victory and peace."

"*Si poétique*," Fleury murmured.

Peggy could feel his breath and lips move against her hair. Her heart skipped over itself.

Rochambeau then tried to present the sachem a beautiful gold medallion. He explained that it was etched with the image of King Louis the Sixteenth, on the day of his majesty's coronation.

But the sachem did not take it. "I thank you, but I wish

not to arouse the jealousy of my brothers or to have them think I am grasping or asking for this distinction."

A gasp of surprise rippled through the crowd.

"*Extraordinaire!*" Fleury breathed.

Yes, very, thought Peggy. As extraordinary as you not taking that Stony Point reward money for yourself. But aloud, she said, "That is their nature."

The sachem was pleased, however, when presented a pipe-tomahawk—a blade on one side, a pipe bowl on the other—made by French silversmiths. Inlaid with silver and engraved, the beautiful creation symbolized both war and its ultimate goal, peace.

In return, the Oneida and Tuscarora gave Rochambeau wampum strings, explaining that in their tribe, the decorative cords represented a warrior's privilege and duty to speak on behalf of their people. Their clan mothers had woven them for the French officers.

"Clan mothers also wear them," Peggy explained, "to show their position of honor and responsibility."

Again, that ripple of laughter. "*Peut-être que vous voulez vraiment être une Oneida.*"

Perhaps what she really wanted was to be Oneida? Peggy turned around and looked at the marquis, thinking he was criticizing or even ridiculing her. But his eyes told her his comment was half-teasing, yes, but also a serious question, laden with respect and curiosity about a culture foreign to him.

"No," she said, drawing out the word. Peggy was not

so naive as to not recognize how hard the Oneida's life was. "But if I were an Oneida woman, I would not have to be a bystander to this ceremonial conference. It is a matriarchal society and invites women to join council circles." Peggy might even have been asked to be its honored translator.

"Extraordinaire!" Fleury murmured again.

Peggy couldn't tell if he was talking about the Oneida or her. It was a glorious riddle.

The Indians remained in Newport for three days. Rochambeau ordered a formal military parade and review in the delegation's honor, complete with the cavalry galloping past and a firing of field artillery. The warriors were treated to a tour of a warship and a banquet on board.

The final night, in tribute to the French and in thanks for such hospitality, the Oneida, Tuscarora, and Caughnawaga would perform a ceremonial dance of alliance. All of Newport gathered to watch. Fleury asked to escort Peggy, that she might explain the traditions to him. Flattered and increasingly smitten, Peggy had dared slip her arm through his to pull the Frenchman with her when she spotted the Oneida sachem again. "Come! Let me introduce you!

"Good sir!" Peggy sang out as she neared the chief.

"It is our sister, the trumpeter swam." The chief smiled and bowed.

Peggy curtsied. She thought of their last conversation, laughing over Tilghman's obvious infatuation with Eliza. She wondered if the Oneida elder would be able to read Fleury's thoughts as well as he had Tilghman's. She'd be grateful if he could. Fleury was a mystery. Were his compliments just old-world gallantries, amusing banter a nobleman might toss easily about at the king's court? Or were they sincere?

But her questions evaporated as she and the Oneida straightened up. He looked so haggard. Shocked, without thinking, Peggy violated all protocol of respect and restraint. She took his hand. "Oh, sir, what is wrong? Are you unwell?"

The sachem shook his head. But he did not draw back. That alone told Peggy how much grief racked the old warrior. "My people are attacked, by the Mohawk and their Tory brothers. They burned our village and castle. Took our cattle, trampled our corn. My people have fled. For safety, your father moves them to Schenectady. But my children . . ." He shook his head. "The enemy have taken my children hostage."

Peggy was horrified. She knew such disaster had befallen his people because of the Oneida's alliance with the Patriots, and in retribution for the Continental Army's attack on Mohawk villages the year before. General Washington and her own father had ordered the scorched-earth assault through the Mohawk Valley to subdue the British-allied Iroquois, who had joined Tories in devastating and brutal raids on Patriot farms. But the Patriots' campaign had only fueled Mohawk anger and resentment with Americans who had continually encroached on their territory. It was a heartbreaking and harsh truth—because of their American Revolution, the Six Nations of the Iroquois Confederacy, who had lived together in peace for decades, and practiced their own form of democracy, were now dissolved into a bitter civil war. "I . . . I . . . I am so sorry, sir."

"I leave tomorrow to offer myself to my enemy in my children's place." He squeezed Peggy's hand before releasing it. "But tonight I dance to honor His Excellency, the great General Washington, and our father, King Louis."

Peggy shook her head and felt tears stinging her eyes now. She knew that being a hostage could bring him death.

"Do not fear for me," the sachem reassured her. "This is what we do for love of family. This life is brief, daughter of Schuyler. We must live it with honor and duty. Or die in shame."

Then he walked away to pray with his fellow Oneida over their fire.

Peggy had witnessed ceremonial dances many times. But never before had she really felt their overlay of potential tragedy and sorrow within their evocation of bravery for battle, the foreboding urgency of their gestures and cries. This was life, stripped of pretense, devoid of polite facades, platitudes, and lukewarm attachments.

The Indians lit an enormous bonfire in the middle of Newport's main street parallel to the harbor waters. As the blaze caught, crackling, engulfing the wood, throwing explosions of sparks and smoke billowing upward, the nineteen warriors entered the fire's ring of light. Peggy's sachem spoke in his native tongue. His voice was rich, resonant, and grave. She knew he was describing his people's history, their victories and pride, and the individual triumphs of the great men of his tribe.

He raised his hands and called out for blessing. Peggy felt her breath quicken, empathizing with the sachem's invocation, his faith in his people and their gods, but also—she could see it on his face in the flickering light—his despair for them.

Peggy looked at the Patriots and Europeans surrounding her. Did they see what she did? Did they understand what they were asking of these men and their tribes? The risks? What they sacrificed for this alliance?

She glanced up at Fleury. She would finally know what to think of him given his expression. If he watched with a tourist's detachment or a European's smugness, he was not for her.

The drums and the dance began.

In the dark night, lit only by the flickering light of the bonfire, the moon and its reflection in the harbor waters, Fleury's face burned with a corresponding lionhearted zeal. Revealed was the man who could rush up a hill filled with spears under a barrage of musket fire to charge to a flagpole and tear down his enemy's emblem. But there was also a grim, knowing respect on that handsome, valiant face. A clear understanding of the harrowing, even cataclysmic costs of bravery.

At that moment, Peggy knew. She was falling in love. She didn't stop to caution herself, or to analyze. She acted on what her heart told her. Peggy clutched the lapels of Fleury's uniform, stood on tiptoe, and pressed her lips against his— that gorgeous mouth she'd watched twitch with amusement, that spoke poetry, and that now she believed echoed the language of her soul.

Then—slightly shocked by her own impulsiveness and panicked about what his reaction might be—Peggy gathered her skirts and ran for the safety of her big sister's house.

FOURTEEN

Late Summer

Alexander Hamilton to Elizabeth Schuyler
Teaneck, New Jersey, August

*Impatiently My Dearest have I been expecting . . . a letter
from my charmer . . . She will there I hope paint me her feelings without reserve—even in those tender moments of pillowed
retirement, when her soul abstracted from every other object,
delivers itself up to Love and to me. . . . I would this moment
give the world to be near you only to kiss your sweet hand.
Believe what I say to be truth and imagine what are my feelings when I say it. Let it awake your sympathy and let our
hearts melt in a prayer to be soon united.*

Dobbs Ferry, New York, August 8

*[W]hy do you not write to me oftener? . . . I write you at
least three letters for your one, though I am immersed in public*

business and you have nothing to do but to think of me. . . .
Love me I conjure you.

Teaneck, New Jersey, August 31

You will think me unkind if I do not come. How will you
have the presumption to think me unkind you saucy little
charmer? . . . Should I not gain more by it, should I not enjoy
more pleasure, feast upon more beauties sweetnesses, and
charms?. . . Yet my love I could not with decency or honor
leave the army during the campaign. . . .

Kiss my little sister for me when she comes. I am happy
on all accounts she is sent for.

A Hamilton

PEGGY DROPPED HER BOOK TO THE FLOOR AS SHE
popped up out of her chair. "What do you mean I am sent
for?"

Angelica looked up from the letter she had just received
from Albany, from their father. "Papa is suffering another bad
round of his gout. He had to leave Congress to convalesce."

"Why can't Eliza help Mama care for him? She's home
in Albany."

"Because Mama is ill herself. Her legs are horribly swollen, so she is mostly bedridden." Angelica skimmed more of
the letter. "This pregnancy is a hard one, evidently."

"Pregnancy?" Peggy flounced back down into the chair, stunned. "Again?"

"Yes. Papa says she will deliver in January—if all goes well."

"Eeeeewww!" She couldn't help it. The thought of her parents being intimate always made her uncomfortable. "Mama is almost fifty!"

Angelica laughed at her.

"But Angelica, she's a *grandmother*. This child will be younger than your children! And besides, her last baby— oh, you didn't see, Angelica, that baby boy suffered so much before he died. Why would she try again?"

Peggy resisted adding what was really bothering her. It would sound so selfish. But she didn't want to leave Rhode Island. Not now! Not now that there was Fleury.

But Angelica knew. She swept to Peggy's side to kneel and embrace her. "Now is a good time for you to leave, little sister. Trust me. Absence makes the heart grow fonder, as they say. Sometimes it is precisely what a courtship needs."

Peggy's eyebrow shot up. *"Really?"* She drew out the word sarcastically. "What idiot says that?"

Angelica laughed lightly again. "Hundreds of poets. And I know it's true. Look at Hamilton for our sweet Eliza. She says his letters ache with love and loneliness for her. Let's see what Fleury writes to you."

"But Eliza and Hamilton were already betrothed when she returned to Albany!" Peggy wailed. And Fleury had not yet spoken of love. Not even after Peggy's impetuous kiss.

What did that mean? Had Fleury found her kiss too forward, or even repulsive?

"Yes, it was quick between them," Angelica murmured, pushing Peggy's ever unruly hair back from her forehead. "Perhaps it would have been better if Eliza and Alexander had come to know each other more before they were engaged. It was only a month's courtship. Eliza definitely leapt before she really looked."

Peggy searched her big sister's face. "Like you did?" she whispered.

Angelica turned away, as if Peggy had slapped her.

"I . . . I'm sorry," Peggy apologized. "I just . . . You seem . . ."

Angelica stood and went to the window, not acknowledging Peggy's question, and said, "I don't think Eliza realizes what she might have gotten herself into. I warned her about Hamilton's prospects after the war. They are . . . questionable. He has no family, no backing, just that . . . that mind of his. Of course, if our Revolution succeeds, we will become a society where effort and intelligence will be what matters most. *If* we succeed." She paused, reflecting on that concept a moment. "Frankly, I sense that Eliza is a bit frightened sometimes by Hamilton's insistence, his intensity, his ardor. Papa hints in this letter that she is succumbing to that nervousness of hers."

Angelica shook her head and concluded, "It will do Eliza good to have you at her side. You are far more patient with her than I."

"Oh, Angelica, when does it get to be my turn? I infuriated Mama by helping you elope and she has never really forgiven me or trusted me since then. Now I am to give up on my own chance at romance to hold Eliza's hand and reassure her about her wedding night? Something I—unlike you—know nothing about? And may never be given the chance to if all of you have your way!"

Laughter bubbled up out of Angelica. "Little sister, I want nothing more for you than happiness, believe me. I have always loved your passion. But it is a double-edged sword. You will learn that."

"Stop laughing at me!" Peggy shouted. "I am not a child anymore. I am the age you were when you ran off with your husband. Come to think of it, remember that awful poem that silly woman who taught us needlework used to make us recite: *At sixteen years come on and woo, and take of kisses plenty . . .*"

Angelica ruefully joined in: "*At eighteen years full grown and ripe, they're ready to content ye. At nineteen sly and mischievous . . .*"

Grinning at each other, the two sisters ended loudly, rebelliously: "*But the Devil at one and twenty!*"

"That's you, sister, twenty-one, the devil," teased Angelica. "Ready to dole out all manner of hell! And I would hope so," she added fondly. Then she shook her head, her mirth subsiding, and murmured, more to herself than to Peggy, "And to think that I was so worried about becoming an old maid!"

"Good Lord, imagine!" Carter strode into the room.

"The beauteous Angelica a spinster? That would never have happened. There would have been a legion of gallants courting you, my dear, had I not materialized." He kissed his wife on her cheek. She did not smile until he added, softly, with his lips lingering in her swept-high hair, "I am the lucky one to have beat them to the treasure of your heart."

He sat and leaned back in his chair. As soon as he spoke, he revealed that he had been listening to their conversation. She could be accused of being nosy herself, but somehow Carter's eavesdropping felt sinister. "Here is a proposal that might make you happy, Peggy. Rochambeau travels to Hartford to confer with Washington in a few days. I go with them, as the conference will be held in my commissary partner's home estate there. Come along. There will be festivities for ladies to enjoy after the meetings. Hartford is halfway to Albany and you will be safe to travel home from there." He seemed to speak with genuine big-brotherly concern.

But then he ruined the moment by adding, "Do not worry, sprightly Peggy, you will have no trouble with your wedding night, I am sure." He paused. "Your . . . heart . . . will tell you what to do."

Peggy felt like vomiting. For all his patina of British courtliness, the man could be incredibly vulgar. Then came a worse thought—could Fleury have gossiped to Carter about her kiss?

Excusing herself with as much dignity as she could muster, Peggy fled the room. She and Fleury had arranged to take a stroll together that afternoon. She needed to think how to tell him—without bursting into tears—that she soon would be leaving.

The air was cool and salty as she and Fleury wandered along streets overlooking the three-mile-wide harbor and the French fleet's thirty-plus ships that bobbed up and down, anchored in it. Peggy had come to be quite fond of the seaside city, the smell of the ocean winds, the push-pull of the tides. It was so unlike the mountains and forests of upstate New York. The waves carried such a sense of freedom as they crashed onshore and then rushed back out to the Atlantic—uncontainable.

She had also relished conversations with the inhabitants. They seemed so open to divergent ideas and philosophies. Rhode Island had been established specifically for religious freedom, breaking off from the more stringent tenets of Massachusetts Puritanism. As a result the city included Quakers, Presbyterians, Anabaptists, Moravians, and Jews. It was a refreshing change from Albany's Dutch Reformed Church strictness. She'd been pleased also by Fleury's liberal response to the religious diversity, especially considering his native land was devoutly Catholic and often persecuted Protestant dissenters. America and her philosophical freedoms were taking hold in him, clearly.

For several minutes now, Fleury and Peggy had walked in silence. Perhaps unsure of his English, the marquis rarely initiated conversation. As he requested, she stuck primarily to English, so he could practice using the language.

Peggy tried to reassure herself that it wasn't disinterest that kept him quiet, since he always answered her questions enthusiastically—mixing French with English. With enough prodding, she had learned he came from a fairly remote southern area of France called Saint-Hippolyte-le-Graveyron. Following family tradition, he had joined the infantry when he was nineteen years old, and eight years later he sailed to America to offer his services to the Revolution. At first Congress didn't want to commission him or the other French officers who arrived in 1776. So Fleury volunteered. Washington quickly recognized the worth of his experience and promoted Fleury to be a captain with the engineers. Before Stony Point, he had been wounded twice, at Brandywine and during the horrifying siege of Fort Mifflin, where he took command after all his superior officers were wounded or killed.

But so much about Fleury remained a mystery. And now Peggy had so little time to find out more.

He was staring out to the ocean in the growing twilight.

"Do you miss France?" she asked.

"Hmm. Yes *et* no. Life is a struggle there. We are of noble blood, but is *difficile* to find security of money. Our lands are rocky for farming. I do not have title enough to find employment in King Louis's court. So I join the army, like my father and his father. I not see my home *pour* . . . mmm . . . ten years." He smiled at her, wistful.

Tell me you want to show it to me someday, she thought. Say you have found happiness here, in America. That you will never leave its shores. But all Peggy could manage was, "Do you like America?"

"*Mais bien sûr!* The country is beautiful. And the women . . ." He pressed his fingers together and kissed them, popping them apart as if throwing the caress into the air in that odd French exclamation of something being perfect.

Silence again.

How Peggy wished Lafayette were still in Newport. He had been recalled almost immediately to Washington's headquarters after the dinner party at Angelica's. Fleury had hinted that his friend's youth and enthusiasms had grated on Rochambeau, that French officers were jealous of the twenty-three-year-old's rank as general. Peggy searched her memory of Lafayette's suggestion in Morristown of arranging a romance between her and Fleury for a hint of what to say next to keep their conversation going.

"Oh!" She blushed as her audible exclamation made Fleury look at her quizzically. Lafayette had said Fleury would be impressed with a woman being interested in his inventions. "There is something I would love to know more of." Peggy hesitated. "But I know it is probably a guarded secret. May I still ask?"

He nodded.

Even though nothing was nearby but seagulls, she lowered her voice, so no one would overhear information about his engineering marvel. "Is it true you were hoping to design self-propelled boats that could blow up British ships? Is such a thing feasible?"

Fleury frowned.

"I . . . I . . ." Peggy decided to be truthful. She didn't want the marquis to think her papa had divulged secret plans. "I know I shouldn't have been eavesdropping. But I heard you describe a rocket boat to Papa. It sounded so interesting, I couldn't help but listen. How do they work? They must be a marvel."

"Paahh." Fleury snorted. "They would have been! I had saltpeter and powder, but I never receive the flat-bottom boats I need. My plan was to fill a chest, a very strong one, with powder. The deck covered with bombs. The direction and velocity will be given to the boat by a strong rocket, like fireworks. A mast sank in the water, horizontal to the stern, bound in a sail, will support the boat and hinder the current to drive it out the wrong way. The head we arm with a strong spur of iron, so it will pierce the British ship and stick. We set the British fleet on fire when the powder blows up from sparks of the rocket—*BOOM!*"

Fleury waved his arms on *boom*, making Peggy jump.

"Oh! *Non, non!*" Fleury reflexively lowered his hands to her shoulders to apologize for frightening her: "*Pardonnez-moi, je ne veux pas vous effrayer!*"

He didn't drop his hands. Peggy did not pull back. Slowly, his eyes traveled from her eyes to her lips.

Oh please, she thought. Prove to me you feel something of what I do. Peggy nodded ever so slightly, trembling, to give him permission.

Fleury leaned toward her, looked in her eyes again, and

then cocked his chiseled face so their lips would meet perfectly, like pieces of a puzzle. Peggy closed her eyes, waiting for the touch of bliss.

CRRRACK!

Peggy and Fleury flinched and fell away from each other at the sound of musket fire. "Damn," breathed Peggy as Fleury pushed her behind him and drew his sword.

"Arrêtez! Arrêtez!"

"This is my town, you stupid frog!" a surly voice shouted down by the water.

Peggy peeped out from behind Fleury to see a sentry squared off with a local fisherman.

"Identifiez-vous!" The French soldier challenged the man to identify himself.

"Let me about my business, or you and all your fancy-dress, wig-wearing fops will starve, ye will!"

CRRACK. The sentry fired another shot into the air as two more French guards came running. *"Arrêtez-le! Peut-être que c'est un espion!"*

Clearly the fisherman didn't understand that the sentry suspected he could be a Tory spy. His response was to drop his basket of cod and pull out his short club that all boatmen carried to twist rope.

"Oh dear," murmured Peggy. As the French soldiers lowered their muskets to aim at the fisherman's chest and other boatmen jumped from their sloops to help their friend, Peggy grabbed Fleury's hand. "Come on!"

This could turn into a brawl. She knew that the locals

were increasingly annoyed by having to navigate around all the French vessels and the officers crowding their homes and streets—no matter how much they welcomed their presence.

As the men closed in on one another, weapons or fists ready, Peggy ran toward the wharf, pulling Fleury with her.

"Stop! *Arrêtez!*" she cried out.

The men all froze, surprised by her sudden appearance, her face red, her bonnet fallen, her hair disheveled from her dash down the hill to the waterside. They stayed squared off, at the ready.

"Good sirs, you misunderstand the French soldiers," she said breathlessly to the fishermen. "The sentry simply asked, 'Who is there?' so that you could identify yourself to him. There are spies everywhere, you know that. The sentry's challenge is simply to keep Newport safe."

The men stuck their lower lips out and nodded, one snarling, "Why didn't the jackass say so, then?"

Peggy turned to the French soldiers. She explained in their language that the boatmen fished the coast and would be coming in and out of the harbor every day.

The sentry insisted the fishermen still needed to answer his question. He had his orders, he told Peggy, straight from Count Rochambeau.

"But you must say it in English so the boatmen could understand." She repeated herself in French, adding, *"Dites,* 'Who is there?'"

"Ou is dair?" the Frenchman repeated.

She laughed. *"Simple, non?"*

The French sentinels nodded, repeating "Ou is dair?"

"Will this do, gentlemen?" she asked the Rhode Islanders.

They shrugged and grumbled about being interrupted in hauling up their catch, and stomped back to their boats.

Well, Peggy thought, not as important a diplomatic moment as Martha Washington had hoped, but a fistfight, or worse, averted at least. She smiled with some pride and turned to Fleury.

He was beaming. "*Extraordinaire*, mademoiselle. You could translate to General Rochambeau when he meets His Excellency, General Washington. I would be honored, like a knight, to have on my arm such a woman."

"Oh, they have Alexander Hamilton for translating," she demurred. But her heart thrilled to hear Fleury say he felt ennobled by being with her. She hoped he knew what he implied by the English words he was choosing—that he felt admiration, perhaps even love, for her.

Peggy took a deep breath. "Marquis, I must tell you something."

"And I must tell you something." His voice was warm and he took a step closer. "*Mais* . . . ladies first."

Peggy hesitated. "You, sir." She gestured for him to speak.

But he refused, insisting on polite formality.

Carefully watching what his reaction would be, she said, "My parents have sent for me. Both are ill. I must return to Albany."

Fleury stiffened.

"But," Peggy rushed on, "I will travel to Hartford first with my brother-in-law, who goes to facilitate the meeting and to procure supplies for your army. Is there any chance you might . . ." She trailed off, realizing that no matter how daring she might be in revealing her feelings to him, she had no right to push Fleury to request Rochambeau include him in a conference with Washington. Fleury had experienced the same kind of envy Lafayette had from the other French officers. Given his prior service in America, he entered Rochambeau's forces as a major—receiving a rank many men who had been with the Saintonge Regiment for years had hoped for and were denied by his elevation. She knew from her father's hurtful experiences with Congress that Fleury being chosen as one of a handful of French envoys to Washington could cause even more grousing about him.

Peggy sighed. Men and rank; it created such discord among them. "What were you going to say?" she asked.

Fleury hesitated, then shook his head. "I will ask to ride in the escort to Hartford. And so, I protect you on the road." He took her hand and threaded it through his arm. "I will tell what I wish to say when we arrive—before you are taken from me."

FIFTEEN

Early Autumn

Alexander Hamilton to Eliza Schuyler
Liberty Pole, New Jersey, September 3, 1780

The little song you sent me I have read over and over. It is very pretty and contains precisely those sentiments I would wish . . . You seem by sympathy to have anticipated [my] inquiries . . . and to have answered them all by this little song . . . [B]e assured My angel it is not a diffidence of my betsey's heart, but of a female heart, that dictated the questions. . . . Some of your sex possess every requisite to please delight, and inspire esteem friendship and affection; but there are too few of this description. . . . [A]nd though I am satisfied . . . that you are one of the exceptions, I cannot forbear having moments when I feel a disposition to make a more perfect discovery of your temper, and character. . . .

When your sister returns home, I shall try to get her in my interest and make her tell me of all your flirtations. Have you heard any thing more of what I hinted to you about

*Fleury? When she returns, give my love to her and tell her,
I expected, she would have outstripped you in the Hymenial
line.*

*Adieu My love
A. Hamilton*

IT TOOK TWO DAYS TO TRAVEL THE SIXTY MILES
from Newport to Hartford, Connecticut. Those precious
forty-eight hours had been deliciously frustrating, with
Fleury riding far behind Peggy's carriage, on duty and in
protective alertness. The French admiral de Ternay was ill, so
Rochambeau rode with him in a carriage as well, rather than
on horseback. The two vehicles jolted along side by side. The
weather was mild enough that the canopies were down so the
Frenchmen could enjoy the splashes of orange, gold, and red
leaves that signaled the coming of autumn. It also released
the smell of onions, eaten to relieve the symptoms of scurvy,
that hung around de Ternay. With the carriages open Carter
could regale his employers with stories and Angelica amuse
them with her winsome chatter.

Peggy, on the other hand, kept looking wistfully back to
Fleury. He would smile but otherwise could not acknowledge
her gaze, being in such close proximity to his commanding general. Each time she squirmed and turned, Angelica
elbowed her in the ribs. By the time they reached their overnight stop, her side was quite bruised.

All day, from Newport to Coventry to Voluntown to

Canterbury to Scotland to Windham and finally to Andover, she had itched to say something, *anything* to him. But even when one of Rochambeau's carriage wheels broke on the rutted road and they stalled unmoving for more than an hour, she was thwarted. Because he spoke enough English, Fleury was sent off to find help.

While they waited, children ran from their farm fields to touch the boots of the beautifully clad Frenchmen, sitting atop their horses. They scattered, cheering, as Fleury returned at the trot, so expert a horseman that he and his gelding appeared one magnificent creature. He had found a wheelwright.

For one beguiling moment Peggy and Fleury were near each other as he explained—with amusement—that the elderly wheelwright had refused to work through the night to repair any carriage, "not even for a hatful of guineas. Not even for the king of France. Then I told him it was to meet General Washington that we travel. *Et voilà!* He says it will be ready by five a.m. tomorrow." He repeated himself in French to Rochambeau.

Rochambeau asked Fleury if Washington was truly that beloved by everyone.

"*Ah oui, c'est vrai.*" Fleury nodded. "*Sa dignité, sa simplicité de manières, son dévouement à la campagne, son visage ouvert et son attitude de défi à l'encontre des Anglais gagnent le cœur de tous.*"

In his native tongue, Fleury put it so beautifully, so poetically—Washington's dignity, his simplicity of manners, his devotion to country, his open countenance and stubborn defiance of the British did indeed win the heart of most everyone. Why couldn't Fleury serve as translator at the conference? Peggy pouted. Why did he have to return immediately to Newport?

Fleury explained there was a tavern nearby—the Sign of the Black Horse—where they could spend the night as the wheelwright worked. Peggy's mood lifted with the thought that surely she and her Frenchman would be able to steal a few minutes together then. But crowded into one room with Carter plus Rochambeau's aides-de-camp and son, Fleury was kept playing backgammon all evening. At midnight, Angelica closed and locked the door of the closet-sized bedroom she and Peggy shared. Fuming, Peggy vowed to find some way to pay back her brother-in-law for detaining Fleury all night.

Now she sat, swaying on the ferry, with Rochambeau's party, crossing the Connecticut River to Hartford. She could see hordes of people on the other side, waving handkerchiefs and homemade flags of blue, white, and red vertical stripes to honor the French troops. How many more minutes did they have? She glanced to Fleury, who was shading his eyes against the water's glare to look in amazement at the thousands of people.

The ferry docked with a bump and an explosion of *huzzahs* from people on shore. Awaiting them was the governor, Carter's partner, Colonel Wadsworth, a dozen city leaders dressed in their finest embroidered vests and purple coats, plus the governor's foot guard, still bedecked in the opulent red and gold-trimmed dress uniforms once given them by King George's *royal* governor.

BOOM! Cannon fired.

BOOM-BOOM. Thirteen rounds in salute and celebration of the thirteen United States. Peggy's heart jumped with each deafening round.

A fife-and-drum corps struck up "Yankee Doodle," and before she really knew what was happening, Rochambeau and de Ternay were astride beautiful warhorses and parading toward the capitol, followed by the musicians, the guard, the city officials, and all the Frenchmen, including her Fleury.

Carter took the carriage reins and struggled to control their horses amid the happily pushing throng, cheering and clapping in time to the music. From every window, on every stoop of the city, people waved and called out and applauded. Peggy could see many of them were crying—that's how starved Americans were for help in their fight. One would have to be dead to not thrill to the euphoria, the sense of hope in all those huzzahs.

From a distance, she could see George Washington standing on the steps of the courthouse, towering over everyone around him.

"There's Hamilton." Angelica cupped her mouth and raised her voice so Peggy could hear her. "See him there, beside His Excellency? He truly is Washington's most trusted man, it seems. Eliza is a lucky girl."

Peggy nodded. She also spotted Lafayette, along with Harrison, Meade, Tilghman, and that insufferable McHenry.

Carter could not get them close enough to actually hear Washington greet Rochambeau—Hamilton leaning into His Excellency to translate the French general's response, and Lafayette doing the same into his countryman's ear. But there were many bows and solemn smiles that made it clear the diplomatic formalities were perfectly executed.

The crowd thundered approval. The leaders got back on their horses, making ready to parade together this time.

"They must be heading to Wadsworth's house now," Carter shouted.

"Do you know the way?" Angelica asked.

"I assume I can follow the masses," he answered with a laugh.

Peggy heard their exchange over the din but had kept her eyes glued to Fleury. She saw Rochambeau speak to him, saw Fleury and Hamilton kiss each other's cheeks in the French custom of *faire la bise*.

As the fife and drums struck up the march "The Road to Boston," she strained to see past the flags and handkerchiefs waving in time to the music. She thought she saw Hamilton and Fleury riding together. Then they disappeared from view. She twisted and peered. There they were! Riding straight for Peggy's carriage.

Hamilton swept off his tricorn hat in greeting. His buff-and-blue uniform was decidedly cleaner than last time she'd seen him, and his hat's decorative cockade fresh—a gift from Eliza. "The Schuyler sisters!" he called, grinning, and held his hat to his heart as he bowed. Peggy smiled back at his chivalrous gesture—he really must think himself a knight of the round table or something equally grand, she mused. Then she realized Fleury was spurring his horse to her side of the carriage. She caught her breath at the urgency with which he moved toward her.

Did she imagine it, or did he say, "*Ma chérie*"? Oh, how she wanted to scream at the multitude to quiet so she could hear.

As the people of Hartford cheered, Fleury leaned over from his saddle, clasped her waist, and pulled her to her feet so he could press his lips to her ear. "There is no time to say all. Rochambeau orders I return to Newport *immediatement* to report his safe arrival. I will write. I have something to explain."

Muskets fired into the air in jubilation and Fleury's horse spooked, half rearing and turning to look about fearfully. The carriage swayed and dipped. Peggy suddenly felt her feet dangling in the air. Fleury held her up, but if his grasp loosened, she'd fall, crushed between carriage and horse!

Fleury's embrace tightened. And there Peggy hovered, five feet off the ground, cradled in his arm. She could feel his muscles tighten and strain as he supported her while trying to calm his horse with his other hand on the reins. She flung her arms around his neck to help, pulling herself close to his chest so they both didn't topple over, tipped like a scale by her weight. They laughed—his rumble and her surprised, nervous giggle melding into one triumphant mutual gasp of jubilation at avoiding disaster.

She waited for him to drop her back into the carriage. But he didn't. Suspended together, Fleury kissed her. Kissed her good-bye with bittersweet urgency, pushing his soul into hers for a fleeting, rapturous breath, a promise of possibilities, of life stolen from catastrophe as the horse danced beneath them.

Then he swung Peggy back into the carriage. She made herself let go. With a gentle caress of her face, a brush of his fingertips on her cheek, Fleury rode away.

The fife and drums played on.

Later that night, after dinner, Hamilton teased Peggy. "Well, that good-bye was certainly impressive, little sister. I can hardly wait to tell Lafayette that he is as good as Cupid."

Peggy smiled absentmindedly. She really hadn't been paying much attention to any comment or anyone that evening. The candlelit parlor, the polite repartee, the women tittering, the men boasting; it all seemed so tepid.

"I admire your . . . abandon."

At that, Peggy was all attention. Her eyebrow shot up, suspecting disapproval.

"No, truly." Hamilton had caught her expression of concern. "Such zest for life, in a woman, is exquisite, intoxicating to behold. And such independence; shall I even say initiative?" He grinned at her. "Remarkable. Mythic. Very like Diana, the huntress goddess who breaks so many hearts."

Peggy ignored the banter in the compliment. This

night, after that kiss, she was only interested in honesty. She shrugged. "Playing games, now, during a war, just . . ." Peggy hesitated. She was slipping into unusually frank and rather taboo conversation with a man. But he was to be her brother, wasn't he? "I just am not particularly interested in flirtation as other girls are taught to be. I never was very good at it anyway."

"Is your sister?"

"Eliza?" She laughed gently. "No." She turned her head to look at him reassuringly, and realized Hamilton was gazing away from her. She followed his eyes and saw that he was looking at Angelica.

Which sister had he meant? What was it between him and Angelica? Was Hamilton falling under her spell as well? Peggy reached out and put her hand on his arm. "Sincerity is the best kind of love, don't you think . . . brother?"

Hamilton's pretty face turned that peach color Peggy had come to recognize occurred when he was embarrassed or caught in a thought. But he decided to follow her lead and be direct: "I just wish Eliza would write me more often. The infrequency of her letters makes me worry someone else is courting her. You must report to me any man who approaches her from now on. Agreed?" He ended on a jaunty tone, but Peggy could tell there was an undercurrent of seriousness in what Hamilton said.

"She's not like that, Alexander. You must trust her. She is a Penelope."

"Well, let's hope I am not an Odysseus, at war for a

decade and then unable to find his way home for another. And those sirens! Calypso!" Peggy didn't take the literary bait of Odysseus's temptations, so Hamilton turned thoughtful. "Tilghman calls her 'the little saint.'"

"Ha!" Peggy nodded. "Well . . . she's not."

"But her letters . . . My letters are . . . hers are . . ."

Peggy laughed at him. She couldn't help it. For such a preening verbal peacock, he was almost childlike in such moments.

Much—Peggy suddenly realized—as she must sound sometimes in her own insecurities, her little-sister competitiveness, her worry that when compared to Angelica and Eliza she came up short, inferior. She hesitated before speaking again. She might have quite a bit in common personality-wise with Hamilton.

But Peggy drew herself back to the point at hand. It was vitally important that Eliza's future husband understand and appreciate her still waters. "Eliza is not a confident writer, Alexander. That's all. She is self-conscious about it since letter writing is deemed a skill that's proof of a lady's sophistication. But you could not be blessed with a better, more devoted and thoughtful wife than my *middle* sister."

Glancing toward Angelica, who had a ring of men about her, Peggy continued, "It can be hard to be the younger sister of a learned and witty and captivating woman. Out of fear of being compared and found wanting, it is safer sometimes to remain quiet. Eliza's choice of words can be simpler than Angelica's, but the ocean of her feeling is vast and deep. Far more lasting than any surface ripples of witticisms or clever turns of phrase."

Hamilton sighed. Nodded. Then he almost whispered, "I worry Eliza does not fully realize that she could be shackling herself to a poor man. I have no property. No personal victory in battle to make my name and my future. Your lover Fleury understands this—it is why he joined the army, why he came to America, to find glory and thus elevate himself."

At this Peggy frowned. Fleury had come because he believed in liberty, the cause. Hadn't he? What did her soon-to-be brother know of the Frenchman she had fallen in love with? "Alexander . . . ," she began to ask.

But Carter sauntered up and interrupted them. "Wadsworth has brought out the grog, my friend. As scintillating as I know our Peggy is, we men have want of you, Hammie, before the dancing begins." The way he pulled out the word *scintillating* made it sound like a sneer. But looking at him more carefully, Peggy quickly realized Carter was tipsy and just beginning to slur his words.

Hamilton stood. What he said next made Peggy like him all the more.

"I have actually been wanting to speak with you as well, sir. This month, the Continental Army has received only four or five days' rations of meal. This distress at such a stage of the campaign sours the soldiery. We lost the port of Charleston in May mainly from the want of a sufficient supply of provisions. And last month, Gates, puffed up with arrogance, foolishly attacked the British in Camden, paying no attention to the fact his troops were ravaged with dysentery for lack of proper food and medicines. As a result, he lost that battle and two thousand Patriots to death or capture by the Redcoats. Our men are beyond dispirited. They need supplies, Mr. Carter!"

Carter was clearly taken aback. "I work for the French army now, *mon ami*," he blustered.

Materializing from thin air, it seemed, came Angelica, a fluttering rush of Patriot-blue satin and French perfume. Peggy suddenly realized that her big sister's tendency to flit about a party from group to group might have more to do with saving her husband from embarrassment and fights than with entertaining herself. Oh, Angelica, what a waste of your magnificence, Peggy thought sadly.

"Gentlemen." Angelica flipped open her ivory-carved fan and swept it back and forth, back and forth, hypnotic. "Governor Trumbull and I were just discussing Thomas Paine and his latest call to action. Have you read it, Colonel Hamilton? He feels the fall of Charleston has called forth a spirit akin to the flame of 1776. That the valor of a country is best learned from the bravery of its soldiery." She smiled. "Surely the men in this room represent that as well as the best and noblest cause that ever a country engaged in."

"Certainly it is among the soldiers that I place my hopes," Hamilton answered.

A stiff silence fell.

"Oh dear." Angelica's throaty laugh sounded like a quick-dazzle run of notes on a harpsichord. "I must have interrupted a serious conversation. I beg your forgiveness." She bowed her head slightly, holding her open fan to her lips—a well-known invitation to kiss someone in the language of fans.

Both men stared at her. Then Hamilton shook his head as if to throw off a daydream. He found his manners. "The truth is I am an unlucky honest man," he apologized, "that speaks my sentiments to all and with emphasis. I was letting my emotions override my manners. Forgive me, Mr. Carter. I hope you will not charge me with vanity." He added with boyish angst and humorous self-deprecation: "I hate Congress—I hate the army—I hate the world—I hate myself. The whole is a mass of fools and knaves."

They all laughed with him.

"But the truth is we are in dire financial straits," Hamilton continued, "even with the French army arriving. The old man will despair if we cannot prod Rochambeau to battle soon, to try to conclude this war as soon as possible. The army is bankrupt. Congress is bankrupt. The country is bankrupt. Washington has exhausted his private resources. He had to borrow money from various persons for us to afford the trip here. I do not know how we will reckon with the bill at the various taverns in which we lodge at Hartford for this conference."

His face clouded with a raw embarrassment at the thought of having to go a-begging for his dinner funds. Peggy's instinct was to hug him, in sympathy and understanding, but could tell that would be the worst possible affront to his sense of honor.

Angelica thought a moment and then glanced toward the governor. "Excuse me," she said, and regally glided toward Connecticut's top politicians, her fan sweeping the air seductively about her gorgeous face.

Within an hour, Governor Trumbull announced his state would be picking up the bill for the Patriots' historic talks with the French. All of them.

That's when Hamilton asked Angelica to dance. Somehow during the effervescent circles and sashays of a cotillion, one of Angelica's garters slipped from her leg and appeared on the floor. Alexander Hamilton swept it up and presented it to her on bended knee, to the applause of fellow dancers. He lingered over the kiss he pressed to her hand as she took the garter from him.

"My knight of the garter," Angelica quipped.

A would-be knight of the bedchamber, thought Peggy. She was being separated from her own lover and sent home in part to assuage Eliza's growing anxieties. How in the world was she to prepare sweet, steady Eliza for such an enrapturing but quicksilver man?

SIXTEEN

Autumn

Alexander Hamilton to Elizabeth Schuyler
Robinson's House, Highlands, Sepr 25 1780

In the midst of my letter, I was interrupted by a scene that
shocked me more than any thing I have met with—the discov-
ery of a treason of the deepest dye. The object was to sacrifice
West Point. General Arnold had sold himself to [the British
and] . . . fled to the enemy.

Could I forgive Arnold for sacrificing his honor reputation
and duty I could not forgive him for acting a part that must
have forfieted the esteem of [his wife] so fine a woman. . . .
Indeed my angelic Betsey, I would not for the world do any
thing that would hazard your esteem.

ELIZA RETREATED TO A SUNNY WINDOW SEAT TO
read a new letter from Hamilton as Philip sorted through a
thick bundle of dispatches the express rider had brought him.
"None for me, Papa?" asked Peggy.

Without looking up, he shook his head.

Peggy sighed and tapped her finger on the checkers board to show her littlest brother, Rensselaer, that her king could take two of his men if he didn't move one of them. She was trying to help the seven-year-old survive checkers with his two older brothers. Jeremiah, five years his senior, would still occasionally play with the child, but defeated him roundly each go, reducing Rensselaer to tears. And John, a cocky fifteen-year-old now, refused to play with the boy until he learned to be a worthy opponent.

"Oh my!" Eliza gasped.

"Damn him!" Schuyler cursed.

Eliza leapt from the window to her feet. Schuyler struggled to his feet with his cane, wincing as his bandaged foot touched the floor.

"What? What is it?" Peggy asked with some alarm at both their reactions.

"Tragedy!" cried Eliza at the same time Schuyler bellowed, "The blackest treason!"

"Poor woman," Eliza whispered.

"The blaggard!" Schuyler shouted. "May he roast in hell!"

"Who? What are you two talking about?" Peggy pleaded.

"Poor Mrs. Arnold!"

"Benedict! The villain, the lying perfidious bastard!"

With both of them uttering such different things at once, Peggy didn't have a hope of understanding. "Eliza, stop." She held up her hand. "Papa, what has happened?"

Looking up from his letter, angry tears falling down his

face, Schuyler raged, "Benedict Arnold has betrayed us. He conspired with the British to give them West Point. I am the one who recommended Arnold for that post." He collapsed back into his chaise, rubbing his leg. "Benedict begged me to help him find a military command after he had recuperated in Philadelphia and married Peggy Shippen. He was so deserving of our honor. He saved Fort Stanwix! He won Saratoga!"

He paused, searching his mind, clearly reliving their conversation. "Good God! Do you suppose he was planning this crime even then? Maybe he wanted West Point because he had already agreed to hand it over. Oh, how could I have been such a fool?"

Schuyler started reading again, his head moving back and forth as if the words were so hard to read he had to use all his strength to push himself through them. Peggy knew better than to interrupt, but her heart was pounding with the fearful question: Had the Patriots lost control of the Hudson River? If so, they were all in the gravest danger—particularly her papa. She tiptoed to Eliza, who was turning her letter over and over. "Eliza, do the British have West Point?" she whispered.

"What?" Eliza looked at her with some surprise.

"Does Hamilton say that West Point is lost?" she hissed.

"Oh!" Eliza quickly reread the first paragraph, while Peggy fought the urge to snatch it and read it herself.

"No, it says here his treason was detected. That he fled and escaped. That is why poor Mrs. Arnold—"

Schuyler exploded again, silencing Eliza. "*Verdomd dwa-zen!*"

Little Rensselaer startled enough at his father's Dutch curse that a number of checkers fell to the floor and rolled about.

Schuyler stood and staggered toward the door, leaning heavily on his cane. "I must write a letter immediately. Lansing!" He shouted for his secretary.

"Is there something else, Papa?" Peggy asked. But what more could there be to add to such a shock?

"They have arrested Colonel Varick. "

Both sisters gasped.

"Colonel Varick? What on earth for?" Eliza asked.

But Peggy knew immediately. The poor, unsuspecting, idealistic man. He was now Arnold's aide-de-camp. Varick had been such an admirer of Arnold and had been ecstatic with the appointment. He never would have foreseen such deviousness. "Papa, they can't suspect Mr. Varick of wrongdoing. You know he would never betray the nation, or for that matter ever do anything he knew would disappoint you."

"I know that," Schuyler answered. "But we also knew that I would never mismanage funds for my army, and yet Congress suspected me of such misdeeds for months and months. They'll believe any conspiracy, promote any cow dung, if it seems to clear them of whatever culpability they had in causing a situation. They humiliated Benedict repeatedly by promoting lesser men over him for political reasons. The British probably offered Arnold riches, and in his bitter disappointments he took the deal." He shook his head. "Poor Richard. I must provide a letter that speaks to Varick's character and integrity for the court of inquiry."

As he limped to his study, Peggy heard him curse again: "Would to God that musket ball that hit Benedict's leg had pierced his black heart instead."

"Peggy, come listen to this." Eliza waved to her and patted the window seat so Peggy snuggled in beside her. She read: *"On my return, I saw an amiable woman frantic with distress for the loss of a husband she tenderly loved—a traitor to his country and to his fame, a disgrace to his connections. It was the most affecting scene I ever was witness to. She for a considerable time entirely lost her senses. The General went up to see her and she upbraided him with being in a plot to murder her child; one moment she raved; another she melted into tears."*

Eliza looked up at Peggy. "Alexander adds that he believes she knew nothing of her husband's plotting until Arnold fled. That Mrs. Arnold was as surprised as they. Poor lady. How horrible. Can you imagine?"

Peggy wasn't so sure she could. Mrs. Arnold's raving sounded a bit like that scene Moses Harris had described to her when he had been desperate to save himself from hanging—tearing open his shirt to bare his chest, telling the British to shoot him, that death was better than being suspected of disloyalty to his king. He'd advised Peggy to remember that if she ever were caught in a beartrap herself: a bit of outraged innocence could get her out of a heap of trouble.

Oh my! What a clever woman Mrs. Arnold was! Thinking on it, Peggy burst out laughing. She couldn't believe that Hamilton was naive enough to believe her hysteria.

Eliza looked aghast. "Peggy, how can you be so cruel? That's not like you."

Peggy peeped over Eliza's shoulder to read a bit of the letter for herself. She pointed to the section in which Hamilton visited Mrs. Arnold the next morning:

"She received us in bed, with every circumstance that could interest our sympathy. Her sufferings were so eloquent that I wished myself her brother, to have a right to become her defender."

Shaking off a strange pang of jealousy that Hamilton wished he were Mrs. Arnold's brother, Peggy said, mirth still ringing in her voice, "In her bed, in her nightgown? Oh, Eliza, think! This is Peggy Shippen, correct? The girl proclaimed the most beautiful woman in all of America. The girl who reigned supreme at all the balls in Philadelphia when Papa was in Congress. Remember the scandalous stories of her being in that Meschianza—that bacchanal the British hosted for themselves before they evacuated the city. There was a jousting tournament, floating barges covered with flowers, an elaborate feast. Didn't she appear in some dramatic staging, dressed like a . . ." Peggy lowered her voice, remembering that Rensselaer was still sitting in the room. "Like a Turkish harem girl? She'd surely be capable of a little theater acting. And we all thought she was a Tory even then, remember?"

Eliza folded up the letter. "You mock me."

"Oh no, no, my dear, I never would do that." Peggy took Eliza's hand and kissed it as apology. "But . . ." She hesitated a moment. She took a deep breath and dared saying, "As beautiful and charming as his writing and conversations are, I do think you will need to be aware of Hamilton's romanticized notions, Eliza. He seems fond of putting everything and everyone into poetical terms or mythology and turning simple events into epics as large as Greek tragedies."

"I know." Eliza's face puckered. "I am so afraid that I will not be smart enough for him."

"Of course you are!" Peggy put her arm around her middle sister. That was not what she had meant for Eliza to feel at all. The fault, if that was the right word, was in Hamilton's tendency to aggrandize everything, not in her sister's intelligence.

"You are one of the smartest, most intuitive persons I know. Nobody sings or plays the pianoforte as beautifully as you, Eliza. That takes such an active, intelligent creativity, analyzing the emotions a composer intends in those scratchy notes on a page, learning and perfecting the technique that gives you the skill to bring those skeletal notations to full-fleshed life in your performance. As far as I am concerned, Eliza, that is the greatest act of intelligence a human being is capable of. Music is air made rapturous, achieving the sublime, capturing the harmony of the spheres for a fleeting moment so we can hear it. It is the closest we get to God. So, therefore, it is pure brilliance of the soul."

"Really?" Eliza's eyes welled up with tears of gratitude. "You believe so?"

"Yes, really." Peggy hugged her. "What bred this insecurity?"

Eliza glanced nervously at Rensselaer still sitting in the chair, swinging his legs, watching them.

"Ren," Peggy cooed at him, "why don't you go see what Jeremiah is doing?"

He grinned at her. "Don't wanna."

"How about checking on Mama, then?"

He shook his head. "She *werps*."

"That's because you're going to have a little brother or sister."

He made a face.

Peggy kept trying. "Where's Cornelia? I bet she'd like to play."

He shrugged.

Eliza put her hand on Peggy's arm and smiled in a watch-this expression. "Well, you'll want to cover your ears, then, my dearest," she said to Rensselaer, "because Peggy and I need to talk about love and girl things."

That sent the seven-year-old running.

The sisters pealed with laughter. "And why do you think you're not smart?" Peggy demanded.

"Because of this." Eliza pulled from her pocket a packet of Hamilton's letters, tied neatly in ribbon. She searched for the one she wanted and opened it.

Peggy noted with a little pang of pity and angry

protectiveness that the paper was dotted with stains— tearstains.

Eliza took a deep breath and in a voice filled with embarrassment read:

"I entreat you my Charmer, not to neglect the charges I gave you particularly that of taking care of your self, and that of employing all your leisure in reading. Nature has been very kind to you; do not neglect to cultivate her gifts and to enable yourself to make the distinguished figure in all respects to which you are intitled to aspire. You excel most of your sex in all the amiable qualities; endeavour to excel them equally in the splendid ones. You can do it if you please and I shall take pride in it. It will be a fund too, to diversify our enjoyments and amusements and fill all our moments to advantage."

"Oh, Eliza, that is nonsense! Who does he think he is? Pygmalion?" As soon as Peggy referenced the sculptor that Greek mythology claimed had breathed actual life and thought into a beautiful but inanimate statue, she knew she had made a mistake.

"You see," Eliza wailed. "Alexander is right. I would never have thought of that story. He will become bored with me." She caught her breath in little sobs. "He would be better off married to you. Or . . . or . . . or to Angelica. Angelica would better satisfy his mind and that quick wit of his. He leaves me tongue-tied."

Eliza buried her face in her hands and wept. Peggy wrapped her arms around her. A dozen scenes of searing glances, wry smiles, heated political debate, and playful repartee between her eldest sister and her middle sister's fiancé played out in Peggy's mind as she kissed Eliza's head and murmured, "You are worrying over nothing, dearest." But was she?

Was that what was between Hamilton and Angelica? An intellectual hunger? Or was it just Hamilton showing off in the feral tomcat way he was legendary for among Washington's military family? Certainly, he flirted unnecessarily with Peggy, more out of habit than any kind of interest. With her sister, was their fiery banter simply the brilliant, well-read Angelica reliving the time she was still free . . . free to choose her path? Suddenly Peggy's heart ached for her eldest sister. Angelica was clearly so unhappy on the road her marriage to Carter dictated she travel.

Then her sympathy switched to her middle sister. What would happen if Eliza sensed the heat between her husband-to-be and Angelica? Surely, it would tear the sisters apart. And what would Eliza think of Peggy if she knew Peggy had suspected the ardor and not told her? What would Angelica feel about her if she tattled her suspicions to Eliza?

Peggy stood in a horrific no-man's-land between them.

A fury filled Peggy. How dare these men endanger their trio's sacrosanct relationship and sully the happiness of her sisters? "The man is patronizing, Eliza," she blurted out. "You are too good for him, I swear. Shame on Hamilton for making you feel less than you are!"

Eliza pulled back abruptly from Peggy. "Take that back."

"What?" Peggy was flummoxed.

"Never say shame on Alexander. Ever." Trembling, Eliza stood up. "He is the most noble of hearts. He is destined for greatness. Martha Washington told me that His Excellency is determined to keep Alexander alive because he will know how to design a new democracy for us when the war is over. We must all safeguard him now."

Peggy reached for Eliza's hand, but her sister clasped hers behind her back. "He was shamed enough in his childhood. Did you know that in Saint Croix he was refused entry to school because he was illegitimate? Everything he knows he taught himself, by reading. Take it back."

"Eliza!" Peggy felt hot, defensive tears stinging her own face. "I only speak out of love for you. Your husband should never make you feel badly about yourself. You especially— you are so beyond reproach."

But Eliza only shook her head. "Take it back," she whispered.

Peggy stared at her sister. She saw their future and it about broke her heart. The Schuyler sisters—like jigsaw pieces that made no sense alone, lacking context, connection, but when linked together depicted all, supported all—would never be the same. There would be truths Peggy could not utter because they challenged Eliza's perceptions of the man she loved and might drive a wedge between Peggy and her.

Peggy swallowed. "I take it back."

Eliza flung herself at Peggy to hug her, squeezing hard. Holding on to each other, they rocked. Just as they had as children when one fell down or had a fright and the other comforted.

Was that to be Peggy's role with her sisters now? To watch in sorrow as they were hurt and then tend the wound? Or was the challenge to watch carefully and intercede when she could tell her sisters were ready to hear uncomfortable truths? Would she not be able to prevent the pain from happening in the first place?

Everything had become so complicated. The only thing she knew for sure was that she must love and stand steadfast on their flank no matter what.

Eliza wiped a tear away.

Well, there was one truth Peggy could share with Eliza that might ease her distress. "You know, Eliza, in Hartford, Hamilton could not stop talking to me about how exquisite your soul is." Peggy left off his complaints that Eliza did not write him enough or passionately enough. "He was quite distressed that you might receive suitors in his absence."

"Really?"

"Yes." Peggy kissed her sister's hand again. "Doesn't he fill his letters with such concerns?"

Eliza smiled. "Yes." She blushed. "And many other things that are . . ." She broke off her words and rolled her eyes with a giggle. "You know."

No, Peggy didn't. She had no letters from Fleury. But she had felt the flush of "you know" in his kiss. What did his silence mean?

"Tell me a good book to read before Alexander gets here for the wedding," Eliza asked, brightened considerably in mood even as Peggy grew disheartened. "Something that will interest him if I discuss it."

"What are you reading right now?"

Eliza wrinkled up her nose with playful embarrassment.

Peggy so loved this humorous side of her sister. "What?" she asked.

Eliza shrugged and covered her face with her hands, then opened them like a window to whisper, "*Pamela.*" Then she covered her face again. "I know you hate it."

That tripe again? Eliza must have it memorized by now. But Peggy burst out laughing with affection. "Come on." She took Eliza's hands. "Let's to father's library."

"But there's only war histories and treatises on geometry and algebra."

"Oh, there's so much more! Whole worlds await in his books," Peggy reassured her. "Worlds you will delight in, get lost in, learn in, cry in. Worlds for your *own* enjoyment, your *own* edification that you can then share with your husband as a common joy, a mutual adventure. You just have to know where to look. Hidden among all those philosophies and biographies Papa also has things like Voltaire's poetry, including . . ." She pulled Eliza to her feet and added mischievously, "His rather shocking one about Joan d'Arc."

"But it's in French," Eliza protested.

"That, my dearest sister, I will happily read aloud and translate for you."

A few days later another Hamilton letter came for Eliza.

"Any other letters, sir?" Peggy hopefully asked the mail rider.

"No, miss," he answered as he tucked into his satchel the letters she handed him from her father for headquarters. "Good day, miss." He tugged the brim of his hat before trotting his horse away down the hill.

Trying to hide her disappointment at still not having a single word from Fleury, Peggy flopped down next to Eliza and asked her to share her letter.

Eliza looked at her with surprise and a blush.

"Not everything, silly. Just the news."

"Well." Eliza skimmed a bit and said, "Alexander describes the trial and hanging of General Arnold's British contact, Major André. How sad it made him because the major was so noble and poetical." Eliza read on, frowned, and then murmured to herself, "Oh dear. You should not disparage General Washington's decisions, my love."

Peggy's eyebrow shot up, impressed at Eliza's recognition. She had a large task ahead of her, safeguarding Hamilton from his more hotheaded opinions.

Eliza continued. *"I wished myself possessed of André's accomplishments for your sake; for I would wish to charm you in every sense."*

"There, you see, my dear," Peggy interrupted. "You

really must stop worrying about how much he loves you."

Smiling shyly, Eliza nodded. "He says that in my eyes he *'should wish to be the first the most amiable the most accomplished of my sex; but I will make up all I want in—'*"

Eliza stopped abruptly, read the next bit silently, and turned red. Then she exclaimed, "Oh, Peggy! This next paragraph is about you: *'How is your little sister? Is she as sprightly as ever? Does she set so much value upon a certain kiss as she seemed to do when we entered the carriage at Hartford?'*"

"A kiss?" Eliza gasped. "What kiss? Did Fleury kiss you?" She giggled. "Have you . . . Have you come to an agreement and you haven't told me, little sister? What is he like? I only know that he is terribly handsome and quite the hero. Oh, how lovely to have a Frenchman as a brother-in-law!"

Peggy stood, her face burning, her heart hurting. "I haven't heard a word from him. I don't want to talk about it." And she fled the house for the garden to kick as many pebbles as possible.

SEVENTEEN

Early Winter

Alexander Hamilton to Eliza Schuyler
Preakness, New Jersey, October 27, 1780

How happy am I to think that one month more puts an end to our long separation; shall I find you my Dear girl as impatient to receive me as I shall be to fly to your bosom? . . . With transport will my heart answer to the question, will you take this woman to be thy wedded wife?

Prepare my charming bride to crown your lover with every thing that is tender, kind, passionate and endearing in your sex. He will bring you a heart fraught with all a fond woman can wish. . . .

God bless you My Darling girl. Mention me affectionately to your Mother and to Peggy. Tell all the family I love them, and assure yourself that my affection for you is inviolable.

A Hamilton

"LET US PRAY FOR SNOW ON YOUR WEDDING DAY," said Catharine, watching their servant Moll pin a sky-blue band along the hem of Eliza's white brocade gown. Eliza was a mass of pins. She wanted the more luxurious flounces removed so her gown better matched the austerity of the Continental Army uniform Hamilton would wear in the ceremony. Her mother had protested but Eliza, in an unusual display of stubbornness, had persisted.

"Oh, Mama, let us not hope for snow," said Peggy. "We had so much last year, I almost wish to never see another flake ever again." She was curled up in the window seat of their bedroom with Cornelia, working through the alphabet with her, but mostly trying to stay out of Catharine's wake. Seven months pregnant, their mother already cut a wide, uncomfortable berth. She moved slowly and painfully and in fretful spurts, her feet and legs badly swollen.

"But snow on a wedding day portends fertility and wealth," said Catharine. No matter how anglicized she and their papa had become in the way they decorated their mansion, dressed themselves, or entertained, Catharine's Dutch heritage slipped out in superstitions. The blue ribbon on Eliza's dress was part of that—it symbolized purity.

"What does fer-fertootully mean?" asked Cornelia, looking up at Peggy. She was about to turn five years old and had become obsessed with whatever her big sisters were doing or saying and the meaning of each and every word uttered around her.

"It means that Mama hopes Eliza is blessed with many

lovely plums like those in our orchard!" Peggy pinched her little sister's nose affectionately.

Grateful for the metaphor, Catharine carried it through to literal plums. "Isn't it a wonderment that there are still some for the wedding party? Your papa is so proud of them." She lowered herself into a chair, rubbing her stomach and sighing heavily. It was midmorning and she still wore her dressing gown, the biggest sign of how physically exhausted their mother was. Peggy earnestly hoped this would be Catharine's last pregnancy. Her body was not as strong as it had been. Carrying a child was taxing for even the healthy and young, plus giving birth, even for a veteran mother, carried so many dangers. Peggy wasn't sure that her papa would survive if Catharine died. His voice still carried honey when he addressed her as "my beloved Kitty."

Despite her physical fatigue, Catharine was clearly delighting in the hubbub of wedding preparations. Eliza had confided to Peggy she'd considered running off to marry Hamilton wherever he was—it was taking so long for him to arrange leave from Washington's staff to make the trip to Albany for their wedding. Thank goodness she had changed her mind—Catharine would have been crushed. And she never would have forgiven Peggy for helping another sister abscond.

Merrily, Catharine chatted on, "The feast will be grand. We will butcher a hog. We will have eel for stew. My only real worry is getting my hands on enough brown sugar for my family's traditional wedding cake. I have hoarded some, as have your grandparents, but pulling together a full two pounds' worth may be challenging."

"Mama, you mustn't use up all the family's sugar on a cake for me," said Eliza.

"Nonsense, my dear! This is your wedding day. It must be celebrated properly and with joy. Consider half the sugar as having belonged to Angelica. Since she chose to forgo a proper wedding and her devoted parents witnessing it, her amount of sugar rightly goes to you." Catharine stiffened, clearly kicked by the baby, and muttered, "I cannot believe Angelica is not coming for your nuptials or for Christmas. Surely that husband of hers can manage without her for a few weeks."

"But what about Peggy?" asked Eliza, ignoring the dig at Angelica. Peggy made her eyes huge and shook her head violently, anticipating what her middle sister would say next. But it was too late, as Eliza added in singsong voice: "You will need to save some sugar for her."

"Oh?" Catharine sat up, smiling broadly. "Is there something I should know?"

"No, there isn't!" Peggy's voice was sharp, despite Eliza smiling at her so hopefully. The hurt of not hearing from Fleury was festering into a gaping wound. Eliza had just rubbed salt into it.

"You will need to curb that tongue of yours, child, to catch a husband," Catharine chastised. "And stop talking politics so much. Men wish to discuss that sort of thing with other men, not women. Such a pity you do not possess your sisters' singing voice."

Peggy glowered at Eliza.

Silently mouthing "I'm so sorry" at Peggy, Eliza tried to repair the damage she'd done. "But Mama, Colonel Hamilton tells me that many officers were quite taken by our Peggy's eloquence and her charming wit and especially her command of . . . French." Eliza emphasized the word *French* as if it were *Frenchman*, smiling at Peggy in her gentle way of teasing.

"*Hmpf.* She does have that. Like her papa. Well, let us hope by the time our Peggy is to be wed, the war is over and trade flourishing again. Surely with Rochambeau's arrival the French and Patriots can end the war by summer."

Peggy bit her lip from responding to her mother's criticisms of her and her lack of understanding that the disasters which had decimated the Continental Army in the South during the summer would most likely keep any spring campaigns to simply being desperate fights to regain a toehold in those states. She stared out the window. Peggy knew she should be accustomed to it by now, but she still brushed away a tear of disappointment at her mother's favoritism for Eliza. She no longer blamed her middle sister for her extra portion of motherly love. Eliza's gentle spirit deserved all the affection she received. But didn't Peggy's loyalty to the family and hard work earn her the same, or at least something equal even if different?

Because she was focusing her gaze to the river, endeavoring to ignore her mother, Peggy heard the sentinel's muffled cry: "Riders to the house!"

She hugged Cornelia and pointed. "See the men coming. What pretty horses!" She watched the riders, recognizing the navy capes, the dark-blue-and-buff uniforms. After a few moments she could make out faces. "Ooooohh, E-li-za," she sang. "Guess who?"

Eliza turned white, then pink, and then darted to the bedroom door, knocking over poor Moll in her haste.

"Oh no you don't!" Catharine hoisted herself up and barred Eliza. "The groom cannot see the bride in her wedding dress before the ceremony."

Eliza looked like she would burst into tears.

"Oh, Mama," Peggy said, "tradition be damned. Poor Eliza hasn't seen Hamilton for months!"

That was a mistake.

Catharine drew herself up to an austere regalness that would shame England's crowned queen. "We will discuss your language later, Margarita. But for now, I need to dress to meet my new son-in-law. Eliza, you—no, you must do as I say." Catharine reached out to take hold of Eliza, who was hopping up and down, desperate to make for the door. "You must put on a different dress. You must. Wear that lovely salmon-colored frock."

Catharine turned to Peggy. "Your papa is in town ordering blankets to be made for the Oneida since they lost everything they had in those raids. Congress, of course, will do nothing for them. He is paying for them himself." She shook her head and muttered something under her breath. "He will not be back for hours. So, you must greet the colonel. With your best manners, mind you. Take Cornelia with you."

Orders issued, Catharine swept from the room. Dutifully, Peggy took Cornelia's hand. Eliza helped Moll up from the floor, begging her pardon and her help in stripping her dress off as quickly as possible! As she headed for the stairs, Peggy could hear Eliza squeal as pins pricked her in her scramble.

Hamilton stood in their wide front hall, hat in hand. Planted on the wall-to-wall floor cloth—painted in large midnight blue and white checks to resemble the grandest of European marble floors—the slender, graceful man looked almost like a statue one would find in a chateau. Motionless, he gazed upward. His eyes wandered over the vaulted ceiling, its richly carved dentil molding, the crystal chandelier, and then down to the elegant wallpaper of hand-painted scenes of Roman ruins that Schuyler had brought back from England. His mouth was hanging slightly open.

For the first time in her life, Peggy felt slightly ashamed of her wealth. Clearly Hamilton had never seen the likes of her family's mansion before. When she called to him and he turned, she spotted fear in those exquisite violet-blue eyes. No greed, no self-satisfaction or sense of new ownership. Rather, a self-conscious intimidation. He masked it quickly, of course. But Peggy had seen it—pitied it—and she promised herself to remember it in the future when Hamilton aggravated her. She was learning his swagger might be more defensive bluster than actual arrogance.

Out of this kindness for her soon-to-be brother, Peggy ignored the comment of his companion, James McHenry, who whispered before they realized she was nearby, "Well, Hammie, you've got it made now." She was really coming to detest the man.

What a shame McHenry had to be the one to stand by her sister's groom. But Peggy knew Harrison was in Virginia because his father had died, Meade was getting married himself, and Lafayette was in Philadelphia meeting with Congress. Tilghman had to remain at headquarters with Washington—how that poor fellow must be drowning in papers as the sole aide-de-camp dealing with the work typically handled by five or six men.

Hamilton's eyes drifted hopefully behind Peggy, trying not to show disappointment that it was she rather than Eliza before him.

"She's coming," said Peggy, approaching the men to curtsy, with Cornelia, suddenly shy, hiding behind her.

Hamilton kissed Peggy and then dropped to his knee. "Is this sister Cornelia?" he asked solemnly.

Cornelia peeped out from behind Peggy's wide skirt to nod.

"I hope we are to become the best of friends," he said.

"Do you know how to get the ball into a Bilbo catcher?"

He smiled. "No. But would you show me?"

The little girl nodded and darted away to retrieve the toy.

While he was still kneeling, Eliza appeared at the top of the landing, she and her rose-tinted gown bathed in sunshine from its window. Their father had so loved his voyage to England that he had ordered the molding on the stair boards be carved to look like waves, the balusters twisted to resemble ship cables. Schuyler couldn't have designed a prettier descending stage for his daughter to sail down to embrace her lover, who staggered to his feet, dumbstruck.

Even McHenry sighed.

A week later, on December 14, Eliza and Hamilton pledged their love to each other in the Schuylers' best parlor. Papered in deep blue and papier-mâché medallions gracing its ceiling, the large room glowed with the hearth's fire, candlelight, and the irrepressible smiles of the groom and his bride. All Eliza's family, save Angelica, stood witness for her, including Aunt Gitty and a beaming Dr. Cochran, who proudly claimed total responsibility for the match. Even the boys stood rapt and quiet as Hamilton slipped onto Eliza's finger a wedding band of two interlocking rings, one engraved with her name, the other with his.

Missing was Richard Varick. The military court had recently cleared him of any guilt regarding Benedict Arnold's treason, and the loyal Dutchman had returned to his home in New Jersey. But what kept Varick from traveling to Albany for the nuptials was the fact he had joined his local militia. Determined to still serve, even though now a low-level foot soldier, he was standing watch every other night. Schuyler explained this to Cochran, who'd asked where Varick was.

"But he sends his best wishes to the lucky groom and his

bride," Schuyler said, smiling with pride at Eliza and then at Peggy, adding, "And he hoped that Miss Peggy's health was excellent."

Catharine perked up. "Now there's a worthy gentleman who would make a girl a good husband! Take good aim when you throw the stocking tonight, my dear." Catharine referred to the tradition of bridesmaids throwing balled-up stockings over their shoulders at the bride. Whoever it hit would be the next to marry.

Rolling her eyes, Peggy took a bite of the wedding cake, refusing to respond.

Catharine had indeed managed to find all its ingredients. The scent of molasses, lemon peel, almonds, raisins, currants, brandy, rum, butter, and a king's ransom worth of sugar drifting from the outside kitchen for the six hours it baked had set everyone's mouths to watering. It had been months since any of them had tasted anything sweet. John, Jeremiah, and Rensselaer had already gobbled up two pieces each.

"Oh, Kitty, don't you know?" tittered Aunt Gitty. "The child's—"

Cochran had been watching Peggy and spoke quickly to interrupt. "Kitty, this is the best cake I have ever tasted. I could use it to revive dying men on the battlefield, I could. Don't you think, my dear?"

"Why yes, husband," Gitty answered, a bit puzzled, and then started to begin again, "The child's . . ."

"The child is no child, Gitty, and she is sitting right here," Cochran said, shaking his head slightly.

How Peggy adored her uncle!

"Indeed the lady," Hamilton chimed in, "has no shortage of suitors, Mrs. Schuyler. Or may I now presume to call you Mother?" His smile was captivating.

Catharine melted and completely forgot what her sister-in-law had been saying.

Peggy would need to thank Hamilton later for that.

As Catharine and he talked, Cochran motioned for Peggy to sit by him on the settee. He took her hand and leaned in. "I know all about your Frenchie, Meaghan-fay-Meaghan. Don't be misunderstanding me. Thank the Lord for the French. They are good allies. Lafayette is the noblest of men. I would take a musket ball for him. Almost did."

Peggy started to protest, but he waved her off. "Your Fleury is a brave man. The lads at Fort Mifflin most like would have been slaughtered without his determined refortifying, night after night, as the British tried to blast them to hell. There's not a man more admirable on the battlefield. But these French noblemen all committed to *liberté* and *égalité*?" Cochran snorted. "That's a bit of a hornet's nest for them once they go back to their country of aristocrats and king, don't you think?" He tilted her chin up so he could look into her eyes as he ended, "You wouldn't want to be living in France now, would you?"

Actually, the idea of traveling to France sounded rather exciting to Peggy! But before she could say so, everyone in the room broke into laughter. McHenry had staggered toward Eliza, his Madeira glass drained, semi-falling to her

292

feet to try to grab her shoe. It was an old wedding game—a way for groomsmen to ransom a bride's slipper back to her in exchange for a kiss—but Eliza was far too modest a woman to enjoy such frivolity.

Peggy was about to tell McHenry to stop being an idiot when Eliza stood and gracefully stepped aside. "Peggy, dearest," she said, "would you mind going upstairs to bring my present for"—she paused and smiled happily—"my husband."

Already, Eliza was different.

Upstairs, Peggy easily found Eliza's wedding present for Hamilton. She had embroidered a gorgeous linen mat to frame a miniature oval watercolor portrait of him. In rainbow-colored-silk threads, she used all manner of crewel stitches—stem, chain, split, satin, French knots—to create fleur-de-lis corners and twines of blossoms, even tiny butterflies. Flawlessly sewn, the delicate art was a visual symbol of how Eliza planned to focus her life and talents on pointing out Hamilton's best attributes.

As Peggy picked up the crewelwork, a letter dropped to the floor from underneath it—another of Hamilton's ardent notes. Peggy reached down to retrieve it and tuck it back into Eliza's carefully ribboned batch, without reading. She was well past snooping into her sisters' love letters but her eye fell onto her own name—*my Peggy.*

Tell my Peggy I will shortly open a correspondence with her. I am composing a piece, of which, from the opinion I have of her qualifications, I shall endeavour to prevail upon her to act the principal character. The title is "The way to get him, for the benefit of all single ladies who desire to be married." You will ask her if she has any objections to taking part in the piece and tell her that if I am not much mistaken in her, I am sure she will have none.

A play about "the way to get him"? Peggy felt her face turn red. "From the opinion I have of her qualifications"—what did Hamilton mean by that? What was he insinuating? Did he think her an artful actress, her feelings feigned? Or that she was . . . she was . . . actresses were considered nothing short of whores by many people. . . . Did Hamilton think, oh God . . . Peggy softened the words she might have used . . . too openly ardent? Despite his compliments in Hartford?

Then worse thoughts: Had Fleury shared an opinion . . . something indiscreet to Hamilton? Did Fleury think these things?

Hands shaking with confusion and embarrassment, Peggy read the next line, to find it directed at Eliza: *For your own part, your business is now to study the way to keep him, which is said to be much the most difficult task of the two . . .*

She felt herself almost growling. There he was again, making Eliza feel like she had to earn his continued interest. But the next lines at least reassured Peggy for her sister's sake: *though in your case I thoroughly believe it will be an easy one . . .*

Did he say anything else about Peggy? Quickly, she skimmed more.

'Tis a pretty story indeed that I am to be thus monopolized, by a little <u>nut-brown maid</u> like you . . . A spirit entering into bliss, heaven opening upon all its faculties, cannot long more ardently for

the enjoyment, than I do my darling Betsey, to taste the heaven that awaits me in your bosom. Is my language too strong? It is a feeble picture of my feelings—no words can tell you how much I love and how much I long—you will only know it when wrapt in each others arms we give and take those delicious caresses which love inspires and marriage sanctifies.

Oh my! Peggy quickly folded the letter up and read no further. No, there was nothing more in that letter that she should read!

But a play? A lesson book for "getting a man"? *Wat de hel?* Dutch curses aplenty jumped into her head as she hurried to the stairs with Eliza's crewelwork.

As she descended, Peggy resolved to pull Hamilton aside to ask him about his meaning. But Eliza's exquisite gift and the beautiful inlaid workbox Hamilton presented her inspired too much praise among the family for Peggy to catch his attention. Before she knew it, the evening was over. Hamilton had retired to the back bedroom with Eliza. The new couple had climbed the ocean of those stairs together, his holding her hand and smiling a gentle, warm reassurance akin to the one Eliza had blessed him with as she coaxed him into a minuet. The look he gave her sister had taken Peggy's breath.

That night, Peggy felt very alone until little Cornelia clambered out of her trundle bed and asked to crawl into Peggy's large canopy one—the one in which she and Eliza and Angelica had giggled and read and cried and shared their dreams as an inseparable trio, and now never would again.

"It's snowing," Cornelia whispered as she nestled against Peggy and fell asleep.

For days, a wondrous happiness of new love permeated the Schuyler mansion. McHenry even wrote a poem that had a few moments of inappropriate innuendo, as Peggy would expect of him, but ended with a pretty hope:

Now genius plays the lovers part;
Now wakes to many a throb the heart;
With ev'ry sun brings something new,
And gaily varies every view . . .
All these attendants Ham are thine.
Be't yours to treat them as divine;
To cherish what keeps love alive;
What makes us young at sixty-five.

Maybe the Irish aide-de-camp wasn't such a jackass after all, thought Peggy. She followed his lead in terms of showing deference for the dreamy haze that hung over her sister and forced herself to wait to question Hamilton about the meaning of his note. But as Christmas approached and mail riders came and left, bearing wedding messages from Washington and Lafayette but no letter from Fleury, Peggy began to grow desperate.

It was as if she had imagined all their encounters—that Fleury was purely a figment of her dreams, or a ghost.

Finally, one early morning before others were awake,

Peggy found Hamilton in the family's yellow parlor, writing letters to headquarters. He would return there after New Year's. "Colonel!" She rushed into the room.

He looked up, surprised. "Alexander," he corrected her.

But she didn't return her brother-in-law's pleasantries. She didn't think about what consequence there might be to Eliza by revealing to her new husband that Peggy had read one of his love letters—even though Eliza had not knowingly shared it. "I need to ask you, sir, why you think I am appropriate to act a drama designed to teach women how to 'get' a man." She crossed her arms and glared.

He looked at her blankly.

She was about to repeat herself when Prince materialized. "Excuse me, Miss Peggy. We have a message that a group of French officers will make the ferry across the Hudson this morning. Want me to send your father's sleigh to the wharf to retrieve them?"

Peggy gasped. "French officers, you say?"

"Yes, ma'am."

Oh, it must be. Finally! Fleury had come!

Peggy felt like she could fly. "Oh, yes, Prince! Harness the horses, but please tell Lisbon to wait for me. I am going to ride to the wharf with him!" Realizing her voice was way too giddy, she made herself sound like a lady of the manor. "One of us needs to greet them properly."

"Yes, ma'am." Prince nodded as he excused himself.

Peggy hoisted her skirts and ran to the door to fetch her cloak and muff.

"Peggy!" Hamilton called after her.

But she was already to the bottom of the stairs.

"Peggy, wait!" he cried.

She ran up the steps two at a time.

"Peggy!" He climbed after her.

She darted into her bedroom. Hamilton dashed into his, where Eliza still slumbered. He reemerged in time to block his new sister as she skipped to the stairs—flustered, ecstatic, wrapped in fur and hope. "Peggy, stop." Hamilton held a letter in his hand.

"Oh, I don't care about that anymore, Alexander! Fleury is here!" she exulted.

She kissed him on the cheek and made for the steps.

But he caught her arm. "I doubt it. You don't want to rush down to the wharf."

She tried to yank her arm away, but he held fast. "I need to tell you something."

"What?" She laughed. "That you are a secret playwright? It doesn't matter."

"Peggy, I'm not sure what you are talking about. But I need to tell you something."

His expression stopped her. He led her to a chair and made her sit in front of a wallpaper medallion of a wrecked temple. Peggy felt her heart sink. "What is it?" she whispered anxiously.

"I need you to hear something that Fleury sent me." Hamilton knelt and took her hand. "He wrote to me of politics mostly and then he . . ."

Peggy snatched away the letter to read for herself:

Mrs. Carter told me you was soon to be married to her sister, Miss betsy Schuyler. I congratulate you heartyly on that conquest; for many Reasons: the first that you will get all that familly's interest, & that a man of your abilities wants a Little influence to do good to his country. The second that you, will be in a very easy situation, & happin's is not to be found without a Large estate. The third (this one is not very Certain) that we shall be or connect'd or neighbors. For you most know, that I am an admirer of Miss Pegguy, your sister in Law; & that if she will not have me; Mr. Duane may be cox'd into the measure of giving me his daughter; this Litle jest is between you & I. It woud be very improper for anybody else.

Peggy looked up, ashen, nauseated. "M–Mary Duane? Or Sarah? Adelia?" Their father, James Duane, was another New York delegate to Congress and a family friend. She knew his daughters—they were lovely creatures. "Fleury has courted one of the Duane girls?. . . As well as . . . as me?" Her hand flew to her mouth to stop herself from retching. The letter was dated late October, well past that good-bye kiss at Hartford. If he really loved her, how could he even consider a second choice?

Head swimming, Peggy was vaguely aware of what Hamilton was saying. "He is a valiant fighter, Peggy. Fleury is quick to act with courage and decisiveness—at every battle, every chance for heroism. He is the best of the professional soldier in this way. He responds with the same zeal to a chance for glory in civilian life as well, for"—he paused— "for conquest. But just as the heat of a skirmish well fought

299

subsides, so do perhaps his affections." Hamilton grimaced as Peggy shook her head, putting her hands over her ears.

Gently he took her hands so she could hear him. "I have also heard that Fleury may be already committed, my dear, to a cousin in France. Not that such an engagement could not be broken. And I do not doubt that you captured his heart, Peggy. I saw it myself. But I also see with what unshaking devotion you can love, with what passion of spirit. You remind me of . . ." He hesitated, and his voice lowered with a sense of tragedy. "You remind me of my mother, my beautiful, fiery mother. She adored my father. But he was shallow in his ardor. It evaporated like a puddle of water in a tropical sun, and he left her. Left her to raise my brother and me alone. Left us with the stigma of being illegitimate in the eyes of the law, bastards."

Gone was all Hamilton's usual posturing. His voice grew raspy. "My mother was much abused by the men in her life. When she dared to leave her first husband—to whom her own mother had essentially sold her into a loveless marriage when she was but sixteen years old—the brute convinced the Dutch court of Saint Croix to jail her for several months for disobedience and alleged promiscuity." He shook his head. "But she was not cowed by them. When they released her, my mother defiantly fled to another Caribbean island rather than return to her husband as ordered. She had a dreamer's heart and a soldier's bravery."

"Much like you." Hamilton squeezed Peggy's hands. "I say this with all brotherly love and admiration: you deserve, my Peggy, to have someone whose gaze is for nothing and no one but you."

Shakily, Peggy stood. She untied her cape. She forced a polite smile and murmured "thank you" before retreating to her room. She wished to let her heart break in private, although Peggy was sure the sound of its crack would rumble like an earthquake.

There was little time for her sorrow, however. By that evening Peggy was helping to play hostess for the four French officers who had arrived to visit—the chevaliers de Chastellux and de Mauduit, Comte de Damas, and the Vicomte de Noailles. Their army settled into its winter hiatus in Newport, the four Frenchmen had decided to spend a month touring the sites of the Revolution. They wished to meet the renowned General Schuyler, to learn of his Canadian expeditions, and to see the battlefield of Saratoga. Given their closeness with Rochambeau, Schuyler needed to fete them well to keep them happy and enthusiastic about the American cause.

So Peggy bubbled like the fermented cider she raised during their toasts. She danced with them as Noailles played the violin. She listened politely to Chastellux discuss his translation of *Romeo and Juliet* into French, in which he had added a happy ending. Far more satisfying that way, he declared. And far from the truth, thought Peggy, but she said nothing.

If Hamilton believed she was a gifted actress, Peggy proved it that night. She was polite, gracious, flattering—while completely dead inside. Until she heard McHenry respond to a comment made by one of the officers who wished Peggy would smile. "Surely then," the Frenchman said, "she would be as beautiful as Mrs. Carter."

Always Angelica, fumed Peggy. She slowed her walk as she passed behind them, to hear what the men said next.

McHenry clearly did not realize Peggy was within ear-shot. "Mrs. Carter is a fine woman indeed," he gushed. "She charms in all companies. No one has seen her, of either sex, who has not been pleased with her."

The French agreed.

"Peggy, though," he continued, "perhaps a finer woman, is not generally thought so. Her own sex are apprehensive that she considers them to be poor things, as Swift's Vanessa did. To be admired as she ought, Peggy needs to please the men less and the ladies more. I have told Hammie he must tell her so. If he does, her good sense will place her in her proper station."

McHenry took a sip of his cider and lowered his voice to finish. "I must tell you, though, you should not desire too many smiles from her. She wants better teeth to be as pretty as her sisters."

Peggy stopped in her tracks. Jonathan Swift's character of Vanessa was condemned and ostracized because of her wishing to discuss philosophy and matters of state with men. She was a kind of literary Diana or Athena, but without the respect granted those ancient mythological figures. And Peggy was supposed to smile at these men, no matter what she was feeling? And her teeth? Her hand shot to her mouth, humiliated. They were a tad crooked and she was indeed missing one or two, but that was how God or Nature had made her. There was nothing to be done—no ribbons, no curling irons, no corsets that could change their appearance.

Had McHenry said these things to Fleury? Had he lowered Fleury's opinion of her somehow with such gossip? Her soul seethed.

Perhaps the heat of her humiliation and fury radiated to them, because the men suddenly turned. The French blanched at seeing her. McHenry smirked.

Peggy lowered her hands from her mouth, balling them into fists by her side. If only she could challenge this jackass to a duel, to avenge her honor. Men could. Why couldn't she? Why did she—required by society's scriptures to be ladylike—have to passively accept such affronts?

But perhaps she didn't. Hamilton's admiration for his defiant mother came to her. And if the Revolution had taught Peggy anything, it was that there were all sorts of tyrannies that needed to be challenged and turned upside down. Carter's quip about the sword of her wit came to Peggy. She drew her weapon.

Taking a step forward, she fluttered her eyelashes as she had seen Angelica do a thousand times, to make what she said next a total surprise attack. She kept her voice silky. "You needn't worry about my ever smiling on you, Colonel McHenry. And I fear with such . . . *gallantry*"—that word she said with steely sarcasm—"few other women will, either. Indeed, Colonel, I worry for you that Swift's Vanessa would

303

consider any man 'a poor thing,' who seeks to entertain and garner the friendship of other men by gossiping and criticizing women. If you are to ever find happiness with a woman, Colonel, I suggest you follow your own advice: please the men less and the ladies more."

Peggy flipped open the feathered fan that hung at her wrist. Fluttering it back and forth, she curtsied to the Frenchmen, gracing each of them with a wry, *close-mouthed* smile.

Then she swept away, leaving them guffawing at McHenry for the rapier hit she had laid him. "*Touché!*" They could use her in battle, they said.

Indeed they could, she thought with a raised-eyebrow smile meant just for herself.

Interlude

THE FIRST LETTER FROM MRS. ELIZA HAMILTON

WITH A PS FROM HER NEW HUSBAND:

Elizabeth Hamilton to Margarita Schuyler
New Windsor, New York, January 21, 1781
Dear Margaret

*I am the happiest of Women. My dear Hamilton is fonder
of me every day. Get married I charge you. . . . There is no
possible felicity but in that state imagined me my Sister. I was
much in want of it. Adieu. Give my love to Papa and Mama
and our friends and the others. With every regard, Eliz Hamilton.*

*PS Because your sister has the talent of growing more
amiable every day, or because I am a fanatic in love . . . she
fancies herself the happiest woman in the world, and would
need persuade all her friends to embark with her in the mat-
rimonial voyage. But I pray you do not let her advice have
so much influence as to make you matrimony-mad. 'Tis a*

very good thing when their stars unite two people who are fit
for each other . . . But its a dog of life when two dissonant
tempers meet . . . Get a man of sense, not ugly enough to be
pointed at—with some good-nature—a few grains of feeling—
a little taste—a little imagination—and above all a good deal
of decision to keep you in order; for that I foresee will be no
easy task. If you can find one with all these qualities, willing
to marry you, marry him as soon as you please.

A. H.

LOOKING OUT THE WINDOW AT FEBRUARY WHITE-
ness, Peggy tapped the pane with a letter just arrived for her
from Eliza and Hamilton. So her brother-in-law was going
to revert to playfulness to give her advice. In her present
mood, she'd prefer his blunt sincerity. How could he expect
her to be lighthearted, given how her romance with Fleury
had vaporized? But certainly Hamilton's banter shielded her
from gossip if the letter fell into enemy's hands along the
mail route. And Peggy could decipher the code in his PS and
the cloaked empathy he was trying to send her. It made her
smile—one of the first to grace her lips in weeks. Perhaps
that had been his aim.

Since he and Eliza left for headquarters—at New
Windsor on the Hudson River, ten miles north of West
Point—Peggy had sunk into sadness and retreated to her
room. Even though she had read Fleury's letter to Hamilton

only once, and that in a flash fire of anguish and shock, his words were seared into her memory. In the heat of that awful conference with Hamilton, she'd focused on the fact the man she had fallen in love with seemed just as content to wed a Duane daughter as he would be her. In her second blaze of grief, though, alone in her room, she'd remembered Fleury's congratulating Hamilton for marrying into the Schuyler family's interest and influence. It would help him *do good in his country.* And then there was Fleury's calculating pronouncement that *happiness is not to be found without a large estate.*

Peggy had been an afterthought all her life. Meet the Schuyler sisters: the scintillating, enrapturing Angelica, the saintly sweet Eliza. Oh, and Peggy, their little sister. Was she also only to be an appendage of her father's, her attractiveness to potential suitors defined by what her papa's wealth and sphere of influence could bring her eventual husband? Clearly, if she were honest about it, such benefits must have occurred to both her brothers-in-law.

No, Peggy certainly would not be "matrimony-mad," as Hamilton put it!

Peggy had laughed outright at his warning her to avoid a man ugly enough to be pointed at! She wondered if Hamilton had written the humor into that line purposefully, suspecting she needed a good giggle.

Several things were quite obvious in the letter, however. Given their messages, both Hamilton and Eliza were happy together. Perhaps now Eliza could shed her worries that she might prove inadequate for the intensity of her new husband's intellectual prowess and poetic passion. Peggy could also tell that Hamilton had not shared with Eliza what he knew about Fleury, or how he had saved Peggy from humiliating herself by rushing to the wharf to meet a lover who had not come. She was grateful for his discretion—especially with her papa.

Schuyler was so busy right now, the last thing he needed was to hear that one of his daughters had been jilted. And by a Frenchman. As much as he loved the language, her papa couldn't quite shed a distrust of the onetime enemy he'd fought in the French and Indian War. And surely he might think less of Peggy if he knew she had thrown herself—literally—at one of them.

Right now Schuyler was serving in the New York legislature and trying to quell a mutiny by troops guarding Albany. The soldiers were threatening to march to Washington's headquarters to demand back pay, which would leave the city naked to attack. Schuyler was extending his own credit to raise subscriptions of grain, meat, flour, and wages to pacify the soldiers.

Congress was also ignoring his plea for clothing and food for the Oneidas and Tuscaroras. He had been horrified when the Iroquois delegates told him of their living conditions. Appealing to Congress's sense of humanity hadn't worked, so Schuyler tried explaining that starving and freezing might drive their loyal Iroquois allies to join the enemy. He was still waiting impatiently for their response. If Congress offered no help, he would somehow have to find funds to supply the Oneidas and Tuscaroras as well as Albany's soldiers.

Peggy worried her papa was working himself into the gout that was crippling him that winter. He was also tense and anxious about Catharine, who was bedridden, due to give birth any minute.

Peggy reread Hamilton's PS one last time. It would require *a good deal of decision to keep you in order; for that I foresee will be no easy task.* There were two ways to read that sentence. First, that Hamilton disapproved of her high spirits. She knew that was false. The second was that he was teasing, in that slightly flirty way of his, to prod her out of her melancholy. To remind her of her pluck.

Peggy chose the second interpretation, knowing that while many damned her tendency to speak her mind as being unattractive or intimidating—that cad McHenry, for instance—Hamilton applauded it. Peggy felt a hint of spring, a reblooming of her rebellious nature.

Hamilton was encouraging her to move on. To not let the world know of her broken heart. That way the fissure line in her steel could be reforged in a way any future opponents would not know where to find the weak point.

Keep her in order? Ha! This was the Revolution.

Peggy folded the letter, kissed it, and tucked it in a drawer. She had been acting like one of those foolish females in *Pamela*. Enough of moping about in her room.

Peggy marched herself downstairs to see how she could help her papa. For right now, her focus would be on the Patriot cause. She was lucky. History was being made all around her, and her papa's study was a hotbed of Revolutionary stratagem and news.

★ PART THREE ★
1781

To guard against Assassination (which I neither expect, nor dread) is impossible—but I have not been without my apprehensions of the other attempt—Not from the enemy at New York—but the Tories & disaffected of this place; who might, in the Night, carry me off in my own Boat and all be ignorant of it till the Morning.

—General George Washington

EIGHTEEN

✸

Winter

Alexander Hamilton to Philip Schuyler
Head Quarters New Windsor, New York, Feby 18, 81
My Dear Sir,

*An unexpected change has taken place in my situation. I am
no longer a member of the General's family. . . .Two day ago
The General and I passed each other on the stairs. He told me
he wanted to speak to me. I answered that I would wait upon
him immediately. I went below and delivered Mr. Tilghman a
letter . . . Returning to The General I was stopped in the way
by the Marquis De la Fayette, and we conversed . . . I met
[the General] at the head of the stairs, where accosting me in a
very angry tone, "Col Hamilton (said he), you have kept me
waiting at the head of the stairs these ten minutes. I must tell
you Sir you treat me with disrespect." I replied without petu-
lancy, but with decision "I am not conscious of it Sir, but since
you have thought it necessary to tell me so we part." "Very
well Sir (said he) if it be your choice" or something to this*

effect and we separated. . . . Thus we stand. . . .
Very sincerely & Affectionately I am Dr Sir Yr. most Obed
A Hamilton

PEGGY FOUND HER FATHER IN HIS STUDY, LEANING
over a snowdrift of papers, his elbows on the desk, bracing
his forehead in his hands. He must be exhausted, she thought.
He had paced the house for hours and hours as Catharine
struggled to give birth to their latest infant. He should be
relieved now—the baby girl was healthy and beautiful and
his beloved Kitty remarkably well.

Her mama was so well, in fact, that she was already
thinking about the christening. She had sent Peggy downstairs to ask Schuyler to write the Washingtons with their
good news. His Excellency and Lady Washington had graciously agreed to stand as godparents to the baby. Peggy
knew her mother was being overly optimistic. General
Washington had not taken a day of leave from his duties
for almost six years since becoming the commander of the
Continental Army in 1775. But perhaps Martha could make
the trip for the baptism.

"Papa." Peggy put her hand on his shoulder. "You should
rest. All is well."

But Schuyler dropped his hands and looked up at her
with distress on his face.

"What is it?" she asked, alarmed. "Not more mutinies?"

Just as her papa had been dealing with Albany troops muti-
nying, General Washington had had to quell an insurrection

314

by the Pennsylvania Line. Those Continentals had actually marched to Philadelphia, muskets ready, to demand Congress pay them what they were owed. Because of his spy network, Schuyler was able to warn Washington that the British were making overtures to the mutineers—promising the Pennsylvanians that the king had money, clothes, and food aplenty to give them. Some of their officers considered playing Benedict Arnold as a result.

Hearing that, Washington had quickly mustered six hundred New Jersey troops out of West Point and rushed to face down their Pennsylvania comrades. It was a disastrous time for the exhausted and ill-fed army to be so dangerously challenged. The general's horse had been so starved it could hardly stand and nearly dumped him down a cliff.

After a tense standoff, seeing their fellow Continentals convinced the Pennsylvanians to peacefully rejoin their ranks. But Washington had had to hang their most radical ringleaders. The events left the army intact, but resentful and suspicious.

"No, no more mutinies, thank God," Schuyler answered. "Not yet anyway." His eyes were sunken with fatigue and dark circles.

"Has Albany's Commissioners for Detecting and Defeating Conspiracies uncovered another plot?" Peggy's father had spent the last week interrogating Tories suspected of colluding with the British stationed in Canada—although what exactly they were up to eluded Schuyler so far. He had been scouring intercepted letters, trying to figure it out.

"No," he said flatly. He handed Peggy a letter. "Hamilton has fought with His Excellency and resigned."

"What?" She gasped.

"See for yourself."

Peggy quickly skimmed Hamilton's account of his break with Washington. She looked up to her father, whose eyebrow shot up, echoing her disapproval of what felt like a temper tantrum on Hamilton's part.

Was her brother-in-law really that thin-skinned?

Hamilton's letter went on to say that when the general sought to apologize for his impatience, he'd rejected meeting with the commander in chief. What insubordination! This was George Washington—the man upon whom the fledgling nation pinned all its hopes and needs. A man holding his army together even though beset on all sides by the plight of starving and ill-equipped soldiers, Tories seeking to ambush or kidnap him, superior enemies, infighting officers constantly wrangling for higher rank, and a thousand men deserting him.

In the midst of all that, Hamilton quit? Simply because the great man snapped at him?

Frowning, Peggy waded on through the long letter—Hamilton's obvious worry was that he'd displease his new father-in-law. He argued in his own defense that he had never wanted to be an aide-de-camp, as it made him too dependent on the man he served. He had only agreed to it, dismissing his *scruples* because he was *infected with the enthusiasm of the times* and an *unfounded* idea of the general's character. Peggy paused. Washington's stalwart and inspiring reputation "unfounded"? She shook her head as she read Hamilton's next line: *It was not long before I discovered he was neither remarkable for delicacy nor good temper.*

"Oh, Alexander," she breathed. "You sound like such a child."

Schuyler nodded. His tone shifted from disappointment to anger as he asked, "Have you reached the part where he claims he has felt no friendship for the general and has never professed any, even when the general has? That his 'pride of temper' would not suffer him to profess what he did not feel?"

"What? His Excellency has been so good to Hamilton!"

"I know!" he growled. "So many Patriots would do anything to be part of Washington's family, to be the recipient of the great man's esteem and friendship." He thought a moment. "Sometimes a man must take a less lauded position to serve a cause he believes in."

Peggy looked up from the letter to assess her father, who had again and again sublimated his own celebrity to aid the American fight for liberty. His expression was a mixture of fury and concern. Clearly, her papa was worrying that his second son-in-law, in whom he had placed such high hopes, might also turn out to be disappointment. At the very least, Hamilton had revealed himself to be mercurial and quick to take offense, rash in his actions and unyielding in his opinion. Not exactly the most steadfast or safe of husbands for their precious Eliza.

Frankly, Peggy felt the same alarm for Eliza. And yet, Hamilton had saved Peggy from humiliating herself by telling her the truth of Fleury. She owed him the same help now with his new father-in-law.

"Well, to be fair," Peggy said cautiously, "General Washington has certainly benefited from the pairing of their abilities. The general can see and speak more clearly, make better strategic decisions, negotiate better through the prism of Alexander. Lady Washington told me so."

"Yes, His Excellency has said the same, repeatedly, to me." Her papa sighed, softening. "I wonder if the boy is soured by the fact right before the wedding, he was twice passed over to be a diplomatic envoy, first to France and then to Russia. I know he believes that happened because he is so in Washington's shadow that Congress doesn't realize his talents—that if he had a command of his own, he would have a larger reputation. I tried to explain to him that wouldn't necessarily make a difference with those delegates. So often there is absolutely no rhyme or reason to Congress's decisions."

Schuyler pointed to the bottom of the letter. "He says he wants to reenter the artillery or join the light infantry."

Peggy drew in her breath sharply. Eliza would be a nervous wreck if her husband did that. Not that he hadn't ridden into the thick of battle beside Washington. But leading a battalion himself would expose him so much more.

She finished reading. At least Hamilton acknowledged that General Washington was a *very honest man* whose popularity was *essential to the safety of America.* But then her brother-in-law ended with a manipulation of her father that Peggy recognized, having used it herself when defending her part in a sibling squabble: *If I thought it could diminish your friendship for him, I should almost forgo the motives that urge me to justify myself to you.*

Peggy dropped into a chair. With this letter, Hamilton put Schuyler in a terrible position with Washington—her papa's close friend, commander, and political ally—and also with his own daughter. Hamilton writing his father-in-law in many ways preempted Eliza being able to reach out for advice from her own father. Peggy wondered if her sweet, believing sister had tried to placate Hamilton's indignation or convince him that perhaps he was overreacting.

And oh, how embarrassed Eliza must be around Martha Washington—the role model her middle sister idolized. "Has Eliza written you about this?" Peggy asked.

Schuyler looked even wearier with the question. "No, she hasn't. But that is proper. Her first loyalty must be to her husband now."

Pensively, Schuyler took Peggy's hand. "I am glad you are still here, child."

Peggy smiled, pushing away the thought he was saying that more out of missing her elder sisters than relishing her company. "How are you going to answer him, Papa?"

"Carefully," Schuyler replied. "I have learned it is a tricky thing guiding a headstrong child. Direct instructions never work. One needs to make suggestions that make her feel like such actions were her choice all along."

Her? Was her papa consciously referring to her sisters? Or to her? And was he speaking with fond bemusement or criticism?

"But"—Schuyler patted her hand before continuing—"such efforts are well worth it, as a stubborn, spirited child lights up a room with life."

Peggy's eyes welled with tears. That was the nicest compliment he had ever given her regarding her outspoken nature. She laughed and responded in kind. "*Moi?* Are you suggesting I am a handful, Papa?"

For a moment his tired eyes twinkled. "Of the best kind, child." He sat up tall. "Now, as one rather impetuous person to another, what would you say to your brother-in-law?"

"Well . . ." Peggy thought a moment. She was already seeing the serious ramifications of Hamilton's tiff with Washington that washed out well beyond the effects on her sister. As Martha had said in Morristown, Hamilton was critical to Washington's communications with Rochambeau. "Perhaps if you compliment Hamilton's importance to the general and play upon his sense of patriotism. The most dangerous impact of Hamilton's pique will be on His Excellency's relationship with the French."

"Precisely my concerns," said Schuyler. "This break between His Excellency and his most trusted and visible aide also suggests to the French court that we are fractured, chaotic. That perhaps Washington does not have the leadership to keep his staff loyal to him." He frowned and shook his head. "I had hoped Hamilton was more . . ." He trailed off.

She wanted to finish his thought with the adjectives: *smart, less egotistical?* But for Hamilton's and Eliza's sake, she chose a less critical word: "More circumspect?"

"Yes." Schuyler picked up a sheet of paper. Dipping a quill into his inkwell, Schuyler scratched out the date and *My dear sir.* Then he stopped and rubbed his hand.

"Is the arthritis bad today, Papa?"

He seemed to suffer most in the coldest months.

"Yes, my dear," he said with resignation.

"Do you wish to dictate your letter to me?" Seeing his surprise, she was quick to add, "It will simply make the writing of it faster for you."

"Thank you, my dear." He stood up and stepped away from the desk so she could take up the quill. Pacing, limping with his cane, Schuyler began. Even though Hamilton's letter surprised and afflicted him, her papa did not suspect him guilty of impropriety. But he did worry that Hamilton's rift with the general might harm the country and he would esteem himself culpable if he remained silent.

"I admire your self-control, Papa," Peggy said as Schuyler paused to collect his thoughts. "I might have called him an idiot."

Schuyler laughed. "Then this is a good lesson for us both, my dear. I am recognizing what a clear understanding you have of important matters of state. And perhaps you are learning a more effective way to get your point across. Ready? Here is where we bait the trap, as it were. With a bit of honey."

Peggy dipped her quill again and nodded.

Schuyler dictated that even before his new son-in-law courted Eliza, he had studied Hamilton's character. It was his opinion that Hamilton alone, of all Washington's aides, had the *"qualifications so essentially necessary to the man who is to aid and council a commanding General, environed with difficulties of every kind"* and whose correspondence was so voluminous and consequential. It was imperative that the wording of all Washington's letters be infused with the wise judgment of a scholar with diplomatic sensibilities—such as Hamilton's.

He paused to instruct Peggy. "See? It is hard for a man to dismiss an entreaty when he has been thoroughly complimented. Next we play to his sense of logic and larger view. Ready?"

"Yes, Papa."

Schuyler urged Hamilton to repair the breach since news of his quitting was sure to produce damaging gossip and doubt. That was particularly true with their all-important French allies who had already observed *"so many divisions between us; they know and acknowledge your Abilities and how necessary you are to the General."*

Then Schuyler was even more blunt. If Hamilton deserted Washington, the general would not have one gentleman left on his staff "sufficiently versed" in French to appropriately convey his concerns or plans. Peggy looked up. Her papa expressed the very same worry Martha Washington had expressed when she asked Peggy to go to Newport and to use her bilingual abilities to smooth over any misunderstandings.

"What think you of my letter so far, daughter?"

Peggy had been fascinated watching her father's mind at work. No wonder he had served as the chief negotiator with the Six Nations of the Iroquois Confederacy for so many years. "It is well done, Papa."

"Now, what is the most effective final stroke in our arguments?"

Peggy thought back to the countless times Eliza had been the go-between when she and Angelica had squabbled. "Time to point out General Washington's side of things?"

"Indeed!" Schuyler tapped his cane to the floor in applause. "Time to play conciliator."

He began again, referencing Hamilton's disclosure that General Washington had immediately regretted his outburst of temper and sent his aide, Tench Tilghman, with his apologies and compliments of Hamilton's importance to the cause.

Peggy still couldn't believe the insolence of Hamilton's refusal to accept General Washington's apologies. She feared the future trouble such self-righteous stubbornness could bring to her new brother and Eliza. But she kept her head down, her gaze on the paper, so she wouldn't reveal her thoughts to her father. She was committed to helping Hamilton as best she could.

Schuyler kept to playing the mediator, pointing out that Washington recognized he had been the aggressor in the encounter and "*that he quickly repented of the Insult.*" He reminded Hamilton that few men passed through life without an unguarded moment of irritation that wounded the feelings of a friend. Attribute it to the frailty of human nature, Schuyler urged, and with heaven's *"recording angel, drop a tear, and blot It out of the page of life."*

Ending with an appeal to Hamilton's obvious patriotism and sense of honor, Schuyler dictated: *"Make the sacrifice, the greater it is, the more glorious to you, your services are wanted."*

"Thank you, my dear." Schuyler took the quill from her to sign his name. He folded the letter carefully. Then he held a wax block over a candle to heat it, wiped a dollop of red onto the letter's back, and pressed it closed with his seal. He looked up suddenly. "I am just remembering that I never asked you how it was several years back when you knew how to unseal a letter without its recipient detecting the trick."

Peggy caught her breath. In the last hour, she'd noticed her father switching from calling her "child" to "my dear." She was desperate to hold on to that hard-won respect for her. What would he think if she told the truth that she'd learned to do so by childishly snooping on Angelica? All Peggy could think to do was to shrug and smile hopefully at him.

Schuyler considered her a moment, his lower lip stuck out in thought. She held her breath until he spoke again. "Pray, give me your opinion on another matter. Do you remember when our friend John Jay was here before leaving for Spain as our new ambassador?"

"I do, Papa. I remember your spending long hours in this library."

"Yes." He nodded. "You are very observant, aren't you, my dear?"

Peggy breathed easier at the "my dear" and felt safe admitting, "I am always curious about the happenings of this room, Papa." She grinned.

"Fair enough," he answered with a snort of laughter. "John Jay went to Spain to elicit their support in our fight. Now that the Spanish have declared war on England, Jay remains, but his mission is . . . a little different. Let us say it is of importance that his letters to me seem innocuous if they are captured on the high seas by the British fleet. So I need a cipher. A key word that would translate his letter. Say we choose KNIFE and we flip it backward and line it up with the alphabet. So in that case *A* would translate to *E*, *B* would translate to *F*, *C* to *I*, and so on. Make sense?"

She nodded.

"But even that cipher has to be coded when I send it to him—in case my letter is intercepted. Almost like a riddle that references something he would recognize but no one else would." He rubbed his forehead. "I am afraid my imagination fails me, I am so fatigued. Any ideas?"

Peggy thought. "What about 'what we call home.' He would know you named our house The Pastures, wouldn't he?"

"Good, good." Schuyler nodded approvingly. "That's the idea. But Tories living in Albany might be able to guess that. Let us think deeper into our household."

Peggy cast her memory back into what she remembered of Jay's visit. Things they had eaten at dinner, conversation at the table. Catharine had served traditional Dutch split pea soup, *erwtensoep* thick enough for a spoon to stand upright in it, paired with *rookworst* sausage and rye bread topped with smoked *katenspek* bacon. Peggy remembered because invariably pea hulls and strands of meat got stuck in her teeth, which was so embarrassing and . . . "Oh, Papa, I have an idea! Prince always passes out toothpicks to dinner guests after a meal."

"Aaah, yes," her papa smiled as she recounted her memory, then suggested, "What if we say: 'the man who every day lays a toothpick by Mrs. Schuyler's plate'?"

Peggy nodded. "Wouldn't Mr. Jay know that was Prince?"

"Indeed he would! Well done."

Fleetingly, Peggy wondered how Prince would feel about their using his name as a key in their battle for liberty. She was growing increasingly uncomfortable with the fact that her family *owned* and enslaved human beings while Schuyler and Hamilton, all their guests and they themselves, philosophized and fought for their own freedom. She had heard Hamilton talk of the abolitionist hopes of his friend John Laurens. Surely that had to be their next battle.

Schuyler crossed his arms and studied her again. "Let me make further use of your hawk eye." He pointed to a bundle of newspapers. "I regularly send agents into Canada to bring back gossip from the streets and their newspapers. Often it amounts to nothing, but sometimes . . ." He trailed off. "I did not spot anything of interest in those Montreal papers. But perhaps you might. Are you game?"

"Oh, yes, Papa!" She felt giddy with approval and inclusion.

Schuyler picked up the papers and handed them to her. "Then by all means. Please have at it."

Schuyler settled down into his chaise to read more correspondence, lifting his leg to rest atop a pillow. Peggy tucked her feet up under her, rearranging her billowing skirts as a cushion, already devouring the front page of the first pamphlet as she did. She heard her father laugh heartily and looked up in surprise.

"Are those my moccasins, my dear?"

Peggy looked down and realized the tips of her feet peeked out from the cloud of her skirts, revealing a hint of buckskin, blue-jay feathers, and colorful beading. She froze, her heart sinking, waiting for a reprimand for stealing them from his closet. "Yes, Papa," she murmured.

He nodded, a wry smile on his face. "Comfortable, aren't they?" was all he said. Then he went back to reading, waving her back to her newspapers. But she could hear him chuckle as he turned over his letters.

NINETEEN

Spring

Dr. James Thacher Journal
late March/early April 1781, near West Point, New York

This vicinity is constantly harassed by small parties on our
side and parties of royalists and Tories on the other, who are
making every effort to effect mutual destruction. . . .

Six of our men . . . were all killed but one . . . we saw
four dead bodies, mangled in the most inhuman manner . . .
and among them, one groaning under five wounds on his head,
two of them quite through his skull bone with a broad sword.
This man was capable of giving us an account of the murder
of his four companions. They surrendered and begged for life,
but their entreaties were disregarded, and the swords of their
cruel foes were plunged into their bodies so long as signs of life
remained. . . .

[The situation of those] who reside on their farms between
the lines of the two armies . . . is truly deplorable, being

continually exposed to . . . horse thieves, and cowboys, who
rob and plunder them without mercy, and the personal abuse
and punishments which they inflict.

PEGGY ROCKED HER NEWEST LITTLE SISTER TO KEEP
her from crying. Dressed in ancient family lace, baby Caty
squirmed against the itch of her elaborate christening gown.

"Will you pray for her, care for her, and by your example
in faith help her walk in the way of Christ?" asked Reverend
Eilardus Westerlo, faltering a bit as he translated the Dutch
Reformed Church liturgy into English for Martha Washington. She, Peggy, and one of Peggy's uncles, James Van
Rensselaer, were standing as godparents. General Washington, of course, could not break from the war to be there for
the service.

"I will," the three answered.

"Will you renounce the devil and all evil, turning away
from earthly things that are against our Lord and his scriptures?"

Peggy felt Martha Washington take in a deep breath as
she tucked her finger into the baby's grasping hand, before
solemnly replying, "I will." She wondered if the general's
wife was feeling the same irony Peggy did in that question.
Certainly war and the killing it required was against the
scriptures even if the minister had used his pulpit to preach
for the Revolution.

As the reverend dribbled water onto baby Caty's forehead

to baptize her, the infant let out a wail that echoed through the vestibule. She kicked and flailed in protest. Peggy had to fight to hang on and not drop her.

"Kindred spirits," chuckled her uncle Johnny, who had escorted Martha from headquarters to Albany for the ceremony. "Your parents certainly chose the right godmamma for this baby," he teased.

After the service, Peggy's family gathered at the house. As they waited in the best parlor for dinner, Martha settled beside Peggy and happily cradled the now slumbering baby. "How I miss this," she murmured. She hummed a little, and Peggy realized silent tears slid down the cheeks of the nation's first and most admired lady.

"Are you all right, ma'am?" Peggy whispered.

"I was just thinking of how my Patsy looked as a baby. She was such a peaceful, beautiful child. Who would have guessed that such pain was to be hers." Martha looked up from baby Caty to Peggy. "I am sure you have heard the stories."

"Only . . . only that you lost her right before the war."

Out of respect, Peggy did not share that she knew Washington's teenage stepdaughter had suffered terrible seizures. So many people said ridiculous things about what caused such convulsions or what they might represent. Just as cruel individuals speculated why Washington had not fathered any of his own children after he married the young widow. As a doctor, her uncle Johnny could explain to Peggy that the smallpox, malaria, and pleurisy His Excellency had managed to survive as a young man might have left him sterile. Per-haps that personal tragedy was part of the reason Washington was so attached to his young aides-de-camp.

Peggy sighed, thinking of Hamilton's petulant break from the great man. Her brother-in-law had totally ignored her papa's plea to his patriotism and sense of responsibility. Hamilton had just written Schuyler that he had even sent his commission to Washington as a demonstration of his resolve to quit the war entirely unless given a field command of his own. Her papa had sadly folded up that letter and not replied.

As a result of Hamilton's departure, Washington was so shorthanded he had taken to dictating letters occasionally to Mrs. Washington. But her spelling was so atrocious that the arrangement couldn't last long. Peggy marveled that Martha had not said a thing about the quarrel and the disappointment her husband surely felt, not to mention the upheaval Hamil-ton's absence caused in Washington's workload.

Instinctively, Peggy reached out to touch Martha Washington's shoulder in sympathy. Martha forced herself to smile. "We had tried everything for our beloved Patsy. Valerian, nervous drops, musk capsules, mercury, Peruvian bark, barley water, bleedings, purges, even an iron ring for her to wear. Nothing helped. The last fit was so violent she died within minutes, George holding her hand and weep-ing." Martha turned her eyes to look out the window. "I do not think he has ever recovered from the loss. He loved her dearly, raising her with me since she was a toddler."

Her gaze turned back to Peggy. "I wear her miniature as

a bracelet, so I can look at her every day." Martha held up her wrist for Peggy to look at a pretty teenage face with round green eyes and a gentle smile, very like her mother.

"Peggy," her papa called. "Please retrieve the Bible from my study. I wish to record Caty's birth and godparents in the presence of Lady Washington, who has so honored us today."

Peggy hesitated, not wishing to leave Martha in her sadness. But Washington's wife nodded and said with perfect for-the-public composure, "Go ahead, my dear. I am content holding this baby. Nothing is as precious as the life of a child."

Peggy flung open the door to the study, unwittingly crushing a guest up against the shelves.

"Zounds!" came an aggravated voice.

"Oh, I am so sorry!" Peggy pulled back the door to discover a young man cradling an armload of books and a red nose from the blow of the heavy wooden panels. "Are you all right?"

The youth shifted the books into one arm and rubbed his nose with the other hand.

Peggy felt terrible—besides displaying a lack of ladylike deportment, she would hate to have marred that beautiful face. Because it was quite pretty—dark, resonant eyes under a mop of soft black curls, an open, heart-shaped face paired with a cleft chin. No beard yet and a youthful flush to his cheeks—which weirdly complemented the red nose she'd given him.

"You need to stop doing that to me, Peggy," the young man joked.

Peggy looked at him with puzzlement. She had noticed him among the congregation at the baptism, but she hadn't really recognized him. Certainly she should since he called her by her first name.

"When we used to gather at our grandparents for berry-picking and picnics, you constantly knocked me over as we all played tag."

Oh goodness! How stupid and rude of her! He must be one of her distant, younger cousins. "Stephen?"

He grinned and bowed.

"I am so sorry, I didn't recognize you!"

She was related to him on her mother's side. Stephen would eventually become the patroon of Rensselaerswyck, an enormous estate granted the clan long ago by the Dutch government. Peggy knew he had been away, studying at Princeton. Plus all the tumult around Albany had pretty much precluded extended family gatherings. It had been years since she'd seen him. Of course, he would be at the baby's christening if he were home. Reverend Westerlo was his stepfather. "Why are you not at college?"

"So quick to be rid of me?" Stephen laughed.

"No, I just . . ." Peggy hesitated, then decided it was fine to be honest with family. "If I had the chance to go to university I would never leave campus except kicking and screaming."

He chuckled with a nice, easy sense of humor. Then he

sobered to say, "There is so much fighting around Princeton, my mother thinks it safer for me to attend Harvard instead. I will leave for Boston in August, when the next term starts. Meanwhile your father was kind enough to lend me your library." He held up his stack of books. "But it is presumptuous of me to borrow so many at once. What would you recommend?"

He laid the volumes out on a table: *The Adventures of Telemachus, The Son of Ulysses*; *Cato's Letters*; a collection of Alexander Pope's writings; histories of New York, Canada, and Sweden; plus Molière's comedies. The boy was ambitious to tackle all this, thought Peggy, as she spread them out. "Papa won't mind your borrowing all this. He is very generous with his library. All these books are fascinating, although"—she laughed as she pushed it to the side—"I might leave off the history of Sweden for now." She'd have to remember to ask her papa why he had that volume. "With Molière, I'd begin with *Tartuffe*."

"Not *Don Juan*?"

"No, that's not one I particularly care for." Reading about a rogue who left a trail of brokenhearted women in his wake was certainly not something that interested her now. "I'd recommend *The Learned Ladies* over that."

"Ah," Stephen answered, "you must empathize with the characters, surely, given the title? My memory is you always have a book with you."

Peggy smiled at the compliment. "Well, it is a bit of a

satire on pretentiousness, so I hope you do not find me in those characters."

"*The School for Husbands*, then?" he asked with a playful tone. "Would I find something instructive in that for our future conversations?"

Peggy looked at him with surprise. Was he flirting with her?

"Ah, so that is what delays you!" Both Peggy and Stephen startled a bit as Schuyler limped into his study on his cane.

"Oh, Papa, forgive me. I completely forgot about fetching the Bible!"

"So I see. I will forgive it because your delay clearly involves books." Peggy caught his glancing between the two of them. What in the world was her father smiling about with such amusement?

"Sir?" One of Schuyler's guards appeared at the door. "There is a man at the back gate, saying he wishes to see you. We checked him for arms." He turned to Peggy. "He says he is a suitor to you, miss."

"What?" she gasped. It felt as if a cannonball had just exploded near her.

It was Stephen who caught her arm and kept her from falling, Peggy felt so faint. Her heart started pounding so hard she could barely hear her father tell the guard to bring the gentleman in or his questioning her as to who this visitor could be. She could only shake her head as Stephen helped her sit in the nearest chair and then excused himself from the room.

Could Fleury have changed his mind? Why didn't he write first?

Breathe! Breathe! her mind hissed, her heart racing. *Calm yourself. You'll look like an idiot!*

Peggy fixed her gaze onto the carpet to focus and stop the house from spinning around her. *Breathe, damn it!*

A pair of boots entered the room. Broken open, dull brown, no flash of white gaiters. Those were not Fleury's boots. Peggy blinked back hot tears. She raised her eyes. It was Sergeant Moses Harris—her papa's double agent.

Schuyler closed the door, sealing them into privacy.

"Begging your pardon, miss," Harris apologized, "for taking liberty with your romantic name and all, but I didn't want no one to suspicion I came with intelligence for the general."

She wanted to hit him, kick him, run him through with a sword. But she forced herself to smile shakily.

"Are you all right, miss?" he asked, squashing his hat in his hand. "I didn't mean to give you a fright. Or . . . or to humiliate you none." He tugged on his waistcoat and his brown jacket, which were far nicer and cleaner than what she had seen him wear before. "I borrowed these togs so I weren't disreputable."

"Very kind of you, sir, a good touch of deception," said Schuyler as he poured and handed Peggy a small glass of Madeira. "My daughter is simply overcome with fatigue. I have been overburdening her with work of late, I am afraid."

She looked up at her father with gratitude. It was bad enough to feel this overwhelmed because of a man who had wounded her; being pitied for it would be like gangrene.

"Should we wait until she feels better, sir?" Harris whispered, clearly thinking Schuyler would prefer Peggy leave the room before he shared what he knew.

"No; please proceed."

"All right then. Well, sir, I done burned the letters I were carrying for fear of being caught with them. Miss Schuyler can tell you what I already been through at the hands of them Tories. Spiteful blokes, they be. Don't much want to be hauled off by your Patriot guard neither. Our ruse last time with them cost me a broken rib. So I committed the messages to memory." He tapped his head.

"Pray, go on, Sergeant," Schuyler said, easing Harris along in his story.

"Yes, sir. Them bloodybacks in Canada are thinking on another invasion. Led this time by old Sir Guy Carleton hisself. Leaving from Montreal and coming straight down Lake Champlain again. They be thinking they can convince Vermonters to join up with them at Crown Point." Harris nodded. "There's their aim, sir."

Schuyler rubbed his jaw in thought. "This coincides with something a deserter told the conspiracy commissioners during an interrogation. And with what an old friend who managed to escape a Canada prison could tell me of talk he'd overheard among his jailers." He paused. "And rumblings of the Green Mountain Boys' disgruntlement about our legislature not carving out a state of their own between New York and Connecticut."

"Then that makes it sound like truth," said Harris.

"But we need much more intelligence for His Excellency to make decisions. Numbers of troops. Exact locations. What artillery pieces." Schuyler hesitated. Peggy knew what he was thinking, even if he didn't trust Harris enough to say it to him.

Recently, Washington had met again with Rochambeau to discuss whether they should join forces to attack New York City—to finally dislodge the British fleet in its harbor and the sixteen thousand troops occupying it—or to travel south to join Lafayette and Lincoln fighting Cornwallis and the turncoat Benedict Arnold in Virginia. Washington, of course, would love nothing better than to defeat and humiliate the traitor he once called friend. But if the British were really mounting yet another full-blown invasion from Canada, either of his plans would be a terrible miscalculation, leaving the northern states open to disaster.

Schuyler considered Harris a moment, obviously assessing if Harris could manage the hundred-mile journey north to Crown Point, or even up into Canada, for a good long reconnaissance. Wiry in build and scrappy in attitude, Harris seemed perfectly capable of that to Peggy. After all, he had done it before—making it to Burgoyne with faked intercepts that Schuyler had filled with false information meant to mislead the British. But such a mission was a lot to ask of a man to do alone these days. It would mean a trek through the wilderness and an area where bands of raiders—nicknamed cowboys and skinners—regularly ambushed travelers and scouts.

"Sir," Schuyler began, "ever since the Oneida and Tuscarora were so brutally attacked and their villages destroyed, I have been loath to ask them to scout as far as I used to. Would . . ."

Harris held up his hand. "Say no more, General. I thought I'd take a little jaunt and look-see along Lake Champlain. Might even trap me some beaver." He put his hat on and tugged on its tip in salute to Peggy. "Sorry to have affronted you, miss."

"Oh, Sergeant Harris." Peggy recovered herself enough to stand and curtsy. "You have flattered me much. I look forward to your safe return."

"Really, miss?" Harris straightened up taller and backed his way out the door, beaming. Out in the courtyard they heard him whistling as he left.

"Remind me, Margarita," Schuyler said with a fond laugh, "to have you in the negotiating room whenever I must ask a man go into battle." He hugged her as he gently added, "Is there anything you wish to tell me?"

"No, Papa."

"Are you sure?"

"Yes, Papa. The curtain has already come down on a drama that is not worth sharing." She ached to tell him she was recovering because she was helping him, doing tangible things, no matter how small, for the Revolution and being included in his thoughts gave her purpose, a sense of individual identity and consequence. But she was afraid to call attention to it, knowing his reliance on her was unusual and a result of war necessity.

"I am relieved," he answered. "I would hate to lose you to someone who does not appreciate you enough to make himself known to me." He kissed her on her forehead. "Now. Let us collect that Bible."

Schuyler played host seamlessly for the rest of the day, but Peggy could tell he was worried. And well he should be.

Over the next weeks, more of his spies came in with alarming reports. A man Schuyler called "Mr. Fox" shared that his Tory friends just north of Saratoga bragged they were about "to make rare work with the rebels." Right across the Hudson from Saratoga, on the river's eastern banks, a Mr. Shipman saw three British boats landing infantrymen. Another agent, going by the name Pierre, reported British campfires at Crown Point that to him suggested two thousand Redcoats were encamped there. A local man doubled the spy's estimate, counting English forces as being closer to four thousand strong. An Oneida scout spotted another fifteen hundred British soldiers near Ticonderoga.

Meanwhile, cattle and hogs were being stolen in droves from the settlements edging New York's wilderness. Barns were burned. Farmers were being pulled out of their beds and from their homes into the darkness of night, beaten, and left for dead.

In retribution, Albany's anticonspiracy commissioners stepped up their arrests of suspected Tories, increasing their threats and confiscations of Loyalists' property to force confessions. Such tactics unearthed, for instance, the fact that five hundred Loyalists and Mohawks were hovering southwest of Albany determined to torch the city. They planned to accomplish that plot with a series of coordinated kidnappings of militia officers that would leave local forces leaderless and in chaos during the larger attack on the city.

Then in late May, a commissioner arrived, breathless and heaving from his climb up the hill to the mansion's front door. The old Dutchman was so agitated, Peggy guided him to her papa's study without waiting to announce him.

"General!" The man nearly flung himself at Schuyler. "I have dire news you must heed!" He was so loud, Peggy worried he would frighten her mother and siblings. She pushed him unceremoniously into the study and shut the door behind them as he hurried on with his story: "We have this from two sources. One is a most perfidious deserter, but a man who knows the worth of intelligence to save his own skin. The other man is a local Tory. This Loyalist is most grateful for previous favors you have done him, and so gives up information to save your life specifically. They both say that just beyond your pastures lurks a band of Queen's Rangers bent on capturing or assassinating you."

Schuyler nodded.

"Truly, sir, you must believe me! It's Robert Rogers' Rangers." Once a legendary American fighter during the

French and Indian War, Rogers had pledged himself and his barbaric guerilla tactics to the British. Mention of his name struck terror in the hearts of New Yorkers.

"I do believe you, sir," Schuyler answered. "In fact, I have been told the British Canadian government has placed a price of two hundred guineas on my head."

The Dutchman fell into a chair. "Two hundred guineas!" He fanned himself. "For that amount, General Schuyler, most anyone might be tempted."

Schuyler laughed ruefully. "Just think of all the salted fish we could buy with that, eh?"

"Papa!" Peggy couldn't help herself. "This is serious!"

"Oh, I know, my dear. I have written General Washington already. He has promised to double our guard." He took her hand and squeezed it. "Please do not worry. Best for you to check on your mama, who might have heard all this hubbub. Please? I need to discuss with the councilman how we can build some bateaux for General Washington. Then will you come back and help me with some correspondence?"

Peggy nodded.

When she returned, her father's bravado was gone. He handed her a letter from Ethan Allen, leader of the Vermonter militia.

"Why is he writing you?" Peggy asked. "I thought you suspected the British of trying to seduce this man and his followers."

Schuyler shrugged. "Allen may have been talking with them. But this letter proves once again that having more than one source for a story is what allows us to determine fact. If nothing else, this letter suggests Allen is aware of our watching him—which may temper his choices. More important, however, as I speak with you now, daughter, is other information he sends, which is of grave importance to our family." He motioned for her to look at the letter for herself.

Peggy quickly read Allen's rough-written statement that despite false rumors he was conversing with the British, he was committed to the welfare of the United States and to Schuyler. As proof he shared that he had taken several British prisoners who confessed "*that they at several different times threatned to Captivate your person, said that it had been in their power to have taken some of your family the last Campain, but that they had an Eye to your self.*"

Peggy looked up at her father. "Do you suppose he is offering you this report to regain your favor, as a way to dispel suspicion against him?"

Schuyler smiled. "You have become quite the analyst, my dear." He crossed his arms and paced. "I did consider that. But given what the good commissioner rushed here to tell me today, I need to give the threat credibility. What I am most concerned about, of course, is Allen's statement that the enemy considered taking some of my precious family captive."

"Papa, did Mama ever tell you that when we were in Saratoga gathering things before Burgoyne reached it, that there were shots fired from the woods and an attempt to invade the house?"

"Yes," Schuyler answered gravely. "I will always be grateful to Richard Varick for his actions that night." He took her hand and sat them down together, facing each other. "I need you to be on guard now, Peggy," he said with urgency. "Do not go wandering through the orchard, as you are wont. Nor go through the pastures down to the river. You must not walk too far from the safety of the house. Keep close watch on your sisters and brothers." He searched her eyes to ensure she was listening, really listening, and heeding him. "Do you promise?"

Peggy nodded solemnly.

"Good." Her papa seemed relieved. "I depend on you. It could be a matter of life or death."

TWENTY

~ & ~

Summer

From John Carter to Colonel Alexander Hamilton
New Port [Rhode Island] May 18th, 1781
My Dear Sir

You do not tell me what your future line of life will be, but
Villemansey tells me he thinks you are to command a Body
of Troops this Campaign. I wish much to be informed, as
independent of myself a certain Lady (who has not made her
appearance this morning) is very anxious for your Happiness
and Glory.

I have been in constant Expectation of Genl. Schuyler's
arrival here to take Mrs. Carter and the little ones with him to
Albany, but I hear not a Word of him. If he does not appear
in ten Days, I must send Mrs. Carter as in her Situation the
Journey in the middle of June will be too fatiguing.

Your Friend & Servant,
John Carter

CATHARINE AND PEGGY HOVERED AS DR. STRINGER, Albany's most-respected physician, punctured her papa's arm with a lancet. Wrinkling her nose, Peggy watched blood ooze from the cut into a cup the surgeon held below Schuyler's elbow. It was the second time that week his surgeon had bled Schuyler to treat his quinsy and to prevent his suffocating. Yet her papa still struggled to breathe, his throat rattling with each raspy gasp.

As soon as the doctor left the room, escorted downstairs to the front door by Catharine, anxious to hear all his instructions, Peggy knelt by her father's chaise. "Papa, this is not working. Leeches, scalpels. You just seem weaker."

Schuyler grunted, putting his hand to his throat. "Better tomorrow," he whispered.

"Papa, do you trust me?"

Schuyler eyebrows shot up, but he smiled.

"Martha Washington told me of a remedy she has for quinsy that she gives His Excellency. She mixes molasses and onions into a toddy."

Schuyler made a face.

"Will you try it? For me?" She grinned at him, adopting a singsong mama voice to say, "If General Washington can drink it, so can my brave papa."

Schuyler laughed, which turned into a cough that cleared his throat. He took in a long, grateful breath. "That's better. What would I do without you, my dear?"

Peggy laughed back. "Who would have known that

being saucy to one's papa could help him breathe? I have found my purpose!"

"Margarita, my beloved child, your spirit—stubborn, defiant, willful"—he paused to pinch her cheek affectionately—"is just what this new nation needs. I wish more men had it."

Peggy's heart swelled. All those adjectives were typically used as criticisms of her rather than compliments, adjectives used as negative comparisons to the sophisticated Angelica, the composed Eliza. She certainly did not want her father ill so that he needed her, but oh, how Peggy had grown up and learned, nurtured by his trust in her. No longer did she feel so overshadowed by her sisters. But that hard-earned place was about to be turned upside down.

"Paaaa-paaa!" a pretty voice called up the stairs. "Mama! Peggy! Where is everyone? I'm hoooo-mmmme!"

It was Angelica.

Two weeks later, Angelica sat in the dining room, a mound of luxurious petticoats and pregnant stomach—voluptuous, rosy, exuding life. An Aphrodite of motherhood, gorgeous as ever, even eight months pregnant and holding her own baby Catharine, a china-doll-pretty toddler, and clambered over by her three-year-old Philip. As always, her vivacious chatter was a scintillating mix of political commentary and gossip, and had everyone riveted.

Across the wide mahogany table from her sat Eliza and

Hamilton, who had just come home as well. Eliza would stay in Albany as Hamilton rejoined the Continental forces in the coming campaign—if Washington granted him a command and then whenever His Excellency and Rochambeau determined what would be the most advantageous line of attack. The Schuyler sisters' circle was once again complete.

"Vicomte de Noailles and his friend fought a duel over a Newport milkmaid, can you imagine?" she said.

Eliza giggled. Then her hand shot to her mouth and she pressed her lips together to suppress a gag. She, too, was pregnant, early on in it. But rather than blooming, she was wretched and violently ill most days. Hamilton reached over and sympathetically patted her hand, but his violet-blue eyes never left Angelica as she continued with her stories about the French forces in Newport.

"One of the officers was determined to show me how on command his horse would rear and stand on his hind legs. But the gelding added a buck that sent the gentleman flying. Oh my." She laughed and then steadied her pregnant belly. "But enough about me," chirped Angelica.

I should say so, thought Peggy, who had had her fill of wondering where in Angelica's stories Fleury might have been. How could her sister not think about how her anecdotes might be tearing her heart apart?

"And so, my dear Ham, what sort of command are you hoping for?" But before he could answer, she added, "Does General Washington know of your daring exploits before joining his staff? Surely you have told him of stealing cannon right out from under British noses as their battleships sailed into New York Harbor and dragging them to the liberty pole at King's College?"

Hamilton smiled.

Eliza's face puckered. "I do not know that story."

"Oh my," said Angelica, "it is quite astounding. There is also the time he led a hundred men in a raid against the British at Sandy Hook Lighthouse."

"We would have taken it, too," said Hamilton, "had Loyalists not tipped off the British regulars to our coming. They were ready for us. We fought bravely for two hours under fire from the ships and the lighthouse. Still, I am proud to say I did not lose a man."

Throughout his eldest daughter's merry monologue and exchange with Hamilton, Schuyler had remained mute. Now he frowned and fiddled with his knife. Peggy knew how disappointed he was that his new son-in-law had totally ignored his urgings to return to Washington's staff. As protective as she had been of Hamilton when he first wrote of his break with Washington, she now felt she should champion her father's hopes. To play mediator as she had in Morristown between the young fifer and Lafayette, and in Newport between the French guard and Rhode Island fisherman. "I am sure General Washington misses your insight and eloquence, Colonel Hamilton, and especially your facility with French."

Hamilton looked at her with some surprise and a flash of irritation. He hid it by correcting the name she used:

"Alexander, little sister." But he did not respond to the content of her comment, which infuriated Peggy. He wouldn't brush aside Angelica like that. And "*little* sister"?

"You know, *Alexander*," she now spoke with some indignation, "it may not be as outwardly glorious, but there are many who have sacrificed much, forgone popularity and individual renown to quietly serve, thereby making all the difference in outcome. Like Papa."

Hamilton shot an anxious look toward Schuyler before saying, "Sadly, that will not gain me accolades enough for employment after the war to support your sister as she deserves." Hamilton kissed Eliza's hand. "If I have my own command I will gain sway among men. That will help me succeed professionally."

"And what profession will that be, Mr. Hamilton?" asked Catharine, in mother-in-law tones.

"I plan to study the law, especially since many of our current lawyers are Loyalists. After the war they should not be allowed to practice. There will be need for a new breed of Patriot attorneys. I will read the law on my own." He tactfully added, "Just as you educated yourself, General."

At this Schuyler sat up and finally spoke. "You may use my library for that very purpose."

Eliza clapped her hands happily. "Why not start now, dearest?"

"Goodness, Eliza," burbled Angelica, "Alexander is not going to want to remain buried in a library during a campaign that may win the Revolution for us. You must not deny him glory. The chance to seize victory and defeat tyranny!"

Eliza glared at their big sister.

Peggy bit her tongue to prevent asking, Why don't you volunteer your own husband?

Angelica ignored both her sisters, speaking directly to Hamilton. "Mr. Carter says it is best you meet up with His Excellency's forces soon. If you are nearby, it will be easier for him to give you troops. You will be like Achilles—brought in to inflame everyone's patriotism, to lead the charge. As you know, Lafayette is promoting you with General Washington. But best be in the right place at the right time. Lafayette's influence with His Excellency is . . ."

"Enormous," Hamilton completed her sentence.

Was there a twinge of jealousy in Hamilton's statement? There had been none before about his friend Lafayette. Peggy tried to assess that beautiful face, but Hamilton's expression was guarded.

"Actually, sir." He turned back to his father-in-law with a fretful look Peggy was coming to recognize as a desire for approval. "I have been doing a bit of writing. I plan a series of papers, titled 'The Continentalist,' arguing that we need a stronger centralized government, a standing national army, if we are to survive. I have sent the first to the *New-York Packet*. It should be published in a week or so."

Schuyler seemed pleased. "Indeed, whenever Congress acts foolishly, it is because one region selfishly considers its own interests over the nation's."

"Yes, sir," Hamilton replied. "We began the Revolution

351

with vague notions of the practical business of government. But it has become obvious in the way our Continental Army is starved that we must have a strong, overarching federal government. If that federal government is too weak, the ambitions and local interests of more powerful members might undermine and usurp the union's overall goals."

"Precisely!" Schuyler agreed enthusiastically. "I have been thinking this is especially true with our monies and how we pay for our nation's needs. We cannot count on the pockets of individual Patriots to continue funding things. Many of us have completely emptied our coffers." Schuyler smiled apologetically at Catharine.

As he and Hamilton talked, Eliza glowed with pride, Peggy hung on every word, and Angelica squirmed, kicked by her unborn baby. Bored, the younger children slipped out of their chairs to play on the floor or skip around the table. Six-year-old Cornelia stopped rocking the cradle holding her infant sister Caty to clasp hands with her eighteen-month-old niece as she toddled around the room. Angelica's daughter was still a bit unsteady on her feet and tripping on the hem of her gown. Three-year-old Philip, though, was quick dash and speed even in his dress. Out the door he scooted, Angelica watching her son with obvious adoration.

Suddenly she shot to her feet, knocking over her chair as she lumbered as quickly as she could toward the door herself, crying out, "Philip, stop! Do not move!"

Startled, everyone silenced. Hamilton rose, moving to help with whatever was so urgent. But Angelica bustled back into the room, furious, holding Philip's hand and dragging a Brown Bess. "Papa! Your grandson was about to pull the trigger on this loaded musket. All arms must be taken to the cellar, right now, out of his reach!"

No one dared disobey her, given her fluster and their own horror at what might have happened. So no one pointed out that the preloaded muskets were propped by the doors because of dire warnings that Queen's Rangers and Tory bands were plotting to attack and kidnap Schuyler.

The debate about Hamilton's rejoining Washington's staff as aide-de-camp or starting to read the law ended abruptly with Angelica's upset. Arguing his choices was replaced with everyone's fears and prayers for his safety when he left for the war, a few days later, determined to gain his own unit of soldiers to lead into battle. Eliza remained upstairs, crying, while Angelica walked beside him on the stairs. Her hand was slipped inside his elbow and the other lay atop his arm, her cheek resting on his shoulder. "I know you will return to us with laurels, like Caesar," she murmured as they reached the bottom of the stairs.

"But without Caesar's plans to become emperor, let us hope," quipped Peggy, who sat in the downstairs hall waiting to say her good-byes. She had watched their descent, a bit alarmed at Angelica's physical closeness to Hamilton. Angelica was like that, always had been, embracing and affectionate, but Peggy wasn't so sure how Eliza would feel about it if she saw them together. "And certainly," Peggy added, "we hope you don't so insult and annoy your comrades as did Caesar that they collude to assassinate you! We don't want Eliza having to play Portia."

Hamilton chuckled. "Thank goodness you are here to keep me in order, Peggy."

"I foresee that will be no easy task." Peggy playfully turned back on him his own warning to her in his postscript to Eliza's letter.

Recognizing it, Hamilton laughed heartily. Taking Angelica's hands in his, he kissed her on both cheeks. Then— did Peggy see this right?—he pulled away slowly so that his face slid along hers, his mouth hovering over her lips for a tantalizing moment before he pulled back. Angelica swayed, closed her eyes, sighed, and reopened them.

"*Adieu, ma belle soeur.* God keep you and your baby safe."

Peggy's stomach churned. There was nothing technically inappropriate in that embrace. It just felt a little too . . . too something. Having been kissed herself, really kissed, she recognized heat.

"My Peggy." Hamilton grinned at her. "Will you walk me to the stable? I need ask a favor of you." He held out his hand.

Peggy clasped hers behind her back, but fell in line beside him as they stepped into the courtyard, sending chickens scattering and squawking.

"So do I have your blessings on my odyssey, fair nymph?" he asked, reverting to the provocative banter he'd used when they were only coming to know each other.

Peggy stopped in her tracks. "Alexander, you do not need to be flirtatious with me. I know it feels a novelty, but you have already won my heart—as your sister."

To her amazement, Hamilton's enormous violet-blue eyes filled with tears. He looked down quickly and flicked dirt from his sleeves, and by the time he raised his gaze back to hers, that haze of emotion was gone, tucked away behind the intensity of his gaze. But the sincerity was not.

"I am not used to having a family. Certainly not a little sister. I apologize." He reached for her hand, and this time Peggy took it. "Watch over Eliza for me, will you? For a heart that so willingly and completely gives, hers is a delicate one. I fear for her and for the child if she frets too much about me. Her anxieties might"—he hesitated—"might . . ."

"I promise to take tender care of her."

He nodded. "The Schuyler sisters' bond is nothing short of mystical. Eliza derives strength from it." He paused. "I know Angelica adores Eliza." He lowered his voice even though Angelica remained inside, out of earshot. "But it is you Eliza trusts, Peggy." He smiled. "You have the best of both of your sisters. Perhaps wrapped in a somewhat biting wisdom"—he laughed—"but also in a fearless loyalty." Hamilton kissed her forehead. "Fleury is a fool," he whispered.

And then he was on his horse and gone.

Peggy watched until she could no longer see the cloud of dust his horse kicked up from the road.

She brushed away a tear. Eliza's life would be shattered

if Hamilton did not return. But hers would have a hole in it as well. Her brother-in-law understood her and knew more of her heartache than her sisters. Peggy already loved him as an ally, a kindred spirit, a needed confidante, a protective big brother. And even though he was out of sorts with General Washington, Peggy sensed that without this slightly reckless, quixotic, and dazzlingly eloquent young man, His Excellency's ability to stand down the British and forge a new nation could be dangerously diluted.

"Godspeed," Peggy whispered, a catch at her heart.

A few weeks later, Angelica sat fanning herself against the August heat. Her baby girl nestled in her arms and batted at the delicately painted fan, chortling, her tiny feet squirming happily. "Thank you for setting supper in the front hall so we can enjoy the evening air, Mama," she said.

"Of course, my dear. I know well how you are feeling. Being pregnant in summer temperatures is hard. It won't be long now, though. I think the baby has dropped, don't you, from the way you are carrying?"

Angelica nodded, rubbing her lower back.

"I wager no more than a month," added Catharine.

"Oh, let it be sooner than that," Angelica said with a sigh. "And how are you, dearest?" she asked Eliza.

"Better, thank you. I can eat now."

Angelica and Peggy exchanged glances. They were both worried about their middle sister. She had passed through the first third of pregnancy so her stomach was no longer constantly at sea. Eliza's wan face these days had nothing to do with expecting a baby and all to do with her anxiety about Hamilton's safety.

But she didn't admit to it, saying, "Just think, Peggy, when you are carrying your first child, Angelica and I will know all about everything to guide you through it."

"*Hmpf*. First she must find a husband," Catharine said. "Have you heard from Mr. Varick, Margarita?"

Peggy rolled her eyes. Varick, always Varick with her mother. With Angelica married to a Brit of questionable identity and Eliza to an immigrant of French-Scottish heritage from the Caribbean island of Saint Croix, Catharine was clearly aiming for a solid Dutchman for her third daughter.

"Look, isn't that a beautiful moon rising over the river?" Schuyler asked, deftly changing the subject.

Peggy stood, hugged her father gratefully for distracting her mother, and moved to the doors flung open to the river's breezes. She drew in a deep breath. "Could we take a walk down to the river, Papa? The moon will be full tonight and the stars clear."

"We'd need a shepherd," Eliza said with a laugh, surveying the flock of children at the table, including five under the age of ten—Angelica's two youngsters, plus Cornelia, Rensselaer, and baby Caty asleep in her cradle. Thirteen-year-old Jeremiah was also with them. The only one missing was sixteen-year-old John Bradstreet, off visiting an uncle.

Schuyler grinned, surveying the wealth of family around his table. "We are blessed indeed," he said proudly.

"You go on," said Angelica. "I will stay here at the house with the children."

Schuyler hesitated. Peggy knew he was worrying over reports that had come in all week of Tory Rangers attacking and kidnapping prominent Patriots in the Albany area, just as his spies had predicted might happen as prelude to an all-out attack on the city. The husband of Ann Bleecker—the poor mother whose infant perished of dysentery along the road from Saratoga during Burgoyne's campaign—had been dragged away from their home, for instance, leaving local militia without a ranking officer. Word was the orders for such raids came directly from British high command in Canada and Barry St. Leger, whom Schuyler and Benedict Arnold had outfoxed at Fort Stanwix in 1777. "He be out for retribution on you, General," Schuyler's agent had warned.

Peggy did a quick head count in her mind. Three of Schuyler's guards were off duty in the cellar and three more were standing post in the gardens. There was also a Continental Army courier on call out back in the courtyard, and several of the family's enslaved male servants eating in the kitchen. Among them was Lisbon, whom Peggy completely trusted to be resourceful and quick to act in trouble. Surely, Angelica should be safe in the house with the children if her papa took a stroll with her to the waterfront.

Peggy was about to say so when Prince approached. "General Schuyler, there's a stranger at the back gate wishing to see you."

Schuyler sighed. "Seems our stroll will need to wait, my dear," he apologized. To Prince, he said, "Show him to my study, please."

Wistfully, Schuyler finished off his wine as a distant shout came from out back by the stables. "*Halt!*"

BANG!

"*Intruders at the gate!*"

BANG! BANG!

"*Huzzah! We're in! Come on, lads!*"

Schuyler leapt to his feet, dropping his cane and the wineglass to the floor with a crash. "Kitty, quickly, the children." He spoke calmly but lifted her out of her chair with some urgency. "We must get everyone upstairs."

BANG! BANG!

"*To arms! To arms! There're at the courtyard.*"

"Prince, bolt the doors!" Schuyler commanded.

Lisbon raced into the house from the kitchen through the dining room, bringing another servant with him to guard the back hall entrance. "The muskets," he cried, "where are they?"

"Oh my God," gasped Angelica. "I had them put the muskets in the cellar! What have I done?"

BANG! BANG!

"No time to worry about the muskets now! Get up, Angelica! Hurry!" shouted Peggy. She grabbed Cornelia and Rensselaer by the hand. "Eliza! Come on!"

Eliza sat frozen, ashen.

"*You men, come with me! Schuyler's inside!*"

Angelica seized Eliza by the elbow and pulled her to her feet, then scooped up her little girl. "Mama," Angelica cried in dismay. "Little Philip!"

Peggy spotted the boy, racing ahead, thinking it all a game. He was heading right for where the attackers would try to enter. The very pregnant Angelica would never catch him. Peggy shoved Cornelia at Catharine, Rensselaer at Jeremiah, and raced after her three-year-old nephew, scooping him up, kicking and shrieking to be let down.

Schuyler reached the staircase, half carrying Catharine, who dragged Cornelia behind her. The boys bounded ahead two steps at a time. Eliza took the kicking toddler from Angelica so she could hoist herself up the stairs as they both struggled to hurry, yanking their heavy skirts up to their knees.

CRASH!

As the Schuylers reached the second floor, the back hall door flew open, smashing against the wall.

"Stand fast agin 'em, boys!" From below, Peggy could hear Lisbon's shout. Then sounds of scuffling, scraping feet, steel being drawn, shoves, shouts, curses.

BANG! A scream of pain.

Stumbling across the wide salon hallway, Schuyler flung his family into his bedroom, slammed the door, bolted it, and raced to the closet to pull out two preloaded pistols.

Panting, starting to cry now in fear, Catharine, Angelica, and Eliza huddled together as far from the door as possible, herding the little ones behind their skirts. Jeremiah took his place as a sentry to his mother and sisters, holding up his hands in fists. The thirteen-year-old bit his lip to control his own terror as Rensselaer wrapped his arms around his big brother's leg, peeking out from behind him.

Schuyler flung open the window and looked into the dark night. "Peggy," he said quietly as he scanned the horizon, trying to spot something in the gloom to aim at. "Take my sword from the dresser and give it to Jeremiah. Son, use that only if I fall."

Peggy pulled her father's sword from the drawer, knowing that recently the weapon had only been used in ceremonies. Was the blade still sharp? But she smiled reassuringly to her little brother as she handed it to him.

Only then, facing everyone who was dear to her, did Peggy realize something terrible. "Mama, do you have baby Caty?"

"Oh my God." Catharine's knees buckled and she fell to the floor. Then she tried to crawl toward the door.

"Kitty, no!" Schuyler scrambled to stop her, lifting her to her feet and holding on to her.

"Peggy," she cried out.

But Peggy needed no prompting. The image of Bleecker's dead baby, an innocent victim of their adult war, had already flashed through her mind. She had prayed that awful day in 1777, among those terrified refugees, that she would have the nerve to protect her family when it most counted. This was that moment. And sharp-edged words were not enough.

Peggy pulled back the bolt of the door. The littlest Schuyler sister, her goddaughter, needed her.

Trembling, Peggy kicked off her shoes so she could skitter across the floor without a heavy tread, alerting the marauders of her family hiding upstairs. *Quickly! Quickly!* her mind screamed. *Before they spot the baby!*

Peggy shoved out of her head stories of Tories and their Iroquois allies killing entire families to terrorize their Patriot neighbors. *They want Papa alive to ransom him. To embarrass the Patriot cause and unnerve the locals. They won't kill the baby. They won't kill us. Surely.*

But she didn't believe herself. After all, her papa had a 200-guinea price on his head.

What Peggy did know with certainty was if the invaders nabbed the baby, Schuyler would give himself up to win her safe release, just like the Oneida sachem had for his captive children. The old warrior had never returned.

BANG!

"Hold them!"

"Help! Help!"

Her heart pounding in her ears as loudly as musket fire, Peggy slipped through the closet-like door to the servants' back steps—a tight, winding, suffocating staircase to the ground floor, no railing, no candlelight. She groped her way in darkness along the rough-hewn walls.

CRASH! The door to the cellar below her was thrown open.

362

"Have at them, boys!"

KA-PING! KA-PING! Shots ricocheted. Mortar exploded and crumbled on the opposite side of the wall from her fingertips.

The baby started to wail.

Please don't cry, Peggy pleaded. *They'll hear you. They'll grab you!*

She tripped on her skirts and nearly fell headfirst down the steps. What she would give to be in breeches. Finally she reached the bottom step.

THUMP! A body slammed against the very door she needed to exit. Peggy clapped her hands over her mouth to silence a startled shriek of fear.

SCRAAAPPE! The body was dragged away.

Peggy took a deep breath, waited a moment, then turned the latch and cracked the door to peep out.

One of Schuyler's guards lay on the floor bleeding. Lisbon kicked at a man who jabbed at him with the butt of a musket. A few invaders were pocketing silverware from the table, while others checked the parlors. Baby Caty was crying and thrashing so hard, her cradle rocked.

One, two, three, four, five, six, seven men that she could see. So many of them!

"Any sign of Schuyler?" asked an officer in Loyalist green, holding a pistol.

"No, sir!"

"Upstairs, then," he commanded. "Take the guards at the staircase prisoner if you can. Let's learn what they know." He pulled back the flintlock.

Hurry! Hurry! Peggy's mind screamed. She had to grab the baby, and then make it back upstairs to warn her papa before these blackhearts reached her family.

The Loyalists gathered together to stride toward the grand staircase. "What about that baby, Captain?" one asked. "We could ransom the brat, don't you think?"

Peggy thought she might throw up.

"Stop right there!" shouted one of Schuyler's guards. Peggy couldn't see him, but she recognized the voice—it was Private Hines. He had gotten Peggy through the blizzard to Morristown—alive. She could trust him to stand fast for the minute she would need to snatch her baby sister. She had to.

"Stand down, man, or suffer the consequences!"

"Back at you, ye bloody bastard!"

More shouts, more scuffling, more grunts of pain.

Now! Do it now! Peggy slipped out of the stair-chute, skittered across the floor, and scooped up the baby, who shrieked with agitation. She turned to dash back.

"Hey! Stop that woman!" shouted the Tory captain.

Peggy pressed baby Caty to her chest, hoisted her skirts around her waist, and made for the steps. *Run! Run!*

"Grab her!"

Peggy—crawling, climbing, scratching her way up—made the second floor, and sprinted across the wide hall. The bedroom door swung open and her papa swept her inside. He threw the door closed behind her, bolting it again.

BANG! BANG!

"Surrender!"

"Papa, they are coming up the stairs." Peggy heaved out the words as Catharine pulled away from the huddle of sisters and toddlers to embrace her and gather up her infant. Never had her mother kissed Peggy that many times.

Peggy fell to the floor, now shaking uncontrollably.

"Ready, son?" Schuyler smiled reassuringly at Jeremiah.

The thirteen-year-old blanched but nodded bravely. Peggy's heart about broke at the sight. "Papa, no, there are too many of them!" They might shoot her brother if he tried to brandish that blade at them. She racked her brain for an alternative. "I wish we could make them think we have guards in here with us. They might think twice about entering."

Schuyler's face lit up. "We think alike, daughter. I set up a signal for the city's watch in case of something like this. Let's try a little subterfuge." He strode to the window and fired into the night, bellowing, "Come, my lads! Surround the house! The villains are inside it!"

By the door, Peggy could hear the Loyalists make the upstairs hall, heavy boots dashing from room to room. "Do it again, Papa," she whispered. She pulled the key from the door and peeped out the keyhole.

He nodded, shot his second pistol, and called, "That's right, my brave fellows! Have at the rascals!" He reloaded and shot again. "This way!"

Peggy saw the Tory captain freeze, then motion to his men and point toward the stairs. She held up her hand to keep everyone in the bedroom silent as she strained to see through the tiny slot. Legs. Backs. The invaders were retreating! Yes! They had bought the ruse! They must think her papa was outside with reinforcements, or was signaling because he saw a Patriot unit coming. "Thank God," she breathed, pulling herself off the floor to stand.

Schuyler remained at the window, looking out to the moonlit night. After moments that felt like a year, he smiled slowly. "It worked." He kept watching. "I can see them heading toward the river. Good God," he cursed. "I count twenty Tories at least. It's that blaggard Waltermeyer. Damn him! He's dragging two of our guard with him."

Peggy shifted her gaze from him to her sisters and the herd of her nephews, nieces, and siblings, still hanging on to one another.

They were all staring at her, their mouths open.

"What?" Peggy asked.

"What?" Angelica burst out laughing, in anxious, relieved hiccup-like gulps. "You! *You* are what." She looked toward their father. "Perhaps Peggy should be sent to General Washington as well!"

TWENTY-ONE

❧ ❧ ❧

Late Summer/
Early Autumn

Alexander Hamilton to Elizabeth Hamilton
Light Camp [New York], Aug. 16. 81

I have received my beloved Betsey your letter informing me
of the happy escape of your father. He showed an admirable
presence of mind, and has given his friends a double pleasure
arising from the manner of saving himself and his safety. Upon
the whole I am glad this unsuccessful attempt has been made.
It will prevent his hazarding himself hereafter as he has been
accustomed to do. He is a character too valuable to be trifled
with, and owes it to his country and to his family to be upon
his guard.

My heart . . . felt all the horror and anguish attached to
the idea of your being yourself and seeing your father in the
power of ruffians as unfeeling as unprincipled; for such I dare
say composed the band. I am inexpressably happy to learn that

my love has suffered nothing in this disagreeable adventure . . .

You have not told me though I have asked it once or twice whether you had received my letter inclosing two others one for [Angelica] one for Peggy. . . . God bless you.

SITTING CROSS-LEGGED IN HER FAVORITE WINDOW-seat perch, Peggy gazed out to the Hudson—in essence standing post after the raid on the house, perhaps perpetually so now. Still in their dressing gowns, Eliza and Angelica were reading letters they'd just received from their husbands. Cornelia was on the floor playing with the little Catharine, baby Caty, and Philip. For the moment all her sisters, her niece and nephew, were at peace and safe.

Downstairs, her papa was undoubtedly worrying over reported Redcoat raids around Niagara and along Lake Champlain, Tory attempts to kidnap General Peter Gansevoort, the hero of Fort Stanwix, and the arrival of new British troops at St. John's—all of which potentially suggested another full-scale attack from Canada, like Burgoyne's.

That morning Peggy had written down a letter for Schuyler to his nemesis, Barry St. Leger, trying to negotiate the release of the two guards his would-be kidnappers had taken prisoner. He'd also dictated a hoax letter for Moses Harris to take directly to the British, as if the agent had intercepted it. Addressed to George Washington, Schuyler's letter pretended to discuss plans for American forces to invade Canada from Cohoe Falls while the French fleet besieged Quebec and other Patriot units made trouble around New York City.

All false and a clever ruse to shield Washington's actual plans to head south, probably to Virginia.

How Peggy longed to tell Angelica and Eliza about their papa's clandestine work and that she sometimes helped in it. But she knew it must be kept secret, even from her sisters. No one could know about any of it.

But Peggy did.

She smiled, satisfied.

"And what are you so pleased about over there?" Angelica asked her. "Are you expecting someone?"

"No," she answered flatly, her smile disappearing. She searched Angelica's face to see if her big sister had meant to take her happiness down a peg. Angelica knew about Fleury and his disappearance from Peggy's life. But looking at her carefully told Peggy that Angelica had simply asked the question by rote. She was rubbing her very pregnant stomach, obviously uncomfortable and preoccupied.

Still, Peggy felt a flare of irritation. Would she now have to suffer comments from her sister as well as her mother about not having a suitor?

Peggy would turn twenty-three in a few days. By this point in their lives, both her mother and Angelica had given birth to two children, and Eliza was pregnant with her first. Peggy, on the other hand, was actually quite fine with not being at that place yet. As long as her papa ran a black chambers operation, she might have work vital to the Revolution to do!

Besides, Fleury had left Peggy bruised and wary of giving

her heart again. And Angelica's marriage wasn't exactly reassuring. From what she could tell, Carter's charms had faded into arrogance and a penchant for gambling and overdrinking. Peggy knew her brilliant eldest sister would have thrilled to know some of the things Peggy did. Angelica's role of influencing great men over dinner, carefully cloaking her more serious thought with scintillating repartee that seemed a tragic cage to Peggy. So who was Angelica to judge her? Peggy fumed silently.

Angelica took in a sharp breath and turned pale.

"Are you all right?"

Angelica nodded, breathing deeply. "This little one must be a boy from the way he kicks. Unless, of course"—she grinned at Peggy—"it is a girl with your temperament. God help me, then!"

Peggy laughed, feeling guilty for her annoyance. She was about to offer to get Angelica some tea, when—to her amazement—Eliza stood, stamped her foot, and crumpled her letter, throwing it to the ground. She started to pace.

"What's wrong?" Peggy and Angelica asked in unison.

Eliza stopped. "Wrong?" she asked with fury in her voice, startling her sisters. Peggy had never seen Eliza really angry, not like this. "Wrong? You tell me."

Angelica rose from her seat. "You must calm down, Eliza, it's not good for the baby. Whatever is troubling you, Peggy and I can help, surely."

"Unless you are the cause."

"What?"

"What?" Eliza mocked Angelica.

Peggy was stunned. That was the kind of snide thing she might have said and done as a child but Eliza never had. The snipe was so unlike her, Peggy knew whatever distressed her cut Eliza to her core. Her stomach churned, suspecting the cause. She looked back and forth between her older sisters. Should she have said something before about her questions regarding Hamilton and Angelica? Either way, Peggy felt like she was betraying a sister.

"What is between you and Alexander?" Eliza demanded.

"Wh-what?" Angelica, fell back into her chair. "Nothing!"

"Then why is he so worried about whether you received a letter he sent you?"

"Eliza, dearest, I do not know what you are talking about."

Eliza scooped her mangled letter from the floor and pulled it open, her hands shaking. "He scolds me in this, saying he has asked me twice whether you received a letter that was enclosed in the one he addressed to me. Why does it matter so much to him? Why? Why does he talk to you about politics and battles?"

Peggy looked to Angelica. She always talked those subjects with men, greedy for knowledge and intellectual discourse. It was her nature. But being the sister of such a sharp-witted and beautiful woman was almost unbearably hard. Peggy had felt inferior and jealous of Angelica, too. But she'd never questioned her own intellect, the way poor Eliza seemed to undercut herself—which was a travesty.

Angelica said nothing.

Her silence was making everything worse, so Peggy spoke up. "Eliza, she engages that way with all men, out of interest in the world. You and I have always known that—since we were little girls. That's all it is." Peggy resolved to tell Angelica later about Eliza's insecurities and how Alexander unwittingly fueled them. Surely, Angelica didn't know, or she'd be more careful in the way she related with Hamilton.

"Why do you defend her?" wailed Eliza. "I thought you'd be on my side."

"Eliza, I . . . ," Peggy began.

"He sent you a letter, too. What was that about?"

"I'm sure it was about taking care of you in his absence." Peggy's answer came quickly because it was honest. "I promised I would. He's concerned that your unease about his safety might make you sick."

Eliza faltered a bit in her anger but continued to glare at Angelica.

"Angelica, say something," Peggy prompted.

"I never received a letter," Angelica said icily.

What was she doing? That wasn't Eliza's question.

"Not the letter he references, no, you wouldn't have." Eliza was going toe to toe with Angelica in attitude. That was new, too. Peggy was impressed. Squaring off with Angelica took courage. "And you know why? Because I burned it."

Angelica gasped. "How dare you burn a letter for me!"

"How dare you expect a letter from my husband!"

"What did it say?" Angelica demanded.

"I have no idea. I didn't read it. It wasn't addressed to me."

"Oh, Eliza." Peggy couldn't help but laugh ruefully. How like Eliza to respect the privacy of someone else's letter, even if its existence infuriated her. Peggy certainly would not have shown that control. Burning it, though, that was pretty audacious! Peggy was quickly coming to learn that where Hamilton was concerned, Eliza was fiery and territorial, stronger and braver than in any other aspect of her life.

Angelica, however, was not amused or forgiving. "Shame on you!" Her typically silky voice grated.

"Shame on *me*?" Eliza stomped toward Angelica. "*Me? When are you going to stop showing off for men?*"

Peggy gasped—the same question had rattled around in her mind, but to say it aloud was so . . . so harsh, so disloyal. "Eliza, don't," she cautioned.

Angelica turned pale.

"What, no clever retort? No dazzling dance away from the question or from responsibility for your actions?" Eliza was now standing over the seated Angelica. Her entire small being was shaking. "I am sorry you are so unhappy. But Alexander is my husband. Mine. And he may die in this battle. He may . . ." Eliza was growing hysterical. "How . . . how could you encourage him to request a battle command? Why is it your business? When will you recognize that it is time to stop being the famed 'thief of hearts'? On your fourth baby?"

373

"Eliza, stop! You are making yourself ill," Peggy said, horrified. She climbed off the window seat, wading through the little children. They had silenced and were watching Eliza fearfully.

Eliza flung one more accusatory question. "Why does he listen to you?"

Angelica stood, rising to her full height and authority. "Because you do not speak to his ambitions. In that regard, sister, you do not meet his needs."

Eliza burst into tears.

"Angelica!" Peggy stepped between them, gathering up Eliza, who now crumpled, murmuring, "He could die, he could die, and never see our child."

"You both must stop," demanded Peggy. "You both must apologize. Our bond as sisters is more important than any letter. Or a man, for that matter! Please, we . . ." Peggy stopped abruptly, seeing Angelica's face. "What is it?"

Angelica looked down, and then bent over in agony, as if punched in her gut. The bottom half of her linen shift was streaked with blood.

"*Haaste je!* Lift her to the bed!"

Angelica bit back a scream of pain as Peggy and Catharine got her onto the mattress. "Eliza," she cried, "take the children away. Please! I don't want them to see me like this."

Eliza shook her head, frozen in her spot. "I'm sorry, I'm so sorry," she repeated over and over.

Angelica groaned and writhed. "Please," she whimpered.

"Elizabeth, do as Angelica says," Catharine commanded. "Peggy, fetch Libby. Tell her to boil water and bring towels. As quickly as possible."

Eliza gathered the children, who now were wailing. For them, she found that soothing voice of hers as she shepherded them out the door. "Come, my dears, let us see what the big boys are doing. Philip, wouldn't you like to play checkers with your uncle Rensselaer?"

Peggy raced to the staircase and shouted down it to Libby, the enslaved woman who had probably saved Catharine's life repeatedly during childbirth. She'd make it all right, she'd help Angelica. "Libby! Libby! Make haste! Angelica needs you. Please come!"

Dashing back to the bedroom, she took Angelica's hand. It was hot, trembling, and sweaty. The sheets under her were already soaked in blood. "Mama, what does the blood mean?"

Catharine was grim as she answered, "The baby's placenta has torn from the womb." She stroked Angelica's forehead and pushed her hair back from that beautiful face, now contorted with pain. "Engeltje, there is no time to waste. To breathe the baby must be born. Right away. Push, daughter. *Duwen*."

Angelica nodded, focusing her eyes on her mother's face for comfort, for strength. "Mama," she murmured, "what if . . ."

"It's all right, child. I am here. Your sister is here."

Catharine turned to Peggy. "Margarita, take her arm, help lift her and brace her."

Together, they hauled Angelica up to a semi-squat. Peggy could see her sister's belly rippling and contracting violently.

"Oh my God," Angelica whimpered, and then closed her eyes and tensed, pushing with all her strength.

"*Goed. Goed. Duw nu hard*," Catharine coaxed.

Angelica strained, hard, and then gasped, her eyes flying open, her head falling back as she shrieked with pain.

Peggy wept at her sister's torment, but held fast to her arm.

"Again, child," her mother urged.

Angelica pulled herself up, held her breath, and bore down again.

"*Goed! Goed!* I see the head!" cried Catharine. "Again!"

Again, Angelica held fast to Peggy, and pushed with all her being, screaming, before collapsing.

Libby hurried into the room with a bucket of steaming water. Eliza was behind her, carrying towels.

"Once more, Engeltje," Catharine ordered. "A long, hard push, daughter."

Angelica was limp, her head wagging back and forth, as if she was trying to keep herself awake. "I can't, Mama."

"You must!"

"Peggy," she whimpered.

"I'm here."

"Tell Eliza," she murmured, "tell her . . ."

Peggy turned to Eliza. "Come! Angelica needs to see you."

Eliza hesitated. Her sweet face was scarred with fear and regret.

Angelica's belly wrinkled and puckered again. She moaned and tried to lift herself, but fell back, her eyes rolling and shutting.

"Now, Eliza!" Peggy urged.

Eliza clambered up onto the bed to kneel in front of the three women fighting together to bring a live baby into the world. "Angelica, my dearest, I am here. Look at me."

Angelica eyes fluttered, open then shut.

"Angelica, Eliza is here. Right by me. She loves you. I love you. We need you. You must push now," Peggy pleaded. "For the baby. For us."

Her eyes still closed, Angelica managed to nod. Peggy and Catharine pulled her up, her head bobbing up and down, loose like a rag doll's, until she opened her eyes and saw Eliza.

Eliza smiled.

Weakly, Angelica smiled back.

"Now, Angelica," Peggy whispered into her ear. "We are all together."

"*Duwen!*" the women cried in one voice, willing Angelica to push with all she had. "*Duwen!*"

And the baby was born in a flood of blood and with a lusty bawl.

"It's a boy!" cried Eliza, holding him as Libby hastened to wrap him in a warm, clean cloth and Catharine cut his umbilical cord with the scissors hanging at her chatelaine, ever-ready.

Peggy turned her eyes from the infant to his mother. "Oh, Angelica, he's beau—" She broke off. "Angelica!" she cried.

Her sister was unconscious.

"*No! Nee, nee!*" Catharine shook Angelica. "*Wakker worden!*"

Nothing.

"Towels, quickly!" Catharine commanded. They packed them around Angelica, stanching the bleeding.

"Now what?" Peggy asked.

"We watch. We pray. It could just be exhaustion." Catharine spoke in practicalities, but with palpable worry. Suddenly, their mother looked old. "Libby," she added, "ask Mr. Schuyler to send for the doctor. He might be at the hospital."

"Yes, ma'am." Libby headed for the door, hurrying past Eliza, who held her new nephew, mewing healthily.

Catharine sat back, stricken.

Hospital. Looking at Eliza, Peggy was suddenly struck with a memory—of the first time she had met Hamilton. At the hospital. And right after seeing Dr. Thacher clean and drain a head wound.

"Mama, all this blood. We need to strip the bed and wash Angelica." She put her hand on Catharine's arm to rally her. "Mama!"

"Yes," answered Catharine, nodding, reenergized. "You

are right, child. We need clean towels, soaked in wine as antiseptic. Quickly!"

The doctor came and went. Angelica did not wake. Peggy and Eliza kept vigil through the night. Through the next day. Checking their sister's breathing. Wiping her down with a cool cloth. Holding their wrists against her forehead to assess her temperature. Each hour that passed without a fever brought them hope.

On the third day, a courier brought several letters for Eliza. The mail routes had become so dangerous letters could arrive out of order, or many at a time, even though written weeks apart.

Anxiously, Eliza opened them, stepping away from Angelica's bedside.

Peggy watched her sister's face, gauging her brother-in-law's words by her reactions.

"He says they are embarking for Yorktown." Eliza looked up. "Where is that?"

Peggy frowned. As hungry as she was to know what was happening, Hamilton should not be revealing such specific troop movements! What if the letter had been intercepted? "It's on the Chesapeake Bay," she answered as she stood and crossed the room to her sister. "Eliza, dearest, may I see that, please?"

"Why?" Eliza's suspicions flared.

"Just the back. I want to look at that wax seal."

"Oh." She sighed. "Of course. I love how my husband

says what he thinks and feels—without reservation. But I am learning I must help him temper himself. Alexander shouldn't have said where he was going, should he?"

Peggy shook her head.

Eliza handed her the letter. "Can you tell if the seal was previously broken as you might do it?"

Peggy looked at Eliza with surprise.

"I was there as you opened a letter when Papa's hands were bothering him, remember? I know you've been helping Papa with"—she paused—"many things. I have been glad of it since I have been away. It was easier for me, knowing you were here for him."

"Really?" Peggy asked. No jealousy?

"Really." Eliza reached out and squeezed Peggy's hand. "Does the seal look all right?"

"I think so. Hopefully it will not matter in any case. Surely our troops are well on their way now."

She handed the letter back to Eliza. "Does he say things that reassure you how much he loves you?"

"Listen and see what you think." Shyly she read aloud: *"What a world will soon be between us! To support the idea, all my fortitude is insufficient. What must be the case with you, who have the most female of female hearts? I sink at the perspective of your distress, and I look to heaven to be your guardian and supporter."*

"There, you see," Peggy interrupted. "That was precisely his concern when he left and what he asked of me right before he rode away. What does he say about the campaign?"

"That they have received news that assures him of success

and that he shall be home by November."

"November! They must have intelligence that makes them confident. That is good, Eliza!"

She nodded. "And he promises me to renounce public life after the war." Pleased, she read, "*Let others waste their time and their tranquillity in a vain pursuit of power and glory; be it my object to be happy in a quiet retreat with my better angel.*"

"Oh my, such words he writes you. You cannot doubt his love. And he is right, Eliza. You are indeed his better angel." Peggy just hoped Hamilton would stick to his statement that Eliza would be more important to him than power or glory. That was yet to be proven, and would require Hamilton to fight against his very nature.

"Eliza," Peggy began, and then paused a moment to collect her thoughts. She knew she had to help her Eliza come to terms with Angelica. Peggy had learned a great deal from helping their papa and watching his mind at work as he negotiated truces and alliances among hot-blooded revolutionists. First compliment, then explain the other side's point of view, and conclude with the need for reconciliation. "Angelica is intoxicating but she is not sustenance, not for Hamilton. You must try to see their conversation as the kind of discourse I imagine happens at a college. But you are his home, Eliza. When Hamilton asked me to look after you, he admitted something I hadn't thought about before."

"What is that?"

"Your husband has never really had a family. His mother died when he was very young. Correct?"

Eliza nodded, adding, "His father ran off."

"I don't think he knows yet how to be part of a family. He'll learn that with you. With us." Peggy laughed. "It's hard to avoid with all of us; we will beat it into him by sheer number."

Eliza giggled.

"Hamilton speaks his heart in his letters. Trust that. And he should come to understand our sisterhood, how close we all are, and that to drive a wedge in it is cruel."

They both glanced toward the bed. "What if Angelica dies?" whispered Eliza. "It will be my fault."

"Oh no, Eliza, it . . . it just happened." Peggy put her arm around Eliza and sat them both down in the window seat.

Sighing, Eliza leaned her head on Peggy's shoulder. "I know Angelica is not happy. It breaks my heart for her." She took in a deep breath. "If such conversations keep her spirited nature alive, I will try not to be alarmed by them." Eliza folded the letter, content. "Thank you for reassuring me, Peggy. I know I can be . . ." She hesitated. "A little anxious sometimes. I am lucky to have you as a sister."

The two sat quietly for a few minutes, while Peggy wondered if she ever really wanted to marry, thinking of how disappointed and limited Angelica obviously felt and how frightened Eliza was of losing Hamilton's love. If Peggy ever married, it would have to be a man who respected and yearned for her as an equal in mind and strength of personality. A next-to-impossible demand in king-ruled colonies, but perhaps possible in a new Republic, a meritocracy that valued individual mettle and common sense.

Suddenly Eliza put her hand to her side and whispered in amazement, "I think I just felt the baby kick!" She grimaced and then giggled. "Oh my, it's strong!"

"That's just the beginning, dearest," came a wan voice from the bed.

"Angelica!" Peggy and Eliza cried. They nearly knocked each other down in their scramble to take her hand, one in each of theirs.

"How are you feeling?" asked Peggy.

"Weak. How is my baby?"

"Absolutely fine. He seems a lusty little fellow. The wet nurse is keeping him happy until you are well."

Angelica nodded slowly, relieved. Her eyes closed, then opened. "I have you two to thank for his life. And mine."

Tears on her face, Eliza hastened to kiss Angelica, and rest her cheek against her big sister's, as Angelica cried as well—an unspoken apology and forgiveness between them.

"I don't know what I would do without you two," Angelica whispered, then added with a feeble laugh, "We are a powerful coven."

"Witches?" Eliza teased her. "Surely not?"

"No," Peggy said thoughtfully, thinking on the way Hamilton had greeted her at the Morristown ball. "No, we are the three Graces."

Once Peggy had thought of their trio like pieces of a jigsaw puzzle, none of their images clear without being linked to the other two. At least that had been how she had seen herself, defined according to comparison or by her relationship to her older sisters—*and* Peggy. But now that she had found her own role, her own identity, Peggy could see that each Schuyler sister had her own talents and personality—they were simply more potent in affecting their individual fates when joined together in purpose.

Yes, the three Graces.

"That makes you Aglaea, then," murmured Angelica.

"The goddess of brightness," added Eliza.

Angelica looked at her with a bit of astonishment.

Eliza grinned back. "I listen to what you two quote from your reading."

"Oh yes." Peggy nodded at Angelica. "That one is full of surprises. Or perhaps we just didn't recognize all her talents before."

"Ah, that is often the way with quiet ones," Angelica answered. She squeezed Eliza's hand.

"And with the youngest ones," said Eliza, looking toward Peggy.

They had come a long way, the three of them, in their Revolution.

The Schuyler sisters hugged—tight, hearing one another's breath, feeling one another's heartbeats. Just as they had done when they were little and jumped into the sweet-cool lake by their Saratoga country home. Just as they had embraced the night Angelica eloped, when the first of them broke away to pursue her own life. Just as they would until the day one of them died.

Postlude

EPILOGUE: JUNE 1782

I have the Honor to inform Congress, that a Reduction of the British Army under the Command of Lord Cornwallis, is most happily effected. The unremitting Ardor which actuated every Officer and Soldier in the combined Army on this Occasion, has principally led to this Important Event, at an earlier period than my most sanguine Hopes had induced me to expect. . . .

I should be wanting in the feelings of Gratitude, did I not mention on this Occasion, with the warmest Sense of Acknowledgements, the very chearfull and able Assistance, which I have received in the Course of our Operations, from, his Excellency the Count de Rochambeau, and all his Officers of every Rank, in their respective Capacities. Nothing could equal this Zeal of our Allies, but the emulating Spirit of the American Officers, whose Ardor would not suffer their Exertions to be exceeded.

. . . Congress will be pleased to accept my Congratulations on this happy Event.

—General George Washington on the American victory at Yorktown

"MISS SCHUYLER, MAY I HOLD MY GODDAUGHTER?"

Peggy looked up in wonderment at the face of General George Washington. He had come to Albany to discuss securing upstate New York from continued British and Tory raids along Lake Champlain and to meet with the Oneida and Tuscarora. Even six months after his victory at Yorktown, the threats from the enemy remained very real.

Of course, Albany had greeted His Excellency with jubilation—a thirteen-gun salute, an illumination of the entire city, a parade and review of troops, and the mayor presenting him with a gold box containing a document representing freedom. Now her family was celebrating him, along with generals Lafayette, Knox, and Greene, with a ball in their mansion's upstairs salon. Little Caty had been toddling and escaped Peggy to run headfirst into the crowd. Peggy had just crouched and crawled after her littlest sister to catch her before someone accidentally trampled her.

"O-o-of course, Your Excellency," she stammered, rising from the floor to hand Caty over. Despite having danced with him at Morristown and his gracious greeting of her that morning, Peggy was still in nervous awe of the man. She prayed little Caty would not be fussy in His Excellency's arms. No matter how intrepid she was physically, the toddler was at that stage where she could be fearful with strangers.

"Hello, little lady," Washington said gently, in that oddly whispery voice of his. "It is my great honor to meet you finally. We are to be fast friends, you and I."

At first Caty's face puckered, but the general swayed and bobbed her, like the expert dancer he was, and she relaxed. She patted his gold epaulets and then grabbed his nose.

Washington chortled.

"Oh, sir, I am so sorry!" Peggy reached to take Caty—the general had a reputation for being standoffish regarding physical contact—but Washington stopped her.

"Do not worry, Miss Schuyler. It is a joy to hold a young child." Caty finally released his nose, fascinated instead by all his buttons. He cocked his head to watch her a moment. "You are as beautiful as your big sister."

"Yes, she does look like Angelica," demurred Peggy. "And Eliza as well, for that matter."

"I meant you, Miss Schuyler." Washington smiled at her—that slightly mysterious tight-lipped expression of his. "I hear she is high-spirited as well. Your papa is a lucky man to have such daughters."

"Thank you, Your Excellency." Pleased but suddenly shy as well, Peggy couldn't think of anything to say other than, "I hope you are enjoying your stay?"

"Very much so," Washington answered. "I look forward to inspecting the fort and hospital, and riding to Saratoga with General Schuyler tomorrow. But I would prefer, in truth, to stay here and play a bit with your sister." He looked over the crowd of guests coming up the stairs from dinner, gathering for dancing. "I hope you will grant me a dance again this evening? One of the highlights of Morristown was our country dance."

He remembered! "Oh yes, please, Your Excellency; it would be my great honor."

"You will have to save one for me. I am sure there are many lads who will duel for the opportunity to partner you."

Ever honest, Peggy blurted out, "Oh, I wouldn't worry about that, General." Then she wanted to clap her hand to her mouth. She shouldn't admit such things at a polite gathering; it begged flattery or pity. But her words couldn't be taken back. She shrugged slightly, embarrassed for herself.

Washington fixed those deep-set analytical gray eyes on hers. For someone who had fought so many battles, witnessed such pain, loss, and betrayals, and had to scrutinize the motivations of countless would-be intimates and foes, they were remarkably kind, those eyes. "Nonsense, Miss Schuyler. The situation simply wants a man of integrity and courage, who relishes a sword fight with an equal." He smiled to reassure Peggy what he said was meant as a compliment. "Remember this—a sensible woman can never be happy with a fool." He paused. "Particularly . . . a French one."

Peggy flamed red. If Hamilton had told His Excellency about Fleury she would strangle him. Instinctively, she looked to the corner where he and Eliza were chatting happily with General Greene. Hamilton had gained the glory he sought at Yorktown, leading a do-or-die bayonet charge into a well-fortified redoubt, clearing the field for Lafayette's full attack. Eliza had safely given birth to a boy, another Philip in honor of their papa. Hamilton was settling into reading the law. But he had a lot to learn about protecting his clients' secrets—if he had indeed betrayed her confidence by telling George Washington, of all people!

Washington noticed her gaze and said, "A general must be observant of those around him, not just relying on reports of trusted junior officers." Then he kept talking, addressing his words to Caty in that overly emphatic, storytelling happy voice adults use for babies, but clearly meaning in message for Peggy. "A beautiful and accomplished lady will turn the heads and set the circle in which she moves on fire. But once the torch bursts into a blaze with a particular gentleman, the lady must ask herself several important questions." He made a face at Caty, as if he expected the child to respond. Her little face dimpled with glee at the game.

"The lady must ask herself: Who exactly is this invader? Have I competent knowledge of him?" Washington continued as if singing a nursery rhyme. Caty giggled.

"Is he a man of good character, a man of sense? Or is he a gambler, a spendthrift, or a drunkard?" He drew out the last words with a growl. Caty laughed outright.

"Do my friends have no reasonable objection to him?" Washington made his eyes big and his face look surprised, and Caty clapped her hands in delight.

"If these questions are satisfactorily answered, there remains but one more to be asked. Are his affections engaged by me and me alone? If my passion is not reciprocated, the man is not worthy of me. Isn't that right, Miss Caty?" He tickled Caty's belly and she squealed with laughter.

Then the general turned to Peggy with all earnestness to

say, "A lady of character deserves a man who looks nowhere but at her." He leaned closer and added quietly, "Like the lad who has been reclining against the door and watching you this entire time."

Washington handed Caty to Moll, who had come to watch the baby so Peggy could enjoy the dancing that was about to begin. He bowed to Peggy. "I look forward to our dance, Miss Schuyler."

Then General George Washington strode into the crowd and a siege of questions: What are we to do about the Redcoats still occupying New York City? Where do our peace talks stand? How will Congress pay all the back wages of the Continental Army? What does land in the Ohio territory look like and when can we Patriots take ownership of it? Pleas of "Your Excellency, sir" echoed over and over throughout the salon.

Peggy watched him disappear into his supplicants and then slowly turned her eyes to the doorframe he mentioned. There stood Aaron Burr, the young Continental Army officer Schuyler was also allowing to use his library to study the law. Burr was talking with dear old Richard Varick. Peggy smiled. Thanks to her father, Washington was now employing Varick as his personal secretary. As such, Varick had arrived with the general's entourage. It was the first she had seen him since Benedict Arnold's betrayal.

Earlier that day he had told her, with great apologies, that he was in love and had an understanding with a woman he'd grown up with. Peggy had been proud of herself for not laughing outright at him, but feigning instead slight disappointment and wishing him well. There would be hell to pay later with her mother, but she'd think on that another time. What lad was Washington talking about?

Shifting her gaze slightly to the left, through a gaggle of locals ogling the military dignitaries, she caught a partial view of a young man, indeed leaning against the door. As she looked, he tilted his face so she could see him better—clearly he'd been watching and waiting for her glance to reach him. A mop of soft black curls fell over his eyes with the movement. It was her distant cousin, the one who had been away at Harvard for the year. Last time she had seen Stephen Van Rensselaer he was a beautiful, slight youth. What a difference a year could make in a boy—he was still slender, still with a peachy hue on that smooth, heart-shaped face. But he obviously shaved now and must have grown two inches taller. As Stephen straightened, pulled himself away from the doorjamb, and strode toward her, Peggy felt herself blush. He had become rather devastatingly handsome—if she cared about that kind of thing.

"Miss Peggy," he said, and bowed, his voice far deeper than before. "I am glad to see you have recovered your strength since last we met."

"Master Stephen." She curtsied. Peggy knew he meant well to ask after her health. After all, she'd almost fainted in front of him, thinking Fleury had come to visit given Moses Harris's ruse that he was a suitor of hers. But she hardly wished to remember or discuss that sudden mixture of gut-wrenching hope and despairing disappointment. She shifted the subject. "How is Harvard?"

"Wonderful," answered Stephen, just as the musicians began to play. They both turned to watch the dance floor. "Ah, His Excellency has chosen your mama as his partner for the first minuet."

Standing on tiptoe, Peggy could see over people's shoulders to Catharine, who was absolutely radiant at the honor being done her by General Washington. Peggy caught her breath—she had forgotten how beautiful her mother could look. Catharine wore a crisp cream satin gown, brocaded with delicate vertical trellises of rosebuds that cleverly thinned her slightly round figure. Beautifully scalloped, pinked ruffles cascaded from her elbows as Catharine held out her arms in a floaty arc, making her a pretty echo of the young, happy, elegant woman captured in her portrait as a bride.

While she pirouetted lightly on her toes, guided expertly by His Excellency, Schuyler beheld Catharine with an adoration that made Peggy's eyes well up. Her papa looked like he might burst with pride in his beloved Kitty. After twenty-five years of marriage, thirteen pregnancies, war's losses and victories, public praise and ridicule, illness and disappointments, fear and jubilation, they were still in love, still *partners*.

"My word, they are an inspiring pair," murmured Stephen.

Peggy nodded. "His Excellency is the most chivalrous of dancers."

"Actually, I meant your mother and father." Stephen

nodded toward Schuyler. "I mean, look at the way he gazes at her—in rapture." He cleared his throat self-consciously. "I suppose I notice it since my father died when I was so young. I never saw him with my mother. I hope to be that in love with my wife when I am that age."

Peggy dared a sideways glance at him. He seemed totally sincere. Stephen felt her scrutiny and turned from watching the dance to smile at her. "Not even Molière, who can satirize anything, would be able to touch them."

"Ahhh." Slowly, she smiled, remembering. "So you read the plays I suggested you take from Papa's library."

"I did indeed. I have to admit that I prefer Shakespeare to Molière's rather biting wit."

So this young man was the earnest type. "*Julius Caesar*, I would guess?"

"Yes, of course. But I also like the comedies."

"Really?" She felt her eyebrow arch. "Which is your favorite?"

"I'd say *Twelfth Night*."

Peggy eyed him suspiciously. "I suppose you enjoy what fools the lovers become, especially Olivia." Peggy felt particular pity for that character, a lady who unwittingly fell in love with a fantasy—a young man who was poetic and courageous. But not what he seemed. Like Fleury. Little did Olivia know that the kind, thoughtful youth was actually a girl pretending to be a young man. And the audience was in on the joke. If Stephen laughed, Peggy would know to put him in the McHenry category. She waited.

"Not really," he said.

"No?"

"No." He grinned at her as General Greene asked Angelica to dance the minuet.

"So what *do* you enjoy most about *Twelfth Night*?" Peggy asked as she watched her eldest sister circle the Quaker general, gliding smooth, calm, like a lily floating along a quiet pond.

"Viola."

Peggy turned back to gape at him—incredulous. "The girl who protects herself after being shipwrecked by dressing and acting like a boy?"

"Indeed yes," Stephen answered. "She is so full of life, pluck, resourcefulness, wit. But what I really like is what she says about love."

Peggy just stared at him. Was this boy real?

"How does Shakespeare put it?" Stephen paused a moment, closed his eyes, and recited, "That a lover should *write loyal cantons of contemned love and sing them loud even in the dead of night.* And that he should 'halloo' his lover's name *to the reverberate hills and make the babbling gossip of the air cry out* her name until she takes pity on him." He smiled down at Peggy, and shrugged. "I am too much of a romantic, I know. I suppose I shall be weaned from it when I leave university."

"Oh, I hope not," said Peggy, shaking her head. "What's the point of loving, if you don't feel it utterly?"

They fell silent, watching Hamilton stride onto the dance floor with Eliza. Peggy was flooded with the memory of their minuet at Morristown, when she had witnessed her sister give her loyal heart to him. There it was again—that look of insecure hunger from Hamilton, Eliza's answer of shy acceptance and loving reassurance, the urgency of their touch, the bittersweetness of their turns away from each other.

Peggy sighed.

"Now that is courtship," Stephen breathed, "as mellifluous as poetry."

She nodded.

As Hamilton and Eliza left the dance floor and walked, arm in arm, toward them, Stephen bowed to her. "Miss Peggy, would you do me the great honor?"

Surprised, she looked up into that beautiful face, unsure why she hesitated, annoyed that she felt fear.

Stephen smiled, bashful, curious, hopeful all at once. "If music be the food of love . . ."

Peggy caught Hamilton's eye as he and Eliza approached, a few feet behind Stephen. Instantly, looking into her face, Peggy's brother-in-law sized up the situation. Hamilton smiled encouragingly and nodded at her in a fond, unspoken way: "Your turn, little sister." Peggy's turn to sweep out into the center of those blue-coated, battle-tested, idealistic Patriots. Her turn to partake in the Revolution's victory, to have all eyes on her—just for a moment.

If music be the food of love?

Taking a deep breath, Peggy put her hand in Stephen's, and whispered to complete the quote: "Play on."

AFTERWORD

In a man's letters, you know, Madam, his soul lies naked . . . whatever passes within him is there shown undisguised . . . nothing is inverted, nothing distorted. . . .

This is the pleasure of corresponding with a friend, where doubt and distrust have no place, and every thing is said as it is thought . . . I have indeed concealed nothing from you, nor do I expect ever to repent of having thus opened my heart.

—*Samuel Johnson (author, journalist, wit) to Mrs. Thrale, October 27, 1777*

WE HAVE ONLY TWO LETTERS FROM ALEXANDER Hamilton to the youngest of the famed Schuyler sisters trio— his introduction and playful plea for Peggy's help in courting Eliza, plus a long postscript attached to a note from her sister right after their marriage. But scattershot throughout his love letters to Eliza are passing references and tidbits of gossip about his soon-to-be little sister, and fond, teasing messages he asks Eliza to pass along to Peggy. Pieced together, they reveal much about the younger Schuyler's high-spirited personality and the quick, intuitive, and affectionate friendship between Peggy and Hamilton. He almost immediately began referring to her as "my Peggy."

To walk through Hamilton's letters is to stroll a lush verbal garden of the most glorious scents and colors: profuse, intoxicating—also full of thorns and stings if he were displeased! I've quoted them and others from the Schuyler circle throughout my novel—misspellings and all, and with signature lines, dates, and locations appearing as they do on the original documents—so you can experience these letters' immediacy firsthand. Within them, you will feel for yourself in vivid descriptions and pleas the palpable heartaches, hardships, and hopes of the people fighting our Revolution. (Also in homage to the epistolary novel tradition of the time, for all you English majors who groaned through *Pamela: Or, Virtue Rewarded*.) In the eighteenth century, people spoke of and to their friends in far warmer and adoring ways than we do today. Their letters are filled with tenderness, compliments, longings to see one another, love advice, and gentle jests. Personas are laid bare in the most delightful ways.

Hamilton's poeticism, insecurities, bluster, and passion rise off the pages of his letters and handed me much of his dialogue in this novel and my ideas for its plot and characters. I immediately knew how to write Peggy's uncle, Dr. John Cochran, when reading his letter calling a fellow officer a "nincompoopa!" And Lieutenant Colonel Varick's constant "please to give my best to Miss Peggy" in his letters from the Saratoga battlefield led me to suspect the earnest Dutchman had quite a crush on the youngest daughter of his commanding general.

Sadly, no letters written by Peggy during this novel's time period survive. What we do know of her is gleaned from what other people have said, including the appearance and disappearance of Marquis de Fleury as a suitor. But what a wondrous skeleton of her life and of her vibrant and savvy personality they gifted me. Carefully cross-referenced, those letters also helped me track her whereabouts, showing she was indeed in the right place at the right time to witness some of the most momentous events of the American Revolution. Given what people said of her, it also felt totally plausible that she could have actively participated in several crucially important war efforts—like her father's spy rings.

Contemporaries called Peggy "lively," "charming," "bright, spirited, and generous," "the favourite of dinner-tables and balls," even "wild" (according to Benjamin Franklin), and possessing "a wicked wit." Hamilton obviously considered her confident enough, possessed with enough charisma and appreciation for satire, to jokingly promise to write a play about matters of the heart in which she would star. In 1795, a French aristocrat who escaped the guillotine to settle in the United States described Peggy as "endowed with a superior mind and a rare accuracy of judgment for both men and things." Madame de la Tour du Pin was not at all impressed by the intellect or sophistication of most Americans she met. But she admired Peggy.

Peggy indeed spoke French fluently, painted, and clearly was just as interested in politics and philosophies as her more famous oldest sister, Angelica. James McHenry's calling

Peggy a "Swift's Vanessa" in a letter to his fellow aide-de-camp, Hamilton, was eighteenth-century code for a woman who was well-read, articulate, and passionate in talking about philosophy and political ideas—conversations at that time deemed more "masculine" than feminine. (McHenry's dialogue in Chapter Seventeen was taken directly from that letter.) Tragically, McHenry dubbed her a Vanessa disparagingly, displaying his own discomfort with a smart, strong woman as well as the societal constraints that must have so frustrated Peggy. If McHenry is to be believed, Angelica was saved from the same negative label because of her lighter, more flirtatious touch, and her ease with other women.

It says a lot about Hamilton that he had such an affinity for intelligent and articulate women. The same can be said of Peggy's father, General Philip Schuyler. All visitors to his Albany mansion, The Pastures, praised the lively and well-informed conversation among his amiable, dark-eyed daughters. Clearly, Schuyler encouraged their learning and discourse. In many ways, he was quite progressive, dividing his primogeniture (his legal right as firstborn son to inherit his parents' entire estate) with his brother and sister. His letters to his daughters typically began with "My beloved child . . ."

Schuyler family documents also unveil a gutsy and loyal young Peggy—detailing her saving her baby sister during the Loyalist kidnapping raid and traveling through the wilderness of upstate New York to help nurse Schuyler. She appears an unflinching caretaker. General John Bradstreet, a father figure and close family friend, is said to have died in the comforting arms of a teenage Peggy, who had stayed by his sickbed. Her younger siblings were often left in her care, even after she married. And, according to a letter from Schuyler to General Heath asking he safeguard his daughters' passage, Peggy accompanied Angelica on the dangerous trip to Yorktown to rejoin her husband—most likely to help tend to her newborn nephew and his young siblings.

Such devotion among sisters was commonplace in the eighteenth century—think Jane Austen novels a few decades later—but seems especially beautiful and symbiotic among the Schuyler trio. Their back-to-back births clearly made them playfellows. Eliza was only eighteen months younger than Angelica, and Peggy thirteen months younger than Eliza. As much as she clearly loved them, and possessed traits of each older sister, Peggy must have struggled for notice given the dazzling, intellectual Angelica, "the thief of hearts," and Eliza, "the little saint" of the Revolution. Hence the theme of Peggy's coming-of-age and finding her own sense of self and agency within this novel.

I speculate the real-life Peggy had a particularly strong, empathetic bond with her father. Madame de la Tour du Pin, for instance, stated that Peggy had learned to speak French so well by "accompanying her father to the general headquarters of the American and French armies." Peggy also suffered the same physical ailments that plagued Schuyler. Plus, she simply seemed to be at home more than her sisters. School bills show Angelica and Eliza in New York City together (without Peggy), and in the letters of 1777 I can find no mention of Eliza being in Albany. Angelica, of course, was already in Boston at that point with her new husband.

All the family events, battles, spies, visits (of Iroquois, French, and Patriot delegations), plus the "celebrity" appearances in this novel are factual. The details of my scenes were gleaned from journals, letters, and news accounts of the time. Much of the dialogue spoken by the novel's real-life characters comes straight from words they wrote themselves—such as George Washington's love advice to Peggy at the end of the novel, which I pulled from a letter he wrote to his grandniece.

Out of their Albany home, Schuyler did run a critically important "black chamber operation" network of Canadian, Iroquois, and New Yorker informants, spies, and double agents. He gathered information on enemy movements and intentions through his scouts and informants and by intercepting British communiqués. He and his staff would open, copy, and reseal these letters and then send them on to their intended recipients, who'd never know the information was compromised. Schuyler also fed his enemies false information and fake letters between him and George Washington. He was probably the Revolution's most skilled military intelligence and counterintelligence officer.

In many ways, Schuyler was Washington's right-hand man—detecting conspiracies for surprise attacks in New York, Canada, and adjacent northern states; guarding our vulnerable back door at the Canadian border; and finding ways to supply the Continental Army when others left its soldiers to starve and freeze. He continued to do so even after his honor was so publicly maligned by Congress and the New England delegates, chiefly John Adams. Besides serving as the commander of the Northern Army from 1775 to mid–1777 and as a New York delegate to Congress, Schuyler was also the Commissioner of Indian Affairs, responsible for negotiating war alliances with the six Iroquois nations.

We forget that the almost decade-long Revolution was also a horrifyingly bloody civil war between neighbors. A third of Americans were committed Patriots, a third were Loyalist Tories, and another third were basically neutral, trying to survive the back-and-forth violence, desperate to keep their farms or small shops operating so they could feed themselves. But there was no avoiding the war and its arguments in the state of New York. Raids on Tory and Patriot strongholds were constant and could be vicious from both sides.

Rangers and marauding "cowboys" and "skinners" attacked any and all travelers and isolated farms. (Those terms came originally from a Loyalist irregular cavalry raised by Colonel James De Lancey, which stole cattle and other livestock from civilians and took them to the British Army in New York City. "Skinners" belonged to a battalion of British refugee volunteers commanded by the former attorney general of New Jersey, Brigadier General Cortlandt Skinner. Eventually the phrase became more indiscriminate, describing all manner of guerilla bands and highway robbers.)

As was true with Patriots, Loyalists were motivated by both idealistic philosophy and self-interested hope for profit and social advancement. Many Loyalists still had family in England and took pride in being part of the British Empire and the constitutional rights it granted its citizens. They feared what they saw as anarchy in the Patriots' actions—especially in Boston with its famous tea party and its mob tar-and-feathering of royal officers and sympathizers—and distrusted what kind of government people who had promulgated such violence could create. Some were xenophobic, fearing the influx of foreigners and radical Protestants who tended to flock to the cause of liberty.

The political rifts could be heartbreaking. During the series of battles at Saratoga, for instance, firing ceased for a moment so that two brothers could wade across a stream to embrace each other, before going back to their opposing sides and the resumed fight.

Tragically, our Revolution ended a peaceful and democratic confederacy that had endured for centuries among neighboring American Indian tribes—the Oneida, Tuscarora, Mohawk, Onondaga, Cayuga, and Seneca—known as the Six Nations of the Iroquois Confederacy or the *Hau de no sau nee* (meaning: people who build). Their longstanding league disintegrated into civil war as well, when four of the tribes decided that allying with the British and Loyalists would better help them keep their native lands, culture, and sovereign autonomy. Colonists had repeatedly violated boundaries established in treaties between the ruling British and the Iroquois—poaching or farming on territory guaranteed to the tribes, lands the Iroquois had traditionally hunted or inhabited. The four "Loyalist" tribes anticipated that a Patriot-controlled government might allow even more encroachment.

They joined the British as scouts and forward raiding parties, greatly helping the British navigate the wilderness of upstate New York. Burgoyne, for one, knew that years of skirmishes, hostilities, and the recent bloodbath that was the French and Indian War had imbedded a visceral fear of Iroquois warriors that he fanned with outrageous proclamations and threats—hoping to cow Patriots and rally Loyalists. Eventually, trying to undercut their ability to fight, Continental troops raided tribal villages, decimating the Mohawk, Onondaga, Cayuga, and Seneca societies. The Oneida and Tuscarora villages had been similarly destroyed by the British and their allied Iroquois.

I don't know that Peggy met Hamilton by Benedict Arnold's hospital sickbed, but it is a legitimate possibility. All three were in Albany at that time. (Legend holds that Hamilton met Eliza during his official mission to General Gates, but there are no records of such an encounter. Schuyler was indeed in Saratoga rebuilding his house.) It is fact, however, that Peggy's father was a friend and admirer of Arnold's, frequently intervened on his behalf with Congress, and supported his taking command of West Point. Arnold's betrayal would have hit the Schuyler family hard as a result.

Tracking Hamilton's mentions of her in his letters to Eliza, Peggy must have met Marquis Francoise-Louis Teissedre de Fleury in Newport, Rhode Island, where it makes sense that she was staying with Angelica and her husband, then commissary for the newly landed French army. I had to really dig to learn much about Fleury. Like Lafayette, he came to the States on his own to volunteer with the Continental Army. And like hundreds of other Frenchmen whose names are lost to history, his enormous contributions to the Patriot cause are largely forgotten—even though Fleury was one of only eight individuals honored during the American Revolution with a commemorative medal (described in Chapter Thirteen).

Born in Southern France, Fleury joined the French Army at age nineteen, serving in Corsica before sailing to America. At first, Congress didn't know what to do with the flood of idealistic French officers, but Fleury was soon a captain with the Continental's corps of engineers. Well trained and a natural leader, Fleury eventually rose to the rank of Lieutenant Colonel. He served (and was wounded several times) at Yorktown, Brandywine, Germantown, Monmouth, the horrific siege of Fort Mifflin, and Stony Point—the attack that earned him a Congressional Silver Medal of Honor. A British commodore wrote of Fleury's charge, "The rebels had made the attack with a bravery they never before exhibited." Fleury did indeed share his reward money with his foot soldiers and showed mercy to his enemy, "a generosity and clemency which during the course of the rebellion had no parallel," wrote the commodore. "Instead of putting them to death, [he] called to them to throw down their arms" and they could expect to be given quarter—a humanity some British commanders had failed to show Patriots in several terrible instances that resulted in massacres of wounded Patriots who had surrendered.

Ingenious as well as brave, Fleury wrote General Washington a marvelously enthusiastic letter, in awkward English, describing self-propelled, exploding fireboats he hoped to launch into the British fleet anchored in the Delaware River and threatened Philadelphia in 1778. (I pull directly from that letter for Henry's dialogue in Chapter Fourteen.) Washington applauded Fleury's "Zeal for the Public Service" and suggested using "some desperate fellows" and "the greatest Secrecy and Caution" to "make the experiment." As far as history knows, nothing came of Fleury's plans. (Perhaps they were discouraged knowing the failure of "the Turtle"—a fantastical eight-foot-long, one-man, egg-shaped submersible—technically the first submarine used in warfare—pedaled through the waters of New York Harbor to try to attach an exploding mine to the hull of a British warship.)

By the way, each year since 1989, the United States Army has awarded individuals who have made significant contributions to army engineering the de Fleury Medal, a replica of the one presented the Frenchman in 1779.

When Peggy met him, Fleury would have been thirty-one. His Newport host described him as "sociable, jocose, and very agreeable in conversation, of a free, liberal turn of mind in matters of religion." It really bothered me that I could never resolve what happened between the two of them after Fleury mentioned his hopes of marrying Peggy in a letter to Hamilton. All I knew was that after the war, he returned to the French Army and fought in a variety of campaigns from South America to India to Europe.

My stubborn quest to gather some hint of what killed their romance led me to heartbreaking letters sent twenty years later, in 1800, from Lafayette (then in France) to Hamilton on behalf of Fleury's widow. While the brief biographies I could unearth about Fleury listed conflicting versions of his death—from being executed in the French Revolution to dying in battle, his body never found—her plea for a pension for his service in the American Revolution states that he committed suicide. I mourned when I learned it.

I finally decided to write his and Peggy's story to reflect the sudden, passionate friendships and love affairs often brought about in the heat of war; the mysteries surrounding what my adult children tell me is a known term used by millennials: "ghosting"; and what I came to believe was Peggy's clear sense of self-possession and self-determination. I think Peggy had the sense to refuse to accept anything but complete and utter devotion. It's what she seems to have offered those she loved. And she waited until she found it.

In June 1783, Peggy married her distant cousin, Stephen Van Rensselaer. Some accounts have them eloping—perhaps because the match scandalized Albany since he was turning nineteen and she twenty-four years old. But her family seemed very pleased. Kindred souls in intellect and devotion to public service, Peggy supported his running for office and becoming lieutenant governor of New York in 1795. He also served as a state senator and US congressman. He inherited one of the largest fortunes in United States history, becoming Lord of Van Rensselaer Manor, the last Dutch land-granted patroon in America. Immediately, Hamilton teasingly nicknamed Peggy "Mrs. Patroon."

Peggy gave birth to three children, but by 1801, at age forty-three, she was chair-bound, crippled with gout and suffering what might have been stomach cancer. Hamilton was in Albany on legal business when her condition deteriorated. Hamilton remained in the city for three weeks, visiting her sickbed almost daily. True to her brave, witty self to the very end, Peggy "was sensible to the last and resigned to the important change," Hamilton wrote Eliza at their New York City home. He seems to have been by his little sister's side as she drew her last breath.

Even then, Hamilton remained loyal to his Peggy, their fates intertwined. He threw his energy into supporting her husband's campaign for New York governor. This pitted Hamilton against Aaron Burr, who promoted Van Rensselaer's opponent. The competition fueled their political animosity.

Three years later, Hamilton died in their infamous duel.

I like to believe Peggy was waiting for him on the other side.

There are many anecdotes—funny, touching, astounding—about the people surrounding Peggy and fighting the Revolution that I wish I could have included. But please see my bibliography for wonderful, deeply humanizing biographies of Hamilton; Washington and his devoted wife, Martha; his aides-de-camp; Arnold; Lafayette; and Philip Schuyler—who truly was an important "supporting" founding father.

I'm sharing two stories about a younger Philip Schuyler because they reveal so much about him, the close bonds the Americans and the British, Patriots and Loyalists, had before the Revolution, the very international complexion of the new nation, the fortitude of its women, and the largesse enemy officers could show one another in the midst of carnage.

During the French and Indian War, Schuyler became great friends with his commander, British General John Bradstreet, eventually even naming his firstborn son for him. Bradstreet remained in America, becoming a surrogate father/grandfather to the Schuylers. So much so, Schuyler was willing to sail to England on business for him, leaving Catharine to oversee the building of their Albany mansion, with three daughters all under the age of five. She was pregnant, too, with twins who perished shortly after their birth while Schuyler was absent.

On that voyage, the captain of Schuyler's ship died. Schuyler took over the navigation, because he was quite smart mathematically. That put him at great peril of being executed when the next mishap occurred—French privateers, or pirates really, captured the ship. But Schuyler managed to negotiate for his life and for the lives of the other British-born passengers because he spoke French so fluently.

Once, during the French and Indian War, Schuyler and his unit had flushed the enemy off a tiny island in the watery regions of upstate New York. The French and American Indians retreated. They mounted a counterattack as Schuyler and his men were canoeing back to the main shore to join their company. In the midst of the crossfire, Schuyler heard a badly wounded French Canadian crying out in agony and begging not to be left there to die. The British soldiers with Schuyler ignored their enemy's pleas. But Schuyler plunged into the waters, swam back to the island, lifted the enemy onto his back, and found a place he could wade across the stream, carrying him. The French Canadian lived. Years later, during the Revolution, he became a spy for the Americans out of gratitude for Schuyler saving his life.

Of course, like so many of our founding fathers, not all about Philip Schuyler is admirable. He bought, sold, and owned fellow human beings, even while he fought to liberate himself. He had as many as twenty-seven enslaved people working in his Albany and Saratoga houses, including two who are documented as having run away, desperate for freedom. Those I mention by name in the narrative are factual, such as Prince and Lisbon, who Schuyler clearly trusted to protect his family, home, and expensive property like horses that were critically necessary to their survival during a war. And while Schuyler fought to protect and supply the Oneida and Tuscarora—often at his own expense—he did support the Continental Army's raids through enemy Iroquois settlements, which devastated their crops and villages, leading ultimately to the collapse of their tribal society and independence.

A brief word about the perplexing marriage of Angelica and John Barker Church, alias John Carter during the Revolution: despite his devolving into a bragging, carousing dullard, when Church met Angelica—if an early portrait of him is to be believed—he was quite handsome, with enormous eyes and thick wavy hair. For a whip-smart, passionate young woman—who had grown up in New York City's lively society and as a constant, pampered guest of the royal governor, Lord Henry Moore—Church's cosmopolitan aura would have been quite alluring. Perhaps his secretive past—gambling debts, a romance gone wrong, a duel—was exciting to her as well. After all, when an impressionable teenager, Angelica had witnessed the elopement of Lord Moore's daughter and its aggrandizing romanticism.

As intellectual and committed a Patriot as her little sister, Angelica must have thought Church would become an important player in the Revolution. He did, indeed, provide critical aid to the cause by finding supplies for the French army. But he also profited as that commissary, making a large fortune for himself. As such, he was a controversial character. At one point, Washington said that all profiteers should be hanged.

In 1783, Angelica and Church left for Paris so he could collect payment for his services to Rochambeau's forces. They then settled in London, where Church became a member of the British Parliament and Angelica a famously charming hostess. She became something of a muse to Thomas Jefferson (then ambassador to France) as well as to her brother-in-law, writing letters to both that were filled with impassioned philosophy and political ideas, doled out in dazzling and affectionate language. She came back to New York on frequent visits, and her close, intellectually intimate relationship with Hamilton was always subject to gossip. Still, she and Church had five sons and three daughters, and Angelica seemed to delight in being a mother. Sometimes she refused to receive visitors if she were in the middle of a card game with her children.

It is said Church owned the pistols Hamilton carried to the duel that killed him—the same pair Hamilton's son Philip died by. Ironically, Burr and Carter had dueled in 1799, both of these men surviving that confrontation.

The double agent Moses Harris is fact—tracked in Washington's and Schuyler letters and verified by his later application for a pension. Much of his dialogue I culled from a wonderful 1878 article (see my bibliography), in which his grandchildren detailed the stories he'd told them, including the rather amazing lifesaving Masonic sign of distress! According to his gravestone in the Harrisena Cemetery, in Queensbury, New York, Harris lived to be eighty-nine years, eleven months, and twenty-four days old.

True, too, is the story of the little fifer, Richard Lord Jones, who also survived to old age, treasuring that three-dollar bill Martha Washington gave him, kept folded exactly as she handed it to him.

The winter of 1779–1780 is still one of the most brutal recorded in America. Snows began falling in the first week of November and didn't stop until April. For the only time in recorded history, all of the saltwater inlets and harbors of the Atlantic coast, from North Carolina to Maine, froze over and for more than a month remained closed to ships. The ice in the Hudson River just above New York City was measured at eighteen feet thick. The red fox that now inhabit our continent are said to be descended from a brace brought to the Eastern Shore by British landowners that were able to walk across the wide Chesapeake Bay frozen solid during that time.

From July 1781 to December 1783, when the war was officially ended, Richard Varick served as George Washington's recording secretary. He stayed in Poughkeepsie, organizing and editing thousands of Washington's letters, dispatches, journal entries, and battle proposals that arrived in trunks under escort of His Excellency's personal guard. It is entirely fair to say that Varick and the scribes he diligently oversaw to produce the forty-four volumes of Washington's wartime papers housed in the Library of Congress are responsible for our knowing what we do about our Revolution. He married Maria Roosevelt, was mayor of New York City from 1789–1801, and lived until 1831.

When describing how Arnold broke the 1777 Siege of Fort Stanwix, I couldn't find a place to tuck in the bodacious defiance of the Patriots inside that ramshackle fortification. Told they would all be summarily massacred when the fort eventually fell if they didn't surrender immediately to the far superior British forces outside their walls, a young Peter Gansevoort refused to yield. Then he and his sick, starving, and ammunition-depleted troops tore up their shirts and stockings to raise a makeshift American flag as the ultimate thumbing of their noses at the British Empire.

I can't help but wonder if his future grandson, Herman Melville, thought of Gansevoort's valiant tenacity when writing his masterpiece *Moby-Dick*.

Ann Bleecker and the death of her baby is also fact, a tragic example of the cost to civilians in any war, particularly for refugee families facing exposure, hunger, dangerous terrain, and unsanitary water. She is also one of those largely forgotten trailblazers in our history. Ann Eliza Schuyler Bleecker was one of America's first published female poets. She wrote about the raw beauties of the wilderness and the devastating tumult of the Revolution. But she also dared to cry out the agonies of loss—the first female poet to acknowledge and therefore raise female anguish to the legitimacy and dignity of grief that epic bards like Homer granted their male warrior-heroes. Her poem "Written in the Retreat from Burgoyne" is haunting in its honesty.

I'll end with admitting that I kind of fell in love with George Washington as I researched. His legendary stoicism and calm was not natural to him. He evidently had quite a volatile temper during his youth that he learned to muffle—mostly. Therefore, his composure was hard-won and a practiced, stunning act of self-control, especially given his huntsmen-soldiers' lack of training and supplies, and the betrayals, jealousies, and constant backbiting among his officers and Congress.

"My old man," Martha Washington affectionately called him—obviously he did not take himself too seriously! He loved, he hurt, he laughed, he joked, he feared, he faltered, but he stubbornly held to his convictions and dragged a new nation to its feet. He did indeed love to dance for hours at a time, to play catch, and to romp with his herd of dogs. And when he loved people he was absolutely devoted to them. He was heartbroken at the death of his stepdaughter, just as Martha describes to Peggy in Chapter Nineteen.

I highly recommend your dipping into the wonderful website Mount Vernon runs (http://www.mountvernon .org/digital-encyclopedia/#personal) to experience for yourself the anecdotes related there that so humanize the "father of our country" we too often represent in cold marble.

Paraphrasing the brilliant Lin-Manuel Miranda, George Washington recognized that history had its eyes on him and all those daring to rise up for freedom. Thank God for those who stubbornly fought on—no matter the disasters, the naysayers, the daunting size and power of the empire they fought, the battles, winters, starvation, and diseases that decimated them, nor the improbability and absolutely unprecedented audacity of their ideas. All of them—including Peggy and her big sisters.

AUTHOR GRATITUDES

"I have more than once compared [Lin-Manuel Miranda] to Shakespeare, and I do it without blushing or apologizing. Lin, in Hamilton, *is doing exactly what Shakespeare did in his history plays. He's taking the voice of the common people, elevating it to poetry—in Shakespeare's case iambic pentameter, in Lin's case, rap, rhyme, hip-hop, R & B—and by elevating it to poetry, ennobling the people themselves. He is bringing out what is noble about the common tongue. And that is something that nobody has done as effectively as Lin since Shakespeare. Yeah, I said it."*

—*Oskar Eustis, artistic director of New York's Public Theater*

LIKE MILLIONS OF PEOPLE, I FEEL AS IF I KNOW Tony Award–winner Lin-Manuel Miranda because he is that open, that passionate about his work—the emotion of his lyrics so palpable. But I have not had the honor of meeting him. Still, I feel I must thank him for his brilliant integration of genres that has revolutionized theater for audiences and artists who follow him, and how his wondrously clever, quick-paced lyrics recount so much history in such a humanizing and compelling way. I hope—just as he says he was inspired after reading Ron Chernow's bestselling biography of Alexander Hamilton to create a musical about an historical figure—that he will take as a compliment my being intrigued enough by Peggy Schuyler's untold story, hinted at in his staggeringly beautiful *Hamilton*, to research and write this novel.

It turns out Peggy was a fascinating woman.

The next bow goes to my wondrous editor, Katherine Tegen, who recognized the thirst for more in lovers of Alexander Hamilton's story, and then entrusted me to do it. She is stunningly astute in recognizing a good story; nurturing and creative in her thinking; and loyal to those she believes in. Her sensitive and adroit editing so strengthened this narrative.

I am particularly indebted to the generosity and enthusiasm of Ian Mumpton and Danielle Funiciello, Historical Interpreters with the New York State Office of Parks, Recreation and Historical Preservation at the Schuyler Mansion State Historic Site in the city of Albany. They graciously responded to my constant questions with their expertise and analysis of the Revolution, sharing first-person, primary documents they've unearthed and their clear empathy and understanding for the Schuyler family whose lives they curate—all of which so enriched this novel. They also were kind enough to read the finished manuscript for accuracy in general and the veracity of nuanced meanings I drew from bare-bones historical facts. If you're interested in learning more about the Schuylers, the mansion hosts tours, an active

Facebook page, and a fascinating blog: http://schuylerman-sion.blogspot.com/.

Many thanks as well to historian Joseph F. Stoltz III at the Fred W. Smith National Library for the Study of George Washington, housed on the Mount Vernon Estate, who kindly guided my study of Philip Schuyler's spy network and counterintelligence efforts. He seemed as pleased as I was to find proof within Mount Vernon's collections of Moses Harris's activities! I am also grateful to librarian Sarah Myers who patiently helped me access the founding fathers' letters and nineteenth-century magazine articles, which added such personal immediacy and rich anecdotes.

Retired Park Ranger Larry Arnold spent hours driving me around the Saratoga battlefield and introducing me to the welcoming staff of the Schuyler House in Saratoga. Morris-town National Historical Park Education Specialist Tom Winslow responded to a long list of questions with carefully culled information about the brutal winter of 1779–80 and George Washington's encampment.

In addition to her perceptive editing comments, assistant editor Mabel Hsu braved the enormous collection of Philip Schuyler papers at the New York Public Library to collect otherwise unavailable letters I needed. There she found evidence of Richard Varick's devoted personality, which added an unexpected and sweet supporting character to Peggy's life. Friend and actor Michaela Kahan read the manuscript with an eye for the platability of Peggy's real-life personality and life arc I researched and presented, given the almost urban legend–level expectations generated by fans of the musical. The unsung heroes of publishing are the production editors and copy editors, especially for a narrative dictated by historical facts and enriched with letters and direct quotes. I am so grateful for production editor Emily Rader's and copy editor Jessica White's painstaking, meticulous, and insightful work.

Finally, as with all the most profound and rewarding aspects of my life, my children—professional creative artists themselves—were inspiration for and integrally involved in this project—researching and guiding the novel's characterizations, plotline, and themes, and reassuring me that I was allowed to imagine plausible scenarios which rippled out from the reams of facts that we pulled in from our wide-cast nets into the sea of Revolutionary War documents.

It was my daughter, Megan—a poetic and ingenious theater director who always manages to diaphanously accentuate the most subtle of a playwright's messages while pulling out emotive and smart performances from her actors—who first introduced me to *Hamilton*. Thanks to her, we wrangled tickets to see the original cast, and I watched dumbfounded and delighted, knowing I was witnessing the transformation of theater and its possibilities. Given the fast turnaround of this project, Megan read almost as much as I did, focusing on researching the roles and challenges facing female Patriots— helping me build as much of a feminist narrative as possible within the reality of eighteenth-century life. She also lent me her nuance of vision and interpretation.

My son, Peter, an exquisite screenwriter and playwright—whose fluid, character-driven scripts always present beautifully complex and compelling personas, revealed deftly and viscerally within riveting action—helped me stay focused on Peggy's individual journey within the wide, engrossing (and therefore distracting!) universe of the Revolution. His suggestions honed my pacing and authenticity of dialogue and helped me crystallize characters. An avid lover of history himself, Peter read and fed me material on George Washington, helping me invigorate the legendary father figure with tangible and very human traits.

Peter's fascination with the past and ability to present it in captivating ways to modern sensibilities was echoed at a White House appearance by Chris Jackson, the actor who so beautifully originated Miranda's George Washington: "In my high school we didn't have a theater program. History was my drama program. I saw each and every moment in history as the most dramatic moment ever—which it was to the people who were taking part in it. Look at it from the perspective of who's the protagonist, who's the antagonist, what's at stake," he advised a teen writer invited by First Lady Michelle Obama to speak with the cast. "You might find a world there to unlock."

I am so grateful to all who gave me the key to Peggy's heart and life.

BIBLIOGRAPHY

These resources guided my research for *Hamilton and Peggy!: A Revolutionary Friendship*. If you'd like to learn more about this fascinating time in American history, these are excellent places to begin your own research. (Also see my website, www.lmelliott.com, for links to historical databases, mini-bios, and other information.)

THE SCHUYLER FAMILY:

Cunningham, Anna K. *Schuyler Mansion: A Critical Catalogue of the Furnishings & Decorations*. Albany: New York State Education Department, 1955. Print.

Cushman, Paul. *Richard Varick: A Forgotten Founding Father*. Amherst: Modern Memoirs Publishing, 2010. Print.

Egly, T.W., Jr. *General Schuyler's Guard*. 1986. Print.

Gerlach, Don R. "Philip Schuyler and the New York Frontier in 1781." *The New-York Historical Society Quarterly* 53 (1969): 148–181. Print.

————. "After Saratoga: The General, His Lady, and 'Gentleman Johnny' Burgoyne." *New York History* 52.1 (1971): 4–30. *JSTOR*. Web. 14 July 2016.

————. *Proud Patriot: Philip Schuyler and the War of Independence,*

1775–1783. Syracuse: Syracuse University Press, 1987. Print.

Grant, Anne MacVicar. *Memoirs of an American Lady: With Sketches of Manners and Scenery in America, as They Existed Previous to the Revolution*. New York, 1845. Print.

Halsey, Francis Whiting. "General Schuyler's Part in the Burgoyne Campaign." *Proceedings of the New York State Historical Association* 12 (1913): 109–118. *JSTOR*. Web. 14 July 2016.

Humphreys, Mary Gay. *Women of Colonial and Revolutionary Times: Catharine Schuyler; With Portrait*. Leopold Classic Library, 1897. Print.

Mayer, Brantz. *Journal of Charles Carroll of Carrollton: During His Visit to Canada in 1776*. Baltimore: Maryland Historical Society, 1876. Print.

Phelan, Helene. *The Man Who Owned the Pistols: John Barker Church and His Family*. Interlaken: Heart of the Lakes Publishing, 1981. Print.

Saffron, Morris H. *Surgeon to Washington: Dr. John Cochran (1730–1807)*. New York: Columbia University Press, 1977. Print.

Tuckerman, Bayard. *Life of General Philip Schuyler, 1733–1804*. New York: Dodd, Mead, and Company, 1903. Print.

ALEXANDER HAMILTON:

Chernow, Ron. *Alexander Hamilton*. New York: Penguin Books, 2004. Print.

Flexner, James Thomas. *The Young Hamilton: A Biography*. New York: Fordham University Press, 1997. Print.

Larson, Harold. "Alexander Hamilton: The Fact and Fiction of His Early Years." *The William and Mary Quarterly* 9.2 (1952): 139–151. *JSTOR*. Web. 14 July 2016.

Schachner, Nathan. "Alexander Hamilton Viewed by His Friends: The Narratives of Robert Troup and Hercules Mulligan." *The William and Mary Quarterly* 4.2 (1947): 203–225. *JSTOR*. Web. 14 July 2016.

Syrett, Harold C., and Jacob E. Cooke. *The Papers of Alexander Hamilton*. Vol. 1 and 2. New York: Columbia University Press, 1962. Print.

HAMILTON: AN AMERICAN MUSICAL:

Miranda, Lin-Manuel, and Jeremy McCarter. *Hamilton: The Revolution*. New York: Grand Central Publishing and Melcher Media, 2016. Print.

WOMEN IN THE AMERICAN REVOLUTION:

Berkin, Carol. *Revolutionary Mothers: Women in the Struggle for America's Independence*. New York: Random House, 2005. Print.

Bleecker, Ann Eliza. *The Posthumous Works of Ann Eliza Bleecker in Prose and Verse: To Which is Added a Collection of Essays, Prose and Poetical*. Gale, Sabin Americana, 2012. Print.

Good, Cassandra A. *Founding Friendships: Friendships between Men and Women in the Early American Republic*. Oxford: Oxford University Press, 2015. Print.

North, Louise V., Landa M. Freeman, and Janet M. Wedge. *In the Words of Women: The Revolutionary War and the Birth of the Nation, 1765–1799*. Lanham: Lexington Books, 2011. Print.

Norton, Mary Beth. *Liberty's Daughters: The Revolutionary Experience of American Women, 1750–1800*. Ithaca: Cornell University Press, 1980. Print.

Stevens, John Austin, William Abbatt, Henry Phelps Johnston, Benjamin Franklin DeCosta, Martha Joanna Lamb, and Nathan Gillett Pond. *The Magazine of American History with Notes and Queries*. Vol. 1. New York: A.S. Barnes & Company, 1877. Print.

GEORGE AND MARTHA WASHINGTON:

Chernow, Ron. *Washington: A Life*. New York: Penguin Books, 2011. Print.

Fleming, Thomas. *The Intimate Lives of the Founding Fathers*. New York: HarperCollins, 2009. Print.

Keller, Kate Van Winkle, and Charles Cyril Hendrickson. *George Washington: A Biography in Social Dance*. Sandy Hook: The Hendrickson Group, 1998. Print.

Philbrick, Nathaniel. *Valiant Ambition: George Washington, Benedict Arnold, and the Fate of the American Revolution*. New York: Penguin Random House, 2016. Print.

Wharton, Anne Hollingsworth. *Martha Washington*. Cambridge, 1897. Print.

WASHINGTON'S AIDES-DE-CAMP:

Beall, Mary S. "The Military and Private Secretaries of George Washington." *Records of the Columbia Historical Society, Washington, DC* 1 (1897): 89–118. *JSTOR*. Web. 1 February 2017.

Lefkowitz, Arthur S. *George Washington's Indispensable Men: The 32 Aides-de-Camp Who Helped Win American Independence*. Mechanicsburg: Stackpole Books, 2003. Print.

Steiner, Bernard Christian. *The Life and Correspondence of James McHenry: Secretary of War under Washington and Adams*. The Burrows Brothers Company, 1907. Print.

Tilghman, Tench. *Memoir of Lieutenant Colonel Tench Tilghman, Secretary and Aide to Washington: Together with an Appendix, Containing Revolutionary Journals and Letters*. 1876. Print.

JOURNALS OF CONTINENTAL SOLDIERS:

Fisher, Elijah. *Elijah Fisher's Journal While in the War for Independence, and Continued Two Years after He Came to Maine, 1775–1784*. Augusta: Press of Badger and Manley, 1880. Print.

Martin, Joseph Plumb. *A Narrative of a Revolutionary Soldier*. New York: Signet Classics, 2010. Print.

Rochambeau, Count de, and M. W. E. Wright. "What

France Did for America: Memoirs of Rochambeau."
The North American Review. 205.738 (1917): 788–802.
JSTOR. Web. 29 August 2016.

Thacher, James, M.D. *A Military Journal during the American Revolutionary War, from 1775 to 1783.* Boston: Cottons & Barnard, 1827. Print.

THE FRENCH AND HESSIANS DURING THE REVOLUTIONARY WAR:

Acomb, Evelyn M. *The Revolutionary Journal of Baron Ludwig von Closen, 1780–1783.* Chapel Hill: University of North Carolina Press, 1958. Print.

Brown, Marvin L., Jr. *Baroness von Reidesel and the American Revolution: Journal and Correspondence of a Tour of Duty, 1776–1783.* Chapel Hill: University of North Carolina Press, 1965. Print.

Chastellux, Francois Jean. *Travels in North America, in the Years 1780–81–82.* New York, 1828. Print.

Jones, T. Cole. "Displaying the Ensigns of Harmony: The French Army in Newport, 1780–1781." *The New England Quarterly* 85, no. 3 (September 2012), pp. 430–467.

Kennett, Lee. *The French Forces in America, 1780–1783.* Westport: Greenwood Press, 1977. Print.

Selig, Robert A. "A German Soldier in America, 1780–1783: The Journal of Georg Daniel Flohr." *The William and Mary Quarterly* 50.3 (1993): 575–590. *JSTOR.* Web. 22 August 2016.

Stevens, John Austin. "The French in Rhode Island." *The Magazine of American History III,* no. 7 (July 1879).

THE IROQUOIS:

Glatthaar, Joseph T., and James Kirby Martin. *Forgotten Allies: The Oneida Indians and the American Revolution.* New York: Hill and Wang, 2007. Print.

MORRISTOWN:

Cunningham, John T. *The Uncertain Revolution: Washington & the Continental Army at Morristown.* West Creek: Cormorant Publishing, 2007. Print.

Mills, Weymer Jay. *Historic Houses of New Jersey.* Bibliolife. Print.

Rae, John W. *Morristown: A Military Headquarters of the American Revolution.* Charleston: Arcadia Publishing, 2002. Print.

ESPIONAGE DURING THE REVOLUTION:

Daigler, Kenneth A. *Spies, Patriots, and Traitors: American Intelligence in the Revolutionary War.* Washington, DC: Georgetown University Press, 2014. Print.

Kaplan, Roger. "The Hidden War: British Intelligence Operations during the American Revolution." *The William and Mary Quarterly* 47.1 (1990): 115–138. *JSTOR.* Web. 23 February 2017.

Nagy, John A. *George Washington's Secret Spy War: The Making of America's First Spymaster.* New York: St. Martin's Press, 2016. Print.

Rose, Alexander. *Washington's Spies: The Story of America's First Spy Ring.* New York: Random House, 2006. Print.

Stone, William L. "Schuyler's Faithful Spy: An Incident in the Burgoyne Campaign." *The Magazine of American History II* (1878). pp. 414–419.

NEW YORK DURING THE REVOLUTION:

Albany Chronicles: A History of the City Arranged Chronologically, From the Earliest Settlement to the Present Time; Illustrated with Many Historical Pictures of Rarity and Reproductions of the Robert C. Pruyn Collection of the Mayors of Albany. Albany: Albany Institute and Historical and Art Society. Print.

Roberts, Warren. *A Place in History: Albany in the Age of Revolution, 1775–1825.* Albany: State University of New York Press, 2010. Print.

Schecter, Barnet. *The Battle for New York: The City at the Heart of the American Revolution.* New York: Penguin Books, 2002. Print.

BENEDICT ARNOLD AND PEGGY SHIPPEN:

Jacob, Mark, and Stephen H. Case. *Treacherous Beauty: Peggy Shippen, the Woman behind Benedict Arnold's Plot to Betray America.* Guilford: Lyons Press, 2012. Print.

Philbrick, Nathaniel. *Valiant Ambition: George Washington, Benedict Arnold, and the Fate of the American Revolution.* New York: Penguin Random House, 2016. Print.

Stuart, Nancy Rubin. *Defiant Brides: The Untold Story of Two Revolutionary-Era Women and the Radical Men They Married.* Boston: Beacon Press, 2013. Print.

CLOTHING IN COLONIAL AMERICA:

Baumgarten, Linda. *Eighteenth-Century Clothing at Williamsburg.* Williamsburg: The Colonial Williamsburg Foundation, 1986. Print.

———. *What Clothes Reveal: The Language of Clothing in Colonial and Federal America.* Williamsburg: The Colonial Williamsburg Foundation, 2002. Print.

Baumgarten, Linda, John Watson, and Florine Carr. *Costume Close-Up: Clothing Construction and Pattern, 1750–1790.* Williamsburg: The Colonial Williamsburg Foundation, 1999. Print.

Riley, Mara, and Cathy Johnson. *Whatever Shall I Wear? A Guide to Assembling a Woman's Basic 18th Century Wardrobe.* Graphics/Fine Art Press, 2002. Print.

VIDEOS:

Alexander Hamilton, PBS.

George Washington, MGM.

George Washington: The Man Who Wouldn't Be King, PBS.

John Adams, HBO.
Lafayette: The Lost Hero, PBS.
Liberty! The American Revolution, PBS.
The Crossing, A&E.

<u>AND LAST, BUT CERTAINLY NOT LEAST:</u>

The Founders Online website, created by the National Archives, is an extraordinary database of letters between the founding fathers and their families, compatriots, and friends: https://founders.archives.gov/.

Also, the New York Public Library's collection of Philip Schuyler's papers have been digitized and are available online: https://digitalcollections.nypl.org.

TURN THE PAGE

for an excerpt from L.M. Elliott's *Da Vinci's Tiger*,
an enthralling historical romance about Ginevra de' Benci,
the real-life muse of Leonardo da Vinci.

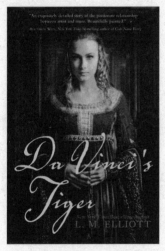

Available now!

1

"QUICK! SHIELD YOUR EYES!" SIMONETTA VESPUCCI CRIED.

Gasping, I raised my hands against a blast of dagger-sharp splinters spewing from the jousting field.

Giuliano de' Medici and his opponent had just raced toward each other, to deafening cheers from the crowd, their lances aimed straight for each other, their horses thundering and snorting toward collision. With a horrifying crash, Giuliano's lance shattered on his opponent's shield, pelting the front row of the stands where I sat with wood fragments.

1

The rider was hurled off his horse. He lay sprawled on his back in the white sand that filled the Piazza di Santa Croce for the joust. Rushing in, his men-at-arms helped him stand and walked him off the lists. The rider's armor had saved him. His exquisite horse, however, writhed on the ground. A huge shard of the Medici-blue lance was embedded in his flank.

Whinnying in agony, the horse kicked out wildly. The crowd hushed as men circled the beautiful animal, trying to decide what to do. Giuliano retreated to a corner of the piazza to await his next round, his own horse prancing in fretful impatience and agitation.

"Poor thing," Simonetta said of the injured horse. "Do you think it will die?" She reached to clasp my hand as we watched.

"Ouch!" My red gloves were spiked with a few azure-colored needles thrown from the shattered lances.

"Oh, my dear!" Simonetta began plucking out the tiny spears. "Thanks be to Mother Mary, your hands saved you. Many knights have died from lance splinters piercing their eyes." She leaned toward me and whispered. "Even so, joust-ing is an exquisite sport, don't you think? So exhilarating to see these men ride at such a pace." She giggled like the girl she was, before shrouding herself again in womanly reserve. "But at such a price." She shook her head as she pulled the last shard from the soft velvet.

I tried not to wince as Simonetta gently peeled off the glove to inspect my hand. She pressed her handkerchief to

2

my palm to stop the tiny ooze of blood from the pinpricks.

"You will ruin that lovely lace with bloodstains," I warned. Such intricate handiwork was imported from Venice and was expensive.

"Your beautiful hands are far more important," she replied. "I have heard them praised by Lorenzo the Magnifico for their delicacy, and for the needlework and poetry they create. We must make sure they do not become infected."

I was a bit vain about my hands, I have to admit. My fingers were long and slender, and I rubbed lemon juice into my skin to keep it fair. So I smiled to hear the compliment, especially since it came from the city's most important citizen-statesman.

Simonetta smiled back. The way her face lit up reminded me why all of Florence was totally besotted with her. With thick golden curls, a long neck, creamy skin, and huge amber eyes, Simonetta Cattaneo Vespucci was gorgeous. Officially, the Medici had organized this joust to celebrate Florence's new diplomatic alliance with Venice and Milan. But Simonetta was its crowned "Queen of Beauty" and its focal point in many ways. The honor was no surprise as Simonetta was also the publicly celebrated Platonic love of the younger Medici brother, the handsome Giuliano, Florence's favorite rider in the joust.

Her image had been the first thing seen that morning as Giuliano and twenty-one other combatants paraded through Florence's streets to Santa Croce. Leading the procession, Giuliano was accompanied by nine trumpeters and two men-at-arms, carrying pennants of fringed blue silk, decorated with the Medici coat of arms. All their tunic skirts were of matching blue silk brocade, their silver-threaded sleeves embroidered with olive branches and flames. As dazzling as his entourage's costuming was, though, spectators couldn't help but stare at the enormous banner Giuliano carried.

On it, Simonetta was depicted as Pallas, the Greek goddess of wisdom and war, over a motto in gold lettering: *La sans par,* "the unparalleled one." The great Botticelli had painted her holding a jousting lance and shield, in a golden tunic and breastplate, looking up to the sky. Beside her, ignored, Cupid was tied to an olive tree.

The banner's message was clear. As Pallas, Simonetta was not distracted or beguiled by Cupid's earthly romances. Follow her gaze and her example to make it to heaven. When Simonetta climbed the grand dais stairs to take her throne, she had received as many cheers as the city's beloved Giuliano would when he rode into the lists to the fanfare of herald-trumpets.

How marvelous to be considered so beautiful, so good and true, that an artist such as Sandro Botticelli would want to paint you, I thought. Jealous, I pulled my hand away and spoke sharply. "It's fine."

The slightest of frowns creased Simonetta's brow. "We must be friends, Ginevra de' Benci Niccolini. I have so few since moving here from Piombino to marry Marco. We are, after all, cousins by marriage. And"—she paused—"I think we will have much to talk about." She giggled again, this time pulling my gaze with hers toward a handsome, debonair stranger sitting next to the great Lorenzo. The man bowed his head in salutation to us as we did. "He has been appreciating you for the last hour."

I felt my face flush. "Who is he?"

"Bernardo Bembo, the new Venetian ambassador."

I was about to turn to look at the diplomat more carefully—something Le Murate's sisters would have chided me harshly for—when a man's voice from behind stopped me.

"Observe! Here comes the Six Hundred."

Men around him laughed.

Again I flushed, mortified. The man was talking about my oldest brother, Giovanni. And not in a flattering way.

Walking onto the field, Giovanni approached the thrashing horse. He circled it slowly, while the other men who'd tried fruitlessly to calm it stepped back. As usual, my brother was dressed to the hilt, wearing a lavish emerald-green-and-gold taffeta tunic, his soled hose scarlet, his fur-lined beret threaded with silver and gold.

"Do you think he has enough florins on his back?" The man behind me kept up his sarcasm.

My brother's love of expensive clothes and fine horses had become the city's gauge for all things ostentatious. Giovanni had purchased a magnificent horse from the Barbary Coast of North Africa for a staggering six hundred florins (an amount that equaled the annual income of ten skilled artisans combined). He raced it in the annual *palio* for St. John's Feast. He

5

also loved to parade about town on the horse. I could hardly blame him. The horse was an incredibly fluid mover and a joy to ride.

But "Here comes the Six Hundred" had become a Florentine slang term for a braggart. A republic city-state of merchants, guildsmen, artisans, and bankers, Florence did not approve of showy everyday displays of wealth, despite its citizens' love of pageantry and spectacles like this joust.

I fumed.

Simonetta put her hand atop mine and patted it to keep me from turning round to glare at my brother's attackers. I wondered if he would cease if he knew who I was. But Florentine men were used to speaking their mind no matter what.

"Well, he is a Benci," another voice said. "His grandfather was Cosimo's best friend and the Medici bank manager. The Benci family earned its wealth. You have to give them that."

It was a typical Florentine assessment of politics and connections, the stuff of many street-corner conversations in a city run by the merchant class. I still wanted to kiss whoever said it. A commoner who made himself a fortune, Cosimo had been much admired in Florence for his generous patronage of artists and for funding the completion of the cathedral's dome. The Duomo had become one of the wonders of Christendom. The respect afforded Cosimo spilled onto my grandfather.

But my brother's critic didn't skip a beat. "Certainly old Benci earned his keep by stuffing the election purse with

Medici supporters to ensure that Cosimo stayed in power—the same as any common whore making her way by bending the ethics of good men."

Simonetta's hand closed tightly on mine. She squeezed hard, warning me to remain rooted in ladylike silence.

Instead, I laughed out loud at the insult. I couldn't help it. I was plagued with an impetuous temper that had always landed me in terrible trouble with the nuns. But this time, I swear the influence of Pallas's mythical intellect saved me. For once, I knew the right thing to say at the right moment.

Leaning toward Simonetta, I said in a loud, staged voice, "Look, Simonetta. My dear, dear brother approaches that poor, suffering, valiant horse." I drew out the adjectives with feminine empathy. "If anyone can save that beauteous steed, it will be my brother. He is a great scholar of ancient texts. He owns the manuscript written by a legendary Calabrian physic to animals, *Liber de Medicina Veterinaria*." The Latin rolled easily off my tongue.

I glanced back at the snide man and his companions, knowing that Florence's obsession with rediscovered ancient Greek and Latin writings granted respect and status to those who possessed them. I recognized the man as a Pazzi—a member of the aristocratic banking family that was the chief rival and a bitter critic of the Medici. I nodded at him, politely, of course. "Through studying that rare, important text, my brother knows everything about tending horses. If the beast is curable, my brother will know how to do it," I said.

With that, all persons within earshot fell silent. If nothing else, they anticipated an interesting display of equestrian husbandry and the value of ancient education. Florentines did so love publicly enacted drama.

Settling back in my seat, I pulled my cloak closer about me against the January chill and buried my nose in the collar's ermine—mostly to hide a self-satisfied smile. I dared to peep over the soft fur at Simonetta to see her reaction.

Her amber eyes sparkled in amusement. "You will go far indeed in this city, Ginevra."

Luckily, my brother proved me right. He moved closer and closer to the convulsing horse, dodging its kicks to stand next to its head. Giovanni knelt. The horse stilled and let my brother touch its muzzle. The crowd was transfixed.

Cautiously, Giovanni lowered his face to breathe into the horse's nostrils, just as horses greet each other. Then he stroked the horse's neck, whispering into its ear. He took hold of the shard of wood with one hand, while the other stayed on the horse's neck. He looked up and nodded, signaling the grooms standing by that he was ready for their help. Quickly, they laid hands on the horse to keep him still. Giovanni yanked the spear out of its side before it realized what was happening.

The crowd cheered. The horse struggled to its feet and let a groom stanch the wound with clean linen. Then, limping, it peacefully followed Giovanni off the course.

"I'll be damned," muttered the Pazzi man behind me.

But it didn't take him long to continue his jabs at my brother. "Now I am sure the Six Hundred will exploit the situation and try to buy that horse away from the defeated rider."

"In truth, that will be a good negotiation for the rider," his companion said. He lowered his voice a bit, since his gossip could be interpreted to be anti-Medici. "He was strong-armed by Lorenzo to compete in today's joust. He told me he was forced into spending enormous sums to properly outfit himself to the Medici satisfaction. He purchased fifty-two pounds of pure gold and a hundred seventy pounds of silver for his armor, his horse's decorations, and livery for his followers."

The men around him whistled.

"So he will be glad for some reimbursement."

I imagined the nods of approval from the gaggle of merchants and money changers behind me.

"But it's not as if that horse will ever be able to joust or race again, not with that wound to its back leg," the Pazzi attacker said, changing tack. "Only a fool would want to buy it. A fool like the Six Hundred."

He would still mock my brother? Even after such a triumphant display of horsemanship and bravery? I turned round and blessed the Pazzi man with the most innocent, demure smile I could muster in my fury. "But good, my lord," I said in a purposely dulcet tone, "would not this horse father wondrous colts?" I paused to allow my listeners time to consider. "After all, his most important . . . mmm . . . . leg . . . was not pierced."

9

The man's mouth dropped open.

His friends guffawed in appreciation. But this time the laughter was with me. Even ladylike Simonetta shook with mirth, but she pressed her lips together to keep from laughing out loud.

I turned back to face the jousting field, having won that round for my family's honor, just as Giuliano charged back into the lists for his next go at glory.

Enthralling and entertaining historical fiction from
L. M. ELLIOTT

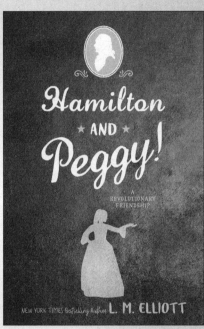

Praise for *Da Vinci's Tiger*:

"An exquisitely detailed story of the passionate relationship between artist and muse, whose spirited yet gentle Renaissance heroine put me in awe of just how far women have had to come in five hundred years. Beautifully painted."

—Elizabeth Wein, Michael L. Printz Honor winner and
New York Times bestselling author of *Code Name Verity*

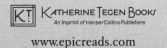

www.epicreads.com

JOIN THE

Epic Reads

COMMUNITY